Separation

Lives Apart: A World War Two Chronicle

Part One

Carole McEntee-Taylor

First Published in 2015
by GWL Publishing
an imprint of Great War Literature Publishing LLP

Produced in United Kingdom

ISBN 978-1-910603-03-1 Paperback Edition

GWL Publishing
Forum House
Sterling Road
Chichester PO19 7DN
www.gwlpublishing.co.uk

Carole loves writing and loves history, so it's no surprise that she writes historical books! She enjoys writing both military history and historical fiction and the idea is to give the author royalties of any military history titles to military charities, whilst proceeds from the fiction go to Carole, to help fund the research into both – at least that's the theory! She currently has five military history books published with Pen & Sword, with more in the pipeline.

Carole lives on the north east Essex coast with her husband, David and, when not writing, she works full-time at the Military Corrective Training Centre (MCTC) in Colchester.

Also by Carole McEntee-Taylor

Herbert Columbine VC

A Battle too Far: The True Story of Rifleman Henry Taylor

From Colonial Warrior to Western Front Flyer: The Five Wars of Sydney Herbert Bywater Harris

The Battle of Bellewaarde, June 1915

Surviving the Nazi Onslaught: The Defence of Calais to the Death March for Freedom

Military Detention Colchester from 1947. Voices from the Glasshouse

Dedication

To my father in law, Ted Taylor, without whom I would never have started writing

Acknowledgements

I would like to thank the following:

My husband David for his continual help and support and for putting up with burnt or undercooked dinners, little or no conversation and me continually forgetting things while my mind was stuck in the 1940s!

My colleagues in the MCTC for encouraging me and Jane da Silva for reading draft copies of the books.

Finally, my publisher, Wendy Lawrance for her considerable perseverance and for believing in me while I re-wrote the manuscript several times!

Cast of Characters

English

Joe Price:	Soldier, Rifle Brigade
Pauline Price:	Joe's mother
Fred Price:	Joe's younger brother
Alfred 'Chalky' White:	Joe's friend
Taffy Jones:	Joe's friend
Frank 'Rob' Roberts:	Joe's friend
Pete Smith:	Joe's friend
Peggy Cooper:	Joe's girlfriend, student nurse at Lambeth Hospital, London
Helen Macklin:	Peggy's friend, student nurse at Lambeth Hospital, London.
Annie Macklin:	Helen's sister
Chris:	Student doctor
Ethel:	Peggy's friend
Colin:	Ethel's boyfriend
Sally:	Peggy's friend
Peter:	Sally's boyfriend
Pam:	Peggy's friend
Olive Cooper:	Peggy's cousin, switchboard operator at Lewisham Council
Kurt Ritter:	Olive's boyfriend
Tom:	Local villain
Kath:	Switchboard operator, Lewisham Council

French

Jacques Servier:	Farmer
Marie Servier:	Jacques' wife
Louis Servier:	Older son of Jacques and Marie
Marcel Servier:	Younger son of Jacques and Marie
Brigitte Fabron:	Louis' girlfriend
Rolf Keller:	German officer
Henri:	Louis' friend
Gerald:	Louis' friend
Pierre:	Marcel's friend
Paul:	Marcel's friend
Antoine:	Marcel's friend
Jean-Paul:	Teacher and refugee
Claudette:	Jean-Paul's wife
Jeanne:	Daughter of Jean-Paul and Claudette
Angel:	Orphan
Gabriel Valence:	Deputy Commissioner, Police
Eve Poitiers:	Receptionist, Police Station

Prologue

Poland

July 1940

The thick, oppressive silence in the dark cellar was only broken by the sound of Rob's rhythmic snoring, a grating cacophony of noise that echoed off the damp, stone walls. Joe moved restlessly on his thin straw palisade, wishing he too could slide into oblivion for a few hours. He envied Rob's ability to sleep when all he, Joe, could think of was his impending separation from his friends. After everything he had endured, just when he'd started to believe things were going to improve, capricious fate had intervened yet again. Finally realising how powerless he was, his destiny controlled by faceless men with swastikas, Joe wondered how long he would survive.

The dark clouds of depression were firmly entrenched in his mind and Joe could find no way of lifting them. Even thinking about Peggy no longer worked its magic; he was beginning to doubt he would ever see her again.

Around him, the flea-infested rats continued their relentless search for food, their claws tapping on the straw-covered stone floor. Joe grimaced. He wasn't sure what was worse: the sharp-toothed rodents who attacked when he was asleep, or the thousands of lice that moved restlessly over his body, causing him to scratch incessantly, day and night.

"You awake, Joe?" The voice was Pete's.

"Yeah, can't sleep," Joe whispered back.

"Me neither," Pete responded. There was silence. Rob's snoring reached a crescendo and Joe kicked out as one of the bolder rats ran across his legs.

"The new place might be better than here." In the inky black darkness, Pete sounded desperate for reassurance. Joe knew how he felt, but he couldn't bring himself to offer the lifeline the other man needed.

"Yeah, and it might be worse."

There was a long silence and Joe began to wish he'd said something more positive, anything to keep the dialogue going, anything to avoid listening to his own desperate thoughts.

"Do you think we'll ever get home?" Giving voice to his despair somehow made Joe feel better.

"We have to believe we will, or we definitely won't," Pete responded, surprised by Joe's lack of faith.

"Yes, you're right, of course. Sorry. I don't know what's wrong with me." Joe was embarrassed he'd shared his darkest emotions with Pete, even though he was a good friend.

"Don't give it a second thought, Joe." Pete sounded much better now. "We'll be alright, you'll see. This time tomorrow, we'll wonder why we were worrying."

Part One

September 1939 - April 1940

Chapter One

"Looks like your call-up papers." Pauline Price wiped her hands on her apron and watched uneasily as her son, Joe, a wiry young man of five feet seven, opened the official envelope.

"Yes, 'fraid so," Joe replied after scanning the page. "I have to report to Winchester next week." He saw his mother's face. "Well, we've known since I received the warning letter back in April that they'd arrive one day. I'm probably lucky I've had this long." Joe tried to maintain his smile, although he was not in the least bit enthusiastic about giving up his life to join the army. Sensing his mother's distress, he put his arm around her. "Don't worry, Mum. I'm sure I'll be alright."

Pauline nodded and tried to ignore the dread she felt whirling around in her stomach. Apart from the danger he would be in, since she and Joe's father had separated a few years earlier, Joe had been the man of the house and she wasn't sure how she would cope without him around.

"You'd better go, or you'll be late." Her voice became brusque in a vain attempt to hide what she was really feeling.

Joe glanced at his watch. "Goodness, is that the time?" he made an effort to pull himself together. "Right, I'll see you later." He kissed Pauline on the cheek. "I'm going to pop round and see Peggy on the way home, so I can tell her I've got my papers. She's moving into her

5

house today, and she'll want to give me the guided tour at the same time. I'll probably be a bit late back."

Pauline didn't reply and Joe realised she was crying.

"Please don't cry, Mum. I'll be alright, I promise."

"Of course you will." Pauline smiled at him through tears which wouldn't stop falling.

"Mum, I'm only going to Winchester for some training. It's not like I'm going off to France, is it?"

"No, of course not." She tried hard to ignore the voice in her head which whispered relentlessly, *not yet, but once you've finished training, that's all the more likely.*

His brother, Fred, three years his junior, was much less sympathetic.

"You lucky sod. I can't wait for my turn. I'd much rather join the army than go to work."

"Don't be silly," Pauline snapped and Joe grinned. This was a much better memory to take with him than everyone standing around weeping.

He put the envelope in his pocket and headed off to work, trying to ignore the sinking feeling in his stomach. He enjoyed his job, liked his workmates and, in general, his life was pretty good. He had worked at Franklin's Engineering since he'd left school at the age of fourteen, some six years earlier and he was settled and content. He was a gentle, considerate, hard-working young man who attended church regularly and loved nature. Although his dad was in the army, he had never wanted to follow in his footsteps and his father had never pushed him, recognising Joe was much more like his mother than him. But, he was a young, fit twenty year-old in a non-reserved occupation and he had no choice.

****

"You can write to me at this address." Kurt Ritter handed Olive Cooper a small piece of paper with a Glasgow address scrawled across it. She looked up at him, a confused expression on her pale, tear-stained face. "I have a friend who lives there and he will be able to get letters to me." Olive nodded. She had no idea how this would work if their countries were fighting each other, but she didn't really care. Kurt was the first boyfriend she had ever had and she wasn't about to let the war break up their relationship. She still found it impossible to believe someone as handsome as Kurt, with his clear blue eyes, straight nose, short blond hair and muscled body, could not only find her attractive, but also fall in love with her and she had to keep pinching herself to make sure she wasn't dreaming.

At thirty-two, Olive's thin, mousy-brown shoulder length hair hung limply around her angular, colourless face, framing cloudy grey eyes which were hidden behind dark-rimmed spectacles that did little to enhance them or the rest of her face. Her only redeeming feature was a rather full mouth. She had worked on the switchboard of the Metroplitan Borough of Lewisham Council for several years, the ideal job for someone who was unsociable, prickly and lonely, because she could listen in to the phone calls and pretend she was someone important.

"Life won't be the same without you." She began to cry again.

"The war won't last forever," Kurt reassured her. "And at least this way we can keep in touch. Think how dreadful our lives would be if we couldn't even write to each other."

Olive nodded. "I know, I'm sorry. it's just that I'm going to miss you so much."

"I'll miss you too, darling." Kurt kissed her, his hands squeezing her buttocks while he pressed her body to his. "Especially the nights."

There was a silence while he began undoing her skirt and she fought with the buttons on his fly. He groaned when she finally succeeded in unbuttoning them and took him in her hand. She knelt down, taking him in her mouth, running her tongue up and down the shaft like he'd taught her.

"That's wonderful." His voice was breathless as her mouth moved quicker and quicker. Within moments, he climaxed, filling her mouth with hot liquid. Olive swallowed and smiled up at him through her tears.

"No more tears." He smiled down at her briefly, then his face grew serious. "Don't forget, Olive. You can't tell anyone about this. My friend would get into lots of trouble and you probably would too."

She smiled back at him through her tears. "You don't have to worry. It will be our secret."

****

Honor Oak Park, London

Twenty year-old Peggy Cooper signed the last of the paperwork, closed the door behind the renting agent and leaned back, a smile of satisfaction on her face. She could hardly believe that, at last, she had a place of her own... well practically her own. She was sharing with two of her friends: Sally who worked for the Ministry of Information and Ethel, a stylist with an upmarket West End hair salon. Until that morning, Peggy had been living in the nurse's home, but because of the talk of war over the last few months, all the student nurses, other than first years, had moved out.

The house was furnished, but Peggy couldn't wait to unpack her own possessions, then the property would really begin to feel like home. She glanced at her watch, an early birthday present from her boyfriend, Joe, after she'd broken her old one.

Peggy ran lightly up the narrow stairs, taking care to keep to the middle of the tread which was carpeted. At the top, she turned left onto the landing and opened the second door on the right. This was the bedroom she had chosen. A good size, the room faced the front of the house and the window overlooked the tree-lined street. She undid her rather battered brown suitcase and hurried to remove her clothes. She had taken the afternoon off, to allow her time to move in. She began hanging her skirts, dresses and cardigans in the large oak wardrobe, and placed her neatly folded underwear in the drawer of the ornate dressing table. Finished, Peggy laid out her hairbrush and toiletries on the surface and stepped back to admire her handiwork. She knew she should be concerned about how she would cope as a nurse when the war started and about Joe probably being one of the first to be conscripted, but for a few moments she wanted to forget her worries and savour her new-found freedom.

****

Lewisham Council Offices, London

Olive stared at the switchboard, a morose expression on her face, her thoughts elsewhere. She'd met Kurt six months earlier in the park while she was walking home after a particularly busy day. She'd bent down to pick up some litter and he'd rushed passed, almost knocking her flying. His profuse apologies and seemingly genuine concern had somehow broken through the wall she invariably erected when men spoke to her. His German accent was quite strong and, at first, she had given monosyllabic answers, until he'd explained he was feeling rather lonely because he didn't know anyone. For some reason she'd felt sorry for him. This was a new experience for Olive; the only person she usually felt sorry for was herself.

He had insisted on taking her for tea at the park café and, while they drank the hot, sweet liquid from old china cups, he managed to make her laugh; an uphill task because Olive rarely saw anything to smile about. Nonetheless, he persevered and eventually persuaded her to allow him to buy her dinner the next evening. Having agreed, Olive almost immediately changed her mind, but he was gone, leaving her no option but to turn up, because she had no means of contacting him to cancel the arrangement.

Despite her misgivings, she made some effort to dress up, even though her 'best' was a rather worn work suit. Olive never went anywhere and had no real 'going out' clothes. The restaurant was quiet, the tables candle lit and the music soothing. Kurt complimented her on her appearance and gradually broke down her reserves and, by the end of the evening, she was enjoying herself. The relationship blossomed. With Kurt by her side, Olive felt attractive and her self-esteem began to rise. Floating through the days on a wave of love, Olive failed to notice the speculative glances and amused gossip in the office, which was probably a good thing, as she would have hated to know she was the topic of everyone's conversation. Keeping herself to herself, the subterfuge worked and her colleagues had no idea who was putting the smile on her face, even though most were sure the dramatic change had to be because of a man. Kurt was quite happy to go along with the secrecy, although he never explained why. In her moments of self-doubt, Olive wondered if he didn't want people to see them together because he was ashamed of her and, after a while, she couldn't actually remember whose suggestion it had been to keep their relationship a secret.

At first, she felt a murderous jealousy towards any other woman Kurt spoke to, or even looked at, but he gradually succeeded in reassuring her that she had nothing to worry about. Time passed, Olive relaxed and then Kurt told her he'd fallen in love with her and wanted them to spend the rest of their lives together. And now their countries would soon be at war and she only had one more chance to see him before he had to leave England.

The switchboard buzzed, shaking her out of her reverie and Olive sighed. What on earth was she going to do without him?

****

As Joe had expected, Peggy was tearful when they said their goodbyes, although he'd not minded much, grateful for an opportunity to put his arms around her and comfort her.

"I'll be back before you know it." He was enjoying the feel of her body snuggling up against his on the sofa in her house. "And you'll be so busy at the hospital, you won't get time to miss me."

She smiled up at him and he leant down and kissed her tenderly. "When will you be home?"

"I'll be finished with my training in time for Christmas and I should get leave then." He made an effort to sound more cheerful than he felt.

"Thirteen weeks just seems like such a long time." Peggy sounded depressed.

"I know." Joe hugged her. "But I'm sure it will fly by and you can write to me. It's not like I'll be on the other side of the world."

"Ahhh. But will you write back, Joe Price? I know what you're like!" she teased and he laughed, pleased to see her looking happier.

"Of course I will. I'll write at least once!"

Peggy's expression changed and she was about to say something, when she realised he was joking. She settled back into his arms and he pulled her body towards him, his mouth eagerly seeking hers. Peggy kissed him back and Joe moved his hands towards her breasts. To his surprise, she made no move to stop him, and instead her kissing became more passionate. Joe began slowly undoing the buttons on her blouse. As the third one popped open, his hands reached inside and he could feel her bra.

"No." Peggy stopped kissing him long enough to push his hands away and start redoing her buttons.

"Come on, Peggy. I'm going away for thirteen weeks."

"What difference is that going to make?" Peggy sounded annoyed. "You know I'm not that kind of girl."

"I'm not going to think any the less of you." Joe tried to keep the pleading tone out of his voice but he was struggling with an enormous erection. "There's nothing wrong with letting me feel your breasts through your bra, we've known each other ages."

"If I let you do that, you'll want to go further." Peggy had moved away from him.

"No, I won't. I promise."

Peggy stared at him for a long moment and then relented. "Well, alright then. If you promise not to try anything else."

Joe pulled her back towards him and renewed his attack on her breasts, this time meeting no resistance when he began rubbing her erect nipples through her bra. Instead, Peggy began moaning, her eyes closed. Joe couldn't help himself. His hands dropped to her skirt and he ran his fingers up her leg until he felt the skin between her stocking tops and her panties.

"See, I knew you'd try to go further." Peggy pulled away and Joe sighed. She looked cross now and he really didn't want to fall out with her before he went away.

"I'm sorry. You're just so irresistible, I can't keep my hands off you." Seeing his flattery was having no effect, he adjusted his trousers and tried to think about something else.

"Let's go for a walk. I don't want to argue with you before you go away." Peggy stood up. Obviously there would be no more petting. Joe nodded. Talk of going to the army had done the trick perfectly.

****

Catford, London

"Let me come with you, please."

Kurt shook his head. "How can you, Olive? In a matter of hours, our countries will be at war. If you come with me, you'll be interned, or worse. And I can't stay here either."

"Then let's go to a neutral country where we can be safe," Olive pleaded.

Kurt looked shocked. "I can't just run away when my country is at war. I will have to go home and fight."

"But you can't…" Olive was aghast.

Kurt rounded on her. "Do you think I am some sort of coward?" His voice was angry and she cowered away, shaking her head. Kurt stared out of the window. "I am a German and my country needs me."

"But how will I know you are safe?" Olive paled at the thought she would never see him again.

Kurt shrugged, then seeing the sadness in her eyes, moved closer and pulled her into his arms. She turned her face up to his and he bent down, kissing her lips, tenderly at first and then with more passion. His hands moved over her body and she stopped him. "Please, Kurt. I don't want you to go. Please take me with you." Her voice was shaky. He stepped back, an angry snarl on his handsome face. Olive hesitated and then began taking off her clothes. His expression relaxed and he watched while she removed her blouse and skirt and stood there in her underwear. The white bra was see-through and he could see her tiny breasts, their large swollen nipples straining against the thin material. His eyes fell to her panties and the curly wisps of tangled pubic hair peeping through, and felt himself grow hard. He undid the buttons on his fly and began stroking his penis, his breath coming in jagged gasps as he stared at her. "My dear Olive." He beckoned her closer, then smiled and reached out with his other hand, pulling her engorged nipples until she was moaning and writhing with pleasure.

The knock on the door bought them both to a sudden halt and the angry expression returned to his face.

"Who's there?" Olive called out, her voice breathless.

"Only Mrs. Smith, dear." The whiny voice never ceased to annoy Olive. "Just wanted to make sure you were alright. I thought I heard voices."

Olive opened her mouth to tell her nosy neighbour to get lost, but Kurt had buttoned up his trousers and was putting on his coat. She didn't want to waste time getting into an argument.

"I've got the wireless on. I was listening to a play," she called desperately, seeing Kurt was already reaching for his hat.

"Alright, dear. Sorry to have bothered you." Olive could hear the elderly woman hesitate outside the door before shuffling away, her slippers scraping on the bare boards and she cursed under her breath. Kurt made to walk past her and she grabbed his arm.

"Please don't go." Her eyes pleaded with him and he relented.

"Just another few moments then," he whispered, removing his coat again.

Chapter Two

Marie stared at her husband Jacques in horror. "Oh my god, not again." Jacques could see the fear in her eyes and he hastened to reassure her.

"I'm sure it won't come to that, my love. We have the Maginot Line and, in any case, no one really wants war, not after last time."

Marie wasn't convinced, but Jacques seemed so sure, she said nothing. She was going to change the subject when the door burst open and Louis, her older son, flew in.

"Have you heard the news, Mama, Papa?" His face was flushed with excitement, his blond hair tousled from the wind. "I'm going to join up straight away," he continued before they had a chance to reply.

Marie felt faint. "You can't!" The colour drained from her face.

"I can do what I like, Mama; I'm twenty. I don't need your permission." Louis' face wore the familiar, stubborn expression she knew well. Marie was about to argue when Jacques placed a restraining hand on her arm.

"Are you sure you want to join up, Louis?" Jacques's voice was calm, his tone reasoned. "Why not wait until they begin conscription. There's no rush."

"If I join up now, I'll get to choose where I go." Louis was not to be swayed. "I thought you'd be pleased, Papa. You were a great soldier; I just want to make you proud of me. I'm going to see Brigitte. She'll be pleased for me, even if you aren't." He spun on his heel and stormed out, slamming the door shut behind him.

Marie watched Louis go and her heart sank. She loved Jacques, but the war had damaged him and she couldn't bear her son to suffer like his father. She hoped his girlfriend would talk some sense into him, but she didn't hold out much hope. Brigitte was shallow, thoughtless and self centred and had already gained a certain reputation in Bethune. Marie couldn't understand why Louis liked her. The only good thing about him joining the army was that he would be separated from the girl and, with a bit of luck, he would find someone else.

"He'll be alright, Marie." Jacques' voice broke into her thoughts.

Marie shook her head, her eyes filled with sorrow. "You weren't alright, Jacques. Why should our son be any different?"

****

Bethune, Northern France

Nineteen year-old Brigitte Fabron slipped quietly through the back door of the butcher's shop and headed in the direction of her father's café. As she negotiated the cobbled street in her high heels, she smoothed down her tight fitting skirt and thought about the money she had just tucked away in her bra and how she would spend it. Her long auburn hair looked windswept, even though the day was still, and her lipstick was smudged, but Brigitte was unaware of this and assumed her appearance was perfect, as usual. Albert was easy to please; she really couldn't understand why his wife didn't spend more time catering for his needs. Brigitte had been sneaking round to see him during his wife's weekly visit to her sister for several months and, providing Louis didn't get to hear about her afternoon activities, she couldn't see anything wrong with the arrangement. Albert was perfectly happy and she was earning very nicely.

She had only just reached her father's café and sat down at one of the pavement tables when Louis rode up on his bicycle. He leapt off, leaned the bike against the wall and rushed over to her.

"Louis! I wasn't expecting to see you today."

"I'm going to join the army!" he burst out.

Brigitte was astonished and then her face lit up. The old crones who were always gossiping about her would have to treat her with a bit more respect if her boyfriend was a brave soldier. "That's wonderful, Louis. When did you decide?"

"We're at war, haven't you heard?" Louis was amazed when Brigitte shook her head. "What on earth have you been doing all day?" Brigitte blanched but, fortunately for her, Louis didn't wait for an answer. "I don't think my parents are very pleased, but I knew you would be."

Brigitte was so relieved he'd lost interest in her whereabouts, she stood up and kissed him. Louis immediately hugged her close to him, squeezed her buttocks and whispered, "I thought we could go somewhere and celebrate? Once I sign up, I'll have to go away and it might be ages before we see each other again."

Brigitte made no attempt to move his hands. She was already planning how she could gain the maximum advantage from his new career. "Of course. Let's go up to our secret place," she murmured in his ear. Louis moved away, grabbed his bike, sat on the seat and helped her onto the handlebars. Once he was sure she was safe, Louis pedalled away in the direction of La Couture.

****

La Couture, Northern France

Marie stared out of the window at the farm she and Jacques had nurtured and waited for Louis to come home. She hoped Brigitte would have more luck than they'd had in dissuading him from signing up, but she doubted it. Once Louis made up his mind to do something, however reckless, it was virtually impossible to talk him out of it. Thank goodness Marcel, her younger son, was more level headed.

Marie sighed. All the talk of war and Louis joining up had rekindled old memories she would rather had not resurfaced. She loved Jacques, even though life had not always been easy. Their problems had started before they were even married. Jacques' family was quite well off and didn't approve of Marie because she was only a waitress in a café; they assumed she was just a gold digger, after Jacques for his money. The irony was not lost on Marie, who had been horrified when Louis had bought Brigitte home to meet them. Remembering how Jacques' parents had done everything they could to stop the marriage and how this had only spurred him on to defy them, Marie had tried hard not to let Louis see how she felt about his girlfriend.

Although she and Jacques had been happy to start with, things had changed after he had been wounded at Verdun in August 1916. The shell fragments they had painstakingly picked out of his body were bad enough, but even worse was the damage the war had done to his mind. Jacques' parents had expected her to collapse under the pressure of caring for him, but she had surprised them. Not long after he was injured, she had given birth to their first child. Sadly the baby, a girl, had died just a few days later. However there had been little time for her to grieve. Jacques was suffering from shell shock and dreadful nightmares and needed constant care. Through the long days and nights of the next few months, Marie nursed him back to health, willing him to overcome the terrifying memories that haunted him. Her obvious devotion to Jacques had finally convinced his parents just how much she loved their son and, at last, they had accepted her. From then on, they had supported Marie and Jacques up until their deaths, treating her like she was their own daughter.

Despite his injuries and the nightmares resulting from his experiences in the war, they had been very happy. The location of the farm, away from any frightening memories, with its rural peace and tranquility had worked their magic. The terrifying flashbacks lessened considerably as the years passed and their two sons had brought them nothing but pleasure. Although they had never had much money, they always had food and clothes to put on their backs. Many of the events in the outside world passed them by, as they lived out their lives in the peace of the French countryside. But all that seemed set to end and it wasn't just Jacques she would have to worry about, not if Louis got his way. She only hoped seventeen year-old Marcel would not be influenced by his older brother's haste.

Thinking about her sons bought a lump to her throat. Louis was like his father, both in appearance and character; impetuous, dashing and brave, but also stubborn and selfish when it suited him. Although Marcel had his father's fair colouring, he was more like her father; resourceful, calm, and thoughtful and always reminded her of a gentle giant.

Marie couldn't see anything of herself in either of her sons, although her friends said they could see her in Marcel's eyes sometimes, and in some of the expressions Louis pulled when he didn't want to listen to good advice. Inwardly, Marie shook herself; she needed to make some sort of decision. If the Germans invaded France, should they go, or should they stay put?

****

La Couture, Northern France

Louis freewheeled through the narrow lane, a broad grin on his face. As he'd expected, Brigitte had been delighted about him joining up and had needed little persuasion to show him just how pleased she was. Louis would miss her when he went away, but the thought of being a soldier was even more exciting. And if she was this accommodating before he signed up, he couldn't wait to see what she would do when he came to visit her in his uniform.

He came to the small hedge that bordered his family's land, lifted his bike over and then vaulted across the thick bushes with ease. As he strolled through the land on which he had grown up and worked, he was sad he would be leaving, but he couldn't suppress his excitement at the new life opening up to him. The farmhouse came into view and his spirits dipped briefly. He could see his mother watching at the window and he sighed. Louis knew Marie didn't want him to go, but

19

he was determined to join up. Just because his father had suffered in the war, didn't mean he would and he hoped she wasn't going to make too much fuss. He didn't want to leave with bad feelings between them.

Reaching the door, Louis let himself in. Marie moved towards him, a troubled expression on her face. She could tell by his demeanour he had not changed his mind and she bit her lip.

"You're still going then?" Louis could hear the emotion in her voice, but he was determined not to weaken.

"Yes, Mama."

"Come here then," Marie reached out and put her arms around him. "Take care, Louis, and come home safe."

Louis hugged her back, relieved she was not going to try and talk him out of joining up. "I will, Mama. Don't worry, I'll be back in no time, safe and sound, you'll see."

Chapter Three

Peggy loved her job, but she couldn't wait for her shift to be over. Joe would be home soon and, although she wasn't seeing him until Boxing Day, two whole days away, just knowing he was only a few miles away was exciting. Because she was a student nurse, she would have to work Christmas Day, but she was looking forward to spending the afternoon on the children's ward. That would be more fun than a day with her elderly Aunt Maud and Uncle Bernard who were rather staid and set in their ways. Even worse, would be a day spent with her cousin, Olive. Peggy had no idea why Olive hated her, but the thinly veiled animosity had never been far from the surface and Peggy had given up trying to make friends a long time ago. Fortunately, they rarely met now they both had their own homes.

Peggy had been training to be a nurse at the hospital for over two years, something she still found incredible. Ever since she was a child, she'd wanted to be a nurse; nothing else had interested her and she could still remember just how nervous she'd been when she first arrived at the hospital. Fortunately, the gate porter who'd greeted her was very friendly and had given her directions to the Sister Tutor's office where she was introduced to the other new applicants including Helen, who also came from London and was soon to become her best friend.

"Are you ready, Cooper?" Peggy jumped. Lost in her thoughts about Joe, she hadn't heard Sister Adams approaching.

"Yes, Sister." Peggy took the lighted candle Sister Adams was holding and followed her up the stairs to the first floor, where all the nurses were getting ready to sing Carols to the children who were too ill to go home for Christmas. The concert began and Peggy pushed dreams of Joe out of her mind and concentrated on making sure the youngsters had a wonderful time. When they finished singing, she and the other nurses decorated the large tree at the end of the ward and helped the children hang up their stockings ready for Father Christmas.

****

England

Christmas arrived so quickly, Joe could hardly believe the thirteen weeks' training was over and the time had come for his first leave. He packed up his 'civvie' clothes, which they were instructed to take home and leave there, and hurried to the Guard House where he had to pass inspection before being allowed out. From there, he went out through West Gate, over the bridge and across the street to the station to catch the train home. He was quite sad to be leaving Winchester. Much to his surprise, he had enjoyed his time there and had made some very good friends. After Christmas, he would go straight to Tidworth to complete his training to be a driver of a Bren gun carrier.

"I can't wait to get home," Joe said to Alfred White, a tall lanky young man, known to his mates as 'Chalky', who was travelling back on the train with him.

"Yeah, me too." Chalky peered through the window. They were pulling into Waterloo Station now and, everywhere they looked, there were sandbags piled up against public buildings.

"Shame we've only got a few days." Chalky's words echoed his own thoughts.

"Still, better than nothing at all." Like Chalky, Joe was only too aware that their short leave would fly by and he was determined to make the most of the time he had before the inevitable return to camp.

"Can you see Joyce anywhere?" Chalky had opened the window and was leaning out, scanning the platform for his wife.

"Look, there she is." Joe spotted her by the barrier. Joyce saw them at the same time and began waving, her face alight with excitement.

Chalky flung open the door, narrowly missing a couple of people standing too close to the edge of the platform. Ignoring their shouts of outrage, he leapt off the moving train, ran towards the barrier, handed his ticket to the collector and swung Joyce into his arms. Turning towards Joe, he waved briefly and then disappeared into the seething crowds.

"Lucky sod," Joe muttered to himself. He wouldn't be able to see Peggy until Boxing Day. His stomach fluttered nervously. He hoped everything was going to be alright. He shook his head. There was no point worrying about something that might never happen. He turned his thoughts to his mum and Fred, and smiled. He'd missed them more than he'd expected over the past few weeks and he was determined to enjoy a family Christmas. The train eased to a halt, Joe stepped onto the platform and strode purposefully towards the exit.

****

La Couture, Northern France

"Hello, Mama, Papa." Louis flung his arms round his mother. "Have you missed me?" Louis had put on weight and was bursting with good health, his uniform smartly ironed, his boots shining.

"You silly boy, of course I have." Marie embraced him, her head turned away so he couldn't see her tears.

"Marcel, it's good to see you, little brother."

Marcel hugged Louis, delighted to see him back safe and sound.

"Come on, Marcel. Help me unpack. I've only got a few days, so let's make the most of our time." Marcel followed Louis upstairs, leaving their parents alone.

"Is the war still boring, like you said in your letters?" Marcel couldn't wait to hear more about Louis' life.

"Worse." Louis pulled a face. "All we do is play football or cards and send up weather balloons. I haven't even seen the Boche."

"Well that's good, isn't it?"

"I suppose so, but I would like to see some action."

"Wouldn't you be frightened?"

"Nah, course not" Louis' response was a little too quick, although Marcel didn't notice.

He gazed at his brother in admiration. "Perhaps I should join up too?"

"You're a bit young at the moment, Marcel. Why not wait a while and see what happens."

Marcel breathed a sigh of relief that his brother hadn't encouraged him to rush off and become a soldier.

"Tell me all the news, then? What have I missed?"

Marcel thought hard. "Nothing really, Louis, although…" He hesitated and Louis looked closely at him.

"Is something wrong?"

"Papa is acting strangely." Marcel stopped, feeling he was being disloyal. Louis didn't say anything, so he felt compelled to continue, "He's started having nightmares again."

"Oh." Louis' face was troubled. "The war's probably bringing everything back."

"That's what Mama said."

Louis punched him playfully on the arm "There you are then! He'll soon get better. Don't worry, little brother. I'm sure he'll be fine."

Marcel opened his mouth to argue, then realised there wasn't much Louis could do to help. "Perhaps we should go downstairs? I know Mama has really missed you."

"Come on, then. I bet I can get down quicker than you!"

They raced each other down the stairs, their laughter filling the house and Jacques turned to Marie

"See, I told you he would be alright." Marie didn't answer. She wanted to shout at him that nothing had happened yet, and what if things changed? As if reading her mind, Jacques reached out and squeezed her hand. "The Germans don't want war any more than we do. You'll see, it will all blow over."

Honor Oak Park, London

"Have you killed anyone yet?" Fred asked. They were sitting around the dinner table, waiting for the food to be dished up.

"Fred, what a question!" Pauline snapped at him as she brought in their plates, but Joe just grinned.

"I was only asking." Fred looked aggrieved. "It's been really boring here. No cinema, theatre or football until a few weeks ago."

"Ah, poor you." Joe wasn't at all sympathetic. "And there's me thinking my life was bad: not allowed to go out without permission; people shouting at me; not able to see Peggy; having to change my whole life." The more he said, the more angry he began to feel.

"No need to get narked, Joe." Pauline glanced at Joe in surprise. He was normally very easy-going. It was most unlike him to get so riled up.

Joe took a deep breath. "Sorry. I'm not cross with you, Fred. Ignore me. Being back home reminds me of everything I'm missing, that's all."

"Well, you have some more rabbit stew and make the most of it." Pauline reached for his half-empty plate and, without giving him a chance to object, she went into the kitchen where the rest of the stew was keeping warm on the stove. "And you stop making him cross, Fred," she added, over her shoulder.

There was a brief silence while Pauline was out of the room, and when she came back with his plate, Joe began tucking in. He was still feeling out of sorts but he didn't want to spoil his precious time at home.

The stew was delicious and he concentrated on enjoying the first decent meal he'd had for ages. Finally realising he couldn't eat another mouthful, he placed his knife and fork together and sat back.

"That was absolutely delicious." He patted his stomach lightly. He was feeling completely bloated. "I really couldn't eat anything else, Mum, honestly."

"Well, if you're sure you've had enough?" Pauline was watching him carefully; he was a little too quiet for her liking. She knew he wouldn't speak out in front of his brother if there was something wrong, so she changed the subject. "Fred's dug up the rest of the flower beds and planted some vegetables." She began clearing away the plates.

"Potatoes and carrots at the moment; I'm going to have a go at growing some cabbage and parsnips too." Fred sounded very enthusiastic, which Joe found quite amusing. Seeing his brother's expression, Fred frowned. "What's so funny?"

"Just the thought of you gardening, that's all. You hate gardening."

"Yeah, well, we've all got to do our bit, haven't we?" Fred was defensive.

Joe grinned. "Well, just as long as you don't kill everything."

"Well, you can talk," Fred laughed. "You put in loads of flower seeds last year. Not one of them came up."

"Ah, but that was the weather; nothing to do with me." Joe was relieved to see Fred was happier now. He felt guilty about snapping at him earlier, but he had suddenly been envious of them all. Yes, their lives were changing, but not to the extent his was and it probably wouldn't be long before he was sent somewhere to fight and then... He made a conscious effort to think about something else. Normally when he was depressed or worried, he turned his thoughts to Peggy. For once, even that didn't cheer him up. He couldn't wait to see her on Boxing Day, but what if...

"Joe!"

"Sorry, I was miles away."

"I just asked if you were alright." Pauline sounded concerned. "You seem really fed up."

Seeing the worried look on her face, Joe felt guilty. His mum and brother were really pleased to see him and here he was behaving like a right misery guts. He made an effort to cheer up. "No, I'm fine, Mum."

"Well, if you're sure?" Pauline wasn't convinced. She knew Joe very well and there was definitely something he wasn't telling her.

Chapter Four

"How do you like being a soldier?" Jacques asked, pouring Louis and Marcel some more wine. They had just finished their Christmas meal, Marie had gone to wash up the dishes and the three men were relaxing at the sturdy oak kitchen table.

"To be honest, there's not much happening at the moment." Louis sipped his glass of red wine. "It's a bit boring really."

"Well, let's hope it stays like that." Marie had her back to them and she missed the wink Jacques gave Louis.

Louis glanced up at the kitchen clock on the wall and downed the rest of his drink in one gulp.

"That was a lovely dinner, Mama." Louis left the table, came up to the sink and gave her a hug. Pulling back, he stretched. "I think I'll go for a walk and work off some of the food."

Marie smiled up at him. "What a good idea, Louis. Perhaps Marcel would like to go with you?" His face fell. "Or was there some other reason you wanted to get some fresh air?"

Louis flushed. He knew his mother didn't really approve of his girlfriend, but he was a man now and who he saw was none of her business. "Well, I did think I might call in on Brigitte."

Marie tried to hide her misgivings. Louis was home for such a short time, she didn't want to fall out with him. She forced herself to smile

28

and she patted him on the arm. "Go on, Louis. Off you go and enjoy yourself!"

Louis grabbed his heavy army greatcoat, pulled on his boots and stepped out into the thick snow. Brigitte had written him several letters in the short time he had been in the army and Louis had spent many a night looking forward to becoming reacquainted with her, so the bitter wind and steadily falling snow did nothing to dent his ardour. He climbed on his bike and pedalled down the lane towards the main road to Bethune.

****

Outside Bethune, Northern France

Brigitte, heavily wrapped up in a warm coat and knitted scarf, her long auburn hair hidden under a fur hat, tramped through the frozen fields, her head down against the cold snow-laden wind. She couldn't wait to see Louis again, especially if he was in his uniform. Brigitte glanced at her watch and quickened her pace. They had arranged to meet in their special place, an isolated barn just outside the town and she didn't want to be late.

"Brigitte!"

Louis was leaning his bike against an ice-coated tree on the edge of the pasture. She waved and he headed towards her. Brigitte increased her pace, wishing the snow wasn't so thick. When she reached him, she flung her arms around his neck and Louis swung her up in the air.

"I've missed you so much," he whispered in her ear before tilting her face towards his and kissing her. Brigitte responded, her tongue seeking his with a passion that caught him by surprise. Louis slipped his hand inside her coat and towards her breasts, his fingers seeking her erect nipples. Giggling, she pushed him away.

"Not here, Louis. I'm much too cold!"

"And here's me thinking it was because you were pleased to see me."
Louis pretended to be hurt and she pushed him playfully. Grinning,

Louis took her arm. "Come into the barn, then you can show me how much you've missed me." Brigitte allowed him to lead her to the large wooden structure, its snow covered roof hanging with icicles.

Louis opened the large barn door and pulled her inside. It was much warmer there, away from the cold easterly wind and she quickly discarded her coat and hat and lay down on the straw, an inviting smile on her face. Louis took off his coat and stood gazing down at her. He could see the rise and fall of her breasts, the outline of her suspenders under her skirt, her shapely legs tapering down to her boots and he could wait no longer. Louis knelt down, straddling her. Brigitte's eyes glazed over with lust as she gazed up at him. With one hand he undid the buttons on his jacket, while the other kneaded her breasts, searching for her nipples through her tightly fitting woollen jumper. Brigitte moaned and reached for him. Louis leaned forward and began to kiss her, his hands pulling at her jumper, until the sweater was no longer tucked in her skirt. Pushing the top up until her cream coloured lacy bra was visible, his hands reached behind her back and, with one easy movement, he undid the clasp, freeing her breasts, her nipples proud as he ran his fingers over them before ducking his head and licking and sucking until Brigitte was moaning and writhing with pleasure.

Feeling himself grow hard, Louis slid his hand down and pushed her skirt up revealing creamy lace knickers. He licked his fingers, then inserted them inside her warm moist opening. She groaned and opened her legs wider. Unable to wait any longer, Louis wriggled out of his trousers and pants and eased himself inside her. Brigitte arched her back and rose to meet him, her muscles tightening round him while he thrust faster and faster bringing them both to a noisy climax.

****

Catford, London

Olive was relieved Christmas Day was almost over. She envied her cousin Peggy being able to work. She had no choice. The council offices were shut for two days, leaving her with two options: spend the days on her own, or go round to her parents. She couldn't face the festive season, enduring the pitying glances and prying questions of her parents, so she'd opted for being alone, having lied and said she was going to a friend's house for the holiday. Fortunately, when she'd arrived home on Christmas Eve there had been a letter from Kurt waiting for her on the mat. Olive had pounced on the envelope like a puppy with a new ball and spent the rest of the evening reading and re-reading the precious prose, planning how she would answer him.

Having eaten her soup and bread – she saw no point cooking for one – Olive pulled out his letter which was beginning to look rather tatty and re-read the words slowly, this time trying to pretend he was in the room with her.

My darling Olive,

I hope this letter finds you in the best of health and missing me as much as I am missing you. I can't believe three months have passed since we last held each other and I pray daily this wretched war will not go on too much longer.

How is London? I miss walking through the park with you. I expect they have erected lots of air raid defences now and I would probably hardly recognise the place. Are there lots of soldiers around? I must confess to being very jealous when I think of you alone with all those men in uniform. I torture myself with the thought that you have found someone else and at this very moment are making love to him like you did with me. Do you remember our love making, my darling? Can you taste me, feel me inside you, thrusting hard while you writhe in pleasure?

If I close my eyes, I can see your beautiful breasts with their swollen nipples and feel how hard they grow against my fingers. I can see my hand lifting your skirt revealing the moist triangle of black hair waiting for me to rouse you to passion. I can savour your own special taste on my tongue and feel you growing wild with excitement. Oh my darling, I need you so much. I do hope you feel the same way?

I think I had better concentrate on something less exciting, so I can calm down!

I am very worried about your safety, my love. The war has barely begun but I feel the fighting will grow worse. You do have somewhere to go if there are air raids, don't you? I know your building doesn't have a cellar. Are you able to go to an underground shelter? Are there men ready to protect you and your home from the death and destruction I have seen in Poland?

Please reassure me you will be safe and you also have enough to eat. There were some worrying reports in the newspapers here saying Britain has very little food left. I can't bear the thought of you going hungry.

I am beginning to fret but I know how you can stop this, if you would, my darling? In each letter you must tell me whether there is enough food and whether you are safe. Then I can relax a little and just concentrate on making love to you in my mind.

I would like to write more but the special post is here and if I miss it, you won't get this before Christmas and I so want you to be reading this, laying warm and snug under the sheets and remembering the precious time when we were together in your tiny bed.

Good night, my dearest love. I await your response with impatience.

Your one true love,

Kurt xxx

Olive placed the letter on the small cupboard by her bed, undressed and climbed under the sheets, pulling the covers over her naked body. Music from the wireless in the sitting room seeped into the bedroom but Olive didn't hear anything. Her eyes were closed, she could hear his voice repeating the words of his letter and she smiled.

Chapter Five

Having spent Christmas Day at the hospital, Peggy hurried round to Pauline's house for dinner on Boxing Day. She hadn't seen Joe since September and she arrived early, eager to spend most of the day with him, before he had to go back to camp. However, Joe seemed edgy and distant and totally unlike his normal self. Peggy asked him several times if everything was alright, wondering if there was a problem at his battalion, although his letters had seemed cheerful enough.

"I've asked him the same thing, but he won't tell me anything," Pauline commented.

"That's because there's nothing to tell." Joe was beginning to sound cross. Peggy glanced at Pauline but she was already heading back into the kitchen. Peggy sighed. Joe was definitely behaving strangely. She was just beginning to wonder whether he didn't want to go out with her anymore and wasn't sure how to tell her, when he suggested they go for a walk. Feeling really nervous, she went to get her coat from the hall stand. Her mind was racing. *Maybe he's found someone else in Winchester.*

"Dinner's at one sharp. Don't be late and it's really cold out there, so wrap up warm," Pauline called from the kitchen.

For the first time since Peggy had arrived, Joe relaxed and laughed. "I'm used to the cold, Mum. I've just spent weeks living under canvas."

"Well Peggy hasn't," she snapped, but she was relieved he seemed more cheerful. Normally, Joe would talk to her but he hadn't and that was really worrying her. What could be so bad he didn't want to tell her about it?

****

Catford, London

Olive spent Boxing Day morning listening to the wireless, reading a rather boring book and composing various replies to Kurt in her head, until she was finally ready to put her thoughts into words.

Picking up her pen and paper she began writing.

My darling, wonderful Kurt,

You have no idea how delighted I was to receive your letter when I arrived home from work on Christmas Eve. I was dreading spending Christmas and Boxing Day alone without you and then you rescued me again. Just like the first time when we met and I finally had something in my life to look forward to.

You don't need to worry about food. We have plenty. Rationing is due to start in January, but there is more than enough food in the country and we are all going to be growing our own soon. No, I don't think you would recognise the park. All the flowers have been pulled out and vegetables planted in their place and there are lots of air defences everywhere. There are even some ack ack guns (I think that's what they're called) in the park and Home Guard and bossy air raid wardens everywhere, shouting at us to remember the blackout. Lots of people are training to be fire wardens to protect buildings and we all have gas attack practice regularly, so you have nothing to worry about.

Life was very boring here without the cinema or decent programmes on the wireless but everything's changed now and at last there are some good comedy sketches on to listen to in the evening and some wonderful shows with very good singers. The news is still bad, though. Poor Mr Chamberlain seems to be under attack from that dreadful Mr Churchill, although I think he's doing quite a good job. There are lots of rumours the Prime Minister

34

really wants peace. Wouldn't it be wonderful if he signed an agreement with Mr Hitler ending the war? Then we could be together again.

I am blushing just thinking about your descriptions of our love making and wish I could write such moving words, I don't think I can, not just yet. Anyway, hopefully I won't have to imagine us together or live on memories too much longer.

I had another run-in the other day with my cousin, Peggy. I really don't like her. She's so prim and proper. I'm sure she thinks she's better than anyone else. Her boyfriend was conscripted right at the beginning of September into the Rifle Brigade. They're based at Winchester in Hampshire and she's always talking about him like he's some kind of god. I can't believe we managed to live in the same house for so many years without falling out more often.

Sorry, I'm getting cross and I don't want to bore you with all my silly problems. How is life in Germany? Have you joined the army yet? You don't say much in your letters about your own life, you must write and tell me, then I can picture everything more clearly.

Well, I suppose I'd better go or I will keep writing this letter forever; anything to feel close to you.

All my love darling, look after yourself.

Your one true love,

Olive. xxxxxxxx

****

Honor Oak Park, London

Peggy put on her coat and followed Joe out into the icy streets. He put his arm around her and pulled her close which made her feel slightly better. She resisted the temptation to ask him again whether there was anything wrong, sensing it would be best to let him talk in his own time. They strolled in companionable silence for a while and Peggy enjoyed the sensation of feeling him close to her, although she was too nervous to really relax. What would she do if Joe had found someone else? They had been together for so long, she couldn't imagine being without him. They were heading in the direction of the river and, when they drew close, Joe spoke for the first time since they had left the house.

"Peggy, you know I love you, don't you?"

Peggy smiled nervously. "Yes, Joe. I love you too."

"Well, I was thinking. We've known each other over four years now and, we both love each other and... Well... perhaps we should... that is... it might be nice to... Do you think we...? Maybe we could get engaged?" There, he'd asked her! Even if he had stuttered and stammered, and the words hadn't quite come out how he'd intended.

Peggy stared at him with a mixture of astonishment, relief and happiness. He hadn't found someone else after all.

"Was that a proposal?" she asked, anxiously.

"Yes." Joe grinned, relieved he had finally managed to do ask but nervous, in case she said no. "Wasn't a very good one, was it?"

"Well, you should really get down on one knee and... Joe!" she shrieked. To the amused stares of the few people brave enough to be out, he knelt down on the frozen river bank, took her hand in his and said, with much more coherence than he had previously mustered:

"Will you marry me, Peggy?"

"Yes, yes, yes! Of course I will." Her delighted response was cut off abruptly. Joe stood up, swung her round in his arms and kissed her. Peggy kissed him back, totally oblivious to the cold and damp. Finally releasing her, they both spoke at once.

"I've been worried sick in case you said no," Joe began

"I was terrified you were going to tell me you'd found someone else." Peggy could hardly hide her relief.

They kissed again and then held each other close, wishing the moment could go on forever.

****

The day after Christmas, not wanting to upset his mother too much, Louis made sure Marie wasn't about before riding to the barn where he had arranged to meet Brigitte again. After making love to her, he glanced at his watch. He would need to go, or Marie would notice he was missing. Spotting him checking his watch, Brigitte snuggled closer and began tracing delicate patterns with her fingers across his naked stomach. He laughed.

"You're insatiable." He turned on his side to face her and took her chin in his hand. Her eyes stared up at him and he leaned forward and kissed the tip of her nose. "I have to go. I said I would help Papa with the milking."

Brigitte pouted, the expression of irritation on her face making him laugh even more. "Don't sulk, Brigitte." He reached down and, clasping her naked buttocks with both hands, pulled her closer. She could feel his penis growing hard against her stomach and she smiled. Louis sighed and rolled on top of her. Her legs parted easily and he positioned himself ready to thrust inside her. Then he changed his mind and sat up. "Turn over."

Brigitte opened her eyes in surprise and then obeyed. Although the light was fading, he could clearly see the outline of her bottom tapering away to her narrow waist. He slid his hand under her pubis and inserted his fingers inside her, feeling the moisture as she wriggled and strained against him. He rubbed gently until she was moaning loudly then removed his fingers, replacing them with his penis. He licked his fingers and, leaning forward, ran them gently over her mouth. "You taste nice too," he whispered, grinding his body against hers, harder and harder until she was crying out. His climax was not far behind and he collapsed back on the straw, panting loudly.

****

Eventually, the cold began to bite and Peggy and Joe resumed their walk. Joe was ecstatic. "When do you want to get married?" he asked.

"I don't know." Peggy wanted to say 'tomorrow'. However, she tried to be practical. "We'll need time to organise a wedding and we don't have a clue where you're going to be or what's going to happen. Maybe we should think about some time in 1941: the summer? Perhaps the war will be over by then. What do you think?"

"I'm not sure if I can wait that long." Joe frowned. "It makes sense, I suppose. Oh, I nearly forgot…" Grinning like an idiot, he fumbled in his uniform pockets. "I bought you a ring." Peggy opened the small box in delight. Inside was a beautiful solitaire diamond on a platinum base which fitted her finger perfectly. Unable to believe she was really engaged, Peggy stared at the ring for such a long time without speaking that Joe became anxious.

"Peggy?"

Seeing the panic on his face, she reached up and kissed him.

"Oh, Joe. I've never seen such a beautiful ring. I'm *so* happy and I love you *so* much."

Relieved, he held her close again and then said with reluctance, "I suppose we'd better go home or we'll be late for dinner."

"And you're starving," Peggy finished for him.

"Well, I am, now I'm not nervous anymore!"

****

La Couture, Northern France

"Sorry, Papa. I got held up in Bethune… some of the men, you know how it is…."

Jacques stared up from the kitchen table, took in Louis' disheveled appearance and the bits of straw hanging from his trousers and an expression of amusement crossed his face. "I certainly do, boy." He glanced down at Louis' trousers and smiled. Louis looked down, hastily removed the straw and blushed, realising his father knew exactly what he'd being doing.

"You promised your father you would help with the milking." Unlike Jacques, Marie was not at all amused. Her hands, resting on the kitchen table, were clenched, her face unsmiling. Louis was about to repeat his earlier lie when he stopped. He was a soldier, a man. Why should he apologise? Marie watched the expression on his face change and sighed inwardly. She hadn't wanted to argue with him but he could be selfish sometimes and that girl was definitely not a good influence on him.

"I don't have to answer to you, Mama." His voice was cold. "I'm not a child anymore."

"It's alright, Louis. I did the milking. You have to go back to camp tomorrow. You should make the most of your time here..." Marcel's voice tailed off when he saw his mother's furious face.

"The boy's right, Marie." Jacques spoke before she could say anything. "He's entitled to enjoy himself. You never know what's around the corner."

Marie flushed and then she nodded. Jacques was right. She might never see Louis again. She stood up so they couldn't see the sudden tears in her eyes. "I was just going to make some coffee, do you want some?" She strode across the small kitchen to the enamel and iron stove and busied herself lighting the gas.

"I'm sorry, Mama. I didn't mean to upset you." Louis's voice was close to her ear. She spun round and enfolded him in her arms.

"Just promise me you'll look after yourself," she murmured, holding him close.

****

Honor Oak Park, London

Joe sighed, he needed to head home and get ready to go to Tidworth early the next morning, although he really didn't want to go.

Peggy followed him to the door and down the stone steps of her aunt and uncle's house into the bitterly cold deserted street. Her guardians had been delighted to hear her good news, so now she just had to tell Olive. Peggy shuddered at the thought, sure her unpleasant cousin would find a way of putting a dampener on her happiness. She pushed thoughts of Olive out of her mind and concentrated on saying goodbye to Joe. An icy easterly wind froze the air around them while they stood outside the house and he held her in his arms. She snuggled into his body, putting her own arms around him and leaning her head on his chest. They held each other in a long embrace, wishing the world would go away and leave them alone. Eventually, knowing time was passing and she would have to let go, Peggy pulled back so she could look straight into his eyes. "You will be careful, won't you?"

"Of course I will. Nothing's going to happen to me. I've got you to come back to and no war's going to stop me." Joe sounded so confident, Peggy found herself believing him.

"I really have to go, sweetheart." With reluctance, Joe withdrew from her arms and kissed her, gently at first, then with more passion until he pulled away, smiling. "Now I really have something to remember you by." Peggy watched him walking down the street, trying hard to stem the tears threatening to engulf her. She couldn't let his last sight of her be one of her crying, so she made a supreme effort and, when he stopped at the corner for one last wave, his final view was of Peggy waving, a big smile on her face.

Chapter Six

Joe groaned. His head hurt and he had no idea where he was. He lay still for a moment, then feeling a mattress underneath him, decided he must be in a bed. Trying to ignore the renewed pounding in his head, he cautiously opened his eyes. No, this was not his room. Above him, there was a solitary light bulb encased in a rather garish lampshade, the window was hidden by flowery curtains and he could smell a musky perfume. He frowned, moved his arm and froze. There was someone in bed next to him. Then everything came flooding back and he groaned again.

He had gone into town for a few drinks with Rob and Taffy. Rob, Frank 'Rob' Roberts, a short, stocky, rifleman with dirty blond hair and blue eyes, and Taffy Jones, a tall, well-built man with thick, black curly hair were his best friends, other than Chalky. Chalky had turned down the invitation to go out with them. Since he'd married, he'd become very boring and they'd left him writing to his wife, Joyce.

Joe had a vague memory of some girls joining them about half way through the evening, but they had been with Rob and Taffy not him; he was engaged, wasn't he? After that, things were rather hazy. He thought they had gone onto some night club and then he had a vision of a girl, Elsie, he thought her name was, allowing him to do all the things Peggy wouldn't.

His stomach lurched. Oh God, what had he done? He pushed himself up on his elbow and stared down at the sleeping face, resting on the pillow next to him. He was mildly relieved to see she was quite attractive with shoulder length blonde hair and even features. She stirred, opened her eyes and smiled at him. Joe remembered her blue eyes. They had entranced him the previous evening, their clarity adding to the intensity of her gaze. He stopped as the image of her writhing body came into his mind and groaned again when he realised he'd been unfaithful to Peggy, and only weeks after they'd become engaged.

He climbed out of bed. "Where are you going?" Elsie looked disappointed and Joe felt even worse.

"I have to go, or I'll be late on parade." He said the first thing that came into his head.

Elsie frowned. "You said last night that you had a couple of days' leave. Never mind, we can go out again next time you're in town."

"Yes, definitely."

"When will that be?"

"No idea, but I'll be in touch." Joe grabbed the rest of his clothes and hurried out of the room.

****

Catford / Lewisham, London

Olive watched the postman walk past the block of flats and turned away from the window. She knew getting post into the country and past the censors was difficult but she'd been hoping today she would receive a letter from Kurt. The last one was nearly a month ago.

Feeling miserable, she put on her coat and made her way to work. The switchboard was busy and the girls were working hard. Olive sat down and answered a couple of calls. She glanced around and spotted one of the younger girls laughing. At first, Olive thought she was having a private conversation with a friend during work hours and she felt her temper flaring. Then she realised the girl was not talking to anyone, just sniggering at something one of the telephone callers was saying. Olive frowned. She frequently listened in to the conversations too, but she'd been there a long time and considered she had a right to do so. Mary had only been there a few weeks. How dare she neglect her work when they were this busy?

Olive stared at the younger girl for a few moments, debating whether she should say anything or not. She was about to stand up when she saw Mary speaking to one of the other girls, a mouthy redhead called Kath. They were obviously friends and Olive changed her mind. Kath was rude and had never showed Olive any respect. Olive knew she could never best Kath in an argument and she wasn't about to risk making herself look stupid in front of the other girls. She would speak to the supervisor instead.

****

The Maginot Line, France

As the big guns were driven towards the front line, Louis watched from his vantage place in the fort and waited for the inevitable response from the Germans. Things were still quiet, apart from a few hours every day when the French fired their guns at the Germans and the Germans retaliated with a barrage of their own.

He couldn't understand why the Germans didn't attack them. They seemed content to sit on the border watching them. He knew why the French didn't attack. The army was geared more to defence than assault and, once the initial excitement had worn off, had been a huge disappointment to Louis. He was beginning to wish he'd joined something else; the Air Force maybe, or the Navy. Or perhaps he should just have stayed at home with Brigitte. He knew she liked him in his uniform but there wasn't much point if she never got to see him. With nothing happening, he really couldn't understand why the generals had cancelled all their leave again. He could be back home with her now instead of sitting in a fort on the German border playing war games.

"Hey, Louis, the post's here. Looks like there's another letter from that girl of yours." Raul, his best friend in the army, handed him a letter. Louis could smell the perfume wafting from the envelope and he grinned.

"Thanks, Raul." He sat back on his bunk, ignored the booming of the guns in the distance and settled down to read.

****

Honor Oak Park, London

Peggy was surprised to find another letter from Joe on the doormat. She'd only received one two days earlier. She pulled open the envelope, wondering if there was anything wrong. She scanned the first few lines and began to relax. He was missing her. She smiled as she re-read the part which detailed how much he loved her and how he couldn't wait to see her again. He was sorry his leave had been cancelled at the last minute, but hopefully he would get some more soon.

Peggy frowned. She didn't know he'd had any leave due. Funny he hadn't mentioned anything in any of his other letters. Maybe they had only been told at the last minute and then something had happened to cancel his days off.

She sighed. She was really missing him too. Perhaps he would be home soon and then they could spend some time together. She'd been thinking quite a bit since Christmas and maybe she should let him go further now they were engaged. The thought made her warm inside and she fought hard to remove the wide grin from her face. She glanced at the clock and gasped. Good gracious! Was that really the time? Mooning around thinking about Joe had made her late. If she didn't leave, now she would miss the bus.

****

Brigitte was bored. She wondered if Louis had received her letter yet. She had written to him every week since Christmas and he had written back almost as regularly. She frowned. She had begun to look forward to hearing from him and she wasn't sure if that was a good idea. Men usually lied to get things they wanted without a second thought, so she wasn't sure she should trust Louis to keep his promises that he loved her and would come back to her. Experience had shown her people couldn't be trusted and she didn't want to get hurt again. On the other hand, he was fun to be with and he didn't seem to mind what people said about her.

Perhaps she should look for a boyfriend closer to home, to keep her company until he returned. She could always dump her new lover, if and when Louis came back and there was no reason for Louis to find out about him, of course. The question was, who? She'd been out with some of the lads in the town already and quite a few had joined up. Then she smiled. Henri, who worked for Giscard, the local landowner, kept giving her the eye when his wife wasn't looking. Perhaps she'd take a walk up to the estate and see if he was about. He would be perfect. He wouldn't want his wife to know he was seeing her, so he would want to keep their relationship a secret too. She had also heard Giscard liked to have special parties at his house. If she could get invited to them, she would be able to meet lots of interesting people and maybe make some more money. Brigitte loved the feeling of security that money gave her. She normally spent most of her earnings on clothes and make up, but just lately, she'd been thinking about saving some for her future instead. She glanced in her wardrobe and wondered which of her new dresses she should wear. Louis was forgotten.

Part Two

May 1940

Chapter Seven

England

After several months in Bournemouth, Joe and his friends left the comfortable boarding house where they had been billeted and joined the convoy heading north east to Suffolk. Joe was relieved to be leaving the town. All the time he was there, he couldn't forget his stupid drunken mistake. Chalky had shaken his head disapprovingly when Joe returned the next morning, while Rob and Taffy had patted him on the back and congratulated him. Joe felt dreadful. He had never intended to be unfaithful to Peggy and he was terrified she would find out. Elsie had proved surprisingly tenacious, tracking him down to the boarding house and refusing to go until he spoke to her. At first Joe had tried to avoid her. However, eventually he'd had no choice but to tell her he had a fiancée and wasn't interested.

Elsie slapped him hard across the face, told him what she thought of him and flounced off. Joe breathed a sigh of relief and wrote another long letter to Peggy, telling her how much he missed her. He'd been about to put pen to paper yet again when Chalky pulled him up. "If you keep writing, she's gonna smell a rat. I'd quit while you're ahead, if I were you. Just forget anything ever happened and get on with your life."

Joe nodded and tried to put the experience out of his mind.

Their journey north was reasonably uneventful, apart from an unscheduled stop in Chelmsford to investigate possible sightings of

German paratroopers. The men piled off the trucks with enthusiasm. At last, here was a chance to fight the enemy. But, despite a thorough search of the surrounding area, they had not found anyone. Disappointed, they climbed back aboard the trucks, assuming the sightings were just another of the many unfounded rumours sweeping the country, in the wake of yet more bad news from Europe.

"Well, that was a waste of time," Chalky grumbled.

"Would have been more worrying if we *had* found them." Joe's reply was thoughtful.

"Yeah, maybe you're right. I just wanted to put our training to use."

"I wouldn't worry." The voice belonged to one of the regulars. "You'll soon get your chance to be a hero. There'll be enough war for all of us."

Chalky flushed and was about to say something, when another regular chipped in, "Yeah, don't be in such a bloody hurry to get yourself killed, Chalky." He carried on before anyone could answer, "Price is right. All the time there are just rumours, our families are safe. The best place to kill the enemy is overseas, not on our own doorstep."

There was no argument to that and, feeling rather stupid, Chalky sat back and said no more.

****

Bethune, Northern France

Brigitte crept up the stairs and hurried along the narrow passageway to her bedroom. She could hear her father snoring loudly and she breathed a sigh of relief. Although she gave everyone the impression she wasn't scared of him, that wasn't strictly true. She was reasonably sure he wouldn't hit her again, not since she'd hit him back a few years ago. She'd been fourteen and he'd accused her of being a slut when she'd crept into the house in the early hours after spending the night with some of the boys from a nearby farm. However, she couldn't be certain. Her father had a temper and, although most of the time he kept out of her way and ignored her behaviour, occasionally he would lose control and shout at her.

As she closed the door behind her, Brigitte shrugged. He'd have Louis to answer to now if he attacked her, she thought, conveniently forgetting that Louis might not be entirely impressed that she had spent the night with someone else, even if that man was the very rich Giscard who owned the small manor house on the west of the town.

Brigitte glanced down at the expensive silver bracelet adorning her left wrist and pulled out a small wad of cash from her black lacy bra. Giscard was very generous when he wanted to be, although he had some strange preferences. A picture of the evening's activities flashed into her mind, making her shudder. She turned her attention back to the jewellery, carefully undid the clasp and placed the bracelet in the small box in the bottom drawer of her dressing table. With the earrings and necklace, she had a matching set. Now all she needed was the opportunity to wear them.

"Brigitte! Brigitte, you lazy cow. Are you up yet?"

Brigitte jumped. She hadn't noticed the snoring had stopped. "Yes. What do you want?" She snapped.

"I need a hand in the café. Renny has joined the army now the Boche are so close and I'm short staffed."

Brigitte frowned, tried frantically to think of an excuse and failed. "I'll be there in a minute." Her lack of enthusiasm was obvious.

Outside the door, Fabian shook his head and wondered where he'd gone wrong. He'd heard her creeping up the stairs and he wondered who she'd spent the night with this time. It was a good job he had plenty of regulars; her behaviour could have killed his business. Even worse, were the pitying glances from his friends. He clenched his fists and headed downstairs to listen to the wireless and open up the café.

Brigitte glanced in the mirror to touch up her make-up and quickly changed into her day clothes. She wished Louis was around, they could go out and have some fun and she wouldn't have to help her father in the stupid café. Her face darkened when she remembered Louis hadn't written to her for a couple of weeks. Bastard! He was just like all the rest. Well, if he thought she was going to sit around waiting for him, he had another thing coming. Giscard had arranged a little soirée at his house for that evening. She would make sure she got some sleep and then she could party the night away. Louis would regret dumping her, she'd make sure of that.

******

La Couture, Northern France

As far as Marie was concerned, the only good news was that the Germans had come through Belgium and not through the Maginot Line where Louis was based. Despite this, she had heard nothing from her elder son and she had no idea whether he was alive or dead. It wasn't just Louis she was worried about. How on earth would Jacques react if the Germans came anywhere near their home? Marie shuddered. She cleared the rest of the breakfast things from the table and then sat down with Jacques to listen to the wireless. She needed to know just how bad the situation really was before she could make any decisions.

The Germans were on the outskirts of Arras and there was a very real danger they would trap the whole of the allied forces on the coast. Her heart began to pound and she was having trouble breathing. If that happened, the enemy would have won and they would all fall under the Nazi yoke. At the moment, Arras was resisting because the French and the British had reinforced the town earlier in the month, but how much longer could they hold out? Their home was only a few miles north of Arras and, if the Germans were heading for the coast, what was to stop them coming straight through their tiny village?

******

"Oh for goodness sake, not another ladder!" Peggy watched the snag creeping down from the top of her leg towards her knee. Frantic, she searched around for some nail varnish to stop the run before it became long enough to show below her uniform. Silk stockings were becoming harder and harder to get now. How she was going to manage if things got worse, she had no idea. The matron at Lambeth Hospital was a real tartar. The slightest hair out of place and she was down on you like a ton of bricks.

Peggy sighed. Obviously today was not going to be a good day; not that there were many of those lately. She had not seen Joe since Christmas, although she'd received quite a few letters. Peggy smiled. Joe was very inconsistent. His letters were usually a couple of weeks apart and then, all of a sudden, she had received three, one after the other. She didn't mind; she was pleased he was missing her so much and loved the photograph he had sent her, with 'All my love, Joe' written on the bottom right hand corner.

Joe looked very handsome in his uniform and Peggy put the picture in a frame which took pride of place on her small bedside cupboard. Saying 'goodnight' to him while she drifted off to sleep and 'good morning' when she woke, made her feel closer to him. At least he was still in the country and not overseas and, for that, she was eternally grateful.

Peggy frowned, remembering that Sally's fiancé, Peter, was in France somewhere. Complete opposites in appearance and personalities, the two girls got on really well and had supported each other through the past six months, when the world seemed to have gone crazy. Peggy was about five feet three inches tall, with gentle brown eyes and shoulder length brown hair, kept tidy with regular cuts, to fit neatly under her nurse's cap. Sally was quite tall, at five feet six inches with long, blonde hair that was forever escaping from the pins she used to keep it in check. Peggy wasn't entirely sure what Sally did, because she didn't talk about her work very much. But she was some kind of secretary to someone vaguely important, with access to quite a lot of reasonably secret information. Despite her dependability at work, her personal life was a different matter. Sally was either on cloud nine or down in the dumps and she often came to Peggy with her problems, treating her like an older, wiser sister. Peggy didn't mind most of the time, although occasionally she wondered if there was something she was missing out on. She didn't always feel wise and sometimes she wished she could let her hair down, lose control and not be the sensible one.

The ladder had now reached her knee. If she kept daydreaming, she might just get her wish and the last thing she needed was to be in trouble today – not when she and Sally were off to the cinema tonight to see *Gone with the Wind*. Like most women her age, Peggy idolised Clark Gable and couldn't wait to spend over three hours gazing at her pin-up in glorious Technicolor on the big cinema screen.

****

Catford, London

Olive ignored the bright spring sunshine and blossoming trees that lined the busy streets. Head down, a sour expression on her face, she hurried to work. It was over three weeks since she'd heard from Kurt and she was beginning to worry. Perhaps there would be a letter today? Her life revolved around them. When she received one, she floated on a cushion of air until the feeling of euphoria wore off and she plummeted back down to the depths of despair again, imagining him dead or injured or with another woman. Her colleagues noticed her violent mood swings but were unwilling to ask if anything was wrong. Olive was a private person who would not take kindly to people interfering in her life, however well meaning. They were all shocked by the rapid advance of the Germans across Europe and they assumed Olive's bad mood was related to that.

Olive had hardly noticed outside events, except to worry that Kurt was among the troops pouring into Belgium and France, which would explain the lack of letters. Even listening in to the council phone calls had failed to improve her mood, although there were some things she could put in her next letter to Kurt that would probably make him laugh.

Chapter Eight

La Couture, Northern France

Marie stood up and switched off the wireless, her heart racing and then collapsed back on the old, rather rickety wooden chair, at the kitchen table. For a brief moment, she tried to pretend she was just having a bad dream and she would soon wake up.

"At this rate, it won't be long before they are on the doorstep," she wailed. The minute the words left her mouth, Marie could have bitten off her tongue. But Jacques was staring into space and didn't answer. Marie was so relieved he hadn't heard her that, although she noticed his rather vacant expression, she didn't see his leg trembling. There was silence, while she tried to think of something to say that would not upset him and, at the same time, bring him back from the past. Then another horrible thought struck her: "What about Louis?" she asked, consumed with fear for her oldest son. There was no answer and she glanced at Jacques with concern. "Jacques are you alright?" Seeing her worried expression, he made an effort to pull himself together.

"I'm fine." She was about to take hold of his hand when he quickly moved his arm under the table out of sight. "Sorry. I didn't hear you," he added, hoping she hadn't noticed that his hand was trembling. But for once Marie was too concerned about Louis to notice Jacques' discomfort. She repeated her earlier question.

"I asked about Louis. Whether he would be alright? With the Germans..." Marie broke off, unable to continue.

"I'm sure Louis will be fine," Jacques replied with a confidence he didn't feel.

His words gave her the lifeline she needed and her own feelings of panic gradually began to subside. "Of course, you're right, Jacques. All his letters speak of playing games and being bored. I'm sure we have nothing to worry about."

Jacques nodded, although he wasn't really listening. His mind was elsewhere, his senses full of the sights and sounds of Verdun: the screaming, the noise, the smell of death.

****

Somewhere in France

Louis stood motionless, his back against the thick oak tree, his rifle cocked and ready to fire. He could hear the German soldiers coming closer, their feet trampling the undergrowth while they searched the woods. Louis licked his lips. He felt beads of sweat forming on his upper lip and tasted the salt trickling into his mouth. The footsteps were much nearer now and Louis tensed his muscles. He was certain that the sound of his heart pounding against his chest was almost loud enough to drown out the crackle of twigs and branches as the German soldiers brushed against them. Louis' finger tightened on the trigger and he held his breath before slowly releasing it. The German had passed within inches of his hiding place. He eased around the other side of the trunk and watched the soldier disappear from sight before bending down to the bushes on the left of the tree where Raul was hiding

"Come on, let's go further in," Louis whispered, pointing into the woods, in the opposite direction to where the German had gone. Raul raised his hand in agreement and the two men lowered their weapons and disappeared deeper into the trees.

Raul and Louis had been running and hiding from the Germans ever since the French Army had collapsed several days before; their orders, 'every man for himself'. They had no real idea what to do;

whether to try and make for the coast and escape to England or to take their chances and go home.

Rumours were rife that the Germans weren't taking prisoners and, although Louis had no way of ascertaining whether or not that was true, he had no intention of finding out.

They tramped on through the woods until the trees began to thin out, thick undergrowth giving way to small fields bordered by hedges and a wide road. Louis and Raul approached the highway with caution, but there were no Germans, just hundreds of refugees.

"What do you think?" Raul indicated the road and Louis shook his head. For some reason, the Germans seemed to take delight in targeting the fleeing civilians. It was probably best to keep away from them.

"No, I think we should keep off the main routes; they're too dangerous."

They waited until there was a break in the endless stream of civilians before crossing over into the grassland opposite. They were just in time. Ahead of them, the shriek of an angry Stuka filled the skies. Louis and Raul threw themselves flat in the long grass behind the hedge and covered their heads, while the air around them echoed to machine gun fire and screams.

"We need to help them!" Raul yelled.

Louis shook his head. "Wait until the planes have gone," he cried. But he was too late. Raul rolled away from the cover of the hedge and onto the grass, firing wildly at the Stuka while the plane passed once more over their heads. The aircraft immediately switched attention towards him and away from the refugees; bullets sprayed the field, ricocheting off the earth. Louis curled up and pressed his body into the hedge. In the field, Raul jerked several times and then lay still. The Stuka finished its murderous run and was already flying away when Louis crawled towards the motionless body of his friend. He stared down at Raul and recoiled in horror. He could see a line of ragged holes in Raul's uniform but there was very little blood. Louis relaxed. He must be alright then. He leaned forward again, called Raul's name and shook him repeatedly. There was no response and the body felt limp in his hands. Louis let go, sat back on his haunches and stared in disbelief at his friend. He was dead.

Louis sat there for several moments before the screaming behind him broke into his thoughts. Wearily he climbed to his feet and headed towards the highway. The sight that met his eyes took his breath away.

****

Honor Oak Park, London

Peggy crossed the busy street and rushed in through the hospital entrance. Once inside, she slowed her pace and headed in the direction of the men's surgical ward, to which she had only recently been assigned and greeted Helen, who was already stripping one of the beds.

"That was close." Helen mouthed a quick greeting. Helen was tall and curvaceous with masses of freckles and a shock of red hair. "Matron was on her way, but got distracted by a new patient in one of the single rooms." She was about to say more, when matron herself appeared at the doors to the ward. "Look out, here she comes," she warned in a low whisper.

"Good morning, ladies." Matron was always unfailingly polite, even when she was reprimanding them. "When you've finished that bed, could you see to Mr Greaves. He had an appendectomy last night and needs watching in case of complications. Make sure you take his pulse, temperature and blood pressure every three hours."

"Yes, Matron," both girls answered in unison. Matron moved on, eyes everywhere, checking for dirt, patients who weren't tucked in properly, badly made beds, in fact anything that wasn't perfect. She headed out of the ward in the direction of the toilets, skirts swishing as she bustled along the length of the ward. Peggy and Helen breathed a collective sigh of relief.

"Probably going to check no one's stuck any fags down the bog." The whispered voice came from Harry who had been on the surgical ward for a couple of weeks. He had a great sense of humour and often had the nurses in stitches.

"Go on with you, Harry." Peggy went over to him and checked his bandages.

"Heard anything from your young man?" he asked.

"No, not yet. He's probably having too good a time in the country," Peggy laughed. "At least he's not in France. We're probably in more danger here than he is." She finished redoing Harry's dressing and, with one last smile, rejoined Helen who had stripped the bed and was in the process of remaking it, ensuring the corners were folded in exactly the right way to satisfy matron and Sister King.

"Going out tonight, Cooper?" Helen finished making the clean bed. Whilst on duty, they had to call each other by their surnames, something which had caused a few problems at first.

"Yes, I'm going to see *Gone with the Wind* with Sally. Why don't you come along?"

"Oh, I'd love to but I'm going out with Jimmy tonight. It's his last leave before he goes to France." Jimmy had been Helen's boyfriend since school. He had joined the RAF when war was declared and was trained to fly Spitfires, which he loved and talked about nonstop when he was on leave.

"Well, at least he gets leave, unlike Joe. Are you going anywhere nice?"

Helen frowned. "Actually, no. We're just going round to his mum's for the evening. He only has a twenty-four hour pass, and he wants to share the time with both of us."

"Oh well, that's not so bad. His mum's really nice, isn't she?" Peggy had heard the rather wistful tone in her friend's voice.

"Yes, but if I'm not going to see him for a while, I'd quite like to have him to myself for a few hours. We can't do too much with his mum sitting in the same room!"

"Macklin! I'm surprised at you!"

"Don't you ever wonder what all the fuss is about?" Helen lowered her voice. "Didn't you and Joe ever want to… well… you know?"

"Yes, but we didn't," Peggy retorted and then relented. "We both believe you should wait until you get married." She frowned, remembering their argument back in September over how far she should let him go. "But perhaps everything is different now…" Her voice trailed off and she glanced around the room. A couple of the patients seemed to be paying rather more attention than bed-making usually warranted. Feeling herself blushing, a reaction which she prayed continually she would grow out of, Peggy changed the subject. "Any idea where he's going in France?" she asked, not really expecting an answer

"Tut-tut, Cooper. You know better than to ask." Helen pretended she was seriously affronted.

Peggy sighed. Talking about France had rekindled her concerns about Joe. Just because he was in England now was no guarantee he would remain safe for much longer.

****

La Couture, Northern France

Jacques realised Marie was staring at him. "We should just carry on as normal. I'm sure they won't get much further."

Marie looked at him doubtfully. He seemed less worried than in the past, although the situation was considerably worse now. Seeing her expression, Jacques was at pains to reassure her. "We have the best army in the world, my love. We have plenty of defences between us and them and thousands of men in the trenches defending us. The Boche will never take Verdun. The men in the trenches will fight to the death. You'll see." He kissed her on her forehead and poured himself some more coffee. Marcel was standing by the kitchen sink and he spun round sharply at his father's words. He was about to say something when he spotted his mother shaking her head at him. Marcel bit his tongue and waited for his mother to say something, but she didn't.

Marie was watching Jacques with a cold feeling of dread. Just as she feared, Jacques was losing his grip on reality. His reference to Verdun and the trenches meant he was back in the Great War again, something he'd been doing with increasing frequency. The nightmares had also returned. During the previous night, Marie had woken to find him standing by the window, shouting orders to men only he could see. She had eventually managed to bring him back to bed and then, an hour later, he had begun shouting again, his eyes crazed, his face covered in sweat. This time it had taken both her and Marcel to calm him. Fortunately, Marcel was used to his father's nightmares, having grown up with them. However, the strain on both of them was beginning to tell. Marie sighed. Not for the first time, she longed to go back to the peace that had been shattered when war was declared

"Perhaps we should call the doctor?" Marcel lowered his voice so his father couldn't hear him. He and his mother had moved to the small outhouse just outside the kitchen door and Jacques was busy reading the paper, or at least he appeared to be.

"There's no point, Marcel. There's nothing the doctor can do." Marie's voice betrayed her exhaustion. "We just have to hope the Germans are stopped and the war ends quickly." Marie tried to speak cheerfully. "Don't worry, he'll recover. He has before. It's just a matter of time." Even while she spoke the comforting words, she doubted their truth. It was a long time since she'd seen Jacques this bad and experience had taught her he would probably get worse before he began to improve. Marie dreaded to think what he would do if the Germans got any closer and she only hoped she would never have to find out.

"Well, if you're sure?" Marcel sounded concerned and Marie shook her head.

"Honestly, Marcel. There really isn't anything we can do." Marcel hesitated and seemed about to ask something else. "What's the matter?" Marie asked, dreading that Marcel might want to go and join up. Although he was officially too young, he was unlikely to be refused.

"I was just wondering about Louis. I know you haven't heard anything, but I was wondering if there was someone we could ask?"

Marie let out a slow breath. She was so relieved Marcel wasn't about to run away and join up himself, she could hardly speak. She pulled herself together. "I don't think there is any way of finding out what's happening. We just have to be patient." Marie paused. "No news is probably good news, Marcel. If anything had happened to him, I am sure we would have heard." She had no idea whether that was true or not, but Marcel seemed comforted by her words.

****

Lewisham Council, London

Olive yawned while she listened in to the man from the planning department. He was complaining to someone at the War Office about the paperwork involved in turning one of the local factories over to shell production. She had tuned out when another buzzer went and soon she was enjoying a much more interesting chat between one of the managers and a secretary from another department. Olive shook her head. Surely the man must know the girls frequently listened in to the conversations? Obviously not, given the nature of theirs, which seemed to revolve around black stockings and what he would like to do to the girl, if she would care to sit on his lap. Olive listened with interest. Unfortunately, she missed the most important part because another line buzzed and, when she returned, the man had gone, leaving the line silent.

****

Lambeth Hospital, London

"Goodness that was a big sigh." The gentle, male voice with a lilting Welsh accent broke into Peggy's thoughts. She'd been so preoccupied that she'd failed to notice the arrival of the latest batch of student doctors and now she glanced up to find a pair of blue sparkling eyes a couple of feet away from her nose. Startled, she stepped back, blushing yet again at the dazzling smile that met her gaze. "Sorry, I didn't mean to startle you," he said.

"That's alright… I mean… You didn't." Peggy was horrified to find herself stuttering. Recovering quickly, she snapped, "Student doctors don't usually bother to lower themselves to talk to mere nurses."

"That's their loss, then." The young man was still smiling, seemingly unaffected by her harsh words. "I shall have a chat with my colleagues and we'll make it our business to always talk to the nurses, especially the pretty ones." Before she could answer, he bowed his head slightly and wandered off to join the other student doctors who were awaiting the arrival of the consultant.

Not sure whether he was making fun of her or not, Peggy looked uncertain. Helen was watching with amusement.

"Looks like you've got an admirer," she whispered, a mischievous glint in her eye.

"Don't be ridiculous." Peggy was unaware she was blushing, again.

Helen grinned. "Well, he's rather dishy and he seems friendly enough. Personally, I prefer my men blond, but tall dark and handsome works too. And as for those blue eyes…"

"If you think he's so wonderful, why don't you go after him?" Peggy pulled the top sheet much tighter than necessary and Helen struggled to hide her amusement. She had never seen Peggy this rattled before.

"Because he's not interested in me," Helen responded. "Anyway, I'm engaged…"

"So am I!" Peggy hurried away towards one of the patients at the far end of the ward, ending the conversation.

****

Somewhere in France

The road in front of Louis was littered with discarded possessions and injured civilians. His eye was drawn to a man lying across the verge not far from where he was standing, his stomach ruptured by bullets, blood seeping slowly into the deep gully by the hedge. Louis stepped towards him, then stopped. The man was dead. Louis felt as though he was in a trance and it was only the screaming that broke through; a long drawn out wail that tore at his heart. He dragged his eyes away from the man and gradually took in the scene around him. Behind him sat a woman, a small boy cradled in her arms while she rocked back and forth, crooning gently, the child unmoving, his head lying at an unnatural angle. An elderly couple sat holding hands on the grass verge. He could hear the man muttering softly to himself, the woman murmuring a prayer, repeating the words over and over again. Turning again, he finally identified where the screaming was coming from: a young woman was frantically trying to revive a baby, her blood stained hands shaking the lifeless body.

Louis shook his head, unable to take in the carnage. Everywhere there was chaos and devastation and there was nothing he could do to stop it. He was standing there trying to decide what to do when a middle aged couple came towards him, their hands outstretched. The beseeching expression on their faces stirred him into action. His uniform was a symbol of authority, the only one in the vicinity and several other people also hurried towards him. Seeing the desperation in their eyes Louis panicked and, searching for a means of escape, he began to back away.

Chapter Nine

"Hello, Brigitte." Marie was just leaving the grocer's shop when Brigitte approached. The café was very busy but she had seen Marie arrive and, when her father wasn't looking, she had taken the opportunity to slip out.

She returned Marie's greeting and then continued, "Have you heard anything from Louis?"

Marie shook her head. "No, nothing at all since the invasion. I take it you haven't either?"

"Oh, Good!" For some reason Marie couldn't understand, Brigitte seemed relieved at her reply. Seeing the confusion on Marie's face, Brigitte hastened to reassure her. "I'm sorry, I didn't mean it was good you hadn't heard. I was worried he was fed up with me and that was why he hadn't written."

Marie was speechless for a moment and then she grew angry. "Don't you listen to the news? The army has been overrun. God knows what has happened to Louis. He could be dead, and all you're concerned about is whether he might be fed up with you?"

For a brief moment Brigitte had the grace to look embarrassed. Then she retaliated, "How dare you talk to me like that! Who do you think you are?"

"I'm Louis' mother and, unlike you, I care about him. All you care about is yourself." Brigitte opened her mouth to interrupt, but Marie didn't give her a chance. "And don't think I haven't heard about you and some of the other men in the village. Louis was just a trophy to you, someone you could brag about to your friends. If I do hear from him, I'll tell him just how concerned you were!" She brushed passed Brigitte, who by now was bright red, and hurried away up the village street.

"Don't bother. He wasn't much of a catch anyway. I only went out with him because he was desperate; a poor little soldier boy!" Brigitte shouted after her.

Marie stopped, whirled around and retraced her steps until she was standing in front of Brigitte again.

"That *poor little soldier boy* may be dead now, fighting to protect the likes of you; a dirty little whore." And with that, she slapped Brigitte hard across the face. The small group of women, who had gathered outside the shop to listen to the argument, gasped as one. Then, nodding their heads and nudging each other, they murmured their approval.

Marie wasn't paying attention. She was hurrying back to where she had parked their dilapidated farm truck, with tears streaming down her face.

Brigitte stalked off in the opposite direction, her face flaming.

****

Somewhere in France

Louis ran through the countryside, head down, his ears closed to the shouts and cries of those on the road behind him, trying to put the horrific images out of his mind. He hated himself for running away, for not helping, for ignoring the plight of the civilians he had sworn to protect and he was ashamed of his cowardice. Eventually, his pace slowed and he came to a halt by a gate that led to a small cottage. Panting heavily, he bent double and tried to catch his breath. How could he have run away and left them to face the Germans? Louis sank to his knees, his head in his hands and wished the ground would open up and swallow him. How would he face his father after what he'd done? Louis remained distraught for several more moments while his mind relived the events of the morning. Then the rumbling of his stomach brought him back to reality. He was on his own and, unless he pulled himself together, he was likely to end up dead.

****

Suffolk

After several days digging sea defences and erecting barricades against the invasion, Joe was pleased to have a day off to relax and play an inter-platoon cricket match. The May sunshine was warm on his back as he crouched behind the wicket and a gentle breeze rustled the new leaves and spring blossom on the cherry trees scattered around the edge of the village green.

With his hands cupped, Joe watched the ball soar through the air towards him. He raised his arms slightly and the ball dropped straight into his open palms. Quick as a flash, he moved to the side and knocked off the stumps while the batsman slid, feet first, towards the wicket, arriving slightly too late.

"Gotcha!" Joe's shout of triumph was cut short. In the distance they heard the familiar sound of an approaching motor cycle. Distracted, he turned towards the sound. So did everyone else.

"Aye, aye – something's up." Chalky also lost interest in the cricket when the motorbike came into view. The heckling stopped and the gaze of the waiting soldiers followed the dispatch rider, who steered the bike off the lane and travelled the short distance across the cricket ground towards the players. He pulled up in front of the major who was umpiring the match, and leapt off his bike. Without waiting to stand it up properly or remove his goggles, he spoke rapidly to the major who immediately climbed on the back of the bike and they drove off. With no one left to umpire, the game stopped abruptly, leaving the men unsure what to do next. Although the day was still warm and bright, Joe felt a shiver of unease.

****

Bethune, Northern France

Brigitte stalked back to the café, her cheeks crimson with embarrassment. Ignoring the amused expressions on the faces of the customers, she stormed upstairs and threw herself on her bed. How dare Louis' mother speak to her like that? Brigitte was incandescent with rage and she spent several minutes plotting revenge against Marie, until a pounding on the door made her jump.

"What the hell do you think you're doing?" Fabian was standing by the door, an expression of fury on his face. In his hands was a checked tea towel which he was gradually screwing into knots. "You know I'm short staffed. Get your lazy backside down there immediately and clear some tables."

Brigitte turned her back to him. "I can't. I'm upset. Can't you see?"

"I couldn't care less." Fabian dragged her off the bed. "I've no doubt you probably deserved whatever you got. Now, I'm not telling you again. Either get down stairs or you can move out."

Brigitte stared at him in astonishment. He'd never threatened to throw her out before. She moved towards the door, making sure to take her time; her only means of defiance. Fabian stormed ahead of her, almost knocking her flying and she grabbed the stair rail.

"No need to push!" she yelled.

Fabian turned back and looked up at her. "I have no idea what I have done to deserve you for a daughter but right now, I don't care. You do know the Boche are almost on our doorstep, don't you?" Brigitte shrugged, a disinterested expression on her face and Fabian let out an exasperated breath. "I give up. God help us if they do reach here." He shook his head in disbelief. "Just go and do some work before all our customers leave."

******

"Have you heard our news, Marie?"

Marie jumped and then relaxed when she recognised the voice of her neighbour, Isabel, who was standing by the back door, looking slightly embarrassed. Marie had been listening to the wireless in the hope there might be some good news. She was also trying to forget her encounter with Brigitte. She couldn't believe she had slapped the girl. Although she was undeniably selfish, Brigitte hadn't really deserved to bear the brunt of Marie's frustration. Marie had taken her fear and worry about Louis and Jacques out on her and, although she disliked the girl and was convinced she was not good enough for her son, she felt guilty about losing her temper. Marie switched off the wireless and turned back to Isabel.

"Sorry. I didn't mean to make you jump. I just came to tell you we're going to stay with some friends in the south until we find out what's happening."

Marie stared at her in horror. "Do you really think things are that bad?" she asked, her own fear rising.

"Of course, we hope not. However, we're not taking any chances. If I were you, I'd do the same."

"But this is my home. We've lived in La Couture since the end of the war. I don't think I could bear to leave."

Isabel shrugged. "We've been here even longer, but I remember the Boche from before. I'm sure I don't need to remind you,"

Marie shook her head. "No, no. Of course not." She hesitated while thoughts of leaving her precious home rushed through her mind. Even if she wanted to leave, she wasn't sure that was possible, not with Jacques the way he was. "I'm worried about Jacques." She voiced her fears. "The fighting is bringing everything back to him. He's already started having nightmares again and…" her voice tailed off.

"Then you should leave now, before it gets any worse." Isabel was definite. "The last thing he needs is to be reminded of Verdun. Take it from me, go south for a while. Don't you have anyone you could stay with?"

Marie shook her head. Jacques' parents had both died a couple of years ago and she was an orphan, her parents having died when she was in her early teens.

"Well, I have to go." Isabel took a step closer. "Take care of yourself, Marie. Hopefully we'll be back soon, but…" She left the sentence unfinished and, after kissing Marie quickly on both cheeks, Isabel was gone, leaving her friend alone and even more concerned for the future. She remembered only too clearly what the Boche were like, but how could they leave their home? If they left, how would Louis find them when the war finished? And what about Jacques? Could he cope if they moved away? She shook her head in despair. If only the Germans hadn't started another war.

Chapter Ten

Somewhere in France

Lost in his thoughts, the sound of gun fire from somewhere nearby him made him jump. Louis threw himself onto the ground, covering his head with his arms. Heart racing, he strained his ears, but there was silence. Cautiously, he raised his head and glanced back. He couldn't see anyone behind him. He looked ahead towards the trees. He couldn't make out any movement. There was no sound and he glanced up at the cloudless sky, hoping he was not too lost. The sun was overhead, giving him no clue as to direction.

He sighed, stood up cautiously and hurried towards the trees. He would wait awhile, until he was sure which way the sun was moving, then he would start walking again. His chest felt tight and he could feel his heart pounding but nothing happened and he reached the wood safely. He ran another few metres then collapsed against a large tree, panting, his eyes closed.

It was the rustling of the leaves that caught his attention. The day was still, there was virtually no wind, yet he could hear fluttering leaves. He opened his eyes and frantically looked around.

****

Marie put together some fresh crusty bread, soft cheese and a small carafe of wine and went to find Jacques. The day was warm and the sun was shining brightly in a virtually cloudless sky. She could hear the birds singing in the trees that lined the first part of her route and the gentle breeze wafted the smell of early lavender in her direction. The gentle aroma of thyme added to the perfume as she brushed past the plants growing wild by the side of the path.

Marie loved this land; it was part of her. When she and Jacques had first moved here, the place had been virtually derelict. The land had been left fallow for several years and the only plants growing were weeds. But this made the soil very fertile and, in the first few years, crops were plentiful. The work was back breaking and had been exhausting, harder because she was pregnant with Louis by then. But the results had been worth the effort. Once the crops had been sown, they had concentrated on making the house habitable. The cottage had been abandoned in the Great War and occupied by German soldiers, so the damage was extensive. But together, they had rebuilt every room until the house took on a homely feel. Marie really couldn't face leaving and starting again from scratch.

******

Somewhere in France

Several metres in front of Louis was a young woman. She was looking directly at him and, once she knew she had his attention, she raised her finger to her lips indicating he should be quiet. Louis let out the breath he had been holding and nodded. The girl turned her head back and stared in the opposite direction to Louis for several moments before making her way carefully back towards him.

"German soldiers," she whispered. "Six of them. They nearly spotted me, so I hid until they'd gone past." She gazed at Louis and smiled. "I'm Lucie. Who are you? I've not seen you around here before."

The girl was pretty with long dark hair and large brown eyes. She was quite thin, with small breasts and tiny hips; not his usual type. However, Louis hadn't seen any women for a while and Brigitte was instantly forgotten while he did his best to impress Lucie.

"I'm Louis. I'm a soldier and I'm on my way home. My best mate was killed when I shot down a Boche plane that was firing at refugees on the road, and I've been on my own ever since." Louis looked suitably sad. He did regret Raul's death, although if he hadn't shot at the plane, he would still be alive, of course. His main regret was being left on his own.

"Louis." She reached out a hand. "Would you…?" Louis never found out what she was going to say because she broke off suddenly. In the distance, they could hear voices coming closer. They both froze and then ducked down into the undergrowth. Louis peered through the tangle of branches and saw the six soldiers Lucie had spoken of. He nudged her and pointed them out. They were heading towards their hiding place. Lucie grabbed his arm and indicated a large bush to their right. He was about to argue when, without waiting for an answer, she began crawling towards the thick foliage. Louis hesitated and then followed. To his surprise and relief, there was a hollowed out space in the middle. They huddled together, Louis aware his heart was pounding, mainly from fear but also from the proximity of her body, lying close to his.

The voices grew louder and they could hear the soft tread of the soldiers' boots coming closer. Louis held his breath: they were standing right by the bush. He could see their shiny boots centimetres from his nose and he felt Lucie tense beside him.

****

La Couture, Northern France

Marie reached the small stile leading into the back field and scanned the horizon. Jacques was in the far corner, fixing one of the fences, totally unaware of anything around him. She watched him for a while; his body was still lean, fit and muscled from the years of hard manual work, unlike her own, whose curves had been accentuated through childbearing. She came close and he turned around, his face beaming a smile of welcome. His skin was surprisingly fresh and he didn't look his age. His hair had not yet gone grey although, just at his temples, she could see hints of the distinguished colour it would become when he grew older.

"Hello. What brings you out here?" Jacques was surprised to see Marie; she rarely ventured up to this end of the farm.

"I brought you some lunch and a drink."

Jacques was even more surprised when he saw the wine.

"I thought we could have a little picnic, like we used to, before the children were born." Marie suddenly wanted to make the most of the rest of the day. Things were changing so quickly, she had a feeling it would be a long time before they were able to enjoy the simple things again, and she was filled with a desire to make every minute count.

"Oh, I see!" A twinkle appeared in Jacques' eye and he reached out and pulled her towards him.

"No, I didn't mean that!" But Marie made no attempt to push him away. For a few seconds, she closed her eyes and enjoyed the sensation of feeling safe in his arms. Then, gently releasing her, he took off his coat and laid it on the ground. "Well, we can't have you catching cold, can we?"

He waited until she was seated, then, sitting down next to her, he reached out and put his arms around her again. Pulling her close, he began to kiss her, gently at first and then with a rising passion until he felt her relax and respond with a fervour equal to his own. Easing her back gently, he sat looking at her for a few seconds. His desire for his wife had never diminished. Although Marie was over forty, she was still a beautiful woman. Her hair was the same shade of blonde it had always been, although if he peered closely, he could see the first few grey hairs. She wore her hair long, but she tied it up during the day and one of his greatest pleasures was to let her tresses down at night when they were alone and run his fingers through the silky locks. She worried she was getting fat but he loved her body. Making love to her was something he would never grow tired of and kissing her still took his breath away. Marie had always been there for him, through the good times and bad. She had given him two beautiful sons and he loved her with all his heart.

Leaning forward, he kissed her again, his hands moving over her willing body, knowing exactly how to arouse her. The sun moved slowly across the sky and the world took another step closer to darkness while they made sweet gentle love, their bodies moving with the accomplished rhythm of experience, only attained by those who are totally in tune, both mentally and physically. Afterwards, they held each other close and lay listening to the gentle sounds of the country, neither wanting to be the first to move and disturb the serenity.

****

Suffolk, England

Back in the village, Major Smiley waited while the colonel summoned his second in command, Major Allen and the company sergeant major.

"We're moving out," the colonel announced abruptly. "The men need to be ready to leave in four hours."

"Yes, sir." The CSM was a professional soldier with considerable experience, but even he was taken aback by the speed of their impending departure. He waited for more information but the colonel had already gone back into his office and closed the door, leaving them to carry out his orders. "No briefing then, sir?" He glanced hopefully towards Major Smiley who shook his head. He was as bemused as the CSM.

"Obviously not, Sergeant." There was a long pause, then he spoke again. This time, there was a hard edge to his voice that had not been there earlier. "Right, let's get on then, shall we?" Although phrased as a question, the CSM knew better than to argue. He saluted swiftly and marched to one of the trucks which was parked up a few yards away.

The driver was sitting in the cab reading the newspaper and didn't hear his approach, but fortunately the CSM was too preoccupied to notice. Instead, he politely asked the driver to take him to the village green. He quickly started the engine and drove the short distance to the centre of the village. The CSM paid little attention to the journey; he had too many plans running around in his mind. There was no time to lose if they were to be ready in less than four hours. It would take them that long to break camp, pack up their kit and equipment, and refuel and board the trucks. He shook his head, a sense of foreboding overcoming his normal calm, unruffled demeanour. He couldn't remember the last time he'd had this little information. The men were bound to ask questions and he didn't have any answers.

"We're here, sir." The driver's voice broke into his thoughts.

"Right, wait here." He climbed out. The training of many years kicked in and he put his misgivings to the back of his mind. The troops were standing around in small groups, chatting. He strode towards them and their conversations stopped. They were already expecting something to happen, so when he barked out his orders, no one was particularly surprised.

"Right, everyone fall in! We're breaking camp. At the double – FORM UP!' His voice echoed across the green to the watching children.

"Bit sudden, isn't it?" Joe murmured to Rob as they fell into line.

Rob was also concerned. "Something must have happened."

"Obviously." Chalky sounded exasperated, then he frowned. "Perhaps the Germans have invaded?"

"No. They would've rung the church bells," Taffy joined in.

"Not if they didn't want to panic everyone," Chalky responded. There was a brief silence, then he added, "Doesn't look like we've even got time to notify our families we're moving."

Joe shook his head. "Perhaps that's the whole point."

****

The soldier nearest the bush swivelled on his heel and began to retrace his footsteps. Gradually their voices grew quieter and Louis began to relax. Now the immediate problem had receded, he was even more aware of Lucie's body. He could feel her hips against his and he fought hard to resist the temptation to reach out and touch her.

"I think they've gone." Lucie turned to face him, her breath warm on his face and, before he knew what he was doing, he was kissing her.

"I'm sorry." He pulled away, mortified, and was about to say more when she kissed him, her tongue urgently probing his mouth, her hands pulling him closer. There was little room to manoeuvre but Louis slid one hand down her body and, within seconds, his fingers were inside her while the other hand was unbuttoning his own fly. Lucie gasped and tried to pull away.

Louis kissed her again. "I'm sorry, Lucie. I thought you wanted me to?" Lucie didn't answer immediately and Louis continued, "We don't have to, Lucie, but I want you so much and tomorrow we could both be dead. We have no idea what the Boche are going to do. Shouldn't we take this opportunity to enjoy ourselves?"

Lucie hesitated and he could feel her weakening. His fingers began stroking her again until she was gasping with pleasure then he climbed on top of her, ignored the branches and leaves poking into him and thrust inside her. Although she was wet, she was also tight and he had to push hard to enter her. He felt something give, she gasped and then suddenly he was inside. He could feel her muscles gripping him and he could hear her moaning in his ear. He began to move faster. For a split second, he thought he could hear the soldiers returning and fear of discovery was all he needed to push him to a rapid climax.

****

While Marie and Jacques enjoyed the fresh bread and sweet wine, Marie confided her plan to him. He listened carefully and agreed she was probably right, although, like her, he hoped they were overreacting.

"Why don't we see what tomorrow brings? The Germans may be held and the French and British may start to drive them back where they belong."

Marie nodded, but in her heart, she no longer believed that was likely to happen. Like the sun beginning its slow descent across the sky to the west, her spirits too were sinking fast. In the distance, she was sure she could hear sporadic gun fire and there was an ominous glow coming from the direction of Arras. She shivered. Marcel should be back by now and she was filled with the need to make sure he was safe indoors.

"Come on, let's go in. You can finish the fencing tomorrow," she urged Jacques, who did not need telling twice. The afternoon's unexpected activity had left him feeling sated and he could think of no better occupation than to sit in front of the range while his wife prepared dinner and his son chatted about the things that mattered in his young life. They strolled back in companionable silence. The shadows were growing longer and the warm day had already passed into early evening. There was a chill in the air that had not been noticeable before and, again, Marie shivered. Her earlier feeling of peace had disappeared, replaced by a restlessness she couldn't explain. She suddenly noticed Jacques was speaking.

"Sorry, I was miles away," Marie apologised.

Jacques pulled her close. He was enjoying the afterglow of their love making and assumed she was doing the same. "It wasn't important. I only pointed out Marcel is back already and busy milking the cows. We should have picnics more often!"

Marie reached up and kissed his cheek.

"I love you so much," she whispered.

"I should hope so." Jacques smiled back at her. It was a long time since he had felt this content and at peace.

Somewhere in France

Once the Germans had gone, Louis relaxed. There was just enough room for him to climb off Lucie and roll onto the ground beside her. He turned on his side and tried to put his arm around her but she pushed him away. Louis frowned. "What's the matter?"

"Nothing." She was doing up the buttons on her blouse with shaking fingers and she looked close to tears. "I have to go. I'll be late and my parents will worry." She pulled down her skirt and began to crawl out of the bush. Louis watched in surprise. He was feeling much happier and the sight of her bottom wriggling away was making him hard again. Perhaps they could find somewhere a bit more comfortable and he could make love to her again. He crawled after her.

"Don't go…" He stood up but she was already several metres away. Instead of turning around at the sound of his voice, her pace increased and, within minutes, she had disappeared into the trees.

Louis scratched his head, a puzzled expression on his face. Perhaps she hadn't enjoyed it as much as him? His stomach growled, reminding him it was several hours since he'd eaten. He glanced up at the sky. The sun had now moved towards the west, providing him with some idea of direction. He put Lucie out of his mind and began walking in the opposite direction to the one she had taken. Hopefully he would soon find some food and shelter for the night.

****

Honor Oak Park, London

Peggy glanced at the clock on the mantelpiece above the fireplace in the sitting room. She loved the wooden sloping exterior of the clock and the Westminster chime that rang out every quarter of an hour. Given to her by her grandmother, she was reminded of her parents every time it chimed. It was one of the few memories of them she had, so the clock was doubly precious. She would just have time for a quick bath if she got a move on. One of the things she missed most since the start of the war, was being able to soak in lots of really hot water. She was on her way upstairs when the front door slammed shut and Ethel came flying in.

Ethel was small, black haired and chubby. Blessed with a calming, happy-go-lucky personality that provided the others with more support than they realised, Peggy was always pleased to see her friend at the end of the day. Soon after the war started, Ethel had left her reasonably well paid job at the upmarket West End stylist to do 'something more productive' and she now worked in the Royal Ordinance factory at Woolwich Arsenal making shells; a particularly dangerous job, although Ethel never complained. "Are you coming to see *Gone with the Wind?*" Peggy called down from the top of the stairs.

"What time are you going?" Ethel asked

"In about an hour; Sally should be back by then. She was going round to Peter's mum's first to see if she's heard anything from him."

"She'll be devastated if anything happens to him," Ethel started to say as the front door opened and Sally came in.

"If anything happens to who?" Sally questioned, exhaustion etched on her face.

"I was just saying I'd be devastated if anything happens to Colin," Ethel improvised quickly. Colin was her boyfriend of nine months. He was a fireman who worked for the Auxiliary Fire Service in the East End of London, near the docks. "We were talking about the war and saying it could be dangerous for the firemen in London if the Germans start bombing."

"Try not to worry, I'm sure he'll be alright." Sally was at pains to console her friend, because she knew how she felt. She was worried sick about Peter; it was unlike him not to write.

"Any news?" Peggy was leaning over the white painted banister. She had heard most of the conversation and, although Sally would have told them the minute she'd come in if she'd heard anything, Peggy felt obliged to ask.

"No, his mum hasn't heard anything from him for a while either. She's worried too." Sally hesitated and then put her fear into words. "This sounds really stupid, but I'm sure something is wrong. Not just because he hasn't written; its more than that. I can feel it here." Sally was holding her right hand over her heart and Peggy could hear the fear in her voice.

Sensing her despair, Peggy came back down the narrow, dark-green carpeted stairs and put her arms round her friend, pulling her close. For once, she couldn't think of anything to say because there was a fair chance Sally was right.

"I'll tell you what…" Peggy made up her mind. "Let's stay in tonight and have a good chat. We can always go and see the film another night."

"There's no need, Peggy, honestly. You've been really looking forward to tonight." Seeing Peggy about to protest, Sally continued, "It'll do me good to go out and the film will give me something else to think about. What time are we leaving?"

"Well, if you're sure…" Seeing the determined expression on Sally's face, Peggy gave in. "In about half an hour then? The first picture starts at seven-thirty. If we're going, we'd better get our skates on. Sure you don't want to come too, Ethel?"

Ethel considered it for a moment. "Oh, why not? It'll be good for us all to go out together."

Chapter Eleven

Catford, London

Olive trudged wearily home. It had been a long day and she was looking forward to putting her feet up and listening to the wireless. She refused to think there might be a letter at home because that might jinx it, instead she thought back over the conversations she had overheard during the day. Most of them were boring, although some, like the manager and his girlfriend had reminded her of what she was missing. She reached the block of flats, took out her key and opened the door. Her eyes lit up. *At last, a letter.* Olive picked up the envelope. She recognised the postmark and the writing and a smile crossed her face. She rushed up the stairs, flung open the door and threw her coat and bag on the settee with one hand. The other was already carefully opening the seal releasing the letter.

> *My darling Olive*
>
> *I'm sorry for the long delay since I've written. The communication line was cut off for a while but it's back in operation again now and I should be able to write every week.*
>
> *I'm not surprised you are very busy at the council, with all the evacuees coming back and all the preparations in case of bombing. I am worried about you, my darling, although I still pray that before long the war will be over and then I can come back to you. My country does not want a war*

with your country, so it seems really silly we are being kept apart like this. I would give anything to be in your arms and I hope you feel the same?

I was quite concerned when you said there were lots of soldiers in London. I would hate you to find anyone else. Are they still there or have they gone somewhere else now? You see how jealous I am, my love?

I was very sad to hear you still don't get on with your cousin, Peggy. Family is very important. Perhaps you should try and make friends with her? After all, it wasn't her fault her parents died and she had to come and live with you. She might be lonely now her boyfriend isn't there either. Has he gone overseas yet? I'm sure her friend's fiancée is alright. If you could find out where he is in France and which regiment, I could try and make some discreet enquiries, if that would help. Of course you couldn't tell them where the information came from, but you could always say you overheard something on the council telephone, couldn't you?

Please keep telling me all your gossip. It's fascinating and reading about your life makes me feel as though I am with you. I can visualise all the places you talk about, especially the factories frantically turning to the war effort. You write beautifully and I look forward so much to receiving your letters.

I am going to have to rush because I don't want to miss the post but I will write more next time.

I love you, my darling, and I pray we will not be apart too much longer. Kurt xx

****

Bethune, Northern France

The evening was in full swing, despite the advancing Germans. In fact, everyone seemed determined to enjoy themselves even more. Brigitte accepted her fifth glass of wine, the room was spinning but the attention she was receiving had almost succeeded in wiping the arguments with Louis' mother and her father from her mind.

Much to her relief, Fabian had not tried to stop her leaving that evening and, when the café quietened down, she had rushed up to the manor house where Giscard had been delighted to see her. He had plied her with drink and introduced her to some of his friends.

"You're very pretty, Brigitte." The man leering at her was tall and thin, a lock of black hair hanging limply over his forehead. Brigitte smiled and took a large gulp of her wine. "Have you seen Giscard's paintings? No? Then perhaps I can show you." He took her arm and led her towards another room. Brigitte went willingly. Giscard had already paid her sixty five francs for the evening and she knew what was expected of her.

The door opened onto a long gallery with portraits of Giscard's family adorning the walls. Brigitte glanced at them, and turned her attention back to her companion.

"This way." She shrugged and followed him along the gallery to a small door leading onto the terrace and stepped outside. The evening air was cool after the warmth of the house but she had little time to feel the chill before he pounced. His hands were everywhere, pawing her breasts and squeezing her buttocks, pressing his bony body against hers. Brigitte closed her eyes and thought about how she would spend the money. He dragged her towards the wall, leaned her against the bricks and began lifting up her skirt. Brigitte opened her legs and watched him try to coax his penis into an erection. After a few moments, she felt sorry for him and, kneeling down, she took him in her mouth. He was flaccid and she could smell the sweat from his hands. She worked harder and, eventually, he came to life only to climax almost immediately.

Brigitte stared up warily. Some men became annoyed when they got there too quickly but she was relieved to see that wasn't the case. He seemed delighted and, after pushing a screwed up note into her hand, he did up the buttons on his trousers and went inside, leaving her to gaze in surprise at the twenty franc note. She stuffed the money into the top of her stockings and hurried back into the main room. A couple more like him and she would earn an absolute fortune.

The waiter walked past with a tray full of glasses of wine. Needing to clear the taste in her mouth, Brigitte downed the glass he handed her in one go. Giscard smiled and nodded to the waiter.

"Brigitte, my love, I have some other friends I would like you to meet." Giscard's words were slightly slurred, although Brigitte was in no position to notice. Everything suddenly seemed slightly out of focus, her legs began to buckle and she leaned heavily on his outstretched arm, giggling wildly.

He led her across the room to a middle-aged couple, the man bald and portly, his waistcoat stretched across his protruding stomach, his wife slim with dark cropped hair and heavily made up eyes that seemed to the drunken Brigitte to look right through her.

"Hello, Brigitte." Her voice was husky and she reached out a gloved hand, taking Brigitte's arm and guiding her gently towards the stairs. Despite her drunken state, Brigitte was confused. She stopped and glanced back but the man was right behind her and she found herself propelled up the steps to a large bedroom at the end of a long corridor.

****

Southern England

It was late by the time the open trucks were finally refuelled, loaded and ready to go. The weary men climbed in to begin their long journey south.

After the warmth of the day, the night air was cool and Joe felt chilly. Although his greatcoat provided some protection, the movement of the trucks increased the cold and he huddled closer to his friends for warmth.

The dark country lanes were quiet and provided little to see, other than the occasional reflection of a fox's or rabbit's eye caught in the dim headlights of the truck when the vehicle travelled around a particularly sharp bend. But this did not happen very often because they had to drive with the headlights off for part of the way and, even when they were on, they were dipped and heavily shielded to prevent any possibility of showing lights to enemy aircraft. None of the drivers had maps and had to rely on the odd signpost to prevent them from getting lost. Joe, like many of his companions, was very tired and, although he attempted to doze, the erratic movement of the truck careering round bends, racing downhill at great speed or over potholes, kept jerking him awake.

Joe eventually gave up on trying to sleep, took out his cigarettes and put one in his mouth.

"Anybody got any ideas where we're going then?" The question was casual enough but, underneath the nonchalance, Joe had a feeling they were finally going overseas. He wasn't entirely sure how he felt, but a mixture of fear and excitement was probably the best description. After all, this was what he had been trained to do and, although he was nervous, a part of him couldn't wait to put the things he had been taught into practice.

"Perhaps we're going to Norway," Chalky suggested.

"No, I think we've blown that one. Hitler's already got his feet in the door there." Taffy opened his eyes just long enough to make his contribution to the discussion.

"Maybe we're going to France," Joe mused. "My dad's already there."

"Didn't think you got on with your dad?" Rob looked at Joe in surprise.

"I don't, not really. He wrote to me just after I was called up and said he was off to France then."

"Doesn't mean he's still there," Chalky responded after a few seconds.

"No, but he could be," Joe persisted. "If he is, he's probably already fighting," he added proudly.

"That explains why we're going, then," Johnston interrupted. "They're probably making a right cock up of it."

"Just ignore him, Joe... bloke's a tosser." Chalky had hold of Joe's arm while he spoke.

Joe took a deep breath and then slowly relaxed, accepting there wasn't much he could do to Johnston, other than thump him, which would have been quite difficult in the confined space of the truck.

"Settle down, lads. Save your energy for fighting Jerry." Corporal 'Woody' Woodhouse decided to intervene before matters got out of hand. "And Johnston…" He paused, waiting until the soldier turned to look at him. "Don't be a prick all your life."

Laughter rippled around the vehicle and Johnston flushed. He was about to say something when a voice from the other end of the truck piped up, "Apparently we're going to Southampton."

"How do you know?" Rob asked.

"I heard a couple of the NCOs talking before we left," the disembodied voice responded. "They were going to tell us once we were underway."

"And how much more *underway* do we have to be?" Chalky muttered under his breath.

"And after Southampton?" Joe asked, ignoring Chalky's interruption.

"Dunno," the voice replied. "I think they'd just been told *Southampton*."

"Right." Joe and Chalky exchanged glances and, for once, neither of them could think of anything to say.

****

Honor Oak Park, London

"I think I'm in love," Sally had a dreamy expression on her face.

"He is gorgeous, isn't he?" Peggy agreed.

"Well, you're both out of luck, because he's mine." Ethel laughed.

"What a wonderful film!" Peggy said. "Definitely worth queuing up for."

"Shame they had to run the newsreel at the end, though." Sally was serious again.

Peggy's good mood evaporated and she felt depressed at the memory of the dreadful images they had all watched on the large cinema screen. Deserted cities, buildings wrecked by bombing, roads crammed with thousands of refugees and their meagre possessions, small children pushing dolls' prams loaded with suitcases, the elderly hobbling along, leaning on sticks, despair and bewilderment on their faces, all fleeing the advancing Germans. Peggy remembered the last letter she'd received from Pam – her friend who lived in Dover – and shivered when she recalled how Pam had talked of hearing the guns across the channel.

"Let's talk about the film instead. That's much more interesting," Sally said determinedly. Peggy and Ethel immediately agreed.

"I really don't understand why Scarlett fell for Ashley Wilkes." Ethel shook her head. "Rhett was so much more…" she paused, hunting for the right word.

"Everything!" Sally finished for her and, linking arms, they made their way back safely through the blackout and, by the time they were home, they had managed to put the newsreel out of their minds.

****

Outside Bethune, Northern France

The small room was full; men and women squashed up against each other while they stared through the window that opened into the large bedroom. Giscard refilled their glasses with expensive wine and warned them to be quiet. The noise dropped to a gentle murmur, the only sound a gentle moaning coming from inside the room. Giscard sat down in the chair he had reserved for himself at the front of the group and beckoned to one of the serving girls who stepped towards him, smiled and sat on his lap. His hand slid up her short skirt and his fingers began stroking her, his attention on the action through the window.

Brigitte was naked and tied to a bed with stockings, her arms and legs outstretched, the bald man astride her. The woman was stroking her breasts with one hand, the other guiding the bald man's penis. Giscard leered drunkenly, pushed the girl off his lap, his hands fumbling with his trousers. She knelt obediently in front of him, but he was too late and he couldn't reach her open mouth in time. His semen soaked the expensive carpet and he gasped, his attention still on Brigitte.

Chapter Twelve

Somewhere in France

Louis had been watching the tiny hamlet since first light. He was exhausted, having walked all night. He was also starving hungry. Despite his unexpected encounter with Lucie, the images of wounded civilians were still fresh in his mind and so was his frightened reaction to their pleas for help. He had tried to justify his actions, but he knew there was no excuse. Every time he closed his eyes, he could see their faces, so he'd finally given up trying to sleep and concentrated instead on finding some food.

In front of him were four houses and a small grassy area with a well. He could see no sign of life. There was an open window at the front of the cottage nearest to him and he crept closer. There was still no sound. He took another step and realised the door was hanging off its hinges. He frowned and edged towards the building until he was close enough to see inside. One glance told him all he needed to know. He stepped back and stared at the other cottages. They were all derelict and looked like they had been that way for some time. Louis cursed and made his way to the well. He lowered the bucket fully expecting it to come back dry so he was pleasantly surprised when he heard the splash. He reeled the pail up quickly and, after a tentative sip, began gulping the water. The roar of aeroplanes from the direction in which he had come made him jump and he dropped the bucket and hurried back into the trees.

****

La Couture, Northern France

Marcel woke abruptly to the sound of gunfire in the distance and the roar of aeroplanes overhead. Shaking his head in disbelief, he leapt out of bed and rushed to the window. To the right, behind the trees, he could see rising columns of smoke and hear the ragged noise of small arms fire, punctuated by the stuttering of machine-guns and the boom of high explosive shells. Overhead, he could hear German planes on their way towards Arras.

"Quick! The Boche are coming!" he shouted, grabbing his clothes and taking the stairs two at a time. The scene that met him was one of normality. His father was seated at the kitchen table where he always sat, staring into space and his mother was cooking some eggs on the range. Not receiving a response to his frantic shout, he peered at them more closely. No, perhaps all was not normal. In fact they seemed to be in shock. "We must leave now!" Marcel appealed to his mother.

"Leave? To go where? The Boche are all around us and there is nowhere to go but the sea." Marcel's heart sank. His mother appeared totally bewildered.

"We can't stay here; we'll be trapped." Marcel shook his head in desperation.

"The French army will save us. There is no need to worry. Your brother will be here soon and he'll know what to do." Marie's lack of coherence was even more disturbing than her belief in the French army. The last letter Marcel had received from Louis had not inspired him with confidence. In fact, it had been so worrying, he had not mentioned it to his parents at all, hoping his brother was exaggerating just how ill-prepared the French were. If the Germans were this close, Louis could already be dead. The thought was sobering as he realised that, whether his brother was dead or not, his parents did not seem capable of making decisions, which meant he was now the man of the house and, somehow, he had to get them to leave.

"Please, Mama, Papa; we really do have to leave. We can go to England. We'll be safe there."

"England?" Marie shook her head. "Our home is here; we've never even been to Paris since your father came back from the trenches. You know what he's like, Marcel." He could hear the resignation in her voice. "How would we manage in a strange country where we don't even speak the language?" She put her arms around him and hugged him. "Don't worry, Marcel. We will be safe here; we are too old for them to think we are a threat." Marcel was relieved the initial shock had worn off and his mother seemed capable of making lucid decisions again. However, her next words stunned him. "You must go, though. Take some food and some money and go to England." She handed him his father's old army backpack. The bag was heavy and, peering inside, he saw some clothes and an envelope containing money. "You will be safe there. When the war is over, you can come back." Seeing his expression, she gently stroked his face. "You are my youngest child; Louis may already be dead. I need to know that you are safe. Take your chance and go now, please." Marcel dithered and she pushed him towards the door, her eyes pleading with him.

Marcel shook his head, panic stricken. "No! I can't leave you. How can I go without you?"

"You must." Marie was insistent. "The Germans won't be interested in us but you are a different matter. You are fit, young and healthy. Think, Marcel," she begged him. "We have no idea what they will do if they occupy France. They might arrest all the young men or, God forbid, even shoot you." Marcel was still shaking his head but Marie wouldn't take no for an answer. "Marcel, I wouldn't do this unless there was no other option." Seeing his stubborn expression, Marie took a deep breath and tried a different tack. "Do you know how hard this is for me?"

"I can't leave you…"

"You have to." Marie finished putting some food into a large paper parcel which she pushed into his hands. "Take this and go, Marcel. It's the only way."

As if in a dream, Marcel took the parcel she was thrusting towards him and put it in the backpack. He realised she had prepared for this, but he still hesitated, unable to face the fact he had to leave his family and his home and go to a strange country, all on his own.

Seeing his hesitation, Marie shook her head. "If there was any other way, Marcel…" She broke off, unable to continue without crying.

Seeing how upset she was, Marcel again tried to reason with her, but she was adamant. The more he argued, the more distraught she became. Eventually, he accepted she would not change her mind and all he was doing was prolonging the inevitable.

He picked up the back pack and then stopped. "What about Papa?" He looked round at Jacques, but there was no reaction. "Does he think I should go too?"

"We talked about this last night and we agreed, if the Germans over-ran this area, you should go."

"Papa, you can't mean this, surely?" There was no response. Jacques was staring into space, his mind elsewhere. Marcel turned back to Marie.

"He can't hear you, Marcel," she tried to explain. "The gunfire has taken him back to the trenches. But, yesterday, he was perfectly lucid." Seeing his stricken face, Marie added, "He did agree you should leave. I wouldn't lie to you."

Marcel shook his head, but he was slowly becoming resigned to his fate.

"Alright, Mama. I will go. But when this is over, I'll be back." He was fighting to hold back the tears. Marie no longer trusted herself to speak. He reached out for her and held her tight. He had no way of knowing when, or if, he would ever see her again. Marcel finally let go and went over to his father, hugged him and kissed him goodbye. There was no response.

"You must go at once, before it is too late." The urgency in his mother's voice was unmistakable and, before he could object anymore, she hurried him to the door and pushed him through into the yard.

Marcel took a long hard look at his home and then, turning away he began the long journey to the coast. Marie watched him go, tears streaming down her face.

"May God protect you and keep you safe, my son." She made the sign of the cross and began praying. Marcel strode across the yard, turned one last time and waved, and Marie's eyes followed him until he disappeared out of sight. The gunfire and shelling were getting closer.

****

Lambeth Hospital, London

"Hello, Cooper." Helen was flustered and completely unlike her normal, calm self. "I'm not late, am I?" She searched the ward for any sign of the sister and then relaxed. She had arrived just in time. When Sister Adams popped her head in, she was busy emptying bedpans, looking as though she had been there for ages. "Phew, that was close," she muttered.

Peggy was about to ask her if anything was wrong when Helen pointed to the empty bed at the far end of the ward. "Come on. Let's strip this bed next." Realising Helen must have something private to say, Peggy hurried after her.

"What on earth's the matter?" she asked.

"There's all sorts of trouble going on at home." Helen checked around to make sure no one could hear. "My sister's gone and married some chap in the Navy. She's only known him a few months. Dad's absolutely furious and says she can't come home and he'll never speak to her again." Helen's face was tired and drawn and her eyes were red-rimmed as if she'd been crying.

"What, Annie?" Peggy was amazed. Annie was the quietest, most demure person she had ever met. She couldn't imagine her doing anything to upset her rather stern father, let alone anything quite so extreme as getting married without telling her family. "Have you met him? Have your parents met him?" she tried to keep her voice down. The patients had very little to do and they loved to listen to the nurses talking.

"No, that's partly the problem. Well, that and the fact she barely knows him herself."

"Didn't he come with Annie to explain?"

"No, they've all been recalled early from leave. He's gone back to his ship."

"If your dad's saying she can't stay at home, what's Annie going to do?"

"She's going to stay with his parents in Kent. They seem quite happy their son has got married, even though they weren't told about the wedding either. Oh goodness, it's all such a mess," Helen wailed.

"Well, maybe your father will come round," Peggy offered, although having met the man, she thought it unlikely. "What about your mum? What did she say?"

"She says whatever Dad tells her to say, but she was really upset." Helen fell silent for a moment before continuing, "Mum's asked me to give her Annie's address, so she can keep in touch without Dad finding out." Helen suddenly seemed petrified. "Don't say anything, will you?"

"Of course not! As if I would!" Peggy tried to think of something positive to say. "Well, at least she had somewhere to go and, if his parents like her, she'll probably be fine." She reached across the bed and put her hand on Helen's shoulder in an attempt to comfort her, without making it too obvious to the rest of the ward that something was wrong. "Try not to worry too much. At least you know where she is and you can go and visit."

Her words had little effect. "That's not all." Helen looked even more miserable. She leant forward and spoke in a voice a little above a whisper. "You must promise not to tell anyone." She waited for Peggy to agree again before continuing, "She's pregnant. That's why they got married so quickly."

"Oh!" Peggy was flabbergasted and, for a moment, couldn't think of any response to Helen's statement, which sounded so unlike Annie she was having trouble making sense of any of it. There was a long silence, then eventually she asked, "Do your parents know she's *pregnant?*" She mouthed the last word, rather than saying it aloud.

"Oh, yes." Helen was distraught. "That was the reason Dad threw her out and called her all sorts of names. You've never heard the like! He was shouting at her and she was yelling back and, when he told her to get out, she said she wouldn't have stayed even if he'd paid her."

"Well people say all sorts of things they don't mean when they're angry," Peggy consoled her. "I wouldn't take too much notice. At least she's married and maybe, when the baby comes, they'll sort everything out. Babies have a great way of bringing people together."

"Are you going to take all day stripping that bed?" Engrossed in their conversation neither of them had noticed Sister Adams approaching.

"Sorry, Sister," they replied in unison and the rest of the day was so busy, they didn't get the opportunity to discuss Annie's situation any further.

****

Bethune, Northern France

Brigitte closed her eyes and groaned. Her body ached, she had a terrible headache and she felt sick when she thought about the night before. She'd been very drunk, but unfortunately not quite drunk enough to block out the memories. She lifted the sheet and glanced down gingerly. Her body looked the same; there were no visible marks and she breathed a sigh of relief. Then she remembered the pile of cash she had been given and felt slightly better. There were plenty of things she could buy with such a large sum of money. On the other hand, perhaps she should start saving and then she could move away, somewhere no one knew her. The idea appealed to her. She could go to Paris and set up her own business. She had no idea what sort of business, but if she continued to make that kind of money, she could do anything. She frowned. Of course with the Germans so close she might do better to go south to Marseilles or Toulouse or even St Tropez.

Feeling much happier, Brigitte pushed the last memories of the previous night to the back of her mind and, by the time she'd washed and dressed, she had convinced herself she'd had the time of her life.

****

La Couture, Northern France

Marie wandered back into the kitchen. Jacques was still sitting there, oblivious to anything except the nightmarish world of his own imaginings. Marie put on the wireless, sat down heavily at the table and waited. With Marcel gone, there no longer seemed any urgency to do anything. The news on the wireless was even worse than the previous night. The Germans were advancing so quickly towards the coast that it seemed nothing could stop them.

The sun was almost overhead when she was brought back to reality by Jacques, who, after hours of inactivity, leapt out of his chair and went into the outhouse. A moment later, he reappeared with his shotgun and a box of cartridges.

"What are you doing, Jacques?" Marie screamed at him in horror.

"We need to dig in, or they will overrun the trench." There was a feverish glare in his eyes and sweat on his upper lip.

"Jacques, we are at home, we are not in a trench. It's 1940. The Great War is over." Marie was patient despite her own panic, although she could see she was not getting through, her task made harder by the sound of the guns outside, which seemed to be coming closer. "This is a different war. You must put the gun down. If the Germans find you with a weapon, they will kill us."

"We have to defend the line, we cannot allow them to advance. Man the barricades, get your gun and fight for the glory of France." Jacques stared into the distance, his eyes feverish and alight.

Seriously concerned, Marie attempted to calm him, without success. In desperation, she tried to grab the shotgun from him but he hit out, knocking her to the floor.

Thoroughly frightened, she yelled at him, "Jacques, for God's sake put the gun down! You'll get us both killed!" Marie tried again to wrest the gun from him, but he was too strong and pushed her away. In despair, she tried to think of something to distract him from the sound of small arms fire that seemed ominously close. She was too late. The door burst open and several Germans stormed in. Seeing the shotgun in Jacques' hands, there was no hesitation. In a split second they had opened fire, killing Jacques where he stood and spraying the kitchen with his blood.

"No!" Marie's scream rent the air and she ran across the room and threw herself on her husband's dead body. "He thought he was in the trenches; he was ill, he didn't know what he was doing." Her protests went unheard; most of the soldiers ran past her into the back of the farmhouse, searching for other occupants. Marie stared into the face of the young man left to guard her, seeking some compassion, anything to show remorse for their actions. She found nothing. He seemed totally oblivious to her pain, to the fact he had brought an abrupt, violent end to the last twenty four years of her life.

Louis and Marcel were lost to her, although she hoped they were both alive, but Jacques was dead and the madness was happening again. Finding the rest of the farmhouse empty, the soldiers ransacked the rooms hunting for food, valuables and anything else they could take with them. They left as abruptly as they had arrived, leaving Marie rocking Jacques in her arms, sobbing uncontrollably, mourning not only his loss, but the loss of her whole life. The silence that followed their departure was only punctuated by the sound of Marie's sobs, and the rhythmic ticking of the clock on the wall.

Chapter Thirteen

Northern France

Marcel strode across the fields towards the highway that led to Dunkirk, about sixty-four kilometres away. To his disgust there were tears rolling down his cheeks. Angrily, he brushed them away on his rough sleeves. A tall, healthy boy with long legs, Marcel soon covered the relatively short distance to the road. He was only too aware of the continuous noise of gunfire in the distance and, several times, he spun around to check there was no one behind him. Every now and again, the earth shook when a shell exploded. The first time, the noise was so loud and seemed so close, he threw himself flat on the ground in terror, cradling his head in his hands. After a few moments, he peered around warily. There was no one in sight. Ignoring the frantic pounding of his heart, he stood up, brushed himself down and continued on his way. The shells continued to fall, but he soon grew used to them and, for the most part, he ignored them, his thoughts on what the future held, until he finally reached the road.

To his astonishment, there appeared to be hundreds of people heading towards Dunkirk. At first, he assumed they were soldiers and he pulled up sharply, frightened they might be Germans. He moved forward, one step at a time, taking care not to be seen, but he needn't have worried. No one was watching him and, when he came closer, he realised they were French soldiers and the remnants of the British Expeditionary Force, wearing the tattered remains of their uniforms.

Many were wearing dirty bandages covered in dried blood, while others had fresh wounds, the blood seeping through onto their clothes. He could see men with blackened faces and blistered skin, their tunics hanging in shreds. Some hobbled along on makeshift crutches made from sticks, or were using their rifle butts to lean on. Marcel watched in horror as he was passed by others carrying stretchers, the wounded staring skyward with blank expressions or moaning in agony. The one thing they all had in common was the expression of defeat in their eyes and Marcel's earlier depression returned with a vengeance.

However, the majority of people on the road were civilians. Men, women and children, young and old, all appeared weary and fearful. There were elderly men and women, stooped by old age, leaning heavily on sticks and on each other, stopping every few metres to catch their breath. There were whole families, the parents pulling carts containing all their worldly possessions, their faces strained with fear, following small children, pushing infants in dolls' pushchairs, their hair tangled, their faces stained with dried tears and their eyes devoid of emotion. There were mothers, carrying their youngest children in their arms and holding the older ones by the hand, their faces grey with exhaustion while they put one foot in front of the other, no longer really aware of where they were going, but consumed with the need to escape the Germans. He even spotted a group of several nuns further ahead, chaperoning ten young girls, walking slowly in pairs, still wearing their school uniforms.

Carts, donkeys, horses, cars, tractors, anything that could be used had been commandeered and loaded full to overflowing. Pots and pans, clothes, furniture, even beds, were tied on to the makeshift contraptions and some people had even brought their cow or goat along with them. There were carts pulled by children full of items of little use in an emergency, but which represented a token of their lives. The roadsides were littered with vehicles which had either run out of petrol or had broken down and, all around them, were abandoned possessions which people were no longer able or willing to carry.

Marcel's attention returned to the soldiers and he scanned the French troops anxiously to see if any were wearing the uniform of his brother's regiment, but it was virtually impossible to identify which units most of the soldiers were from.

"Excuse me, is there anyone from the 128th Fortress Infantry Regiment here? I'm searching for my brother, Louis Servier. He was on the Maginot line. He was… is serving at Ouvrage Brehain near Brehain-la-Ville," he tried asking two soldiers who were passing him, their eyes staring straight ahead.

The older one gazed at Marcel, his expression blank for a moment, before answering, "I'm sorry; I have no idea who is here. The French army is defeated; it's every man for himself." Seeing the despair on Marcel's face, he repeated, "I'm sorry. You should leave France if you can. We're going to the coast to try and get some boats to England. You should do the same. If your brother is alive, he'll probably make for the coast too." The soldier went on his way, leaving Marcel standing on the grass verge. Eventually, he decided he might find out more if he followed the refugees, rather than watching them stream past.

Marcel joined the long queue of people and was about to ask where they were going and if they had any news, when he heard the sound of aircraft in the distance. He watched in astonishment as everyone around him abandoned their possessions and animals and dived into the drainage ditches which ran on either side of the highway.

"Quick! Get off the road! They'll shoot you!" an older man yelled at Marcel from his prone position in the ditch, where he had thrown himself, together with a lady who was probably his wife. Beside them, Marcel noticed a girl who seemed about his age.

Marcel stared at them in disbelief. "We're just civilians; children, old people. Why would they shoot us? You must be mistaken."

"Look around you! I'm telling you, they'll shoot you if you stay there!" Seeing Marcel's hesitation, he gave up. "Don't say I didn't warn you." And, putting his head down, the man disappeared out of sight.

****

The transit camp, three miles from Southampton docks, was very busy when Joe and the rest of the men arrived and, although it was raining, they were delighted to be able to get off the uncomfortable trucks and stretch their legs. They had not had much sleep on the long, tiring journey and had only stopped twice, the first time to refuel, the second to cook and eat breakfast. The vehicles, with their drivers and the dispatch riders were sent straight to the docks where their transport and equipment were to be loaded onto the ships. The rest of the men settled down to eat

"This is more like it." For once Chalky forgot to complain; he was too busy tucking into a large plate of delicious meat and vegetable stew.

"And it's finally stopped bloody raining," Rob chipped in between mouthfuls.

Joe was too busy eating to speak, but he could feel his uniform drying out in the sunshine that had now come out from behind the clouds, and his spirits rose. They finished their meal and, while they waited for further orders, Joe took the opportunity to go and have a shave and a wash. Feeling revitalised, he wandered around until he found Chalky.

"Writing to Joyce?" he asked.

"Yeah, I'm not sure what to say, though." Chalky looked troubled. "We're not allowed to say where we're going, even if we knew, although I could make an educated guess. I don't want to worry her but, at the same time, this might be the last time I get to write." Seeing the horrified expression on Joe's face, he added, "For a while, I mean... we might be too busy or... well, we might just not get another chance for some time," he finished.

Joe nodded. "I couldn't think what to write to Mum and Peggy either. When's the baby due?"

"End of September or thereabouts. Hope I'm home by then." Joe had been best man at Chalky and Joyce's wedding in November. Because of the war, they had only had a few hours off and Chalky had to return to camp by the next morning. "She'll be getting quite big now. I should be at home with her, not here and about to go God knows where."

"She'll be alright, mate." Joe searched for the right words to reassure his friend. "She's staying with her family, isn't she? And anyway, you'll be home before you know it."

"Yeah, I'm sure you're right." Chalky tried hard to rid himself of his pessimistic mood. "How's Peggy? Have you sorted out a date yet?"

"Not really. We haven't seen each other since I proposed; all we've managed to agree is summer next year – hopefully. Personally, I think we should just nip down the registry office but Peggy wants a proper do. Can't blame her, I suppose."

"Maybe she'll change her mind?"

Joe shrugged but before he could answer, Taffy interrupted, "See, hen pecked already and he's not even married!" Taffy was quietly envious. He hadn't yet met anyone he wanted to go out with more than twice, let alone marry and he was beginning to wonder if he was a bit odd. He was certainly in the minority. Most of the lads seemed to be either going steady, engaged or married, some with children. *Even Rob has managed to find himself a girlfriend and, surely, no one in their right mind would ever want to go steady with Rob. Still, if Rob's managed to find someone, then there's no reason why I shouldn't.* He decided his next leave would be the one where he would meet the girl of his dreams.

****

Northern France

Marcel dithered for another couple of seconds and then decided that, unbelievable as it sounded, the man must be telling the truth. Why else would everyone have dived into the ditch when they heard the plane coming? Just in time, he threw himself off the highway, landing a few feet from the man who had shouted the warning. Within seconds, the air was filled with the sound of machine-gun fire, followed by bullets hitting the tarmac, as the Stuka dived low and flew along the length of the road. Marcel covered his ears with his hands and curled up into a ball, trying to make himself invisible. He was absolutely terrified. The sound of metal tearing up the road was followed by the ear-shattering shriek of another Stuka strafing the refugees, the bullets ricocheting close to where Marcel lay.

Like everyone else, Marcel stayed where he was for a few minutes after the planes had disappeared into the distance. Already, the noise of the aircraft had been replaced by the sounds of screaming and crying. Finally daring to raise his head, Marcel saw the total devastation the machines had left behind. The air was filled with acrid smoke and dust; several carts and cars had been hit, leaving rips and holes in tyres, clothes, beds, and anything else in the line of fire.

A small child lay, as if asleep, on the grass in front of him, her shocked mother sitting silently by her tiny body. She appeared to be completely untouched, but was obviously dead. Marcel averted his gaze and peered ahead of him. A man was lying wounded on the verge. Even from where he lay, Marcel could see the man's leg had been blown off. The roadside around him was littered with blood and bits of flesh and bone. Marcel looked away, feeling sick and dizzy. Turning, he noticed for the first time, close behind him, a horse had been hit, the contents of its stomach and intestines spilling out onto the highway, while its eyes stared sightlessly into the distance. Already, the smell was appalling and it was this that finally finished Marcel. Again, he tried to fight down the rising bile but lost the battle and he retched violently, throwing up the contents of his stomach.

There was a gentle pat on his shoulder. He turned to see the man who had warned him. "Are you alright, boy?" he asked. His voice was gruff but sounded sympathetic.

Marcel shook his head, unable to speak. His mind could not come to terms with the contrast between the rural peace of the French countryside where he had woken up only a few hours before, and this total carnage in front of him.

"Why?" was all Marcel could think of saying.

"I wish I could give you an answer," the man sounded weary. "They have been strafing and bombing the busier routes ever since we left Arras." The despair and disbelief were written all over his face. "My name is Jean-Paul, by the way." Once his companions had stood up, he continued the introductions: "This is my wife, Claudette and my daughter, Jeanne."

He waited for Marcel to say something, but there was no answer and the boy showed little sign of having heard. Realising he was in shock, Jean-Paul tried again, "What's your name, boy?"

Marcel finally refocused his gaze on his companion, the need to answer the normal, mundane question helping to steady him. "Marcel, Marcel Servier. I live... lived in a farm house just outside La Couture. My parents wouldn't leave, but they made me go." He stopped for a moment, the confusion and shock etched on his face and then he added, his voice cracking with defiance, "I want to go to England and join the army, then I can come back here and drive the filthy Boche out of my country." While he spoke, his voice rose and he found he was shaking.

"How old are you, Marcel?" The question came from Claudette who was smiling at him kindly.

"Twenty," Marcel replied quickly. Then seeing their expressions he confessed, "Alright, I'm only seventeen but I'm nearly eighteen; old enough to fight."

"Of course you are." Jean-Paul was relieved to see the colour returning to Marcel's cheeks and that he seemed less shocked and more in control of himself. Most of the refugees had picked up their belongings and resumed their journeys. Jean-Paul called to his family, "Come on, we must get moving before they come back." He turned to Marcel. "Would you like to travel with us? I would be glad of your help and I am sure Jeanne would be happy to have some company nearer her own age."

Marcel hardly hesitated at all. "Thank you. I would like that very much." Although he felt shy, he was pleased he was no longer alone. He followed them back onto the road and, trying to ignore the carnage left by the German attack, they continued on their way. Behind them, soldiers stopped to help the wounded civilians, while those who had survived unscathed continued their weary journey towards the coast.

****

Bethune, Northern France

Brigitte was already bored. She had received word that afternoon that she was not going to be invited to any more parties. She wasn't sure whether this was because of the proximity of the enemy or because Giscard had no further need for her after last night. She didn't mind not going to the parties; Giscard's strange sexual proclivities were becoming too much even for her. However, she was concerned about where she could earn some more money. Even the café was quiet; everyone was worried about the advancing Germans, including her father who had taken several bottles of expensive wine from the cellar and buried them in the small garden.

"Do you really think that will stop them?" she asked, an expression of disdain on her face.

"Providing no one tells them where they are, yes I do." Fabian fixed her with a steely glare and Brigitte looked away.

"Where's that soldier boyfriend of yours?" he asked suddenly. "Have you heard from him?"

Brigitte shook her head. "No, it's nearly three weeks now." She waited for him to make a sarcastic comment, but was astonished at his next words.

"He's probably on the run from the Boche, you know hiding and living rough. Or he might be fighting somewhere." He sensed her desolation and, for once, he felt sorry for her. "He seemed like a nice lad. Don't give up on him too quickly, eh?"

Brigitte nodded, surprised her father was saying something pleasant to her. Then her thoughts darkened again. If Louis really wanted to get in touch, he could have done. They had a telephone in the café and he knew the number. No, Louis was long gone. He'd taken what he wanted and moved on to the next girl who would keep his bed warm. Men were all the same.

Brigitte sighed and stared out into the empty streets. She needed another source of income. The thought that she could be stuck in this god forsaken town for the rest of her life horrified her.

****

Northern France

The further Marcel and his new friends travelled towards Dunkirk, the worse the bombardment became. The instances of strafing increased as did their intensity. The continual noise took on an air of normality and only during the brief silences did Marcel recall that this was how the French countryside should really be.

Jeanne had fallen into step beside him and he found her silent presence strangely comforting. They traipsed mile after long, tiring mile and Marcel despaired of ever getting to Dunkirk. They seemed to be spending more time in the ditches, hiding from the marauding planes, than moving towards the coast.

On the approach to Merville, the German planes attacked yet again. This time, the ferocity was so great that Jean-Paul decided they would be safer leaving the main highway and trying to skirt around the town. That way, they could avoid the seething mass of refugees who seemed to be attracting the Germans' animosity. Examining the map, he considered their best chance would be to try and get through the Forêt Domaniale De Nieppe, which would at least afford them some cover from the planes.

****

Olive had spent all day thinking about Kurt's letter and, in particular, about making friends with her cousin. At first, she'd been annoyed he could even suggest such a thing, but then she had finally admitted to herself she was lonely and maybe having a friend wasn't such a bad idea. She congratulated herself on having such a caring fiancé and wished she could tell everyone about him. However, she knew she couldn't, so instead she took the bus to Honor Oak Park. She would visit Peggy and try to bury the past.

She alighted at the stop opposite Peggy's house and, taking a deep breath, crossed the road, went up to the front door and knocked loudly. There was a brief pause and then the door opened.

"Hello, Olive." Peggy stared at her in astonishment, then her face paled. "Is anything wrong? Aunt Maud…?"

She didn't get any further before Olive interrupted, "No, nothing's wrong. I just thought I should pop by and see where you're living. After all, we are cousins and I've never been invited…" Olive stopped, realising her words weren't coming out as she'd intended. She took a breath and started again. "I thought perhaps we could have some tea?" Olive noticed an expression of irritation pass briefly across Peggy's face. "I didn't mean you had to do anything," she continued quickly. "I know you've had a busy day…" She didn't get any further; the damage was done. Used to Olive's pointed remarks, Peggy immediately assumed she was being sarcastic.

"I can't tonight, Olive. I'm going round to Pauline's, you know my *fiancé's* mum." Having emphasised the word 'fiancé', Peggy glanced pointedly at her watch and then back up at Olive who almost froze at the wintry expression on her cousin's face. Feeling her own anger rising, Olive stepped back.

"Well don't let me keep you. I would hate to hold you up from such an important engagement. Goodbye, Peggy." Before Peggy could say anything, Olive had turned on her heel and was walking back down the path.

Chapter Fourteen

Northern France

Still shocked, and having little idea of where he was going, Marcel was content to follow where Jean-Paul led. Night approached and they found themselves on the outskirts of Hazebrouck. All around them, they could hear the sound of small arms and see the flashes of mortar fire in the evening sky.

"If they've already reached this far," Marcel said, voicing what they were all thinking, "how on earth are we going to get in front of them to reach Dunkirk?"

"Maybe we should go towards Calais instead?" Claudette suggested.

Jean-Paul took out his map. "We could double back and go to Calais, but there is no guarantee that will be any better. We are much closer to Dunkirk. I think we need to keep going in that direction, at least for the time being." Jean-Paul folded up the map. "Come on, let's try and find some food in one of these abandoned houses."

However, others had already done the same. Every house they came to had been completely ransacked and there was no food left at all.

****

Peggy soon put Olive out of her mind. She had spent the day looking forward to seeing Pauline and Fred who only lived a few streets away. They were great fun to be with and more like a family than her elderly aunt and uncle, and Olive. The evening was mild for the time of year; the birds were singing, the shadows were gradually lengthening and the sun was just beginning its slow slide westwards as she approached the house.

"Peggy! We thought you were never coming." Fred's delighted shout reached her just as she opened the gate. "She's here, Mum!" he shouted over his shoulder, opening the front door wide to let her in.

"I don't usually get such a rapturous welcome," Peggy remarked to Fred in amusement. "What's all the excitement?"

"Dinner's nearly ready and we've got braised beef. My favourite!"

Pauline appeared from the kitchen. "Come and sit down, dear, and have a rest. You do look tired," she said, leading the way into the dining room where Peggy sat down at the table. She was delighted to take the weight off her feet and the dinner smelled delicious. Pauline was an excellent cook and Peggy thoroughly enjoyed coming round to dinner.

"This is absolutely wonderful, Pauline. What's in it?" Peggy asked after a couple of mouthfuls.

"According to those women's magazines, you're not supposed to ask until we've finished eating," Fred answered before his mother could say anything.

Pauline laughed. "Actually, I found the recipe in last month's Good Housekeeping Magazine. I'm glad you like it, Peggy. Remind me before you go and I'll give you the recipe."

"Thanks, Pauline. How's work, Fred?"

"Not bad," he replied in between mouthfuls. "They call me Joe because I'm doing Joe's old job and that way I don't get mixed up with the other Fred who works there."

"Oh." Peggy wasn't quite sure how to answer him. Eventually, she asked, "Isn't that confusing?"

"Not really. At first I kept ignoring them, but it's alright now."

The dinner and the conversation lived up to expectations and, afterwards, they sat around the wireless while Pauline did some sewing. To their relief, the early evening news reported Arras had been recaptured, after a spirited fight by elements of the French and British forces.

"Perhaps the tide is turning." Pauline sounded optimistic. "That's the first good news we've had for a while. I keep hoping we'll switch on the wireless and find the war's over and we've won."

****

Bethune, Northern France

The fighting sounded closer than earlier and, for the first time since the news of the German invasion, Brigitte began to feel scared. The café was empty, apart from a couple of her father's friends who were huddled together with him by the bar. Their voices were lowered and, whenever she approached, they stopped talking, obviously not wanting her to hear their conversation. Irritated by their secrecy, as if she was interested in their boring talk anyway, Brigitte wandered down to the street door, watching the empty road outside and wishing someone would come in.

For some reason, the conversation she'd had with her father about Louis popped into her head and she felt sad. She'd really liked Louis but he had left her, preferring to go and play soldiers instead and then he'd stopped writing. He could hardly expect her to sit around waiting for him could he? Her heart hardened as she imagined him making love to other women and not giving her a thought. Well two could play at that game.

****

They were queueing to board the *Daffodil*, a small, flat-bottomed paddle steamer, normally used as a ferry, when Joe overheard a conversation going on near him.

"Busy?" The officer was obviously making small talk with one of the loaders.

"Nah, not really," the dock worker replied. "Not many ships going to France at the moment, not likely to be either, from what I hear." He sniffed. "Looks like you lot are going in the wrong direction. Only my opinion of course," he added, seeing the officer's expression darken.

"Yes, well let's hope you're wrong, shall we?" The officer's reply was sharp, his eyes reflecting his fury when he realised several of the men had overheard the conversation. "We don't need that kind of defeatist talk."

"What on earth are we letting ourselves in for?" Joe asked with a worried frown on his face.

"God only knows," Chalky responded and proceeded to pass on the conversation to Taffy and Rob, who were just in front of them. The conversation was soon repeated, with embellishments, throughout the ship.

****

Northern France

As they left the fifth empty house, Marcel remembered the parcel his mother had given him. He had totally forgotten about the food. The scenes on the road had killed his appetite and he realised he hadn't eaten anything since the previous night.

"Jean-Paul, I have some food. I'm so sorry. With everything that's happened, I completely forgot."

Jean-Paul was genuinely relieved. "That's wonderful, Marcel." Seeing the doubtful expression on the boy's face, he explained. "If you had remembered the food earlier, you would have eaten it. Now, instead of trying to sleep with empty stomachs, we all have something to eat, no matter how small." Marcel slid his rucksack off his back and was about to get out the food when Jean-Paul stopped him

"No, not here. Let's find somewhere safer." He steered them out of the last house, concerned that if they stayed there, they could be attacked and robbed. He was worried about his ability to protect them all. Although Marcel was a big lad, he doubted the boy had ever had to fight to defend himself. He would be easy pickings for some of the less salubrious people who were travelling these roads. Rumours were rife among the refugees that the French authorities had just opened the prisons, releasing thousands of convicted prisoners to mingle with the hordes of fleeing civilians.

They retraced their steps until they came to some trees next to a hedge. Glancing around, Jean-Paul decided this was as safe a place as any, given their current circumstances.

"This will do nicely." He pulled off his jacket, offering the garment to Jeanne to sit on.

"No thanks, Papa. You'll get cold." Jeanne shook her head, sitting down on the grass next to Marcel. Seeing her father's rather startled expression, she continued, "I'm not a child anymore and I'm quite happy to sit on the grass like everyone else. Thank you anyway," she added, smiling at Jean-Paul. She loved him dearly and didn't want to hurt him, but she didn't want Marcel to think she was a child.

Jean-Paul could see Claudette smiling at him and, after she too refused his offer, he shrugged, pulled his coat back on and sat down next to his wife. Putting his arm round her, Jean-Paul drew Claudette close and kissed her on her nose.

"Papa!" Even in the semi darkness, lit only by the flares and flashes from the shelling, Jean-Paul could see his daughter blushing. Marcel smiled; it was the first time he had found anything to smile about since waking up that morning.

"Here; this is the food my mother packed before I left home." Marcel took the package out of his bag and gave it to Jean-Paul who was touched by both his innocence and generosity. Another boy, having witnessed the appalling scenes of the day, might well have kept his food and, if he had shared it at all, doled it out himself. Pleased that his initial assessment of the boy had proved correct, Jean-Paul accepted graciously.

"We mustn't eat everything," he admonished. "We don't know where we'll find any more, so we must ration it." Opening the package, Jean-Paul found a loaf of bread and some cheese, sausage, two small tins of meat, fruit, biscuits and a bar of chocolate. There was also a large bottle of water. "Goodness, Marcel. Your mother has done you proud. We'll eat some of the bread with the sausage tonight and, if we don't find anything else, we can eat the rest of the bread with the cheese and apples tomorrow. The biscuits, tins and chocolate will last longer. We can refill the water bottle from one of the houses before we leave, if there is still a supply. If not we will use the canals and rivers." Seeing the expression of distain on Claudette's face, he added, "If you're thirsty, you won't worry too much about where the water comes from, I can assure you." He broke the loaf in half, put one part back in the bag and divided the other and the sausage into four pieces while he was speaking. "If you eat slowly and chew every mouthful carefully, you will feel more full up."

****

Catford, London

Olive was furious. How dare Peggy speak to her like that? Angry thoughts whirled around her head. She was nothing; just a jumped up little tart who thought she was something special because she had a *fiancé* and was a nurse. *Trainee* nurse, she corrected herself angrily. Peggy had no idea of the suffering Olive had gone through after Peggy's parents had died. The child had moved in and everyone had run around after her, relegating Olive to the background. *Poor Peggy the orphan; Poor Peggy, the one who didn't have anyone.* "That didn't give her the right to take my family," she cried in anguish before she fought to bury the pain and hurt that had coloured her whole life since Peggy's arrival in their home.

She had confided in Kurt about her feelings for Peggy one night when they were in bed. She had shared her deepest thoughts with the man she trusted and a small part of her felt betrayed that he seemed to have forgotten how deeply affected she'd been. Then she realised he was only trying to help. If she and Peggy had been able to make friends and put the past behind them, it would have been beneficial to her. Once again, Kurt only had her best interests at heart. She began to relax. Well she had done as he asked and she could tell him in her next letter that his suggestion hadn't worked. The thought crossed her mind briefly that he might be annoyed, but she soon decided that was ridiculous. Why on earth should he care? He was just being thoughtful.

****

Southampton, England

The *Daffodil* finally sailed in convoy with the two vehicle ships, but only to the end of Southampton Water. The men were not given any reason for the delay, the decks were very crowded and uncomfortable and they were given very little to eat. Once they were finally underway again, the sea was quite calm, but several of the men suffered from seasickness and had to either scramble to the rails to be sick over the side, or throw up where they stood. Joe was grateful his stomach was unaffected by either the sea or the men retching around him.

"Want a fag?" Joe gratefully took the cigarette Taffy was offering and, lighting up, drew the smoke deep into his lungs.

"Thanks, mate. This isn't much fun, is it?"

"Well, at least we're on deck. The ones below aren't even allowed to smoke." Taffy's response made Joe feel a bit better, although he wasn't sure being close to the rails was much of an advantage, because people kept climbing over him to throw up over the side.

"Look, mate, I'm really sorry you're ill, but could you please go somewhere else to chuck up," he said, exasperated at having to move for the fourth time.

"Sorry." The face staring back at him was a curious shade of green and, for a moment, he didn't recognise Sparky.

"Sorry, Sparky. I didn't know it was you. Do you want a fag?" he asked, his tone slightly more considerate.

"No, thanks. I think a cigarette might make me feel worse." Sparky really was a strange colour and Joe felt rather mean for having moaned at him. Trying to make up for his harsh words he asked, "How's the wife and kids?"

Sparky brightened up; he always did when anyone asked after his family.

"Alright, last I heard. She's living at her mother's in the country, near Hailsham. Apparently the kids are fed up, though. They miss their friends and the locals keep treating them like lepers." Sparky stopped for a moment, closed his eyes trying to ignore the unpleasant churning in his stomach. "To be honest, I think she's the one who's fed up, not the kids." He let out a large belch. "Sorry. Anyway, where was I? Oh yeah, the kids. They're perfectly happy not having to go to school; they spend all their time running wild. She was on about going back to London but I talked her out of it. No point asking for trouble, is there? Just because nothing's happened yet, doesn't mean it's not going to. Do you want to see some pictures of them?"

Sparky had three children: two girls called Sarah, ten years old and Mary who was eight, and a boy, Frank, who was six. Joe, like everyone else, had seen the pictures of them numerous times; Sparky was a very proud father and they had an unspoken agreement among them all not to ask him about his family.

"No, you're alright mate. It's a bit windy on deck, you don't want to risk them going over the side," Joe hastily improvised.

Chalky and Taffy turned away so Sparky couldn't see the broad grins on their faces and, once he'd returned to the middle of the deck, Taffy muttered, "That was a close call. Good thinking mate!"

Joe smiled back. He didn't really mind listening to Sparky going on about his family; at least that took his mind off other things, like where they were going and what they would be expected to do when they got there.

Chapter Fifteen

Northern France

Marcel awoke with a start, aware of a particularly loud bang that not only deafened him, but also made the ground shake. He sat up, gazing into the darkness in confusion. Jean-Paul put a reassuring arm on his shoulder, until he could see Marcel was fully aware of where they were.

"I think we need to move." Jean-Paul shook Jeanne awake. "I can't believe she slept through that," he muttered to himself.

"What about your sleep?" Marcel asked, surprised to find he was completely alert. Normally he took ages to wake up. "You must be very tired."

"We'll stop later, I can always rest then. At the moment, we need to move." Jean-Paul led them through the trees and back to the carriageway. There were already other people making their way towards the coast. "We should follow the road during the hours of darkness but, once daylight comes, I think we should head across country. It'll be safer."

No one argued. The highway was littered with corpses, abandoned vehicles, possessions and empty shell cases. The full moon lent an eerie light to their progress, but enabled them to avoid stepping on the scattered bodies that were starting to swell, giving them a ghostly, unreal appearance. They were also starting to smell and Marcel found himself holding his nose while they made slow progress along the heavily shell-pitted road.

****

Olive woke early. She'd intended to write to Kurt when she returned after her abortive visit to Peggy, but she was far too angry. Even the prospect of writing to him had failed to calm her down, so instead she undressed, switched on the wireless, climbed into bed and tried to listen to the evening concert. Her mind would not be still, however, and within moments was churning with angry thoughts repeatedly taunting and mocking her, reinforcing her feelings of inadequacy. She finally fell into a restless sleep and woke well before the alarm.

Having washed and dressed, she sat down at the small pine table, picked up her pen and dipped the nib in the ink. There was just time to write to Kurt before she left for work.

> *My darling Kurt,*
>
> *I was relieved to hear from you. I began imagining all sorts of things when you didn't write. There was no one I could ask, so I just had to hope each night when I came home from work there would be a letter from you.*
>
> *I did what you suggested with Peggy but alas she was very rude to me. There is no point trying again. I was going to write to you last night after I returned from her house but I was very upset and I couldn't bring myself to put pen to paper. Instead it is very early in the morning and, having woken thinking about you as I always do, I thought I would write now. I miss you so much, I sometimes wonder how I manage to get through each day. Oh, darling, how much longer is this stupid war going to keep us apart?*
>
> *I know you said we couldn't be together before the war ended, but I have been giving our situation a lot of thought. If I moved to Southern Ireland, you could come and live there, too. Then we could be together. Please think about this, my love. Even if I could come for a short visit? I would give anything to see you again, for however brief a time.*

There's not much news to report here. Everyone is quite sure the BEF will beat the Germans eventually. I can't say 'beat you', because I don't really associate you with the enemy. I'm finding life very hard because I have no idea if you are involved in the fighting against the BEF and I worry constantly. How can I support them if that could mean danger to you? So I say nothing and just listen, praying all the while that you are safe. There are some really stupid rumours about fifth columnists floating around at the moment and we are all being cautioned to 'keep mum' in case the person next to us is a spy. Isn't that ridiculous?

The Home Guard have regular practice sessions to deal with parachutists and they have increased restrictions on visits to the coast, including Southend, which is such a shame. Do you remember our day there, how we walked along the pier and you saved my hat from blowing away in the strong wind? Most of the beaches are mined now, of course, and they have built all sorts of defences which I'm sure is a complete waste of money. Even worse, the council is drawing up plans to remove all the road signs in case we're invaded. I've never heard of anything so stupid. How on earth will we be able to find our way about?

I had a good laugh yesterday. One of our managers has lost the rehoming document which lays out all our strategies to deal with people who might be displaced by bombing. He's a really nasty man, very rude most of the time, so I was rather pleased to hear him on the receiving end of a good telling off for a change. He was straight onto his girlfriend afterwards, moaning about his boss and trying to win her sympathy. He succeeded in the end, because she invited him round for his tea. Some girls will fall for any line, won't they? I am pleased I have someone like you, who cares so deeply for me.

Well I suppose I'd better go, or I'll be late for work and that wouldn't do. The buses sometimes run early because a lot of the businesses have left London and gone further north. I did hear they were talking of moving the Woolwich Arsenal armaments factory north too. I'm not sure when though.

All my love, darling and please think about my suggestion.

Yours, now and forever,

Olive xxxxxx

****

Northern France

Dawn broke and Jean-Paul pulled up sharply. Ahead, was a hastily erected German roadblock, consisting of a coil of barbed wire strung between two vehicles, behind which they could see several soldiers manning machine guns.

"Quick, into the bushes!" The panic in his voice was evident as Jean-Paul pushed them into the undergrowth. They lay completely motionless for several minutes, while Marcel wondered why Jean-Paul was so frightened. He watched other people approaching the Germans and they were just turned back. The same would have happened to them, surely? He was about to ask, when Jean-Paul indicated they were safe to move again. They picked their way through the brambles and weeds until they found some cover in a small copse of trees and, once he was sure they were completely hidden from the road, he pulled out a map and tried to work out an alternative route.

"There's no need to panic. We still have several options. The Germans may be here but they may not have reached Dunkirk yet, which is several miles away to the north." There was silence, and he continued, "We can try going around them and carry on to Dunkirk. Or we can go towards Calais, or one of the other channel ports, Boulogne maybe? We can go west towards Le Havre and try to get to England that way. If we're lucky, we might be picked up by a naval ship. We can even try making for the Channel Islands and get a boat to England from there. If we keep off the main routes and skirt around any roadblocks, we should be reasonably safe. But we do need to make a decision and make one quickly."

"I think we should aim for Dunkirk." Marcel's earlier question about why Jean-Paul was so keen to avoid the Germans was forgotten. He had set his heart on going to Dunkirk, because the French soldier had suggested he might hear news about Louis there.

Claudette and Jeanne exchanged glances and eventually Claudette said, "Whatever you think is best, Jean-Paul."

Jean-Paul studied the map for a little longer, then began leading them deeper into the French countryside. "We'll keep on a bit further. If we're careful, we can bypass the Germans and reach Dunkirk by means of the back lanes and across country."

The deeper they moved into the countryside, the less they could hear the shelling. Like any constant noise, the fighting gradually faded into the background and they were only really aware of particularly large shells exploding. Aircraft activity was also less obvious, although they hid every time they heard a plane anywhere near them. Occasionally, they watched from their hiding place as a dog fight between English and German planes took place over their heads, or hid when they heard the ominous rumble of German tanks in the distance.

****

Dover, England

Joe held his rifle tight and waited for the order to disembark.

"This is it then." His voice was hoarse with nerves.

"Looks like it." Chalky was pale and Joe was grateful he wasn't the only one who was anxious.

In the very far distance, Joe could hear the sounds of gunfire and the muffled booms of heavy shelling; he winced as a particularly loud bang rent the air.

Joe tensed. The shore was covered with coastal defences, sea gulls circled lazily overhead, calling and shrieking while they searched for food and he could hear the water gently lapping against the hull. The sky was blue with hardly a cloud in sight and Joe was struck by the similarity between England and France. From his position on deck, he saw aerial masts on the top of the cliffs and, on the beaches, there were enormous piles of scaffolding.

Joe held his rifle even tighter. Why hadn't they been given the order to disembark? He'd expected to go ashore immediately. They waited and nothing happened. Joe's arms started to ache and he was finding it increasingly difficult to maintain his stance. Then, to his disbelief, a paper-boy appeared on the dock announcing loudly, in English, that the Germans had over-run Holland.

"For fuck's sake, we're still in England!" His church upbringing meant Joe rarely swore, but the realisation they had gone no further than another English port was a bit of a shock. He also felt really stupid, especially when he saw some of the older men were fast asleep.

Chalky also looked rather sheepish. "Right bunch of wallies we are," he said, the tension draining out of him.

Rob was smiling. "Oh well, easy enough mistake to make, I suppose."

Joe shrugged and then saw the funny side. "I really thought we were in France. I couldn't understand why the place looked just like England."

"Me too." Chalky could hardly speak, he was laughing so much.

"You did go very pale," Rob joined in. "You looked like you were going to crap yourself!"

Chalky threw his empty cigarette packet at him and Rob ducked. Eventually, they calmed down and Rob spoke, his tone more serious: "Can't say I'm too disappointed, though."

Joe nodded in agreement. He wasn't in any hurry to start fighting either.

However, relief they were in England soon turned to frustration.

"God, I'm bored and bloody uncomfortable. Are we gonna sit here all day?" Chalky grumbled, trying to get comfortable; something that was very difficult to do in full kit.

"I wouldn't be in such a hurry if I were you," one of the other soldiers piped up. He was an older man, one of the regulars who had seen action in the Great War.

"Oh, and why not?" Chalky answered peevishly. "Anything has to be better than waiting here in full kit and going nowhere."

"Oh, really?" The man puffed on his pipe. "There's German E-Boats patrolling the English Channel; can't say I'm in much of a rush to meet up with one of those. Not to mention all the mines protecting the French ports."

"Are you sure?" Joe sounded worried.

"Oh, he's just repeating rumours," Chalky snapped. "Haven't you heard the advice about defeatist talk?" he snarled back at the soldier, who shrugged and puffed hard on his pipe again, covering them all in thick smoke.

"Well don't say I didn't warn you. I'd enjoy the peace and quiet if I were you and not be in such a bloody hurry to get yourself killed."

Chalky flushed and was about to say something else when Joe kicked him. "What the 'ell did you do that for?" he snapped.

Joe shook his head and indicated the soldier who appeared to have fallen asleep.

"Perhaps he's right. Maybe we should be grateful for any delay."

Chalky opened his mouth to argue but the fight had gone out of him. He closed his eyes and tried to pretend he was somewhere else.

****

Lambeth Hospital, London

On arrival at the hospital, Peggy was surprised to see patients being moved out of their wards. "Ah, Cooper." Sister Adams called her over the minute she walked through the door. "I'm glad you're early today. We have a lot of cleaning and sprucing up to do. From tomorrow, you and all the other qualified nurses will be working in the emergency department." The sister dropped her voice. "We're expecting quite heavy casualties in the next few days."

Peggy found there was a lump in her throat and she couldn't think of anything to say in response.

Seeing her worried expression, the ward sister hastened to reassure her. "I'm sure we'll all rise magnificently to whatever challenges we have to face. Try not to worry too much." A veteran of nursing the wounded through the Great War, Sister Adams had a fair idea of what they could expect, but saw no reason to frighten her nurses.

Helen arrived at the end of the speech and, seeing Peggy's expression, raised her eyebrows in question.

"Good morning, Macklin. Cooper will explain what's happening. When she has finished, perhaps you could make a start with the beds. They need stripping and new sheets and blankets putting on. The porters will be bringing up some more beds and they all need to be placed closer together. I'll leave you to organise that while I get on. Thank you." She strode off and Peggy quickly repeated the sister's words. Helen went pale.

"I think Jimmy's going to France today."

****

Bethune, Northern France

Brigitte watched the Germans driving through Bethune from her bedroom window and wondered what would happen to them all. She was too young to remember the last war, although she had heard her father talk about the horrors of the trenches. For a brief moment, she thought of Louis and then turned her attention back to the enemy. The armoured cars had passed and they were followed by ranks of men marching, their boots clattering on the cobbles. There was a noise behind her and she jumped.

"Thought I'd watch the bastards from up here." Fabian's voice was hoarse with emotion. "I can't believe they've got this far." He muttered under his breath.

Brigitte shrugged. An idea had just come to her, although at the moment she didn't know how to put her plan into action. She watched the soldiers disappear out of sight and then turned to her father.

"I'm just popping out for a few moments." She was gone before he could object and he shook his head. He didn't know who was worse… his daughter or the Germans.

****

Louis kept to grassland, meadows and woods and away from the main highways. He could hear the crump of the heavy guns in the distance and he wondered how close behind him the Germans were. His stomach growled again. He would have to find some food soon; he couldn't remember when he'd last eaten. He was also thirsty. Once the German planes had gone, he had returned to the well and filled his water bottle but that was all gone now. In an attempt to distract himself, his mind wandered to Brigitte and their last meeting. Despite his current circumstances, the memory of their love making bought a smile to his face. He began to make plans for the future. Perhaps he should go to Brigitte's house rather than going straight home. If he went there instead of going back to the farm, he wouldn't have to face his parents and Marcel knowing he was a coward. Brigitte wouldn't care if he wasn't a very good soldier; she loved him for who he was. Maybe the two of them could try and escape to the south or even across the mountains to Spain. Then they would be safe. He was sure the Germans wouldn't get that far. He looked up at the cloudless sky, promising another hot sunny day.

"Hey! You there!" The shout caught him by surprise and he spun round, his finger on the trigger of his rifle.

Chapter Sixteen

"Right! Other than those manning the guns, everybody get below." The order was followed by much grumbling and moaning while they made their way below decks.

"Christ, it's fucking hot down here." Taffy wiped the sweat from his forehead

"Bloody crowded, too," Joe complained

"That's twice you've sworn today," Rob remarked mildly. "Most unlike you."

Joe shrugged but said nothing. He didn't like the claustrophobic feeling that being below deck was giving him. With all the hatches and doors closed, he felt hemmed-in and the constant throbbing of the engines was making him feel sick. To make matters even worse, they weren't allowed to smoke either.

"I didn't think life could get any worse," Chalky grumbled.

"Here, Sarge," Joe called out. "How long are we going be stuck down here?"

"As long as it takes, Price, and no longer." Sergeant Miller's response was curt. Privately, he agreed with the moaning and grumbling going on around him. "Sort yourselves out as best you can and try and get some shut eye. Might be a while before you get the chance again. Settle down lads!" He raised his voice above the growing din.

Joe, Chalky, Rob and Taffy finally managed to find themselves a space together on one side of the ship. Relieved they could take off their backpacks, they sat down and Taffy took out a pack of cards.

"Who's in?"

"Me." Sparky had joined them. He appeared a much better colour and seemed to have found his sea legs.

"And me." Woody made his way over to them from the other side of the ship, a journey not without difficulty as he tried not to tread on legs, arms and various other parts of the men's anatomies, not to mention random bits of kit.

****

Lambeth Hospital, London

Peggy squeezed Helen's arm sympathetically. "Come on, let's start on the beds. No point standing here worrying about things." Helen nodded and, together, they began the back breaking work of stripping and remaking bed after bed.

"Any news from Annie?" Peggy asked.

"No, nothing. Dad says we're not allowed to mention her name in the house ever again. We're to act like she never existed." Peggy's jaw dropped opened in disbelief. "Have you ever heard anything so ridiculous? It's 1940 not 1840!"

"How's your mum?"

Helen shook her head. "Devastated. She knows better than to argue with my dad, though. He's likely to thump her one. I only hope he doesn't find out she's defied him and is keeping in contact with Annie. Or that I gave her Annie's address." Helen seemed worried for a moment and then she shrugged. "Still, there's no reason for him to find out, if we're careful."

"Will her husband's parents mind all the secrecy?"

"No, I don't think so. Annie didn't seem to think there would be a problem. I'm sure she's explained to them about Dad's temper. I'm going to write to her tonight." She hesitated. "Peggy, can I ask a favour?"

"Yes, of course you can."

"She can't write to us at home for obvious reasons. Would she able to write to us at your address?"

"Of course she can. Just tell her to send her letters to you care of my home and I can bring them in for you. If you want, you can arrange to meet her there too. Your dad isn't likely to turn up at my house. I doubt he even knows where I live."

"Oh, thank you. Mum'll be ever so relieved." Helen's gratitude was touching and Peggy leaned across the bed and gently squeezed her arm.

"I'm delighted to help. Have you got my address?"

"No, not the postal address."

Peggy took out her notebook and wrote quickly. She tore out the page and was handing the piece of paper to Helen when a thought struck her. "I know this sounds a bit over dramatic, but perhaps you should memorise the address and then throw the paper away. You don't want to risk leaving anything lying around for your father to find." Peggy was a bit worried this precaution sounded a little extreme, however she had seen Helen's dad lose his temper once before and she wasn't under any illusion about how he would react if he found out they were all in some conspiracy against him.

****

Northern France

Jean-Paul and the others approached the smallholding on the corner of a barley field. Although they had some food left, Jean-Paul considered they would be wise to stock up whenever they could. From a distance, the farm appeared deserted but they still approached with caution. They climbed over the low fence into the yard that stood eerily silent and were in the process of walking towards the farm door when a shot rang out. The discharge was so close, they felt the air move as the shot whistled by their heads. Terrified, they all threw themselves to the ground.

"What do you want?" The voice was gruff, with a hint of fear, but was at least French. Marcel and Jean-Paul gingerly raised their heads. A man, wearing dirty overalls and a beret, with a scowl on his unshaven face and carrying a shotgun, had appeared around the side of a building next to the farmhouse. The gun was firmly aimed at Jean-Paul's head. Jean-Paul stood up, keeping his eyes firmly on the man's trigger finger, and raised his hands above his head.

"We're a family. We don't mean you any harm. We're trying to get to Dunkirk and we were hoping to buy some food."

"Bah!" The man twisted his head to the side and spat contemptuously on the ground. "Money's no good to anyone now. I don't have any food for sale, so get lost."

"We only want a little bread and cheese and some milk, just enough for a small amount each." Jean-Paul tried again. "We have been on the road for two days. If we pass anyone else, we won't tell them where we got the supplies from."

"Are you deaf?" The man's finger tightened on the trigger and Jean-Paul stopped abruptly. "There is nothing here for you. Go away, before I shoot you all." They began to move past him when he shouted, "Not that way – go back the way you came." The gun was pointed straight at Jeanne's head now and Jean-Paul was taking no chances. The man was scared, nervous and trigger happy. It wouldn't take much for him to carry out his threat.

"Alright, we're going." He stepped backwards warily. "Follow me, all of you… slowly, don't make any sudden moves." Jeanne was crying, tears falling silently down her cheeks. Jean-Paul bit his lip, ignored the red mist threatening to overwhelm him and held back the angry retort he wanted to make. The most important thing was to get them all out of there alive.

Once they had reached the safety of a nearby field, Jean-Paul slammed his fist into his palm and swore. Seeing their frightened faces, he tried to calm down.

"Sorry," he said. "I was very angry. At least we're safe. Come on, let's keep going." As Jeanne and Marcel began walking away, he put his arm around Claudette.

"Do you think he knew about us?" she whispered, her eyes wide with fear.

Jean-Paul hesitated, then hastened to reassure her. "No, I don't think so. He was just a very unpleasant man."

After this, they were wary of going close to any of the other small farms they passed. However they were low on food and, although Marcel had refilled his bottle at a stream they passed earlier, they had very little water left to drink. Their clothes were also torn and muddied from having to keep throwing themselves into ditches and down the sides of embankments to avoid being seen by passing German patrols. Jean-Paul was very tired and he knew he would start to make mistakes if he didn't rest soon.

****

La Couture, Northern France

Marie had no idea how long she had sat there rocking the dead body of her husband in her arms. She didn't notice the darkness that surrounded her when night fell, nor the sound of the birds singing when dawn broke the next day. She was still sitting there when her neighbours found her in the late afternoon of the following day.

Madame Christine Laval and her husband Georges lived on another of the small, isolated farms outside the village and their land bordered that of the Serviers. Georges had been out in the pastures early in the morning, checking his livestock and making sure the Germans hadn't done too much damage to his crops. He had expected to see Jacques doing the same and his concern had grown when the day wore on and there had been no sign of him. Returning home early, he discussed his thoughts briefly with Christine and they decided to go and check on their neighbours.

"Maybe they've left, like many of the others?" George suggested for the umpteenth time while they made the brief journey on foot through the fields.

"Then we don't have to worry," his wife replied. "But I would like to make sure just the same." Christine and Georges had bought their farm not long after the Serviers and because they were all 'outsiders', they became firm friends very quickly. The Lavals approached the yard. They could hear the Servier's cows stamping and calling from the barn and see their two horses wandering loose, eating the flowers and vegetables in the beds outside the farmhouse. There was no other sign of life and Christine glanced at Georges, a worried expression on her face.

"There's something very wrong," she said and they quickened their pace. Georges reached the back door first and, after knocking loudly and receiving no answer, he pushed open the door. Half expecting to find the place empty, it took him a few seconds to take in the scene before him. Then he rushed across the floor to where Marie was sitting, her arms holding her dead husband. She was totally unaware of his presence.

"Marie?" There was no answer, so he tried again, this time a little louder. "Marie? Marie, can you hear me?" One glance at Jacques was enough for Georges to know he was dead and had been for some time. He was more concerned about Marie. She did not seem to be physically injured in any way he could see, but she was obviously in shock.

"Where's Marcel?" Christine asked in a whisper, frightened of the answer.

"Stay with Marie and I'll have a look around." Georges was worried about what else he might find and he didn't want his wife stumbling on something even more gruesome.

Christine nodded and came closer. The heat of the farmhouse in the hot May weather, coupled with Marie's own body heat had kept the air around the body warm and the corpse was beginning to smell. Resisting the temptation to hold her nose, Christine knelt down beside Marie and gently began to prise her arms away from the body of her husband. At first, Marie resisted but then she suddenly crumbled and allowed Christine to lay Jacques down and lead her away to the sofa in the corner. Marie seemed totally unaware of her surroundings, her movements like those of someone in a dream. Having sat Marie down, Christine searched for something to cover Jacques and, spotting a large blanket thrown over one of the worn armchairs, she carefully placed it over his body.

Marie appeared to be in a trance, so Christine went and made some strong sweet coffee which she poured into a large cup and took over to her. She gently guided the cup to Marie's mouth and, as the warm liquid went down her throat, Marie's eyes gradually cleared and she finally focused her attention on Christine. Georges came back into the room. His eyes met Christine's and he shook his head. She wasn't sure whether to be relieved or not. At least Georges had not found Marcel's body. Maybe the Germans had taken him with them, although that didn't seem very likely. Georges helped himself to some coffee and came and sat next to Marie. Gently, he took her left hand in his and asked carefully, "Marie, where is Marcel?"

Marie didn't answer for a minute and then, to their relief she said clearly, "I made him go. I told him he should try and make for England. I had to make sure at least one of my boys was safe. I haven't heard from Louis for weeks and…" She stopped.

"And?" Georges gently prompted her.

"The Germans killed Jacques." Her voice was calm. "They thought he was going to shoot them. I tried to tell them he thought he was back in the Great War; I told them his mind had gone, but they didn't listen to me."

Georges nodded slowly, the broken shotgun on the floor beside Jacques now made sense.

"Come back with us. You can't stay here on your own at the moment. I'll go and milk the cows and tether the horses while you go back with Christine. Then I'll make some funeral arrangements. Now, you go with Christine… don't argue." He held up his hand as she started to protest. "We can leave a note for Louis and Marcel telling them where you are, in case they come back. Off you go, I need to deal with the livestock.'

Too shocked to really argue, Marie allowed herself to be guided towards the door and, with Christine's arm supporting her, she stumbled across the farmland towards the Laval's cottage.

Chapter Seventeen

Calais, France

Joe stared around in dismay. The docks were a shambles with untended fires raging in some of the buildings and civilians and soldiers milling about, seemingly without purpose. The harbour was littered with abandoned kit from those non-combatants who, trapped on the continent by the German's swift advance, were racing to get aboard the ships which the incoming troops were vacating. Joe was horrified at their battered and dishevelled appearance and the expression of defeat in their eyes; hardly the ideal welcome for the disembarking soldiers.

"Doesn't look much better out there." Joe peered in the direction Rob was pointing and his heart sank. He could count at least eight or nine different places on the horizon where smoke was rising and flames could be seen. There was broken glass everywhere and an air of desolation. Joe didn't have time to take in anything else because, as they began to disembark, a lone Heinkel flew over, dropping bombs and strafing anyone in the open. He ducked instinctively, but not before he saw the loaders running for cover, leaving their vehicles and equipment untended and unloaded. The Heinkel flew off and they continued their disembarkation, Joe now able to see the situation more clearly.

"Looks like the cranes aren't working."

"That would explain why the unloading's taking such a long time," Rob answered. "P'raps they're broken?"

"Probably no power. The enemy have been quite busy." For once Chalky wasn't moaning, just stating a fact.

"Could be sabotage," Taffy suggested.

"Well whatever it is, it's going to take a long time to get all our stuff off." Woody had joined them. Already exhausted, Joe, Chalky, Rob and Taffy exchanged glances. The sounds of shelling, mortars and gunfire were ominously close and the acrid smell of cordite caught in the backs of their throats, making them cough.

"Right, muckers, if we want our equipment, we'll have to get the stuff ourselves. Now, we've not done this before, so be careful. We don't want any accidents." The captain's orders were met with considerable muttering and cursing.

"Bloody good this. Not only do they want us to fight for them they want us to do all the ruddy unloading too." Chalky wasn't amused. Other soldiers broke open some of the packs that had already been unloaded and began to dole out the linen bandoliers of bullets to anyone who wanted them. With rounds of ammunition slung round their necks, and bent double with the weight, they soon began to look more like bandits than soldiers.

"Still no sign of the transport ships and the tide's beginning to go out." Joe sounded anxious. "If the water gets much lower, they won't be able to get in at all. Not much point being a motorised battalion without motors."

"Maybe the Jerries got 'em," Rob answered. "It was pretty rough out there."

"Nah, they've probably got lost or stopped to do some sight-seeing." Taffy sounded more cheerful now he had some ammunition. "At least we're off that bloody sardine tin and our feet are on solid ground again."

"Doesn't help though, if we haven't got most of our equipment." Chalky refused to be cheered up.

"God, you're a misery, Chalky. Do you moan like this when you're with your wife?" Taffy was determined to be positive. "We're alive, uninjured and we've even got our emergency rations. We've also got smokes, water and our rifles. What more could we ask?"

"Beer, hot food, transport, women… Do you want me to go on?" Rob muttered under his breath, but at least they were all smiling.

****

Bethune, Northern France

Brigitte followed the Germans through the town at a safe distance, her high heels echoing off the otherwise silent cobbles. The rest of the population was safely behind closed doors and she wondered briefly whether she might be better off doing the same. She'd had every intention of remaining with her father but then the thought had occurred to her that the Germans would have plenty of money and, if they were going to stay, they would be a good source of income. The decision to follow them had been made on the spur of the moment and she was already beginning to regret her impulsiveness.

Out of the corner of her eye, she could see curtains twitching and she was acutely aware of the eyes of the townsfolk on her back. The feeling unnerved her and she speeded up, trying to escape their disapproving gaze. She was about to turn back when she spotted the end of the convoy disappearing around a corner. Her fears forgotten, she hastened up the hill after them. She knew fraternising with the enemy would be frowned upon, but the need to be wanted and the lure of making enough money to move away was too much to resist, so she closed her ears to her misgivings. The first task would be to discover whether they were staying in the town or just passing through.

****

Lewisham, London

"She's always listening in." The younger girl, Mary, looked fearfully around the large ladies' washroom with its numerous toilets, to make sure Olive was not in sight.

Her friend, Kath, patted her hand. "I know, luv. Don't let her get to you. She's a right miserable cow and she had no right taking out her bad mood on you." Kath peered into the long, badly lit mirror, carefully finished a thin layer of eyeliner to her eyelids and then added some bright red lipstick to her pale lips. "A definite improvement," she muttered, admiring the finished result which was totally different from her normal demure work look.

"I can't afford to lose this job." Mary wrung her wet handkerchief in her hands and gazed tearfully at her friend.

"Well, you haven't got the sack, he just threatened you, so providing you keep your nose clean the matter'll soon be forgotten." Kath was at pains to reassure her. "The next time she's copping an earful, perhaps we should report her."

"We couldn't!" Mary looked shocked and Kath smiled.

"Come on, wipe your eyes and put some lippy on. You'll feel much better. You coming down the Red Lion tonight? There's a dance in aid of the Spitfire Fund."

Mary looked troubled. "I'd love to, but I don't know whether I should. I mean, I don't know if I'm gonna lose my job or not, do I?" She dissolved into noisy tears again.

"Look, Mary, I've told you. Stop worrying. You've still got your job and providing nosy parker doesn't report you again, you've got nothing to worry about."

Mary stared at her friend and then nodded. "I suppose you're right." She sniffed and took a deep breath. "Thanks, Kath. I think I will come tonight. Do me good to get out. Can't let that horrible cow win, can I?"

"That's the spirit." Kath handed Mary the lipstick.

Mary patted her eyes, borrowed Kath's lipstick and eyeliner and was soon feeling better. The two girls left, chattering about the fun they would have, their earlier conversation forgotten.

A few moments later, the toilet door at the far end opened and Olive came out. She hadn't intended to listen in but, once they started talking about her, she was trapped because she was too embarrassed to come out and face them. She washed her hands and gazed at her reflection in the mirror. Her normally pale face was flushed, her eyes filled with pain and fury. Olive stared at herself for a few moments. Those two would regret their conversation. She would get them both the sack. After all, she couldn't leave them where they were, they might tell the supervisor that Olive was listening in to the phone calls too. And then, what if they found out she had a German boyfriend and was writing to him? In her mind, everything began to spiral out of control, even though there was no logical reason anyone should find out about Kurt. Her own tear-filled eyes gazed back at her. She couldn't lose him. She would do anything to stop that happening… anything.

****

Honor Oak Park, London

Ethel was already home when Peggy arrived and, after making herself a cup of tea and kicking off her shoes, she collapsed onto the comfortable settee in the front room. Although she had enjoyed living in the nurse's home when she first started her training, she loved coming back to her own house.

Ethel glanced up from the previous Thursday's *Woman* magazine.

"Hard day?" Ethel took in the exhausted expression on Peggy's face.

"No, not really." Peggy yawned. "No worse than usual, I suppose. We had to strip and remake loads of beds. Most of the patients have been moved to hospitals further north and, starting tomorrow, I'll be working on the emergency wards."

"Just you?" Ethel asked

"No, lots of us have been transferred. We've been told they're expecting heavy casualties. Still it's not the first time. They did the same thing at the beginning of the war, then when nothing happened, they moved everything back again." She changed the subject. "What was your day like?"

"The usual, really." Ethel sounded fed up. "Working in the munitions factory might be useful, but it's very boring. I'm thinking of trying something else. There are rumours production is going to be moved up north in case the Germans start bombing London. The Arsenal would make quite an easy target. If I really don't want to move hundreds of miles away from here, I'll have to find something else. I saw a poster today asking for spotters. I think I might apply."

"What on earth's a *spotter?*" Peggy was curious.

"Someone who spots enemy aircraft and helps the gunners line up on them apparently. I asked someone else, because I'd not heard of them either."

"Sounds a bit dangerous to me."

"Yes, but isn't everything nowadays? At least being a spotter is helping to save lives. I'm doing the opposite at the moment. I think I'd feel happier saving lives rather than taking them."

"I can't say I disagree with you. How do you go about becoming a spotter, then?"

"The poster said to speak to your local Government Training Centre. So I'm going there on Friday. I've swapped my day off with one of the other girls. You've got a half day off too, haven't you? Why don't you come with me?"

"Yes, alright. I will."

******

Northern France

Jean-Paul looked up at the early evening sky, where a particularly vigorous air fight was taking place above them. They had finished the cheese, fruit, chocolate and biscuits and he was worried about where they would get fresh supplies. Hopefully they would come across another farmhouse soon, one with friendlier residents.

No sooner had this thought gone through his mind than the rattle of machine gun fire caught his attention. The noise sounded like the gun was right on top of them. Spinning round, frantically scanning the horizon, he could not see anything. Then he realised the sound was coming from two planes circling each other lazily in the sky directly above their heads.

"Quick, out of sight!" His warning was unnecessary. Jeanne, Claudette and Marcel had already thrown themselves flat onto the ground where they were standing. Lifting his head and desperately searching for some better cover, Marcel pointed to some small bushes on their right. "Over here!" He crawled towards them, pulling Jeanne with him. Jean-Paul and Claudette followed.

From their vantage point, they watched the Hurricane finally gain the advantage and the Stuka exploded, its shattered, burning remnants falling to the ground. But their silent cheers were short lived when they saw the tell-tale puff of white smoke coming from the rear of the Hurricane. In horror, they watched the plane begin to tail spin, the screaming noise growing ever louder. Then, to their relief, they saw a parachute emerge and they watched the pilot slowly pirouette to earth, not far from where they were hiding.

Before Jean-Paul could say anything, Marcel was up and running towards where they had seen the pilot land, followed closely by Jeanne and Claudette. Jean-Paul hesitated and then followed more cautiously.

The pilot landed a few hundred metres away and they soon reached him. He was busy trying to fold up his parachute when he heard them. Spinning round, he pulled out his gun and took aim.

****

Somewhere in France

To Louis' relief, he was approached by a group of French soldiers. They came closer and Louis slowly lowered his rifle. There were four of them: one had his arm in a sling, another was using a tree branch for a crutch.

"Thought you were the Boche!" He tried to ignore the pounding of his heart.

"You'd be dead if we were," one of the soldiers replied. "We've been trailing you for ages and you didn't notice!"

Louis blushed then snapped at him, "Why didn't you shout earlier, then?"

"Come on, lads, there's no need to argue. We've got enough to worry about." The wounded soldier with the crutch eased to a halt and wiped the sweat from his brow. The men fell silent, the only sound the boom of heavy artillery in the background. Now he was closer, Louis could see the stripes on this man's arm. "Where are you going?" the sergeant asked.

"I don't know, sir, to be honest." The strain of the past few days showed on Louis' face. "We were told it was every man for himself, then my mate was killed by a Stuka and I've been on my own ever since." There was a brief silence. "I was going to try and get home."

"We're trying to do the same," the sergeant answered. "Where do you live? We're heading towards Arras if that's any help?

"I live in La Couture, several miles north of Arras, in the same general direction though."

"Good, then you can travel with us for a while, if you want?"

"Thanks, sir." Louis cheered up. At least he would no longer be on his own.

"Good lad." The sergeant turned to the others "We need to find some civilian clothes. Any properties round here?" he asked Louis.

Louis shook his head. "I haven't seen any for the last few hours but I've kept off the main roads."

The sergeant sighed. "Right, well let's get going and keep your wits about you." As he finished speaking, a particularly loud explosion rent the air and he ducked. "Come on, the Boche'll be here soon."

Now he was with other soldiers, Louis soon forgot his earlier fears.

"Seen any Germans?" the sergeant asked while they tramped deeper into the woods. Louis recounted his experience on the road.

"I had to do something to protect the refugees, so I fired up at the Stuka. Unfortunately, the bastard came after Raul and me and started firing at us. He didn't move quick enough." Louis went quiet, remembering Raul's selfless action and his motionless body and, for a brief moment, he felt guilty for lying. Then he began justifying his version of events, after all Raul was dead, the truth wouldn't matter to him anymore.

The sergeant misread his silence for grief and patted him gently on the shoulder. "Never mind, lad. You did the right thing. Go on."

"The Boche plane flew off and I went back up to the highway to help the wounded." Louis held the sergeant's eyes.

"Right little hero, ain't he?" one of the other men muttered to nods of agreement from his friends. Louis ignored them. In his mind, the fantasy had become the true version of events and Louis was the brave dashing soldier he'd always wanted to be.

****

Northern France

"Don't shoot!" Marcel raised his hands and shouted in French, only afterwards realising the Englishman probably didn't understand. Jeanne had also reached him by this time and the delight on her face left the Englishman in no doubt they were not the enemy.

"Do you speak English?" he asked, more out of hope than any belief he could be that lucky. Although he spoke some French, he wasn't sure his limited vocabulary would be enough to make himself understood.

"I do... a little anyway." Jean-Paul had appeared on the scene "Welcome to France!" The Englishman gave a wry smile and, putting away his gun, stepped towards Jean-Paul.

"Flight Lieutenant Griffiths, Charles Griffiths. Pleased to meet you." He glanced around before adding, "Perhaps we should move away from this area a bit sharpish." Jean-Paul appeared confused so Charles rephrased his comment: "I think we should move away from here quickly."

Jean-Paul agreed and hurriedly led them back to where they had been hiding. Quickly gathering their meagre possessions, he introduced his family and Marcel, checked the map and started walking, gesturing for Charles to fall in beside him.

"We can talk while we walk. We're trying to get to Dunkirk. Have the Germans reached there yet?"

"No, although they're not far off." Charles sounded grim. "Perhaps you should turn back."

Charles' words were worrying, but Jean-Paul was still convinced going to Dunkirk was the best thing to do. After all, they were already more than half way there. Even with a rest overnight, they could reach the port by the following evening.

"Are there any French army personnel there?" Marcel asked when Jean-Paul had finished translating for them.

"Yes, and some Belgians and a few Dutch," Charles added seeing the hopeful expression on Marcel's face. "Has he got relatives in the French army?" he asked Jean-Paul.

"His brother was on the Maginot Line," Jean-Paul explained. "He's not heard anything and his mother told him to try and escape to England, which is how we came to find him on the route to Dunkirk. We've been travelling together ever since." Jean-Paul glanced around. The sun would disappear soon, leaving them in darkness. "On a more practical note, we need to get some food and I need to rest." He quickly told Charles about their experiences at the farmhouse earlier. "Still, you are armed, so we may have more luck at the next one. We also need to get you some clothes; you can't wander around the French countryside in your uniform; you will be captured and we could all be shot."

"Sounds good to me," Charles agreed and they continued walking while the sun began to sink lower, finally dipping below the treetops. Then Marcel pointed. "Look, there's a house over there."

In the distance, there was a fairly large property, fringed by trees and a neatly tended garden.

After a few seconds, Jean-Paul spoke. "We'll try here." They approached cautiously but couldn't see any sign of life. Jean-Paul didn't want to risk putting his wife or daughter in danger and was about to tell Claudette and Jeanne to hide behind the small outhouse to their left when the front door opened.

Chapter Eighteen

Eventually, with no transport in sight and the tide going out, they were ordered to the sand dunes between the north side of the Bassin de Chasses and the sea. Here they could keep watch for the transport ships.

"Right, lads. Fall in. Keep alert and let's get dug in quickly." Sergeant Miller's orders were welcome. They were becoming increasingly restless just standing around doing nothing other than providing a good target for marauding planes. Feeling slightly happier now they had some purpose, they fell in and headed towards the dunes.

As they marched through the Gare Maritime, they could see the remains of bombed out railway trucks on the train lines and rows of stretchers on the platform. There were untended fires raging in some of the buildings and a strange smell in the air. Joe peered more closely, noticing many of the stretchers were covered completely and he was suddenly aware of his heart pounding uncomfortably against his chest. Obviously the men lying there were dead. This was the first time he'd seen a dead body, let alone rows of them.

They were passed with increasing frequency by bearers carrying the injured and wounded to ships that would take them home to England. For Joe, the moans and screams of the wounded were worse than seeing the lines of dead bodies. He could hear those in pain or dying calling out for their mothers or for something to kill the pain. Others were just screaming, a continuous wave of unintelligible sounds conjuring up his worst nightmares; only he was wide awake and this was real.

"Eyes front!" Sergeant Miller yelled. Despite their discipline, they only half obeyed the order; it was impossible not to stare at the injured as they passed. "Eyes front, lads," Miller repeated. "They don't need you gawping at them, do they?" This time his words had more effect. Trying to ignore the noise and the smell, they concentrated on looking ahead while they continued into the dunes.

****

Northern France

Standing in front of Jean-Paul was a middle-aged lady whose initial apprehensive expression was soon replaced with a big smile and who, upon hearing their story, invited them in without any hesitation. Her name, she said engagingly, was Madame Antoinette Vignet and she was a widow of some three years. She was particularly pleased to see Charles who reminded her of her son who was away fighting. After their last encounter, Jean-Paul was delighted to find not all his countrymen had gone mad.

Antoinette smiled. "At times like this we have to stick together and help each other." She changed the subject. "You must be hungry and I am sure you could do with a wash and a change of clothes. Come with me and, while you are doing that, I will prepare some food." Unable to believe their luck, they followed her up several stairs and past numerous doors, until she opened one of them.

"This is where I have stored all my husband's clothes," she explained to the men. "Help yourselves to anything useful. When you have found something to fit you, go to the second door on the right and you will find some sheets and blankets. Take them to this room." She pointed to yet another door. "You will be able make up your beds for the night."

She turned to Claudette and Jeanne. "You and I are of a similar height and build." She eyed Claudette up and down. "You won't have too much trouble finding something to wear and I am sure there will be something we can adjust for you, chère," she said to Jeanne. She opened the door to a beautiful bedroom, bathed in the dying glow of the evening sun and pointed to the large wardrobe running the whole length of the back wall. Before she left them, she showed them the bathroom and their bedroom.

Claudette and Jeanne gazed into the vast wardrobe full of expensive clothes.

"I don't know where to start." Jeanne was overwhelmed. "Are you sure this is alright, Mama?"

After a brief hesitation, Claudette nodded. "Yes. We would be churlish to turn down such generous help, especially when we are in obvious need. Just take a couple of outfits and some underwear. It's always a good idea to have something in reserve. Before you do, go and have a good wash. The bathroom is the second door on the left."

Jeanne entered a light airy bathroom with a large inviting bath in one corner. She started to run the water, adding a few crystals she found in a large jar on the shelf near the window. The room began to fill with gently perfumed steam and, for the first time since they had fled their home, Jeanne felt safe. Taking off her filthy clothes, she climbed into the steaming bath and sank beneath the water level, closing her eyes in pleasure. She was just starting to drift off, when the door opened and her mother came in.

"I'll get in after you, then there'll be plenty of hot water left for the men and we won't be abusing Antoinette's hospitality." Seeing Jeanne's sleepy expression, she apologised. "Sorry, love, were you dozing off? There'll be time for sleep later. We should get a move on. The men need to use the bathroom too."

When Jeanne finished, Claudette eased herself into the warm water, enjoying the opportunity to soak and relax for a few moments before washing. She closed her eyes and thanked God for providing them with such luxury and asked for His continuing protection in the days ahead. Realising she was in danger of falling asleep herself, Claudette opened her eyes, washed herself in the rapidly cooling water and climbed out.

After drying herself on one of the big fluffy towels Antoinette had left them, she carefully put on the clean clothes she had chosen. Antoinette was right; they were of a similar size and fitted beautifully. Jeanne was also dressed and, feeling human again, they washed their clothes in the bath before emptying the water and leaving the bathroom for the men. Claudette took the wet clothes downstairs to find somewhere to hang them.

Antoinette was busy laying the table and Claudette immediately offered to help. Antoinette shook her head. "No need. There's nothing left to do, other than let the meal cook. You can hang your things over there." Antoinette pointed towards some clothes-drying wires suspended from the ceiling and stretched across the back of the kitchen. "The warmth from the stove should dry them enough for you to take them with you tomorrow."

Claudette hung up their belongings and again offered to help. Antoinette shook her head. Then, seeing Jeanne coming down the stairs, she greeted her. "You look lovely, Jeanne. The dress fits beautifully."

Jeanne was delighted to be told she looked nice. The last few days had been so fraught with danger and discomfort, the last thing she had worried about was her appearance. Antoinette turned back to the range. "You sit down and rest while I enjoy having someone to cook for again. I thought I would make a chicken stew. It will warm you up and provide plenty of nourishment."

Antoinette made Claudette and Jeanne some coffee and they sat down at the table, chatting about all sorts of things, except the war.

****

Somewhere in France

Louis was so relieved he was no longer on his own, he was unaware of his new friends' animosity. They headed deeper into the trees and he fell in beside them, trying to make conversation.

"I'm going to make sure my girlfriend's alright." Having decided to go to Bethune first, his thoughts were full of Brigitte.

"Bet she's really special. Got to be, having a hero boyfriend like you." The man with his arm in the sling's voice was laden with sarcasm.

Louis didn't notice though, and nodded with enthusiasm. "She's gorgeous." He motioned a figure of eight with his hands. "And she loves the fact I'm in uniform." He was too busy remembering to notice the others sniggering.

"Well, let's hope she's keeping herself for you and not sharing it around." This was from the man he'd snapped at earlier.

This time the laughter was loud enough to elicit an angry, "Sshhh, keep your voices down and your eyes open!" from the sergeant who was in front of them.

Louis shook his head, a serious expression on his face. "No, she's not like that. She loves me. We're going to get married." As he said the words, he realised getting married would be an excellent idea. Once he reached Bethune, he would ask her and he was sure she would say yes.

****

Bethune, Northern France

The soldiers drew to a halt at the edge of the town and Brigitte could hear shouting. She edged closer, using the shadows of the last few properties on the outskirts to hide her movements. She watched some of the men begin erecting a roadblock while others spread out into the surrounding countryside. Although she didn't know much about the army, she assumed they were some kind of sentries because she could see them standing at various points surrounding the makeshift camp springing up in one of the fields.

Now she was here, Brigitte had no idea how to put her plan into action. She couldn't just go up and start talking to them, not with the officers around anyway. Perhaps she should come back later. She was about to retrace her steps when a couple of officers began heading towards her. Terrified they had seen her, she turned, removed her shoes and began running quickly back down the cobbled streets.

****

Catford, London

Olive let herself in to the empty flat. She was seething about the two girls. She was also worried. Olive had worked on the switchboard for a very long time and she'd had a couple of warnings about listening in to conversations over the past few years. The black marks were bound to still be on her record. Even if the supervisor couldn't prove the girls' accusation, he might decide to sack her. The thought terrified her so much, she couldn't think clearly. Having begun her working career just before the depression, the struggle to find work was fresh in her mind. She couldn't face telling her parents she had been sacked, or Peggy for that matter. Olive paled in horror as she pictured her cousin laughing at her behind her back. Then there was Kurt. What would he think of her?

Her mind whirled and she tortured herself with thoughts of losing everything, including Kurt; then an idea came to her. Maybe she could deny all knowledge of the complaint against Mary and instead persuade Mary to believe that Kath had reported her. That would drive a wedge between the two girls and make them less likely to support each other in any complaints about her. The more she went over the plan in her mind, the better sense it made.

There was no time like the present. She didn't want to talk to Mary at work, because Kath would be hovering around. She would have to speak to her tonight. Maybe she could catch her on the way home from the dance.

Olive cut some bread, spread the thin slices with butter and a scraping of jam and, while she was eating, she plotted what she would say. She would have to be convincing or she would make matters worse.

151

Chapter Nineteen

The inviting aroma of the stew reminded Jean-Paul, Charles and Marcel of just how hungry they were. They were all wearing clean clothes and, apart from Charles' uniform, which they had packed away, in case he needed it to prove who he was, the others had been washed and were soon hanging on the wires, drying with the women's.

"Sit down at the table, the food won't be long." Antoinette pointed to the wine rack. "Perhaps you would like to open a bottle, Jean-Paul?"

Jean-Paul didn't need telling twice. He could hardly believe they were about to eat a civilised meal. "You are very generous, Madame. I'm not sure we can ever repay you."

Antoinette shook her head. "I don't want repaying. At times like these, we should be helping each other." She took the large earthenware casserole dish off the stove. "The stew's ready; there is some bread on the table. Please help yourselves to as much as you want." She put the casserole in the middle of the table and put a large ladle next to the dish. They were hungry at first and they ate in silence. Then, gradually, they sated their appetites and began to talk, first about the worsening situation, then about other things.

They discovered Antoinette's husband had been quite a successful artist until he had died of tuberculosis three years earlier. Antoinette proudly showed them some of his paintings which seemed vaguely familiar to Jean-Paul.

"Has he ever exhibited in Paris?" he asked. "Only I'm sure I have seen this style before."

Antoinette was pleased. "Yes he did, although I can't remember the names of the galleries. They weren't the top ones, but he made a reasonable living from his paintings, so you could have seen them. Do you come from Paris?"

"We used to live there a long time ago but when Claudette was expecting Jeanne, we decided to move out to somewhere smaller and we moved to Amiens. I was a school teacher there and Claudette was a nurse."

"Were you living there when the war started?" Antoinette asked with interest. "I've never been there, but I have heard Amiens is very pretty."

Jean-Paul nodded. "When we heard the Germans had overrun the border, we decided to try and get to England. However, our car ran out of petrol after about thirty miles because we weren't able to fill up before we left and there was no petrol to be had once we were on the road. We left behind anything we couldn't carry and started out on foot." He stopped and took another mouthful of stew.

Antoinette waited until he had finished before asking, "And Marcel and Charles?"

Jean Paul relayed their stories. "Anyway, enough of us! Are you going to stay here?"

Antoinette's response was emphatic. "This is my home. My husband is buried in the orchard. I am not leaving him to some filthy Boche. I saw how they left our homes after the last war. I will be quite safe." Changing the subject, she asked, "What will you do when you get to England?"

Before Jean-Paul could reply, Marcel interrupted, "I'm going to join the British army, if they'll let me or maybe the French army, if they're regrouping in England."

"Good for you." Antoinette was struck by how very handsome Marcel he was. The fact he was totally unaware of his own charm only added to his appeal and, if she wasn't mistaken, he already had an admirer, although he was too caught up in the present events to have noticed. He and Jeanne would make a very attractive couple, she thought and then glanced down quickly at her plate, not wanting them to see her sudden smile. *What a silly old woman I am. We are in the middle of a war and these two young people have only just met and already I have married them off.*

"And you?" she asked Jean-Paul and Claudette.

Claudette answered, "We'll try to find work. Jean-Paul could teach and I will enrol at a hospital, if they'll have me. Jeanne should have no problem finding some work; she's very clever and I am sure, with a war on, everyone who wants to work will be welcome."

Antoinette was about to ask more when she then saw their white, tired faces. "It's getting late and you are all exhausted. Go and get some rest. You have a long day ahead of you tomorrow. We can talk at breakfast, before you leave and we can always meet again after the war has finished and continue our conversation in peace."

They were all too exhausted to argue and, thanking her again, they left the table and went upstairs to the rooms she had given them where they said goodnight.

****

Lewisham, London

The dance was in full swing when Olive arrived. She fought her way through the revellers and spotted Mary at the other end of the pub, near the bar. She was with Kath and two young men. Olive frowned. She hoped the men wouldn't offer to walk the girls home; that would make approaching Mary much harder.

Realising she would draw attention to herself if she stayed there much longer, Olive left and wandered across to the other side of the road, where she could watch the door.

****

It was much quieter in the sand dunes. The sea was lapping on the beach and there was a moderate on-shore breeze providing cleaner air. Relieved to be away from the chaos of the docks and the depressing sights in the station, the men began the laborious task of digging themselves in. Then the heavens opened and, before long, they were soaked by driving rain. Fortunately the sand was soft enough for them to use their bayonets to dig shell scrapes, as all their tools were still on the transport ships. Eventually, the trenches were ready, the rain eased off and the soldiers settled down to wait for their transport. Other than eight Bren guns, which would have to be divided between them, they had very few armaments.

"What are we going to do if our transport doesn't arrive, Sarge?" Chalky was sounding rather mutinous and the others listened with interest.

"Manage without any, White. Haven't you been in the British Army long enough yet to know you do the job with whatever you've got? The British Army never has enough equipment, but better men than you have managed without it."

"Consider yourself told," Rob muttered under his breath.

"Do you have some pearls of wisdom you want to share with us, Roberts?" Sergeant Miller glared at him.

"No, Sarge. Not me," Rob replied. "I was just agreeing with you, Sarge."

"Mmm." Sergeant Miller wasn't overjoyed either. Unlike them, he couldn't say so. "Now you're dug in, get yourselves a brew and a smoke and have something to eat."

Unable to do anything else, they took his advice.

Sipping his hot sweet tea, eating his bully, biscuits and chocolate, Joe began to relax. Although he could hear shelling in the distance and the dock area was occasionally lit up with the flashes of mortar fire, he felt much safer than he had on board ship. The stress and excitement of the day drained away and Joe began to feel tired. He yawned

"Right, I'm going to try and get some kip, while I can," he announced. The others agreed and, after finishing their tea, emptying their dregs in the sand and smoking their cigarettes to the end, they dug themselves into their holes and closed their eyes. A life-long Baptist, Joe always prayed before he slept and tonight was no exception. He had the feeling tonight his prayers were needed more than ever, not only for himself and his family, but also for all his friends. He was just dozing off when his thoughts returned to the brief conversation he'd had with the sergeant when they had marched through the station:

"What's that awful smell, Sarge?" The somewhat sickly stench had been puzzling Joe ever since they arrived.

"Burning bodies." The sergeant sounded grim. Joe had swallowed nervously as they marched past the dead and the dying, the words of the loader back in Southampton, prophesying they were going in the wrong direction, even clearer in his head. The feeling of foreboding had been reinforced when he'd watched the speed with which other soldiers, officers and civilians hastily boarded the *Maid of Orleans*, like they really couldn't get away fast enough. His last conscious thought before dropping off to sleep, was that everyone, except them, was going in the other direction.

****

Honor Oak Park, London

Peggy was making some cocoa when there was a knock on the front door.

"Are you expecting anyone, Ethel?" Peggy shouted.

"Only Colin. He was going to pop by, if he had time. I'll go."

Peggy heard an exclamation of pleasure, followed by Ethel's voice chattering away and responses in a deeper tone and, smiling, she went back to the saucepan.

"Shall I put some more milk on?" she called.

"Yes, please," Ethel replied.

A few moments later, Colin was standing smiling in the kitchen doorway, one arm draped round Ethel's shoulder. "Hello, Peggy. I hope you don't mind me calling in?" Colin was always polite.

"Of course not. You're welcome anytime." Peggy poured the hot milk onto the cocoa powder. "You'll need to stir them well. For some reason this cocoa seems to be lumpier than usual."

"Probably because there's a war on." Colin and Ethel spoke in unison. This was the universal response to any problem at the moment and, as usual, made them all chuckle.

"Come on." Peggy handed them their cups. "Let's go in the front room and sit down."

Ethel and Colin sat next to each other on the sofa and Peggy sat on the armchair opposite them. She was pleased to see her friend happy. Colin was tall with brown hair and green eyes. His nose was a little crooked where he had evidently fallen off his bike as a child and broken it, something he was very conscious of. No one else noticed, except when he tried to hide his nose by putting his hand over his face. He had a very broad smile and was quick to find humour in every situation. He was making Ethel giggle now by regaling her with tales of supposed accidents that happened at work when they were practicing their fire drills.

"I don't believe a word you're saying!" Ethel shook her head while he told her a particularly funny anecdote that obviously couldn't be true. "You must spend hours thinking up these stories."

"I just like to see you happy and, anyway, most of them have got some truth in them." He winked at Peggy.

They sat and chatted for a bit longer and then Colin stood up to go.

"I have to get up early tomorrow and I know you both do. I really came round to ask you to come to the cinema with me on Friday night, Ethel. There's a new film out called *Irene*, with Anna Neagle and Ray Milland."

"As long as it's not a war film or a western!"

"It's a musical romantic comedy according to the trailer I saw last week."

"I'd love to. Roll on Friday. I like musical comedies, the funnier the better."

"I'll pick you up around seven o'clock then? Perhaps we could go out and eat afterwards?"

"Sounds lovely." Ethel turned to Peggy. "I'm sorry, Peggy, we're being very rude. Would you like to come too?"

"I wouldn't dream of playing gooseberry! If the film's good, I can always go next week. You go and enjoy yourselves."

Colin said goodnight and let himself out. Ethel was glowing and couldn't keep the big smile off her face.

"Someone's going to have good dreams tonight…"

Ethel blushed but didn't deny it. "Goodnight, Peggy. Sleep well."

****

Lewisham, London

"At last." Olive breathed a sigh of relief. She'd begun to wonder if they were ever going to leave. Her relief was short lived, though; Mary was not alone. She was accompanied by one of the young men Olive had seen her with earlier. She cursed under her breath. She would have to follow them and hope to get an opportunity to speak to the girl. They set off towards Mountsfield Park with Olive following close behind. She could hear Mary giggling and see the boy's hand squeezing her buttocks through her skirt. Olive pursed her lips in disapproval. Then he began kissing her. Wondering how long she was going to have to wait before getting Mary on her own, Olive watched while his hands roamed over the girl's body and then began hitching up her skirt. To Olive's surprise, Mary started trying to push him away.

"No. I said, no. I'm not that sort of girl." Although Mary's words were slurred, the meaning was clear. However, the boy did not seem to be taking any notice. Olive watched him tighten his grip on her arm and he began steering her away from the path and towards some bushes. Mary started struggling, but he was much too strong for her and, as she opened her mouth to scream, he hit her. Olive gasped and, without thinking, stepped forward out of the shadows where she had been hiding.

"Are you alright?" She remembered at the last second not to say Mary's name.

The boy sprang back at the sound of her voice and then, seeing a rather thin, harmless looking, middle aged woman, he snarled, "What's it got to do with you, you nosy old bat?"

Olive was about to answer him, when she realised Mary was moving away. She ignored the man and hurried after the girl. He watched for a brief moment then shrugged and turned back the way they had come, leaving Olive to follow Mary.

"Mary! Are you alright?" she called.

Mary turned towards her in astonishment. "Yes, thank you." Her words sounded slurred and then she peered at Olive in surprise. "Oh, it's you." Her voice rose. "Why are you here? Are you following me?" The words sounded so preposterous she laughed, a loud cackling sound.

Olive winced. "I wanted a word." She was now close enough to smell the alcohol on the girl's breath. "I just wanted to tell you I did not speak to the supervisor about you. It was Kath."

Mary peered at her in confusion and then shook her head. "Don't be ridiculous. Why would Kath do something like that?"

"I think she's jealous of you." Olive said the first thing that came into her head and wished she'd thought it through properly. She wasn't expecting to have to rescue the girl and all her carefully rehearsed words had vanished.

Mary stared at her for several seconds before answering, then laughed. "You're sick." She was too drunk to wonder how Olive knew she'd thought her guilty of speaking to the supervisor. She was beginning to feel quite ill and all she wanted to do was to go home.

Mary tried to push past, but Olive caught her arm. "Please, Mary, I'm telling you the truth. If you tell the supervisor about me, I'll get the sack." Olive slammed her mouth shut wondering why on earth she had told the girl the truth. Mary stopped and leered drunkenly at her.

"*You'll* get the sack?" She stared for a moment and then laughed. "And there was me thinking I was the one about to lose my job." She began to stagger off. Olive hurried after her.

"Mary, wait. I need to know if you're going to speak to the supervisor." Olive could feel her anger rising even while she pleaded with the drunken girl in front of her.

Chapter Twenty

It took Joe several minutes to wake up when he, Chalky, Taffy and Rob were called in the early hours and given new orders. He'd been dreaming he was back home, so he was rather shocked to find himself in a rather damp shell scrape. Grumbling about not having time for a brew, they left the relative safety of their dugouts in the sand dunes with another platoon and made their way cautiously to the Dunkirk road. All around them, the shelling of the town was intensifying, the sky was alight with the flashes of mortar fire and heavy artillery, and the tap-tap-tap of rifles and the louder chatter of Bren guns was punctuated by booms from heavier shells.

By the time they arrived at their destination, between Le Beau Marais and Marck, the sun had risen. Having been told to await further orders, the men moved under cover while the tanks went on ahead. They were only gone a few moments and, on their return, the tank commander informed Brigadier Nicholson there was a heavily fortified German roadblock further along, set among the houses and allotments. After a brief discussion, the platoon sergeants made their way back to the men.

"We need to clear the roadblock, or the convoy won't be able to get through." Sergeant Miller pointed to the group of men nearest him which included Joe, Chalky and Sparky. "Let's get going."

Joe tried to ignore the nervous fluttering in his stomach, put his head down and followed the others in the direction of the Germans.

Progress was painfully slow while they edged forward in a line along the side of the road, hoping to get as close as possible to the Germans before being seen. Joe could feel the sweat forming on his skin. The houses backing onto the street to their left were quiet and, other than the gentle buzzing of early morning insects, the singing of the birds, the muted sound of voles and other tiny mammals scurrying out of their way and the odd scraping of the men's boots on the rough ground, there was silence. However, they had not travelled far when they were spotted by the Germans, who immediately let loose a barrage of artillery and mortar fire. Reacting automatically, the men dived into the little cover available: a narrow ditch and a few sparse bushes. Joe, Chalky and Sparky threw themselves flat on the ground, hoping the Germans hadn't found their range. They were lucky. The shells flew harmlessly overhead, exploding with a furious noise, shaking the ground and hurting their ear drums.

"That was a little too close for comfort," Joe murmured to Sparky, who was lying prone on the grass next to him.

"A miss is as good as a mile, my old mum used to say." Sparky tried to disguise his nerves.

Within minutes, another barrage began and this time the shells fell much closer. The ground shook even more and Joe could feel his heart racing. Other than being showered in clods of earth, he was still uninjured, but for how much longer? The shelling intensified and then, to Joe's relief, word came down the line for them to withdraw to the relative safety of some bushes further back. Keeping low, Joe, Chalky, Sparky and the rest of the men inched their way back and, while the shells roared over their heads, the sergeant examined his map and considered their options.

"We'll split into two sections, cut across country and come up on them from the rear. "You." He pointed to Woody, Joe, Chalky and seven others. "Go up the railway line there. Keep under cover as much as possible." He pointed out the directions and surrounding undergrowth on the map. "Then come up behind them here." He showed Woody an exact position. The corporal memorised the details and began to lead the men towards the railway line. They had no sooner begun their perilous journey than the Germans spotted them and immediately opened fire with a machine gun.

Again, the men dived for the little cover available. This time they were too late. Joe felt something scrape his helmet and threw himself flat on the ground. He could feel his heart pounding rapidly against his chest. "Christ that was bloody close," he swore, turning towards Sparky who was behind him. To his horror, he saw Sparky lying a few feet away, blood pouring from a head wound.

****

Catford, London

Olive's breath was coming in short bursts as she covered the brief distance between the park and her flat. Thankfully, she didn't pass anyone and, once inside, she scrubbed and scrubbed at her clothes. However, the blood still wouldn't come off. Her mind was racing, her heart pounding against her chest. What on earth had she done? She'd never meant to hurt Mary but the girl wouldn't stop taunting her. Olive shook her head, trying to clear her mind of the images replaying themselves, over and over.

Ignoring her pleas and still smirking, Mary had turned her back to walk away and it was then that Olive had spotted the tree branch, lying like a gift on the dry ground. She vaguely remembered picking up the branch and then everything went black. One moment Mary was stalking away from her, drunken laughter wafting back towards her and the next, the girl was lying face down, her head covered in blood. Olive had stared down at the body in disbelief for several seconds before leaning down and feeling for a pulse. There wasn't one and she'd stepped back, horror dawning on her face. Oh God! She had killed her.

Glancing vaguely around her room, Olive took a deep breath and tried to calm herself. She stripped off her clothes and put them in an old paper bag. She would have to throw them away somewhere, a long way from home. She finished scrubbing the sink and looked around again. The flat was pristine, everything neat and tidy; there was no blood she could see. Olive began to relax. She was reasonably sure no one had seen her. Providing she disposed of the clothes carefully, she would be safe. She would never speak of this to anyone, not even Kurt.

Olive washed, put on her nightdress and climbed into bed, remembering at the last minute to wind the clock and set the alarm. She was shocked to find there was barely any time left until she would have to get up for work. Her heart had finally slowed down, although her mind was still racing while she searched for anything that could give her away. Eventually, she was convinced there was nothing to lead the police to her. They would probably arrest the young man Mary had left the dance with and he was bound to mention seeing her. However, no one was likely to believe him. They would assume he was lying to save his own neck. Provided she behaved in a perfectly normal way, she would not be under suspicion.

****

Calais, France

It was painfully obvious to Joe that Sparky was dead. The bullet had scraped his own helmet, ricocheted and then killed his friend. Shocked to the core, Joe froze and for several seconds he lay there staring at his friend, unable to believe he was really dead. Then he pulled himself together. There was no time for him to take in his friend's death or to grasp just how close he had come to dying himself. They had taken at least two other casualties and, while Chalky frantically tried to stop the bleeding of the man nearest him, Joe concentrated on firing in the direction of the Germans. The noise was tremendous; not only the deafening sound of the bullets bouncing off the railway lines and the ground in front of them, but also the constant shouting of the men from both sides, giving directions or warning of danger.

Somewhere to the front, he could hear the incoherent murmuring and screams of German casualties who were too badly wounded to get back to their own lines, while their comrades were unable to come forward far enough to reach them.

He closed his ears to their pain-filled shrieks and tried to concentrate on the job in hand. The barrage continued. Somehow, they managed to remain where they were, returning fire doggedly, ensuring every bullet counted.

"You'd think they'd give up, wouldn't you?" Blanketed by thick swirling smoke and ear-splitting noise, making contact with any of the others was difficult, so Joe had begun talking to himself. He and the rest of his platoon had been pinned down on the railway line for several hours and, despite being outnumbered, they were more than holding their own. They had successfully adapted the ditch alongside the railway line into a defensive trench and this enabled them to successfully beat back three attempted infantry assaults with no loss. Each time the Germans sent their men forward, the British riflemen had little difficulty in picking them off, one by one. The ditch was narrow and, because they had dug quite deep, the continuous mortar and artillery fire sailed harmlessly over their heads. In fact, from his position, peering across the raised railway line, Joe could see German casualties were steadily mounting. Despite this, they were determined not to be beaten and were now sending over some small high explosive mortar shells.

"Bloody Nora, that was close. Where the 'ell is our artillery?" Although he couldn't see Chalky, Joe was relieved to hear his friend's voice, even if he was complaining.

"Everybody alright?" Woody shouted while several more shells exploded harmlessly behind them.

"Yes, Corp."

"Aye, Corp." The responses continued and Woody breathed a sigh of relief.

"Then hold your positions until I give the word. I think we've got them on the run."

****

Northern France

Exhausted from their long journey, Jean-Paul slept until nearly ten o'clock. For a few seconds, he was disorientated and he struggled to work out where he was. Then he remembered the events of the past few days and, cursing under his breath, he leapt out of bed. He first checked under the mattress to make sure their money belts were still there. Having assumed the French currency would lose its value very quickly in the chaos, Jean-Paul had changed much of his cash into diamonds and other small jewels and had sewn these into money belts which they were all wearing under their clothes. Although they had felt very uncomfortable at first, everyone had soon grown used to the belts and were now rarely aware of them. They had removed them to change their clothes and he had placed them all under his mattress for safe keeping. Jean-Paul also had several hundred Francs left, although he was not sure how much longer he would be able to use them or whether they would be able to buy anything.

He crossed to the window and pulled open the curtains. The scene that met his eyes could have belonged to another era. The sun was shining and, below him, he could see some chickens pecking around in the dust of the yard. Not far from the farmyard, the birds were singing cheerfully in the trees, the branches covered in the new fresh green leaves of spring. This bright green cloak was punctuated in places by patches of stunning pink blossom standing out against the green, making everything seem even more vital and alive. There was a dog barking somewhere close by and he could hear cattle lowing in a nearby meadow.

He resisted the urge to stay and enjoy the tranquil view and, turning back to Marcel and Charles who were asleep in the other beds, he called loudly, "Marcel. Charles. Quick! Get up."

Without waiting for a response, he went out into the corridor searching for his wife and daughter. The landing was silent and, seeing several doors, he took a chance and opened one. For a moment, he stood watching his sleeping wife and daughter, before calling them gently.

"Claudette, Jeanne. We have to get moving. You need to get up and dressed." For a moment, there was no reaction, then Claudette opened one bleary eye and peered at him. Like him, she was confused to start with, then recognition dawned and she sat up.

"We've slept really late. We need to start out soon or we won't reach Dunkirk tonight." Jean-Paul's voice held more than a hint of urgency. Claudette was alarmed, knowing their only chance was to get to the coast and to England: they would be in danger all the time they remained in France. Hurrying out of bed, she pulled herself together. There was no time to dwell on the future; she needed to wake Jeanne, who had already proved she could sleep through an earthquake.

She shook her daughter gently and, when that did not provoke a reaction, her shaking became more persistent.

"Chère, you must wake up. We have to leave."

Jeanne groaned but didn't open her eyes. "Oh, I was having such a lovely dream. Just a little while longer, please Mama."

"I'm sorry, Jeanne. You must get up. Once we are safe, you can sleep for hours, but now we have to move."

Jeanne grimaced and, grumbling to herself, went over to the wash bowl. Pouring in some cold water, she wasted no time in washing her face and hands and dressing in the clean clothes Antoinette had given her. Putting on the elegant tweed skirt and crisp cotton blouse made her feel better and she smiled at her reflection in the mirror.

"There's no time to admire yourself, Jeanne." Claudette spoke more harshly than she'd intended. "Go and use the bathroom quickly and then come back here and we'll go down together. No arguments, please,

just go. We don't have a lot of time if we are to reach Dunkirk tonight."
Claudette watched while Jeanne went out of the door. She was sure
they were safe at the moment, but she didn't want to take any chances.

****

Lambeth Hospital, London

To Peggy's experienced eye, the hospital seemed busier than normal
and there were ambulances pulling up with increasing regularity. Helen
had just arrived and the emergency department was frantic, the beds
already full of young men in various conditions. Amongst the general
unwashed odour, Peggy could smell the sickly aroma of gangrene. Even
worse was the age of the patients, many of them in their early twenties
or younger. Some were crying out in pain or staring into space, others
quietly waiting for attention.

"Ah, Macklin, Cooper." The ward sister called them both over. "We
are starting to receive some of the wounded men from the fighting in
Belgium and France. We've had word this may just be the start of quite
heavy casualties. I know you won't be used to dealing with injuries like
this but I'm sure you will do the best you can. Could you start with bed
six please, Cooper? The young man has severe leg injuries and some
very filthy bandages. They need removing so the wounds can be
cleaned. Macklin, if you would go to bed four, the young man with the
head injuries. He's lost an eye and is also delirious."

Peggy took a moment to glance around before attending to her
patient. Everywhere she looked, nurses were cleaning wounds,
changing bandages and comforting the badly injured.

****

Ten minutes later, Claudette and Jeanne were both ready and they went down into the dining room. The men were already there, tucking into an enormous breakfast Antoinette had cooked for them.

"You have a long, uncertain journey ahead. You must eat properly before you go." She pointed to the seats they had occupied the previous night and they sat down, amazed by how hungry they felt. When they had eaten everything they could, she handed them a large brown paper parcel. "I packed you some food for your journey."

"We can't thank you enough for your kindness." Jean-Paul tried to hand her some money. Antoinette refused.

"It's only food; my little bit for France." The last few words were said with pride and with tears in her eyes. "Now you must go. You have a long journey ahead of you."

"Before we go, I think we should make arrangements to meet again after the war," Claudette declared.

"What a good idea." Antoinette clapped her hands together. Then she frowned. "How though?"

"Perhaps we could meet here on the first Sunday of May following the end of the war?" Jean-Paul suggested.

There was a brief silence while they all agreed. Then there was nothing else left to say but *au revoir*.

"I will look forward to seeing you all again. I wish you all safe journeys."

"And we wish you safety until we see you again." Claudette hugged her, more grateful for the brief respite than she could ever express.

After hugs all round, they took their leave and went out into the warm mid-morning sunshine. If not for the sounds of war coming ever closer, it could have been any spring morning. However, in the distance they could hear gunfire and every now and then the ground would shake from the pounding of the German shells.

"Do you think she'll be safe?" Claudette asked Jean-Paul. "I asked her to come with us again, but she was adamant there was no need."

"I hope so. You don't often meet such a lovely, generous person. I only hope I would've been as kind if the situations had been reversed."

"I can answer that." Marcel was standing behind Jean-Paul. Apart from his brief responses at the dinner table the night before, he had been very quiet while they were in the farmhouse. He felt totally overwhelmed, not only by the events of the previous days, but by the lady who had invited them into her home whilst knowing nothing about them. "You took me in, when you could've just ignored me, left me to get hit by those German planes. Even then, you didn't have to let me come with you."

Claudette squeezed his arm, unable to speak for a moment. This was the worst time of her life, yet she had met the most wonderful people. *Life is very strange*, she thought. *It often gives you something good to balance the bad, if only you can see it.*

"I really think we should get going." Charles was becoming increasingly nervous. He hadn't understood the conversation but he was conscious of the need to keep moving. Although he felt safer in civilian clothes, he was very much aware that, out of uniform, he could be considered by the Germans to be a spy. He had struggled with the decision. If he stayed in uniform, he would be picked up more quickly, although he would probably be treated as a prisoner of war. Out of uniform, he was more anonymous, but if captured, he could be tortured and imprisoned or even summarily shot.

Jean-Paul nodded and they began the trek towards Dunkirk. The countryside was beautiful and, if not for the noises all around them, they could have fooled themselves into thinking they were not in the middle of a war zone. The trees swayed gracefully in the gentle breeze and the sun climbed higher and higher into the cloudless blue sky, encouraging them to shed their outer garments in an attempt to cool down. Whilst they were more comfortable travelling in the sunshine than the rain, the heat made them thirsty and, before long, they were low on water and searching for somewhere to refill the bottle. They tried to avoid the main roads, although occasionally they needed to cross them. They approached each one with caution, the men taking it in turns to check for signs of activity while the women remained hidden.

Consulting his map, Jean-Paul reckoned they must be about a ten hour trek from Dunkirk. They could make better time if they stuck to the main highways, but that would be very dangerous. He was also aware Claudette and Jeanne were struggling to keep up the pace set by the men. Reluctantly, they slowed down.

****

Somewhere in France

The small cottage was deserted and the exhausted soldiers entered with a feeling of relief. While the sergeant went upstairs to the two small bedrooms to try and find them some civilian clothes, the men searched for food. They found some bottles of beer and tins of soup in the larder, but not much else. Louis shrugged, beer was better than nothing. He had given up trying to make friends with the other men. For some reason, they didn't seem to like him. He'd tried telling them all about his plans for the future, how he and Brigitte were going to get married and run his farm but their attitude hadn't changed. He'd not intended to lie about the ownership of the farm, but they weren't likely to visit, so he carried on, hoping they would be impressed that he was a man of property.

"What are you going to do when the Boche try to take your farm?" The man with his arm in a sling was really fed up with Louis and was convinced he was a liar.

"Just let them try!" Louis snapped. "No one's going to take my farm."

"Gonna fight off the whole Kraut army by yourself then?" One of the others joined in. "Shame you weren't in charge of our forces. We wouldn't be in such a mess."

Louis opened his mouth to say something and then realised they were making fun of him.

"Well, at least I've got something to fight for." He was growing angry. He hadn't done anything to them.

"Try these on." The sergeant had returned with several items of clothing. He ignored the atmosphere and began changing his own outfit. Relieved at the interruption, Louis started searching through the clothes trying to find some trousers to fit him.

"Looks like you'll have to wait until we find somewhere else." The sergeant wasn't being unkind, just honest. All the trousers were much too short for Louis and the shirts too small. "Cheer up, lad," he added, seeing Louis' crestfallen face. "It's not the end of the world. I'm sure the next place'll have something." He glanced at the other men. "Stop bickering you lot. We've got one enemy, we don't need to fight amongst ourselves, do we?"

"No, Sarge." The man with the sling sighed. "Come on, Servier, let's grab the rest of the beer and get moving. We need to find you some civvy clothes."

Chapter Twenty-one

Bethune, Northern France

"Faster, faster, don't stop!" Albert gasped and groaned and Brigitte sucked harder. With the Germans camping outside the town, his wife, Estelle was no longer visiting her sister, but had gone that morning to check on her mother and, seeing Brigitte strolling past the butcher's shop window, Albert had wasted no time in calling her in. He had closed the shop temporarily and they were in the small back room, Brigitte on her knees while Albert stood by the sturdy table he used to count his money on.

Brigitte had demurred at first, concerned Estelle might come back. However, Albert had insisted she would be at least an hour and he would pay extra. Against her better judgment, Brigitte allowed herself to be persuaded. She wished he would hurry up; she had no desire to be caught by his wife. Still, the fear of being discovered seemed to be exciting him more than usual and suddenly he stopped, pulled out of her mouth and told her to bend over the table. Brigitte obeyed and he shoved her face down, one hand on her back while the other fumbled with her expensive lace panties and then he plunged inside her making her gasp. She began to groan and writhe in the way she knew he liked. Her mind was elsewhere, planning how she could bring herself to the attention of the Germans, when she heard the door behind her suddenly burst open. Her heart leaped into her mouth and she felt him pull out and turn away from her. Brigitte didn't need to look to know that his wife was standing there; her father could probably hear the woman yelling at the other end of the street.

While Albert's wife's attention was on her husband, Brigitte tried to grab her knickers and sneak out, but Estelle wasn't about to let her get away so easily. She stepped back into the shop, grabbed a large knife from the counter and began slashing at Brigitte's blouse and skirt, leaving her partially naked.

Brigitte screamed and Albert stepped forward to protest. Estelle gestured towards him with the knife and Albert gasped and covered himself with his hands. He retreated, horror on his face, leaving Brigitte to the mercies of his wife.

"Get out, you whore!" Estelle yelled at her.

"I haven't been paid," Brigitte muttered, standing her ground. Then, seeing the murderous look on Estelle's face, she changed her mind. With as much dignity as she could muster, she pulled the remnants of her clothes around her and ran up the road, back to the café, the raucous laughter of those who'd come out to see what all the fuss was about, ringing in her ears.

****

Outside Calais

For the next four hours, Joe and his colleagues held their positions and then the enemy defences started to crumble and they began to advance. Progress was painfully slow but eventually they had overrun their original objective by about three and a half thousand yards, forcing the Germans back.

"This is a bit more like it." Chalky sounded quite pleased for once and Joe was about to comment, when the word came up the line that they were to withdraw.

"That can't be right, surely?" One of the soldiers near Joe spat noisily on the floor. Joe shook his head in disbelief.

"Sorry, lads. The order comes from the top." Woody sounded just as disappointed. "There's probably things going on we're not aware of," he added in a vain attempt to make them feel better.

"I can't believe they've ordered us back." Joe was fuming. His nerves were long gone and all he could think about was carrying on the attack.

The men continued grumbling, although inwardly most were relieved they had survived. Carefully, making sure the Germans were unable to use their retreat to overrun them, the remains of the scouting party returned to the rest of the troops who were waiting at the original position.

They were only just in time; everyone was preparing to withdraw. The initial German shells that had soared harmlessly over their heads, had exploded further back onto the main party. One had scored a direct hit onto a truck, killing three men and wounding four others. Joe could see the truck alight and smouldering over by the bushes, so he was relieved to see both Rob and Taffy were unharmed. Still high on the adrenaline of the battle, he was about to tell them about Sparky when Woody appeared.

"Seems we were in danger of being surrounded," he explained. "That's why we were called off. Shame though; we were close to breaking through. No doubt we'll have plenty of other opportunities to beat the bastards." He grinned and patted Joe on the back.

Feeling vindicated that the failure of the assault was not their fault, the men fell in and, together with the main party, began the long march back to Calais.

****

Lewisham Council Offices, London

Olive gazed around and licked her lips nervously. She'd heard Kath asking the other girls where Mary was and had seen them shaking their heads. She wondered if the police had found the body yet or whether Mary was still lying there. She'd been tempted to try and hide her, but then she'd reasoned, if she did that and was caught, she would have less chance of saying the whole thing had been an accident. She'd not touched Mary at all, other than to feel for her pulse. The phone lines began buzzing and she reached out automatically.

"Lewisham Borough Council, which department do you require?"

"Planning please, Miss Gresham."

"Putting you through." Olive connected the call, making no attempt to listen in. She'd recognised the voice as one of the councillors she knew was having an affair with Miss Gresham, one of the secretaries, but for once she had no interest in eavesdropping on their intimate conversation.

The police arrived at the council offices late in the morning and, before long, the news was circulating around the building that Mary's body had been found in the park. Like everyone else, Olive appeared shocked and, although she was careful not to seem too distressed, because that might seem suspicious, she did pass on her condolences to a devastated Kath, who was busy blaming herself for inviting Mary to the dance.

The police interviewed them each in turn and once Olive told them she didn't really mix with her work companions and knew nothing about Mary's private life, she was immediately discounted as being anyone of importance and she returned to work, grateful that she didn't have any friends amongst the other girls.

Kath gave the police a description of the man Mary had left the pub with and the police departed. The switchboard gradually returned to normal and Olive slowly relaxed.

****

Lambeth Hospital, London

As the day wore on, more young men arrived. Not all of them were English, which made them harder to comfort because Peggy couldn't understand everything they were saying. She was also keeping an eye out for Peter, although the numbers were such that she wasn't able to check all the admissions; there simply wasn't time.

Many of the young patients were in shock and, while some just lay in silence staring up at the ceiling, others were more vocal. They talked of continuous bombing and shelling and German planes strafing the thousands of refugees who were trying to escape their advance. Peggy listened to their stories with a growing sense of horror while she cleaned their wounds, many of which had become infected. Although most of the men were from the Army, there were also casualties from the Navy and Air Force as well. The injuries ranged from shrapnel and bullets wounds, to burns and blistering and, in the worst cases, missing limbs. Some of the men had already been treated in the hospitals and dressing stations in Calais and Boulogne; others hadn't.

Peggy became more and more demoralised. It was difficult to remain optimistic when all she saw were wounded men reporting the inability of the BEF to halt the Germans.

"Maybe there is more to the talk of invasion than they've been telling us," she said to Helen, while they were taking a short break; there were too many casualties for them to take their full lunch hour.

"I'm really worried about Jimmy; he's gone over there and they're all coming back." Helen was even more depressed than Peggy. "I was cleaning up some shrapnel wounds of one of the young chaps who was fighting near Calais and he began telling me there were lots of dog fights in the skies above them while they were battling on the ground. He was describing some of the fights and how the planes exploded without the crew being able to get out. I wanted to tell him to stop but I couldn't." She was near to tears and Peggy immediately put an arm around her.

"Why don't we go and get some fresh air; we've got a few minutes more before we have to be back." Helen allowed herself to be propelled towards the exit and out into the bright May sunshine. The day was warm, the sky a brilliant blue. Gazing up, they saw white, fluffy cotton-wool clouds floating lazily above them. The birds were singing away and they could smell the blossom on the nearby trees. The traffic was just a gentle murmur in the background and both girls gradually felt their spirits rise.

They stood there for some time, eyes closed, just breathing in the fragrant spring air and basking in the warm sunshine, until Peggy said with reluctance, "I think we'd better go back in or we'll be in trouble."

Helen sighed and they both hurried back to the emergency wards. Many of the earlier patients had been treated and moved up to wards and new patients awaited them.

Peggy found herself in a cubicle with a young man in his early twenties. His eyes were closed and he was whimpering softly, his eyelids flickering with delirium. His face was filthy and he had a minor head wound. It wasn't infected and cleaning and covering the injury was a relatively simple process. Peggy then began the painstaking process of removing some filthy bandages from his left fore-arm. They were covered in dried blood, mud and something else she couldn't identify. The blood and mud combined, made the bandages difficult to unravel and too thick for her to cut through easily.

Peggy finally removed the last of the bandage and saw, to her horror, the injury was infested with maggots. The smell was dreadful and she struggled not to retch. The wound was obviously infected and Peggy went to search for the Sister Adams, but couldn't find her. Although she asked several other nurses, no one seemed to know where she was. Peggy started to panic. She wasn't really supposed to talk to the doctors, she was meant to talk to the ward sister who would relay the message. She tried each cubicle in turn yet still there was no sign of Sister Adams and every doctor she found was already busy and could not be disturbed. Frantic, Peggy searched up and down the ward again, then to her relief spotted the sister by a bed at the far end. Peggy headed towards her when she noticed she was setting up a drip. Peggy could feel her heart pounding. She couldn't disturb her but she needed help urgently. Peggy stopped in the middle of the ward and stared around in desperation.

****

Louis examined the rather tatty trousers and loose shirt he was wearing and felt relieved to no longer be wearing his uniform. They had finally found him some clothes in a virtually deserted village several miles on from the cottage. They were all now dressed in civilian apparel, although Louis doubted that would help if the Germans spotted them. He was still wearing his army boots and two of their party carried wounds but, at least from a distance, they might pass for farmers.

"I think we should split up." The sergeant's words struck fear into Louis' heart and he spun round in horror. "Together, we look like soldiers pretending to be farmers. We'll stand a much better chance if we travel separately." His words echoed Louis' thoughts, but that didn't make the order any easier. Seeing the terror in his eyes, the sergeant patted him gently on the shoulder. "Don't worry, lad. Just stick to the back lanes and use the meadows and farmland wherever you can. We would have parted at some point, because we all live in different places. Just keep your head down, keep out of trouble and you'll soon be home."

Louis nodded, not trusting himself to speak. The men shook hands, wished each other luck and then they headed off into the surrounding countryside. Louis was on his own again.

****

Calais, France

While they made their way back under the continuous shelling and gun fire, the reality of the fighting he'd experienced hit Joe. That had been his first time under fire and, once the battle had started, there hadn't really been time to feel scared. Like the others, he initially felt buoyant he had survived and performed well and he had not disgraced himself. However, now he was away from the immediate action, the shock of Sparky's death began to hit him and his legs started to shake. He tried to ignore his trembling limbs but the bullet had been so close. Another inch and it would have been him lying in a ditch in France, not Sparky, whose only mistake was to have the misfortune to be standing behind him.

"You alright, mate?" Chalky was standing beside him. One side of his uniform had patches of dried blood from the man he had been trying to help and there were several rips in his trousers. Glancing down, Joe saw his own clothes looked just as bad. He probably had a dent in his helmet too from the bullet, although he couldn't see because it was on his head.

"Yeah, just a bit shocked really. That could've been me."

"Yeah, but it wasn't, was it?" Chalky patted him on the back and Joe tried to put the incident out of his mind.

****

Lambeth Hospital, London

"Hello again, can I help?" Peggy whirled round. Standing in front of her was the young student doctor who had spoken to her before.

Relieved to have found someone more senior to take over, Peggy forgot her normal reticence and grabbed his arm. "Please, I've got a young man whose arm is crawling with maggots. I think some of the flesh may need to be cut out and I can't find a doctor who is free."

"Right, let's take a look." His calm voice reassured her and she began to feel less fraught. She suddenly realised she was still holding his arm and she let go as if she'd been scalded, her face crimson. But the doctor did not appear to have noticed. "Where is he?" he asked and Peggy forgot her embarrassment and led the way back to the patient who was still unconscious.

After a quick examination, the young student doctor gave the man some morphine and attached a saline drip to his other arm. Turning round, he saw a porter coming towards them.

"Porter," he called. "Can you please take this young man to the operating theatre. He'll have to wait a while, there's a long queue, but he's better off there than here." He turned to Peggy. "Although they may have to amputate his arm, they should be able to save his life." Seeing her pale face, he said with concern, "It's been a hell of a day, hasn't it?" Normally his language would have offended her, but his words were such an appropriate way to describe exactly how she felt, Peggy hardly noticed. He glanced around to make sure there were no sisters or matrons about, and said in a conspiratorial tone, "I'm Christopher, by the way. My friends call me Chris." His smile was appealing and she found herself responding.

"I'm Peggy." She smiled back, then remembering where she was, she continued in a more formal tone, "Cooper. Thank you for your help."

"My pleasure. Any time." Then, with a twinkle in his eye, he added, "I'd better let you get back to work *Cooper* and go and do something myself, or we'll both be in trouble."

Without giving her time to answer, Chris headed towards another cubicle, leaving Peggy disconcerted.

****

Calais, France

The harbour finally came into view and they stared at the station yard which was ablaze with cars, ambulances and ammunition lorries burning away. Once again, they were deafened by the thunderous noise of the ammunition exploding.

"Looks like our transport and weapons have arrived," Chalky pointed to some of the other soldiers who were standing around a couple of Bren gun carriers. He was about to say more, when they were given the order to halt. Chalky gulped some water from his bottle and wandered over to the two soldiers from the 60th Rifles.

"They finally got here, then?"

"Yeah, the ships arrived yesterday afternoon but, because the tide was out, they couldn't get in until early evening," one of the soldiers answered

"Have they unloaded everything yet?" Joe asked.

"Shouldn't think so." The soldier shook his head. "The Krauts had got the range by then and were pounding the docks with everything they had. Our guys were worn out from unloading all the BEF rations and the bloody Frogs did a runner every time the Krauts started bombing."

"They also had to unload all the petrol before they could get to the transport," the other soldier chipped in. "Whoever decided to store all the petrol in jerry cans should be shot."

"But all our weapons, ammunition and equipment are on the transport." Chalky was aghast.

The first soldier shrugged. "Now you know why the Krauts are winning."

There was no answer to that and Joe began to feel totally demoralised. However, before he could say anything else, Chalky asked, "Are they still unloading?"

There was no mirth in the soldier's laughter. The second one answered him, "You gotta be kidding, mate. The ships are going back home; orders of the War Office."

Chalky and Joe stared at each other in disbelief.

"They've only unloaded half of the equipment, but they're going back home?" Joe was incredulous

"Yep. That about sums it up." The first soldier was shaking his head. "A monumental cock up." He sighed. "Not the first one and probably won't be the last either."

Chapter Twenty-two

The switchboard was busier than normal and the girls were subdued. Olive concentrated on her work and kept one eye on the door in case the police returned. She couldn't quite believe she'd killed someone, but sadly every time she thought about Mary, her only real feeling was one of relief that she had stopped the younger girl causing trouble. She glanced up and was surprised to find Kath watching her, a speculative expression on her face.

Olive glared at her, refusing to be intimidated by the girl, although her heart was beginning to pound against her chest. Kath held her gaze and then looked away. Olive realised she'd been holding her breath and she let it out, chiding herself for being stupid. She was letting her imagination and guilt run away with her. How on earth could Kath know she'd killed Mary?

****

Calais, France

Shaking their heads in disgust, Joe and Chalky made their way back to the others, explained about the ship and settled down to watch the activity on the dock. Despite the pessimistic words of the soldiers, they were still hoping their equipment would be unloaded. However, the

Gare Maritime continued to come under increasingly heavy shelling. From their position, they could see the decks of the *City of Canterbury* were covered with wounded and the bombardment was getting worse. Eventually, the ship departed at half past eight without unloading the other half of the desperately needed equipment. The *Kohistan* remained until noon, whilst all the non-fighting men were released to join her, then she too left under heavy shellfire.

"You'd better take the opportunity to eat." An NCO came round and began handing out emergency rations. Joe took his without any enthusiasm. Although several hours had passed since he'd eaten, he wasn't hungry. He kept seeing Sparky lying on the ground behind him with a gaping hole in his forehead.

Chalky noticed Joe wasn't opening his rations. "You'd better eat, mate. Starving yourself won't bring him back."

Chalky was right but Joe couldn't bring himself to behave as though nothing had happened. Feeling Chalky's eyes boring into him, Joe finally gave in, opened his rations and took a small bite. The bully beef was surprisingly tasty and one bite was enough. Once Joe started eating, he appreciated just how hungry he was and, within minutes, he had finished all of his food.

"I never dreamed emergency rations would actually taste good." He was beginning to feel better.

"Well the chocolate's quite tasty. Not sure about the bully beef and biscuits." Chalky examined the remains of his ratpack carefully.

Joe drank some more water and then lit a cigarette. He checked the packet anxiously and was relieved to see he had about fifteen left and another couple of packets in his bag. He breathed in the nicotine with a sigh of pleasure and tried to block out the horror of the morning. All around him, the shelling grew fiercer and the Germans moved closer. Buildings were collapsing on all sides, covering them with dust and debris and, before long, they were ordered to move back.

****

Brigitte stared up at the ceiling from her bed where she had flung herself several hours earlier, her face streaked with tears and mascara. She was not upset because Estelle had caught her, but because of the humiliation of having to run the gauntlet of the townsfolk laughing and jeering at her and the fact that Estelle had ruined her favourite clothes. She had paid a lot of money for a skirt that was now completely unwearable, large slits across the front making it indecent even for Brigitte's lax standards. The blouse was also torn to ribbons, the pieces flapping in the gentle breeze as she'd hurried home. The only good thing was, she had managed to reach her bedroom before her father had seen her, although she was sure he had enough customers who would be delighted to paint a picture of her discomfort for him.

She was also angry Albert had made no effort to defend her. She had never said 'no' to him, the arrangement had been his idea after all and yet, when she had needed help, he'd ignored her, leaving her to his wife. She could scream at the sheer injustice and then her face flushed again when she remembered her ignominious exit. How on earth was she going to live this down? She turned on her side and closed her eyes.

"Brigitte, get your fat lazy arse down here!"

Fabian's angry yell broke into her thoughts and she shrank back on the bed. Her father sounded really livid this time.

The door flew open and he stood there, his face red with fury. He strode towards the bed and Brigitte tried to shrink away from him. He reached out and grabbed her arm, pulling her to her feet.

"You needn't think you're going to hide yourself away up here. Take these rags off, get dressed and come downstairs and give me a hand."

Brigitte shook her head. "I can't." Her eyes were large with terror and, for a moment, he almost felt sorry for her. Then he hardened his heart.

"You made your bed, or lack of a bed, you lie on it, girl. Ten minutes, and if you're not downstairs I'll drag you down, whatever you're wearing." He turned tail, slammed the door behind him and went back down to the café.

Brigitte stared at the door for several moments, then turned towards her wardrobe and began looking for something to wear.

****

Calais, France

They had only just settled into their positions nearer the dunes when Sergeant Miller approached with new orders. "Corporal, I want you to take your men and make your way to the canal where the Queen Vics are pinned down. Take over from them, give them some covering fire. They need to evacuate their wounded. Then follow them back here."

"Yes, sir!" Woody turned to Joe and the others and they spent a few minutes familiarising themselves with the area both on the map and through field glasses. Then they prepared to move out. The shelling was even heavier than before, the sky was continually alight with brilliant flashes coming from heavy mortar fire and the air was thick with black, choking smoke.

"Keep a sharp eye out for snipers." Woody ignored the expressions on their faces. "There are a lot of fifth columnists in the town. Those who weren't already here probably came in with the refugees. Keep your eyes peeled."

They made their way very slowly, through the streets to the canal. Every now and then, a swarm of German planes would fly over, dispensing death and destruction in equal measure. However, other than forcing them to take cover until the danger had passed, they had little effect.

The air was thick with dust and smoke, but even if they hadn't known where the canal was, they could have found the waterway by following the sound of artillery and small arms fire which intensified when they grew closer. Relatively unscathed, they reached the survivors of the Queen Victoria's Rifles.

Joe slid into the narrow hole next to one of the territorials, making him jump. The man was about to shoot when he recognised the uniform. "Look out, lads! Here comes the ruddy cavalry!" he yelled, his teeth shining white in his smoke-blackened face. There was a ragged cheer from the few remaining survivors who were running very short of food, water and ammunition.

"Are we pleased to see you?" he said to Joe. "We've had no bloody kip for two days and the tosser in charge seems to think we can hold back the whole ruddy German army and all the refugees with no bloody weapons, no transport and very few men." Seeing the expression on Joe's face, he stopped. "Sorry. Things've been a bit fraught, to say the least. Still, now you're here we can go and get some shut eye. You never know, perhaps our motorcycles have finally arrived from England."

Joe didn't want to put a dampener on things but he felt he owed the soldier some honesty.

"I wouldn't bank on it. They only unloaded half our vehicles and equipment before turning round and hightailing it back to Blighty."

The man stared at him and seemed about to say something before changing his mind and muttering, "Oh well, I'm sure they know best." They shook hands and, before Joe could comment, he'd crawled back out of the hole, leaving Joe totally bemused. He was quite sure they had no idea what they were doing but who was he? Just a humble rifleman.

****

Somewhere in France

Louis watched his new friends disappear into the gloom and tried to ignore the growing feeling of despair. His first task would be to find somewhere safe to sleep. He stared across the large open field in front of him, scanning for anywhere that could provide him with shelter. There was nothing other than the hedge on the other side. He turned around to look back the way they had come but behind him there were only the woods. He stood still for a few moments weighing up his options. The countryside was quiet, although he could hear the guns in the distance. Eventually, deciding he would be safer sleeping amongst the trees rather than in the open, he retraced his steps until he came to some thick undergrowth near a group of trees. He sat down and placed his small bag next to him. He regretted leaving his backpack with his uniform, even though he could knew the pack would have given him away. Despite the warmth of the day, the ground felt damp. He ignored the discomfort, pulled out the biscuits they had taken from the last farmhouse and, leaning back against the tree, he began eating.

The biscuits were slightly stale but he didn't mind; they took the edge off his hunger. Louis lay down and closed his eyes. He decided the safest option would be to doze for a while and then walk through the night.

****

Northern France

Jean-Paul and the rest of their small party were skirting along the field when, a little way in front, they saw some other people doing the same, heading towards a solitary cottage in the distance. They watched the small party of one man, two women and a child approach the dwelling and saw a large portly man come out. He greeted them with enthusiasm and invited them in, but only a few minutes later the sound of shots rang out and screams could be heard. To their horror, they saw the two women and the child come running back out of the house, followed by the owner who was brandishing a shot gun. He fired at them, killing the women, reloaded and fired again, killing the child. He then strode over to the bodies and began searching them.

The horrific events happened so quickly, they had no time to intervene and they were completely stunned. For several moments, they couldn't move. Eventually, Jean-Paul pulled himself together. He pushed Jeanne and Claudette unceremoniously back into the ditch and hurried them out the other side. Speechless with shock, Marcel and Charles followed.

The small party continued in silence for some time. Marcel finally put their thoughts into words. "How can people behave like that?"

"I don't know, Marcel." Jean-Paul sighed. "Unfortunately, I think this may be just the tip of the iceberg. Wars either bring out the worst or the best in people." He glanced briefly at Claudette while he was speaking, but did not say anymore.

****

Calais, France

With no tools, sandbags or wire, Joe soon realised they were at a severe disadvantage. The east side of the canal had little cover to offer and he began digging frantically into the earth with his bayonet, trying to enlarge the shell scrape he was in.

Chalky arrived a few moments later, followed immediately by Rob, Taffy and Woody. The shelling continued and they copied Joe and hastily dug themselves in. Feeling safer, Chalky retaliated with a couple of rounds in the direction of the Germans, and then ducked back down, when a particularly ferocious round of machine gun fire whistled dangerously close to his head. The exchange of gunfire went on for some time, getting closer with every succeeding barrage. Bullets rattled around their heads and ricocheted off the surrounding banks, throwing up earth and stones, adding to the general noise and confusion.

"The Queen Vic's need more time to get their wounded out of here, so we need to either find some more cover, or make some," Woody shouted. "We're going to be slaughtered otherwise."

"There's some potato sacks over there." Joe pointed to some houses behind them while yelling at Woody. "We could fill them with earth and use them to build a defensive wall."

"Good thinking, Price. You and Taffy go get them; Chalky and Rob'll cover you," Woody shouted back.

Joe counted to three and, on Chalky's shout, ran full pelt, at a crouch, back to the house where the sacks were and threw himself flat on the ground while bullets rattled round him. Rob slithered to a halt beside him and the two men grabbed the sacks and then searched frantically for some soil. There was nothing close to hand; the nearest earth was in the gardens on the other side of the street. "Shit," Joe cursed. "How the hell are we going to get over there? There's no cover at all."

Rob shook his head. "Let's get back to the others; no point hanging around here."

They waited for a brief lull and ran rapidly back to the canal, throwing themselves into their shell scrape just in time, more bullets bouncing off the ground they had just covered. Panting from the exertion and the smoke and debris filling his lungs, Joe shouted to Woody, "It's no good, Corp. The nearest earth is across the road and there's no way of getting there."

There was no response for a few seconds, then Woody yelled, "Those houses over there? Can we get into them? Are they empty?"

"Don't know, Corp." The continual shouting was making Joe's throat sore. "I didn't see anyone, unless they've got cellars." The smoke was also making him really thirsty but he daren't drink, he only had the one water bottle and the canal didn't seem particularly appetising, especially since the item floating past him looked suspiciously like an arm. He frowned. Woody was saying something he couldn't hear.

"Say again."

"Gawd blimey, Go!" Woody shouted in exasperation. "See if you can break into one of the houses. Don't take all day about it, or we probably won't be here." He ended as a particularly vicious barrage came over.

Joe and Rob repeated their half crouching zig-zag run back to the houses behind them, wondering when the bullets they could hear following them would finally find their mark. Somehow, they managed to reach one of the houses safely. Then their luck deserted them and, despite frantic efforts with their rifle butts, they were unable to break the sturdy locks on the doors. Joe took a deep breath and tried the next house, while Rob moved on to the one after. The result was the same. They headed back to the canal.

"What the hell are you doing back here?" Chalky shouted in surprise, seeing Joe slide back into the hole beside him.

"Can't open the bloody doors. The locks are too strong."

"Fuck!" Chalky swore loudly. For once Joe didn't notice. "What do we do now, other than keep our heads down? Oh shit…"

Chapter Twenty-three

Somewhere in France

Now he wasn't in uniform, Louis decided he might be safer mingling with the refugees fleeing the Nazis, rather than travelling on his own. He headed towards the nearest road and turned north. To start with, he saw few refugees and those he did pass were travelling south, then ahead he spotted the tail end of a long column of people. Increasing his pace he caught up to the stragglers, a family of six: parents, grandparents and two children, one leading a horse, the other a cow. The weary parents were dragging a cart on which was seated an elderly woman, her black shawl and dress contrasting sharply with the brightly coloured blanket that formed her seat. An elderly man, leaning heavily on his stick, held her hand, the procession making its slow passage along the uneven lane. They spun around at the sound of Louis' approach, concern on their faces, then relaxed when they recognised he offered no threat to them.

"Have you seen the Boche?" the woman asked, fear in her eyes.

Louis shook his head. "No, not for a while. Where are you heading?"

"The coast. There's talk we can get a boat to England there."

Louis made no comment and the man peered at him through his thick spectacles. "Are you a soldier?"

Louis shook his head. "No, not me. I'm heading home, I was visiting some relatives near the border when they crossed over, I've been trying to keep one step ahead ever since."

Louis didn't give the man any time to argue; instead he said goodbye and speeded up, leaving the small family to struggle on alone.

****

Calais, France

Joe didn't need to ask what Chalky meant; the whining drone of a squadron of Stukas clearly heading in their direction needed no explanation. Hands covering their heads, they tried to make themselves invisible while the Stukas dive-bombed the area repeatedly. When they finally flew off and Joe felt safe to remove his arms from over his head, he was surprised to find himself uninjured. Hearing crackling, he gazed back at the surrounding houses he and Rob had been unable to break into. Those still standing were engulfed in thick black smoke and dust with flames shooting several feet into the air. He could see people's possessions burning, along with their furniture. He watched walls crumbling, exposing glimpses of a peacetime life that seemed so long ago. He was grateful now they had been unable to get in. If they had, they would probably be dead.

He checked around and to either side and was relieved to see Woody, Chalky, Taffy and Rob were also unhurt. They were in the minority. Several riflemen had died in the attack, their bodies lying lifeless, blood seeping slowly into the earth beneath. Joe stared in disbelief at Andy Merchant who had been talking about his female conquests and making bets with Taffy, only two days ago. At first glance, Joe had assumed Andy was alive, it was only on closer inspection he realised his body was only being held together by his uniform. Joe tried to stem the rising bile and made himself turn away. All around him there were reminders of the murderous barrage. He turned back and tried to focus on the living, ignoring the sight of the disembodied limbs and parts of bodies he didn't recognise.

However, the dead were only one part of the horror. Other riflemen were severely injured. A few feet to the left, Taffy was trying unsuccessfully to stem the bleeding wounds of the man next to him whose leg had been severed at the knee. Joe realised the man was Johnston. He could see Taffy talking to him but it was a few minutes before his ears cleared enough and he could hear the words.

"Hang on, Johno," Taffy was urging him. "We'll get you out of here, back home eh? They'll soon have you on the next ship, back to your family… just hang on… no, don't go to sleep… you've got to stay awake, mate. Just a bit longer… you can do it… hold on a bit longer." Running out of things to say, he raised his head and caught Joe's eye. Joe scrambled into the hole beside him and tried to help, using the bandage out of Johnston's medical pack to add pressure to the bleeding stump which was all that remained of his left leg.

"Come on, Johno. Molly'll be waiting for you. Don't give up, just hang on a bit longer, mate…" Johnston began jerking, his body in spasm, blood pouring from his mouth and Joe stopped talking. Johnston's body stilled and he opened his eyes, staring straight at Joe.

"You'll tell her I'm sorry?" There was a long pause and then, "I can't wait for her. Sorry."

Joe felt his hand being gripped hard. "You can tell her yourself mate, I …" He stopped mid-sentence. Johnston was no longer listening. Joe swore loudly, picked up his rifle again and switched his attention back to the action.

There was no time to grieve, no time for anything other than to carry on fighting. The Poles who'd escaped to Britain had told tales of atrocities on the battlefield by the Germans which made them all the more determined to fight to the death. If they were going to die anyway, they might as well take some of the bastards with them. His thoughts were interrupted by a frantic shout from Taffy: "Bloody hell, they're coming back again."

****

They had travelled a few more miles when they came across a gentle stream burbling along contentedly across a bed of large, flat stones. Willow trees provided shade and cover and an ideal place for them to take some rest, have something to eat and replenish their water supply.

"I think we'll stop here for a little while." Jean-Paul could see the exhaustion etched on all their faces. They sat down on the warm grass and Jean-Paul took out the large parcel of food Antoinette had given them. Inside, there were some small loaves of fresh bread, tomatoes, apples, cheese, sausage, pickles and several slices of cold meat. He handed them all a small portion of bread, meat, tomatoes and pickles and they began eating.

"Charles, do you have a girlfriend?" Claudette's question caught him by surprise.

"Yes. Her name is Debby. She lives in Folkestone and she's in the WRENS," Jean-Paul translated

"WRENS?" Jeanne questioned

"The WRENS is the Women's Royal Naval Service." Charles answered, showing them a small picture of a smiling girl in a smart uniform.

"She's pretty," Claudette exclaimed.

"I think so." Charles replaced the photograph in his pocket. "And you, Marcel? Do you have a girlfriend?"

Marcel shook his head "No, not yet." He hesitated "Could I ask you something?"

"Of course, Marcel. Go ahead."

"Could you teach me English?"

"Of course I can. Perhaps you can help improve my French at the same time."

Jean-Paul translated and Marcel smiled. "Thank you."

"Can I learn too?" Jeanne asked.

"Why not? The more the merrier," Charles responded. "It'll give us something else to think about, other than this blasted war."

"Come on, we should start walking again." Jean-Paul was pleased the two younger members had something to occupy their minds. It would make their journey much easier and would be very useful for them both when they reached England.

****

Lambeth Hospital, London

Peggy didn't have a chance to speak to Helen again until later that afternoon.

"Have you heard from Annie?"

"No, nothing at all," Helen answered. "I saw you speaking to your admirer earlier."

"He's not my admirer. One of the patients had maggots in his wounds and I couldn't find anyone to help." Peggy was immediately on the defensive.

"You know who I'm talking about, then?" Helen's eyes were alight with mischief.

The guarded expression left Peggy's face. "He *is* rather nice and very helpful." She sighed. "I'm not interested, though. How could I be? I'm engaged to Joe." She shook her head as if to remove any memory of Chris.

"We'll see." Helen wasn't about to resist the temptation of teasing her friend. "He's here, and Joe's not and what he doesn't know…" She left the rest of the sentence unspoken.

"Helen, that's awful!" Peggy was shocked.

"Why?" Helen really couldn't understand why Peggy was horrified. "Although you're engaged to Joe, he's not here and we're not talking about running away with someone else and getting married, or even going out with them in that way. All we're talking about is maybe going out for a drink or to the pictures as friends." Helen was no longer joking. "The war could go on for years. I'm not going to spend every night sitting in being miserable and Jimmy won't either. Like my mum says, wartime makes things different. None of us can be sure we're going to be here tomorrow and you're a long time dead," she finished.

Peggy appeared doubtful and Helen could see she wasn't convinced.

"Well, it's irrelevant anyway. It's not like he's asked me out. We've only spoken twice!"

"But he is quite nice, isn't he?"

"How can I answer that? I don't know him!" Peggy snapped. "Now, can we please change the subject?"

Peggy was delighted to see her friend had cheered up, although she didn't agree with Helen's views. On the other hand, Joe hadn't written in ages and she was getting a little fed up to think she meant so little to him that he couldn't be bothered to write her even a few lines. Perhaps Helen was right. Maybe she was just too convenient. Perhaps if Joe thought she had another admirer, he might show a little more interest. She made up her mind she would accept, if Chris did ask her out. After all, there was no harm in going out for a drink, was there? Peggy smiled. He hadn't even asked her and already she was planning their evening.

****

Calais, France

Taffy didn't need to shout, despite the shelling, grenade and mortar fire; they all heard the dreaded droning of the Stukas and were already curling up into the foetal position in an attempt to make themselves invisible. They waited. The expected bombardment never came. Joe looked up gingerly and stared in astonishment at the pieces of paper falling gracefully from the sky. Leaning over he picked one up and read the English words exhorting them to save themselves and surrender. "Stupid bastards." He muttered.

"Ah well, it'll come in handy for bog roll." Rob's words made Joe smile but within minutes the artillery barrage had restarted. "Is it me, or are the bastards getting closer?" Without waiting for an answer, he carried on, "I'm getting low on ammo, what about you, Joe?"

"Yeah, I've only got three clips and a couple of rounds left in this one. Chalky?"

"I've got four clips left, then I'm done" Chalky raised his voice above the shelling: "Corp, we're running low on ammo."

"How much have you got left?" Woody listened to their responses and rapidly came to a decision. "Right, we've covered the Queen Vics' withdrawal. It's time to start pulling back." Woody's order was a welcome relief. "Let's go. Cover us, Taffy, until we get to those buildings, then we'll cover you."

Taffy changed clips and let loose a murderous burst, spraying the surrounding area with a hail of bullets, causing a brief lull in the enemy fire and using up the rest of his ammunition. Joe and the others took the opportunity to crawl rapidly towards the relative protection of the few buildings still standing and, once there, opened fire to give Taffy some cover to pull back. Whilst Joe and Chalky fired and reloaded, ensuring the Germans kept their heads down, the others threw hand grenades and fired mortars into the enemy lines. Taffy grabbed the useless Bren gun and, half running, half crouching, sped towards the buildings where they were waiting. He had just reached them when another squadron of Stukas flew over their heads strafing the ground where they had been entrenched only a few moments earlier.

Chapter Twenty-four

Somewhere in France

Louis tried to ignore his conscience which kept reminding him of the poor family he had left to struggle on alone. He needed to concentrate on his own survival. If he stopped to help everyone in trouble he might never get home and he was becoming increasingly worried about Brigitte. She was a very attractive girl and he didn't want any dirty Germans getting ideas. She was his girl and he would kill anyone who hurt her. The strength of his feelings surprised him, but just the thought of her warm loving arms could make him forget all the horror of the past few days. He began rewriting the episode in his mind and, before long, he was congratulating himself on just how much help he had given the refugees. From finding food and water to amusing the children, Louis had been a Godsend and although he had eventually found some other people to help them, they had been very sad to see him go.

Ahead was a bend and he approached it cautiously. Although all was quiet, he crept round, expecting at any moment to find himself looking down the barrel of a German rifle. There was no one there. The road in front of him was totally deserted, there were weeds sprouting in the centre and the lane was growing narrower as it dipped into a small hollow before rising up into another sharp bend. Louis followed the road a little longer then came to a stile leading into a large hedged field with a small copse of trees at the far side. He climbed over and, after checking there was no one in sight, he made his way along the edge. His thoughts fixed firmly on his reunion with Brigitte and how pleased she would be to see him, Louis soon managed to put the small family completely out of his mind.

****

Northern France

The afternoon sun was quite high in the sky and Marcel was enjoying the feel of its warmth on his back while they hiked across the open countryside. The relentless pounding of the German bombardment had long since become background noise and even the occasional shake of the ground seemed normal. Trying to teach each other their languages proved to be a huge distraction and caused plenty of merriment when they attempted to pronounce words and phrases. Putting sentences together was even funnier and Jean-Paul found he was so busy translating and laughing, he wasn't giving his full attention to their journey. Fortunately, their route kept them away from any of the major highways and the countryside they were passing through was strangely devoid of people. It was much later in the day, when the warmth of the sun was starting to fade and the shadows were beginning to lengthen again, before they saw anything to worry them. They were coming to the edge of a small copse of trees and, in front of them, were a couple of pastures and then some more woods.

"Hold it!" Charles stopped and put out his arm to warn the others. "I'm sure I saw something moving over there." He pointed in the direction they were heading.

Immediately, they all stopped and threw themselves flat on the ground. Jean-Paul cautiously raised his head. "Whereabouts?"

"Over there. On the edge of the trees." Charles was busy scanning the horizon, though he couldn't see anything out of the ordinary.

"Stay still for a while." Jean-Paul was watching the trees for any sign of movement. They waited for several minutes, but couldn't see anything. Eventually Charles spoke.

"I must have been mistaken." He didn't sound convinced though. "I could've sworn…"

He didn't get any further; Marcel nudged his arm and whispered something in French. Charles frowned, although his limited French was not sufficient to translate Marcel's words, he could hear the urgency in his voice. Jean-Paul answered Marcel and then turned to Charles. "You were right. Look carefully at a position about two on the clock and you'll see movement. I think it's soldiers. We couldn't see them because they're camouflaged against the trees. They are either waiting to ambush someone or they are hiding; I can't tell which. Neither can I tell from here if they are German."

****

Lewisham, London

"Are you sure?" The tall swarthy man lit another cigarette and stared at Kath. They were in The Red Lion public house and Kath had outlined the plan she had spent all day formulating to her old friend Tom, a local wide boy who had fingers in several pies and would do pretty much anything for money.

"Definitely. Mike said he spoke to Stan this morning before Mary's body was found. Mike said Stan was really pissed off because she'd led him on and then changed her mind. He would've pushed it with her but some snotty middle-aged lady interfered. The description fits Olive Cooper."

"Surely, he'll tell the police that?" Tom was unconvinced.

"Yeah, they're not likely to believe him though, are they?" Kath laughed. "They've got several witnesses to say he left the dance with her and why would some woman kill her? Much more likely Stan did, 'cause she wouldn't give him what he wanted."

"Why would this Olive Cooper want Mary dead?"

"I think she thought Mary was going to say something about her listening into council phone calls. She's already been hauled over the coals for earwigging before, so she'd probably get the sack. And, let's be honest, all she's got is her job."

He was still dubious. "Yeah, but is that really worth killing over?"

Kath shrugged. "I saw her in here, standing by the door, then she went and stood over the road and she was watching us. Why else would she be there? Not likely she was looking to pick up a bloke, is it?" Kath laughed again. "She probably didn't mean to kill her. It's more likely to have been an accident. Perhaps she wanted to talk to Mary, you know, make Mary change her mind about reporting her. Mary was pretty pissed and you know what a big mouth she's got on her when she's drunk. Perhaps she wound the old girl up. Anyway, whether she killed Mary or not, she's not gonna want the police knowing she was watching Mary is she, not now she's dead?"

Tom grinned, revealing yellowing teeth and red gums. "How much do you think it'll be worth to her to keep us quiet?"

Kath smiled back. "I don't know, but she's got sod all to spend her money on. Why don't you go and find out. I'll meet you in here later." She handed him a small piece of paper. "That's her address."

****

Somewhere in France

Louis lifted his head and stared at the farmhouse which appeared deserted. After watching carefully for another few minutes, he crept forward and cautiously pushed open the door. It looked like the occupants had left in a hurry; there were a couple of dirty plates with the remains of food and two half-full glasses of wine on the table. Ignoring them, Louis made his way further into the kitchen and searched for the larder, stopping only to turn on the kitchen tap. He lowered his head to drink the clear refreshing liquid and put his head under the running water, allowing it to cascade over his hair, cooling and cleansing him. Feeling better, he resumed his search for food.

From the sink he stepped towards another door, which he opened. To his delight, the larder contained a small quantity of cheese, eggs, meat, chutney, biscuits and bread, enough for a feast. There was no milk but some bottles of wine lay in a small wine rack. Louis picked up a bottle, cracked the top on the sink to break the neck open, found a clean glass in the large dresser that lined the back wall, poured some wine and gulped it down. He shoved the dirty plates out of the way and cleared a place for himself, grabbed some provisions from the larder and sat down at the table. The wine flowed and he tucked into the food.

He thought back to his encounter with Lucie and grinned. The war wasn't all bad if it was going to present him with opportunities like that. Shame she'd been in such a hurry to get away afterwards. He would have liked to make love to her again. He shrugged, finished the rest of the wine and went to look for another bottle. Still, not long and he would be home. He couldn't wait to see Brigitte again.

****

Honor Oak Park, London

The post was on the floor. Peggy picked the letters up without much interest, then smiled. Thank goodness: there was something from Peter. Sally would be so relieved. She skimmed through the others. There was nothing from Joe. There was one for her from Pam in Dover and one for Ethel. She put Ethel's and Sally's letters on the hall table where they would see them when they came in and took the one from Pam into the kitchen to read while she made a cup of tea.

Having put the kettle on to boil, she opened her letter, eagerly scanning through Pam's news.

Dear Peggy
Sorry for the long delay in replying; you know I'm a lousy letter writer.
How's everything with you? No doubt you're quite busy, unlike me. I am

*bored rigid, to be honest. Not only am I helping the WRVS, but mother now
has me helping out at numerous charity events, raising money for Spits and
various other good causes. I must admit, most of them are not much fun,
although I have met some rather dishy RAF pilots in the past few weeks. In
fact, I'm thinking of joining the WAAF. Got to do something for the war
effort and at least the uniform's smart. What do you think?*

Peggy grinned. Pam was great fun, although she was totally
undisciplined. Peggy had doubts that she would last the pace in the
WAAF. Daisy, one of her friends from church had joined and she was
always complaining about how strict they were. Peggy wasn't sure
joining up would give Pam the excitement she craved, either. Then she
felt guilty: maybe she was misjudging Pam, after all the WAAF might
be perfect for her. Peggy turned her attention back to the letter.

*It will also help me to understand what that good-for-nothing brother
of mine is talking about. Talking of Tony, he is really enjoying himself. He
talks non-stop about his beloved Spit; I do wish he'd get a girlfriend instead!*

The kettle boiled, Peggy made the tea and went back to the letter.

*When are you coming down again? I'd love to see you, I've missed you,
Peggy and it really is very boring here! We always have such a good laugh
when we get together. I can't wait to sit down and have a good old catch up
and you can give me all the gossip.*

Peggy considered Pam's request for a few moments. Maybe she
could go down the following month. If she only went for the weekend,
it wouldn't use up too much of her holiday. She needed to keep some
for when Joe was on leave. She reached the end of the page:

*Well that's about it for my news. How about you? How's Joe? I hope
he's a better letter writer than I am. Have you set a date for the wedding yet,
or are you going to wait until the war is over? The way things are going,*

that might be some time; maybe you should reconsider? Don't forget I'm available for bridesmaid duty and I can even help organise the wedding if you're too busy! Something else we can talk about when you come down. You can see I'm not taking no for an answer! Just get some time off and we can have a good old chinwag.

Well, I'd better go. It's time to get ready for yet another charity bash.

Love from your very dear friend,

Pam

The signature was scrawled large across the bottom of the page and Peggy smiled. Pam's letters always cheered her up.

"Peggy, I've had a letter from Peter!" Sally's excited voice carried into the kitchen, interrupting her thoughts.

"I know." Peggy called back "Do you want a cup of tea? The pot's still warm." She didn't wait for an answer, but poured out the tea anyway and stepped into the hall, following Sally into the front room. "What does he say? Is he alright?"

Peggy watched Sally tear open the envelope and take out the letter. There was a brief silence; her eyes rapidly scanning the text.

"Yes, he's fine. They've not had an opportunity to write because of… oh that bit's censored…" She carried on reading for a while and then, beaming with happiness, threw herself lengthways on the sofa and, kicking off her shoes, gratefully took the tea Peggy was offering. "Oh, Peggy, I am *so* relieved. I was getting concerned something had happened to him." A thought occurred to her. She turned the letter over and saw the date was the 13th of May. "You don't suppose anything's happened to him since the thirteenth, do you?"

"Sally, you've had a letter saying he is fine. There is a war on for goodness sake! Post is bound to be a bit slower than normal."

"Yes, of course you're right. I'm just being silly." Sally hugged the letter to her chest and closed her eyes. "I just couldn't bear anything to happen to him."

Ethel came in through the front door. "Hello, Sally." One glance at Sally's smiling face told her all she needed to know. "You've had a letter?"

"Yes, Ethel. Finally!"

Ethel looked relieved. "I gather he's absolutely fine and we've all been worrying for nothing."

"Yes, he says he is. The letter's just taken longer than normal to reach me." Sally was so delighted, she missed the quick glance that passed between Peggy and Ethel.

Chapter Twenty-five

Bethune, Northern France

"Are you alright, Fräulein?" the German accent took her by surprise and she raised her eyes to find three German soldiers blocking her path. Her father had sent her to buy some more bread and, with her earlier humiliation fresh in her memory, Brigitte was taking care not to make eye contact with the women who were congregating in the square. Despite this, she could feel their eyes on her and hear them gossiping about her.

"Yes, thank you," she murmured. The German touched his cap in a gentle salute. Brigitte stared up into his brown eyes and noticed he was rather handsome. Seeing they were about to move on, she forgot her argument with her father and treated them to one of her very best smiles. "Are you billeted in Bethune?" she asked.

The second soldier answered, "Yes, Fräulein. We are camped just outside the town. We are on our way there now."

Brigitte's face fell. "You are not staying in the town then?"

The Germans exchanged a glance and then the first one answered, "No. Not yet anyway. But we will be patrolling. You looked disappointed, Fräulein, when we said we were not staying in the town. We did not expect anyone to be friendly towards us."

"You're here." She shrugged. "It's not our fault our countries are at war. There's no reason why we shouldn't be friends, is there? I'm

Brigitte." She could feel the animosity of the women who were watching her and defiantly held out her hand.

The soldier smiled, clicked his heels together and, bending over, kissed her hand. "Wolfgang Schmidt and these are my friends, Helmut and Klaus."

Brigitte turned her back on the women and smiled at the men. "My father has a café, La Bienvenue in Rue de Lille. Come on, I'll show you, then when you're next in town you can come and visit me."

****

Northern France

Charles focused his attention on where he had seen the movement and, once his eyes had adjusted to the shapes and silhouettes of the surrounding countryside, he could see the soldiers quite clearly. There were three of them; two were lying down and the other was standing against a tree. However, like Jean-Paul, he couldn't tell which army they were from.

"What do we do? Unless we go all the way back to the stream and circle round behind them, we have to go through there. We'll lose hours." The despair in Charles's voice echoed Jean-Paul's own thoughts. Needing to examine the map, Jean-Paul motioned them to crawl backwards into the thicker trees behind.

"Move slowly and carefully, try not to disturb any of the bracken. We're lucky they haven't spotted us – they must have been facing the other way."

Once under cover of the trees, Jean-Paul took out the map and began to search for an alternative route, hopefully avoiding both the soldiers and the need to retrace their footsteps. Charles was reading over his shoulder and pointed.

"We could follow this stream which seems to start back there somewhere." He indicated the way they had come. "And comes out on the other side of the woods."

Jean-Paul followed Charles' finger on the map. "It could work. We wouldn't have to go all the way back and we should come out behind them. Means adding a few hours onto our journey but I don't think we have any alternative."

Marcel, Claudette and Jeanne began to follow Charles towards the stream which was situated down a steep bank and was virtually dry. Scrambling down, Charles held out his hand to help Claudette while Marcel offered his hand to Jeanne who gave a shy smile and, taking his hand, began to inch down towards the stream. Although the stream itself was nearly dry, the bank was damp and slippery. Jeanne was about halfway down when she slipped and began sliding towards the bottom of the bank. Marcel immediately moved forward to stop her fall, using his body to break the downward movement and reaching out his arms automatically to encircle her body. She slithered to a halt and found herself pressed up against him with his arms tightly around her. For a moment, neither of them moved and then, embarrassed, Marcel stepped back.

"Are you alright? You haven't hurt yourself?" he asked, conscious of the feel of her body against his.

"No, I'm fine, thank you." Jeanne blushed. Glancing around to make sure no one had seen, she carefully negotiated the last few steps to the bottom. Marcel followed. Although he was embarrassed, he also felt strangely elated. He had never held a woman in his arms before and the feeling was like nothing he'd ever experienced. Jeanne was very attractive. He had been too preoccupied with everything going on around him to really see her. Now he was only too aware of her. He glanced sideways to where she was standing with her mother. She was facing him, her clothes were dirty again and, although her long blonde hair was tied in a ponytail, some wispy tendrils had escaped, curling gently as they framed her face. Her green eyes were sparkling and her hands moved expressively while she chatted about something with her parents. As he watched, Jeanne laughed, her generous mouth showing even, white teeth.

Charles smiled. He'd seen the expression on Marcel's face and he didn't need to speak French to know the boy was smitten. Watching

Jeanne's body language, Charles was pretty sure the feeling was probably reciprocated, although she too was undoubtedly unaware of her feelings. He sighed, watching Marcel and Jeanne reminded him of Debby. It was all very well wandering around France with Jean-Paul and his family, but their chances of reaching England safely were diminishing hour by hour. Still, there was no quicker way to get to the coast.

The stream was still flowing in places and, although little more than a trickle, it was enough to soak through their shoes. They took them off and carried on with bare feet which felt nice until the sun started to go down, the shadows lengthened and they began to feel the cold.

Finally, the stream dried up completely and Charles scrambled carefully up the bank to see where they were. The others put their shoes back on and waited in silence; the sun dropped even lower and they began to shiver. Charles was only gone a few moments before reappearing with a big smile on his face.

"We've come up near the end of the woods. The soldiers are over there somewhere." He pointed back in the direction they had come. "And Dunkirk is over there." He indicated the direction they were going. "Come on, I'll give you a hand up." He put out his hand to Claudette. Jean-Paul scrambled up himself and Marcel held out his hand to Jeanne.

Once they were back up in the woods, the temperature rose slightly. Night was not far off. Jean-Paul glanced up at the sky and then ahead. In front of them was a large meadow and then a main highway. By the time they had crossed the field, they would be in darkness, which would make crossing the road easier and, on the other side, there were more trees. The sensible thing would be to stop for the night and try to get some sleep in the cover of the woods. They could then start again when the sun came up. With an early start, they might make Dunkirk by the middle of the next day. At least in daylight, they would be able to see where they were walking and, with luck, they could be on a ship to England and safety by the evening.

Calais, France

By the time Joe and his companions reached the rest of the battalion and dug in for the night, the sun was sinking in the west. Exhausted from their experiences, conversation was limited. Joe might have wanted revenge in the heat of battle, but away from the fighting, he was not finding it easy to come to terms with killing another human being, even though he'd had no option if he wanted to stay alive.

The sun gradually sank lower and lower. Joe ate his rations, drank some water and smoked. The setting sun added its own crimson hue to the skies over Calais, already glowing red from the many uncontrolled fires still raging and the constant shelling from the advancing Germans. All around him, smoke, clouds of dust and the ever-present smell of cordite were joined by the sound of falling masonry as buildings collapsed into piles of unrecognisable rubble.

****

Somewhere in France

Louis had no idea how long he'd slept, but when he woke, the room was dark. For a moment he couldn't work out where he was and then he remembered he was in one of the bedrooms in the abandoned farmhouse. After eating and drinking his fill, he'd stumbled upstairs and collapsed on the large double bed. Within moments, he'd fallen into a deep dreamless sleep. He was about to turn over and close his eyes again when he heard a noise.

****

Honor Oak Park, London

The salty smell of kippers had filled the house by the time Peggy came downstairs, wearing one of her older dresses, a soft green cotton with pleats and a polka dot pattern. The evenings were quite chilly, so she was wearing a cardigan over the top and, on her feet, she had a pair of long socks and her favourite crocheted slippers which the others always made fun of.

"I love the smell of kippers." She sniffed appreciatively. "Are we listening to *ITMA* tonight?"

"Have we ever missed an episode?" Sally was horrified. "And Vera Lynn is on afterwards. I've got a favour to ask. Can we give the news a miss tonight? It's always depressing and I'd quite like to hold on to my good mood." Peggy and Ethel didn't hesitate. Sally's words pretty much echoed their own sentiments and one night away from the events of the outside world couldn't hurt.

Their meal finished, they cleared up, went into the front room, switched on the wireless and sat down expectantly and, within minutes, they were roaring with laughter. The programme drew to a close and they noticed the light had gone.

"Goodness, we haven't put up the blackout!" Peggy jumped up and rushed to the front window. "Can you do upstairs, Sally, while Ethel and I do down here?" Peggy was already putting up the curtains while she spoke and Sally rushed upstairs. It was nearly nine o'clock by the time they finished and they had only just sat down when there was a loud insistent knocking on the door. They looked at each other in surprise. Peggy stood up

"I'll go. Are either of you expecting anyone?"

They both shook their heads and Peggy went out into the hall. They heard her talking and then the door to the front room opened. There, pale and tear-stained, was Peter's sister, Mona.

****

Somewhere in France

Hardly daring to breathe, Louis moved his head in the direction from which the noise had come, and stared into the darkness. He could just make out a shadow near the window and he gasped.

"You're awake then?"

The voice belonged to a woman and he struggled to sit up.

"Who are you?" His voice sounded hoarse and he cleared his throat.

"Shouldn't that be my question? After all, you are in my house."

"I'm sorry, I was trying to hide from the Germans and…" His voice tailed off as she laughed.

"It's alright. If I'd thought you were a threat, you wouldn't be lying there." She closed the curtains and he heard her moving across the floor. The next second, he heard a click and then the room was flooded with light. Louis blinked, his eyes adjusting to the sudden brightness and he focused on the woman standing in front of him. She was quite tall and smartly dressed in a brown close fitting jacket over a cream blouse and matching skirt. Her auburn hair was tied up neatly in a bun above clear green eyes, a retrousée nose and full lips. Louis judged her to be about thirty.

"Perhaps you would like a bath?" she suggested and Louis immediately felt ashamed of his unkempt appearance. "I'm Gabrielle and you are?"

"Louis. Louis Servier. I'm… I was a soldier. Now I'm just trying to get home." He was surprised he'd told her the truth and he waited for her to throw him out. She didn't. Instead, she stood watching him for a few more moments before turning away.

"Well, Louis, I suggest you go and have a bath and a shave, find some clean clothes in the bedroom next door and then come downstairs. We can talk more then."

****

Catford, London

"Excuse me, Miss Cooper?"

Olive opened the door in surprise. She had been about to go to bed, relieved the long day was over when the knock on the door had sounded. "Can I help you?" She automatically adopted her official voice.

The man was tall with a swarthy complexion and dark narrow eyes. His hair was greasy and slicked back, and there was an unpleasant smile on his full lips. "You most certainly can, Olive. You don't mind me calling you Olive, do you? And you can call me Tom."

Olive was furious. "How dare you?" She stepped back, prepared to shut the door in his face but he was too quick for her. He placed his foot over the threshold, pushed past her and closed the door behind him. To his amusement, she had left the key in the lock, so he quickly turned it and placed it in his pocket, locking them both in the flat. He looked around the rather spartan space and then indicated the two chairs placed neatly at the small table.

"Why don't you sit down and I'll explain."

"If you don't leave, I'll scream." Olive's voice trembled but she held his gaze. "They'll hear me downstairs and call the police."

Tom smiled. "Be my guest, Olive. I'm sure the police would love to know how Mary died." He watched her carefully. Now was the time for her to say she didn't know what he was talking about. If she did, he would be stymied. He had no evidence, except Kath's suspicions.

Olive paled. That was all he needed. Tom pressed home his advantage. "Just as I thought. Now sit down and listen carefully." The smile had gone, his voice was authoritative and Olive obeyed automatically.

Chapter Twenty-six

Northern France

"This will do," Jean-Paul suggested after he had tripped over a branch in the semi-gloom for the second time. "If we keep going in the dark, we'll end up hurting ourselves or breaking something. Let's stop here and have something to eat and then we'll get some rest. We should also keep our voices down. Sound travels a long way in the dark and, now the shelling seems to have ceased, we don't want to draw attention to our presence."

They sat down, tried to make themselves comfortable and ate sparingly from the remains of their food. They had plenty of water, thanks to the stream and, because they were very tired, they ate for the most part in silence. By the time they'd finished, the light had gone and they could only just see each other.

"Time we got some sleep, I think," Jean-Paul consulted Marcel and Charles. "We need to keep watch overnight. I think there are about six hours until dawn; so that's two hours each. Who wants to go first?"

"I will," Marcel volunteered.

"I'll take the next one," Charles offered.

"Then I'll take the last watch." Jean-Paul was busy trying to identify the best place for the women to sleep. "If you lay down here, you will be sheltered from any rain and wind." He indicated a space on the ground where the roots had disturbed some of the earth, making a shallow dip, which would protect them from the wind. The space was under the canopy of the tree to provide them with shelter from any rain. He kissed and hugged his wife and daughter goodnight and found himself a space around the side of the same tree so he was close to them if they needed him.

Claudette and Jeanne lay down and tried to provide each other with some warmth, whilst Jean-Paul, Marcel and Charles worked out the best place for the sentry to sit.

****

Honor Oak Park, London

"No, I don't want to know!" Sally's scream reverberated off the walls of the small front room. She covered her ears in a childish attempt to block out their voices.

"Sally, he's alive, but he's wounded." Mona repeated the sentence twice before she finally broke through Sally's panic.

"He's alive?" Sally repeated, her eyes full of fear. "You're sure?"

"Yes, although he is quite badly wounded." Peggy used her 'hospital' voice, firm, calm and confident.

"How badly?" Sally was quieter now, her eyes fixed on Peggy's face.

"He's lost a leg." For a moment, Sally stared at her, unable to take in Peggy's words.

"He's alive though, and he's going to be alright?" she repeated.

"Sally, did you hear me?" Peggy repeated the words, this time more gently. "Mona says he's alive but he's lost a leg. He trod on a land mine just outside Arras. He was brought out on a hospital ship this morning and he is in Lambeth hospital."

"Can I see him?" she asked.

"Not yet." Mona was relieved Sally seemed to be back with them. "They were going to operate tonight. His other leg was damaged and they want to try and save it." Mona glanced at Peggy, not sure what else to say. Until they were able to go to the hospital the next day, they wouldn't know any more.

216

Although she was shocked, Peggy had reverted to her hospital self, realising her responses needed to be practical not emotional.

"I'll put the kettle on and make us all some hot sweet tea. Do you want a cup, Mona?"

"No, thanks. I've drunk enough tea tonight to sink a battle ship." Mona had a faint smile on her lips.

Peggy went into the kitchen where she was joined by Ethel.

"I thought you might want a hand. Besides, I couldn't think of anything to say to Sally," Ethel whispered.

"There's not much any of us can say until we know more. Things won't be the same, whatever Sally thinks. It might not make any difference to the way she feels about Peter but I've seen people who've had limbs amputated after accidents. Sometimes they think no one can possibly love them because of their injury." She stopped speaking, suddenly aware Mona was standing behind her. She didn't know how long the girl had been there, or how much she had heard.

"It's alright. Mum said everything would depend on how Peter coped with losing his leg and it was important Sally didn't appear horrified or anything when she saw him…" Peggy could hear the slight question in Mona's voice.

"Sally loves Peter more than anything. I am sure she won't want to do anything that would make things worse for him or upset him in any way." Peggy reassured her. The kettle whistled and she busied herself making the tea. "You take Sally's for her." She handed Mona a steaming mug.

Back in the living room, Sally took the mug and began to drink automatically. Peggy smiled at Mona who went and sat down on the settee. There was silence while they drank the tea and then Mona got up to go.

"Are you sure you don't want to stay, Mona?" Peggy asked the young girl.

"No, Mum's expecting me back, thank you anyway."

"Do you want me to walk you home?" Ethel asked.

"No, thanks. It's not far. Will you come round in the morning, Sally?"

Having drunk her mug of tea, Sally seemed to have pulled herself together.

"Yes, Mona. I'll be round early." She got up and gave the younger girl a big hug. "Thank you for coming to tell me. I know it can't have been easy." She released Mona from the hug and looked her straight in the eyes. "He'll be alright. You'll see."

Mona gave a watery smile and let herself out, leaving Peggy and Ethel to shepherd Sally up to bed.

****

Somewhere in France

Louis stared at his reflection in the mirror. Now he'd shaved, he could see how much weight he'd lost. It was strangely quiet. Maybe the war was over? That would probably mean the Germans had won: he couldn't imagine there had been a miracle and the French and British had driven them back. He went into the other bedroom and was surprised to find some clothes laid neatly on the bed. He dressed quickly, appreciating their good quality and hurried downstairs. Gabrielle was listening to the wireless, a glass of red wine in her hand. She poured one for Louis and, after handing the glass to him, indicated for him to sit down at the table, which was now spotless.

"Have they said why it's gone quiet?" Louis asked. Gabrielle shook her head.

"No, but it's unlikely to mean the Boche have given up and gone home."

There was silence. "I'm sorry for breaking in here," Louis apologised.

Gabrielle drained her glass, reached across the table and took his hand. "I'm not. My husband is away fighting somewhere and I'm lonely."

Louis stared at her in disbelief, then he grinned. "Perhaps I can do something to help?"

"Not much point telling you to wash and scrub up otherwise, was there?" Her eyes bore into his and then she came over to stand in front of him. She took his wine and placed the glass on the dresser, then turned back to him. "I cleared the table for a reason, you know."

Louis needed no second invitation. He stood up, his left hand grabbing her hair, forcing her head back so he could kiss her, his lips bruising hers with their intensity. Gabrielle was already undoing his belt and pulling down his trousers when he eased her back onto the table and shoved her skirt up, forcing her legs apart. He slipped his hands under her buttocks and with one easy movement slid inside her. She writhed under him, her moans and cries of pleasure mingling with his long drawn out groan. The war was forgotten.

******

Northern France

Marcel didn't feel tired. For some reason, his mind was full of Jeanne and wouldn't be still, even though he tried to think of other things. Staring into the darkness, Marcel relived all their conversations and the few moments when he had held her close. He'd never felt like this before about a girl. Perhaps this was love? He hoped Jeanne felt the same way about him or life could be very awkward if he said something. She might take offence and then Jean-Paul and Claudette might ask him to leave and travel on his own. He heard a sudden noise and he spun round, but it was just Jean-Paul turning in his sleep.

Always supposing they reached England safely, Marcel began thinking about what was he going to do when he got there. Lost in his plans for the future, the time flew by and, before long, his two hours had passed and he woke Charles.

******

Brigitte stood up, straightened her skirt, fastened her blouse and blew a kiss to the young man who was busy doing up the buttons on his fly.

He reached over, kissed her cheek and disappeared into the night, leaving her alone in the alleyway. As she let herself into the back entrance of the café and made her way up to her bedroom, Brigitte smiled to herself. Wolfgang was great fun and seemed to like her. Brigitte knew her father wouldn't approve of her friendship with the Germans, and she didn't care: her father was a pig. Brigitte grinned, remembering the expression on his face when she'd arrived with the Germans earlier. He was furious, but too much of a coward to say anything to the occupying forces. Instead he'd hovered by the open doorway listening to them promise Brigitte they would be back later, then he'd turned on her. Brigitte had just laughed at him and flounced into the café leaving him shaking his head in disgust. Wolfgang and his companions had reappeared a few hours later and ordered drinks which Brigitte served them with a smile on her face, much to the locals' disgust.

Determined to make the best of the company, Brigitte had been at her most accommodating and eventually Wolfgang had suggested they step outside. Delighted, Brigitte had taken his arm and led him to a small alleyway behind the shops. She did wonder whether she should ask for some money first, however, he was in a hurry and she liked him. Once they were out of sight of the road, Brigitte was quick and eager to kneel down on the dusty cobbles and take him in her mouth. She was a little disappointed he had climaxed so fast, but he blamed the alleyway. Brigitte nodded, an understanding expression on her face and explained how to sneak past her father to her bedroom.

Brigitte opened her bedroom door and slipped inside. She could hear voices in the café below but there was no sound of her irate father coming up the stairs and she breathed a sigh of relief. Pulling out her small compact, she gazed at herself in the magnifying mirror and patted some powder on her face, followed by some bright red lipstick.

Pouting, she admired her reflection and thought about Wolfgang. He had gone to get some more wine and wait for an opportune moment to slip past her father and up the stairs. Brigitte sat down on the bed and opened the top button of her blouse again. Leaning back, she rested her head on the pillow and waited for his return.

Chapter Twenty-seven

Calais, France

Although he was exhausted, Joe couldn't really relax. He was constantly on the alert, aware the reduction in fighting was probably just the calm before the storm. He was right. Dawn broke, the shelling resumed and, by sunrise, they were once again under a fierce artillery barrage. The fighting all around them was becoming desperate and, with only a few scout cars, light tanks and Bren gun carriers to support them, they knew they would not be able to hold on too much longer.

"The Germans are trying to cross the canals." Sergeant Miller sounded defeated and was no longer trying to appear upbeat in front of the men. "According to my briefing, the rest of Calais Force are managing to hold their own at the moment, but it's unlikely to stay that way. Unless there's a miracle, the sheer weight of numbers will eventually overwhelm them. We need to be on our guard. There's also been fresh sniper activity in this area, so keep your eyes open."

******

Somewhere in France

Louis yawned, stretched and reached for Gabrielle who was lying prone next to him. The floor was littered with their clothes and several empty bottles of wine and his head ached. He was also thirsty. Leaving the sleeping Gabrielle on the floor, he stood up, went to the sink and turned on the tap. The noise of the running water woke her and she peered sleepily up at him.

"God, look at the time!" To Louis' astonishment she leapt up, ignoring the pounding in her head and began pulling on her clothes. Louis walked over to her, a smile on his face, but seeing his nakedness, she shrieked.

"Quick! Get dressed. You need to leave before my husband gets home."

Louis stared at her. "I thought you said he was away fighting?"

"I lied. He's out screwing his mistress. Well? What are you gawping at? He'll be home in a minute and he'll kill us if he finds you here."

The urgency of her tone finally broke through Louis' confusion and he began to dress hurriedly, one eye on the lane outside the kitchen window. He had just finished buttoning up his trousers when he heard the sound of a vehicle coming down the track. Gabrielle froze.

"Quick! Out the back and across the fields."

Louis hesitated "What about…?" he indicated the mess.

"Don't worry. I'll just say I got drunk. Now for God's sake, go."

With one boot on and the other in his hand, Louis climbed out through the window at the back of the kitchen and began hopping across the yard. Hearing the truck pull up on the other side of the house, he speeded up and vaulted over the small fence and into the meadow. He pulled on his remaining boot and quickly laced them both up. In front of him was a stream and some shrubs; behind them, a sloping wooded hill. He waded through the water and sank down behind the bushes struggling to catch his breath. His headache had increased, but he was beginning to see the funny side of his encounter. At least he'd had some sleep and something to eat and was now wearing clean clothes of a much better quality than those he'd worn on the previous day. All was quiet in the farmhouse behind him, Gabrielle must have got away with her lie. Reluctantly, he stood up and began making his way up the hill. Ahead, he could hear the sound of guns and his pace increased.

****

Just before dawn, the air was rent with the howl of mortars and the ground shook again. Waking with a start, Claudette and Jeanne glanced around fearfully and were relieved to find they were alone. Marcel also woke with a start, thinking they were under attack.

They were all bitterly cold, although the sun was starting to rise through the mist covered ground where they had been laying. There was no warmth yet though and they had to resort to jumping up and down on the spot to get the circulation going in their arms and legs.

"Let's get moving. We'll warm up better and we won't be wasting energy. We can stop to eat further on," Jean-Paul urged. "We need to find out where the Germans are and whether we can still get to the coast." The guns sounded very close and, every minute they expected the enemy to appear from the trees in front of them. They grabbed their belongings and followed Jean-Paul northwards. Before long, they'd reached the edge of the woods and, examining the map, they saw only open countryside and the Germans stood between them and Dunkirk.

The early morning mist had given way to the smoke of the guns, the noise was tremendous and they wanted nothing more than to cover their ears with their hands. There was obviously an intense battle going on for Dunkirk and they were only a few miles in front of the Germans which meant their shells were landing in front of them while the outward facing fire from the BEF was landing behind them. They were in the midst of hell.

"If we go out in the open, we'll be like sitting ducks," Charles shouted. Seeing Jean-Paul's confused expression, he amended, "We'll be an easy target."

"I agree. We'll have to make our way around the edges of the fields," Jean-Paul yelled back. "Although at some point, we'll have to join one of the main routes to stand any chance of getting to the beach area."

"That's where the Germans are going to be concentrating most of their fire power." Charles sounded uneasy.

"Do you have a better plan?" Jean-Paul exploded, then relented. "Sorry, I didn't mean to snap. I'm serious, though. If you can think of a better plan, I'll be happy to follow it."

"No, I think you're right. We have no option but to head for the beach. Come on then. Let's get going."

****

Honor Oak Park, London

Peggy slept badly and, when she woke, she took a few moments to recall the events of the previous night. When she did finally remember, she sat bolt upright.

"Oh, goodness. Poor Sally." Peggy leapt out of bed, dressed and went downstairs to find Sally sitting by the window in the front room, staring into space. She appeared to have been there some time and didn't move when Peggy came in. The wireless was on quietly in the corner and, without turning, Sally announced that Boulogne had fallen and fierce fighting was continuing, with the Germans trying to cut off the BEF communication lines. She seemed unnaturally calm.

"Have you had any breakfast?" Peggy asked, more as a way of making conversation than in any hope Sally would want to eat.

"No… no, thanks. I'm not really hungry. I was waiting for you to get up, so we could go round to Peter's mum and then on to the hospital. I was hoping you would be able to come with me?"

"Of course I can," Peggy reassured her. "I'll need to talk to my ward sister first to make sure. I can do that when I get there," she added, seeing the panic on Sally's face. "Let me just have something to eat, or I'll be really bad tempered all morning. I'll make some toast. You should have some too. I know you don't want any, but you do look a bit pale and you don't want to feel faint while you're visiting Peter, or they'll make you leave."

"Oh. I hadn't thought of that. I'll just have one slice then, please."

Peggy went into the kitchen and sliced and toasted the bread. She used up all of their butter ration, figuring they would both need the extra calories and then added some jam.

****

Lewisham, London

Olive stared into space, the ringing phone ignored while she relived the events of the previous evening. The man had not told her his name and had informed her he would not go to the police, provided she helped him out. Olive had felt a momentary relief which was quickly crushed when he told her to get out her post office savings book so he could see how much money she had. She'd wanted to refuse, but she couldn't find a good enough reason. Trying to look unconcerned, the only way she could keep some pride, she'd done everything he asked and watched, humiliated, while he worked out a payment plan in which she would give him ten pounds the next day and then a regular payment of one pound and ten shillings each Saturday evening.

She'd argued that, with rising prices, she would struggle to meet his demands. He'd laughed and then, as if to reinforce her helplessness, he'd reached out and run his hand over the outline of her breasts and then grabbed one, squeezing hard until she gasped. "Of course, you could always pay me another way." He released her. "But I prefer money. I'll be back tomorrow for the cash. Make sure you've got it." Then he was gone, leaving her trembling and alone. For a brief moment, she had considered going to the police station, then the moment passed and she sank back on the chair, looking and feeling older than her years.

She suddenly realised the other girls were staring at her and she reached out to answer the ringing phone, but not before she caught a glimpse of Kath's face. Unlike the other girls, who were confused at Olive's vacant expression, Kath was smiling.

****

Bethune, Northern France

Fabian handed Brigitte the tray full of glasses and pointed her in the direction of a table at the front of the café. He waited until she returned with the money and reached out, holding her arm. Brigitte stared at him and tried to pull away.

"I need to tell you something." Fabian leaned forward until his face was close to hers. "Louis' father was killed by the Boche a few days ago. His mother is staying with the Laval's while they sort out the funeral. You might want to go and visit her, see if she's alright?"

Brigitte nodded, even though she had no intention of going anywhere near Marie; the memory of their last encounter was too fresh in her mind. In any case, she doubted Marie would want her to visit and Louis had made no attempt to contact her, so she couldn't see why she should bother.

Chapter Twenty-eight

Lambeth Hospital, London

Going in through the main doors, Peggy went over to the front desk to find out where Peter had been taken. Morag, another student nurse, was looking down at the signing-in book.

"He's on one of the surgical wards. They're on the second floor... " She raised her eyes. "Oh sorry, Peggy... of course you know where that is." Morag indicated Peter's family and Sally. "I'm not sure they'll let them in, though; it's not visiting time."

"I'll ask when I get up there," Peggy responded. "Thanks, Morag." She turned back to Sally. "I just need to see if there's anyone in the emergency ward to explain why I'm a little bit late this morning. Do you mind waiting here for a few moments, or do you want to go up on your own?"

"No, I'd rather stay here, if it's all the same to you." Sally glanced at Peter's mother who inclined her head in agreement.

"I won't be long," Peggy said and she hurried towards the emergency ward to which she had been assigned. Although quite busy, the ward was nothing like as frantic as in the past few days, but there was no sign of either the ward sister or matron. Beginning to despair, she was relieved to see Helen coming in through the entrance at the other end of the ward and heading towards her.

"Macklin!" she called.

Helen looked up in surprise and came towards her. Peggy quickly explained about Sally.

Helen frowned. "I'll tell Matron, but you know what she's like."

"Thanks. I'll take my chances. I can't let my friend down at a time like this. I won't stay long; just till we find out how he is."

"You go." Helen made up her mind. "I'll tell her I'm prepared to cover for you, that should help."

"Thank you. I'll do the same for you."

"You've already helped me more than enough. Go on, go… or you'll be even later!"

Peggy hurried back to the main entrance, where Sally and Peter's family were waiting. Seeing Sally's white face, Peggy squeezed her arm for reassurance and then led them towards the stairs. They climbed up the two flights in silence, each lost in their own thoughts. The second floor was noisy after the quiet of the stairs and Peter's mum, Mona and Sally looked around in confusion.

"This way." Peggy led them down a long corridor with several doors along its length. Sally glanced into a couple of the rooms as they passed. There were six beds to each room and all the patients were young men with various parts of their bodies covered in bandages. One had most of his face covered and gazed back at her with his good eye.

"'Ello, darling. You come to visit me, then?"

Sally smiled at him. "Not this time, but you never know your luck!"

The other patients in the room laughed.

Peggy smiled to herself. Sally was going to be absolutely fine. Now, all she had to worry about was Peter's reaction to his injuries. She carried on down the corridor to the end, then through a set of double doors and into another hallway. There were several doors leading off this corridor on both sides and Peggy stepped toward the third door on the right and opened it. Peter was lying in the bed nearest the window. He was facing away, toward the window and she couldn't see his expression. The bedclothes were raised and she couldn't tell whether they had amputated both legs or just one. The other patients glanced up with interest at Peggy, who smiled and closed the door.

"I need to go and find the ward sister first and make sure you can go in." Peggy ignored the impatient expression on Sally's face.

Fortunately, Sister appeared at that moment and Peggy hurried over to explain the situation. They watched while she inclined her head and then pointed to her watch. Peggy returned to the others.

"We can see him for ten minutes and then we'll have to go. Visiting hours are from three o'clock to five and again this evening from seven to nine." Before she'd finished speaking, Sally was through the door and heading purposefully towards Peter's bed. The others watched, but they need not have worried. Within seconds, Sally had her arms around Peter and he was hugging her back, his head on her shoulder. His eyes were closed and he was smiling.

"Perhaps we should wait out here for a few minutes," Mona began, but Sally was already calling them in and they crowded round his bed, leaving Peggy alone holding open the door. She hesitated briefly, then made her way towards Peter.

"Hello, Peter," she said. "I'm pleased to see you're safe. You gave us a bit of fright. I'll leave you all to catch up. If you need me I'll be in the Emergency Ward or I'll see you back at home, Sally."

****

Somewhere in France

The sun was shining and Louis' headache gradually cleared. He grinned to himself. The war was definitely improving. The last couple of days had been much better than the first few and he was getting closer to Brigitte with every step. He ducked under a low hanging branch and strode quickly across the small clearing until he was back in the cover of the trees again. Ahead, he could see a hill and he approached the incline with confidence.

The bullet missed him by inches and he threw himself flat on the ground. His heart was pounding and he crawled towards the base of the hill for protection. He had no idea where the shot had come from, other than the general direction which appeared to be to his left.

Another bullet whistled passed him, narrowly missing his nose and Louis glanced around frantically for somewhere to hide. The sniper had chosen well. The hillside was bare, with little vegetation, other than a few sparse bushes further to his right. Louis looked back to where the shot had come from and spotted a portly man with a peaked cap striding towards him. Louis frowned. The man was French. Why was he trying to kill him? He stood up.

"What the hell are you shooting at me for?" he yelled.

The man raised the rifle and aimed at him. Louis could feel the sweat forming on his upper lip and he cursed himself for presenting the man with such a good target.

"You fucked my wife," the man shouted back.

Louis stared at him in disbelief. Half the German army were likely to descend on them and this man was shooting at him because he'd slept with his wife.

"You've made a mistake." Louis tried hard not to sound desperate. "I'm a soldier, I'm trying to get back to my girlfriend before the Germans get there. I don't have time to mess about…" He stopped as the man's finger tightened on the trigger. "Look, I really have no idea who you are. You've got me mixed up with someone else, I swear."

"Then why are you wearing my clothes?"

Louis opened his mouth but nothing came out. He couldn't think of anything he could say to get himself out of this mess.

"For God's sake, Etienne, he's not the one. He's just a soldier I gave some clothes to. I told you, the soldier I slept with went in the other direction."

To Louis' relief, Gabrielle had appeared and was running towards her husband who turned to her, lowering his gun. Louis decided not to wait around to see what would happen next. He began running towards the trees on his right. He was going in the wrong direction, but didn't care. The trees would provide cover and he could double back when that gun-wielding maniac had gone. He waited for the shot but there was silence. He disappeared into the trees and risked one quick glance back. Gabrielle and her husband were standing arguing in the middle of the field and he was forgotten.

****

Dunkirk, France

Although skirting the edges of the fields took longer than taking the more direct route, their patience paid off and they reached the outskirts of Dunkirk without incident. Once there, the situation changed. Within minutes, they were confronted by a solidly constructed road-block manned by British troops who refused to let them come through. Charles showed them his dog tags which he was wearing under his civilian clothes and argued, but to no avail.

"Sorry, mate. You're service personnel, you can come through, but we're not allowed to let civilians past. No exceptions." The soldier sounded tired and resigned. "There's no point them coming through anyway. None of the ships can get across here, and those that can – and there aren't many of them – aren't taking civilians. Orders are to evacuate the military, otherwise the whole bleeding BEF will be in German hands and then there'll be nothing left to stop them invading Britain next." Turning to Jean-Paul, he raised his voice and spoke slowly, "You'd do better to go home and find somewhere to hide until the fighting stops. It's not likely to be long: we can't withdraw any further than here and the Frog army has pretty much surrendered."

"I can vouch for them," Charles pleaded. "They saved me from capture when my plane crashed."

"Look, mate." The soldier glared at him. "I'm not trying to be deliberately rude, but we've seen thousands of refugees in the past few days. We're short of supplies and ammunition and the Jerries keep trying to use the refugees to smuggle in fifth columnists. I'm sure this lot are fine and dandy but our orders are not to let *any* civilians through. Anyway, I already told you, there's no point," he added before Charles could argue again. "Like I said, the ships won't take them, even if I did let you all through. Their best bet would be to go home and wait for the surrender." Charles stared at him, aghast. "We're on the run and there's nothing to stop them once we've left. *Our* priority, is to get home and protect our *own* country."

While they were arguing, the shelling grew heavier and the air was filled with Junkers, Stukas, Hurricanes and Spitfires fighting for air supremacy. Several times, the small party had to throw themselves into the ditch and the British soldiers took cover, while Stukas flew low overhead strafing the road.

Seeing their entry was barred, Marcel slumped by the side of the verge. He was tired, hungry and dispirited. He would never find his brother in all this confusion and, if they weren't taking civilians across the Channel, how could he get possibly to England?

Jean-Paul beckoned to Charles

"You should go through and take your chances, Charles. There's no point us trying. We'll have to head towards Calais and see if we can get a boat from there."

Charles was shocked. He had assumed they would all travel together. It had not occurred to him his French friends would not be allowed through. He gazed around, trying to find inspiration from somewhere. Jean-Paul watched him, a sad smile on his face

"You are welcome to come with us, Charles. However, there's not much point, is there?"

There was a short silence while Charles finally accepted there was no other option, then he shook his head. "You're right. Much as I would prefer to come with you, I think duty demands I stay here and help with the defence and hope I'll be evacuated with the others." He stretched out his hand to Jean-Paul. "Thank you for all your help and I do hope you get to England safely. If you do, please look me up. I wrote my address down earlier in case we were separated. If you need anyone to vouch for you, then please give them my name." There was a brief whispered conversation between the two men, before Jean-Paul took the piece of paper Charles offered and something else, which Jean-Paul secreted surreptitiously into his pocket. Then, ignoring his outstretched hand, Jean-Paul gave Charles a hug. He was quickly followed by Marcel and the women, before they began heading back the way they had come.

"Good luck," Charles called, watching them retrace their steps. "I think you're going to need it," he muttered quietly to himself. Turning towards, Dunkirk he murmured under his breath, "And by the looks of this lot, so will I." He hurried back to the barrier, where the soldiers let him through without argument.

"I should head towards the beach area, mate," one of the soldiers shouted after him. "That's where they're trying to evacuate from. Keep your head down though… them bloody Stukas and Junkers keep strafing and bombing everyone." He was about to turn back when he added, "Can't think where the ruddy RAF's got to!" Charles ignored the jibe and headed in the direction of the beach to join the thousands of others hoping to be rescued and taken home to England.

****

Bethune, Northern France

"Did you go and see Marie?" Fabian asked.

"Yes, I rode over on my bike, I've just got back." Brigitte lied. She'd been up to visit the Germans and had been wondering how she could account to her father for her absence. She'd not been able to find Wolfgang at the makeshift camp that was growing rapidly, however the two sentries on duty had been more than helpful. She patted her pocket to make sure the money was there and met her father's eyes.

"She was very upset, of course, but grateful I had come up to see her. She said she'd let me know when the funeral was." Brigitte was quite pleased with her improvised answer. There was no way her father could guess she was lying.

"Good girl." Fabian smiled at his daughter. Perhaps the war would make her grow up and start behaving responsibly. "Had she heard anything from Louis?"

Brigitte shook her head, her face darkening in anger when she recalled how long it was since she'd heard from him. "No, nothing, but like you said he's probably too busy trying to escape the Germans."

Fabian mistook the anger on her face for grief and he reached out and patted her arm. "I'm sure he'll be alright, Brigitte. Try not to worry too much."

Taken by surprise, Brigitte couldn't immediately think of an answer, so she smiled instead. She had no intention of worrying about Louis. She had better things to do.

****

Lambeth Hospital, London

While she retraced her steps back to the emergency wards, Peggy yawned. Her restless night had left her tired and she would've liked nothing more than to go home and put her feet up with a good book. Thank goodness she had the afternoon off and Ethel was doing the shopping. She reached the bottom of the stairs and was about to head towards the Emergency Ward when a familiar voice hailed her: "Hello, we don't often see you up here." Intent on not being any later, she hadn't heard anyone approach and she glanced up in surprise.

"Hello, Christopher."

"Chris," he corrected.

"Hello, *Chris*." Peggy smiled and then explained, "My friend's fiancé was brought in last night. He's had his leg amputated and I just came to give her some moral support."

Chris frowned. "I'm sorry to hear that. How is he?"

"I don't know, to be honest. Once I saw my friend was alright, I left her and his family to it. They didn't really need me standing around watching." She began to walk away.

"Wait, Peggy. How would you feel about coming to the pictures with me, or for a drink one evening?"

She hesitated, thinking of Sally and Peter. "Thank you very much for asking Chris, but I'm engaged and I'm not sure whether I should."

"I only meant as friends, nothing else." He backtracked rapidly.

Despite her earlier intentions to say yes, Peggy still wasn't sure. There might be all sorts of good reasons for Joe not writing to her, although she really couldn't think of any. She made up her mind. "Okay then. Thanks, I'd love to," she blurted out. Chris was almost wrong footed by her answer. He'd expected to have to work harder. However, he was determined to strike while the iron was hot.

"How about this weekend?"

"I'll give you my address." Peggy was rapidly regretting her hasty decision but she wasn't sure how she could withdraw her acceptance. Perhaps an excuse would come to her before the weekend.

"I'll pick you up at half seven on Saturday evening and we can go for a drink," Chris persisted. Peggy nodded and searched around for an escape. There was no-one in sight. Thinking hard, she found a way to change the subject. "How's the young man who came in yesterday? The one with the maggots in his wound?"

"As a matter of fact, I've just come from there. He's doing very well. They operated last night and caught the infection just in time, so they didn't need to amputate. He should make a full recovery."

"Oh, that's wonderful. I'm glad."

She glanced around again and this time, to her relief, she saw Sally bounding down the stairs behind her. She appeared much more like her old self and Peggy smiled. "I gather everything is alright, then?"

"Yes. They managed to save his other leg and they are going to give him an artificial one. The damage was only from the knee down, so it's not too bad." She suddenly noticed Peggy had been talking to someone and turned to look at him more closely. "Hello, I'm Sally," she introduced herself.

"Hello, Sally. I'm Chris. I gather the news is good about your fiancé?"

"Yes, I think so. We'll know more tomorrow. I haven't interrupted anything, have I?"

"No. Chris was just saying hello and I was on my way downstairs to do some work." Peggy began, steering Sally towards the main entrance. "Goodbye," she added over her shoulder.

"Goodbye, Peggy." Chris sounded as if he was smiling. Blushing furiously, Peggy headed for the door.

"He's nice." Sally glanced sideways at Peggy. "Who is he?"

"No-one important, just a student doctor." Peggy changed the subject. "Is everything is alright between the two of you? You were very quick?"

Sally was much happier "I thought I'd better let Mona and his mum get a look in. I've arranged go back later during visiting hours. Then we can be alone for a while." She smiled at Peggy. "You were right about him thinking his injury would change everything. That was the first thing he said, I shouldn't tie myself down to a cripple." Peggy was concerned but Sally laughed. "Thanks to your warning, I had my answer ready. I told him not to be ridiculous. I never wanted to marry him for his appearance anyway. I love him because of who he is and he hasn't had his personality amputated, just part of his leg. So there's no reason for him to consider anything has changed." Peggy was amused at the defiant expression on Sally's face.

"That told him then?"

Sally grinned. "Yes it did, rather. I could tell he had been worrying quite a bit. Aren't men silly sometimes? Right," she finished. "You need to go back to work and I had better make the effort to go into the office and let them know about Peter. If I don't, I won't have a job to go back to and then I'll have to join the women's land army or something, God forbid!" She hugged Peggy and disappeared out of the door in the direction of the tube station.

****

Dunkirk, France

The others didn't speak until they were back in the relative safety of one of the fields off the main highway. The heavy shelling and continual thudding of mortar rounds seemed slightly less intrusive here. The black smoke resulting from the intense bombardment swirling around in great clouds over Dunkirk was also thinner, making breathing easier. Jean-Paul took out his dog-eared map and studied it carefully while the others took the opportunity to sit down.

"Right, the coast road goes direct to Calais. However, I think that will be very unsafe and probably full of refugees who will be a target for the German planes. If we back-track to the woods, we can cross this lane here." He pointed to a small track cutting across the countryside. "And then head in the general direction of Calais across country. There are no wooded areas I can see, but we will probably come across farmhouses: maybe we'll get lucky again." Seeing their downcast expressions, he tried to cheer them up. "Come on, the situation's not so bad. We're alive and we're in with a chance. The sun is shining and it's a beautiful day."

Marcel stood up and Jeanne moved towards him, falling in by his side. Claudette held out her hand and Jean-Paul took it gratefully. Marcel and Jeanne walked in silence for some time until Jeanne asked him about his brother.

"Louis is great fun. Everything a brother should be." Marcel smiled.

"Does he look like you?"

"No, he's a lot thinner. He does have blond hair and blue eyes though. I always think he resembles my mum, but she can't see it. Maybe his mannerisms remind me of her..." Marcel went quiet. He was feeling homesick and missing his family more than he could ever put into words. Lost in his memories, he wasn't immediately aware that Jeanne had taken his hand, like it was the most natural thing in the world. When he did notice, he squeezed her hand in thanks. Neither of them spoke and they continued hand in hand, feeling strangely content and at ease with the world. Marcel finally broke the silence. "I really like you, Jeanne."

"I should hope so, since you haven't let go of my hand for the last ten minutes." Jeanne's eyes were laughing as she gazed up at him.

"Do you think your parents will mind?"

"No, I am sure they won't. My parents like and trust you or they would not have let you stay with us."

Claudette nudged Jean-Paul. He looked at her and then to where she was pointing. In front of them, Marcel and Jeanne were walking hand in hand. Pleased to have something else to think about, Jean-Paul smiled.

"Do you remember when we first met?"

Claudette nodded. "Yes, I do. You were insufferably arrogant and assumed I would fall in love with you automatically, just because our parents had arranged it." She frowned. "We were very lucky, weren't we? I just want Jeanne to be happy like we were before this awful war started." She snuggled closer to him. "We will get out, won't we?" She sounded scared and Jean-Paul stopped and tilted her chin up, so she was looking straight into his eyes.

"I can't guarantee anything, but I can promise I will do everything within my power to make sure you're both safe. You and Jeanne are my life. I would protect you both until there was no breath left in my body." He stopped. "Come on, we're getting maudlin and those two will be out of sight if we don't get a move on."

****

Calais, France

By lunchtime, the situation across the part of Calais that remained in Allied hands was becoming increasingly chaotic.

"This is fucking ridiculous." Joe nearly fired at some civilians who were trying to find refuge from the bombing. "I can't see who I'm shooting at." Some more figures appeared through the smoke, Joe raised his rifle again, only to lower it in disgust when he realised his targets were unarmed French and Belgian soldiers.

"Instead of running away, why don't you get some weapons and help us?" he shouted in frustration. Joe's words fell on deaf ears and the foreign soldiers passed through their lines towards some empty buildings behind them.

"There must be thousands of the bastards just hiding instead of fighting." Chalky was furious.

"Makes you wonder why the hell we're here, doesn't it?" Joe yelled back.

By early afternoon, the fierce fighting became hand-to-hand in the tightly packed streets, and the British troops were forced back. Soldiers lobbed grenades from doorways, bullets ricocheted off buildings, firing was coming from all angles and all around Joe, men were dying. He wiped the sweat from his smoke-blackened face, wondered how much longer he was going to survive uninjured and prayed for a break in the relentless fighting.

Then, at three o'clock, the shelling stopped abruptly and an eerie silence replaced the bombardment.

Joe stared around in astonishment. Cautiously, he put his hands up to his ears. Perhaps he had gone deaf. Then he noticed everyone else was just as surprised. A few seconds later, they heard the sound of falling bricks in the distance. Joe breathed a sigh of relief until a thought struck him. Perhaps they had surrendered.

"What's going on?" he asked Chalky.

"'ow the 'ell do I know?" Chalky answered in exasperation. "Make the most of it. I'm sure they'll start again soon enough."

"Here, have a fag and a drink and, like Chalky says, let's enjoy the rest." Taffy handed Joe a cigarette and they sat down and tried to relax.

"God, I'm thirsty. I'd give anything for a couple of pints of cold water." Joe closed his eyes and drew the smoke deep into his lungs.

"Got anything to eat?" Chalky was eyeing Rob's remaining rations.

"Thought you didn't like the bully beef and biscuits?" Rob retorted.

"Only when I'm not *really* hungry." Chalky's sarcastic reply fell on deaf ears.

"Here, you can share mine," Joe broke the last of his biscuits in two.

"See, that's a true friend. When the chips are down, you soon find out who your mates are, *Rob!*" Chalky was exhausted, but he managed to smile at Joe. "Nah, mate. You're alright. You eat them. I'm not hungry, really. I'd much rather have this fag."

Joe shrugged. "Well if you're sure..." He ate the remains of his rations, drank some more water and then lit another cigarette. The smoke curled slowly up to the sky and he closed his eyes.

"Better fill your bottles with the last of the water." An NCO arrived with a large container. "Make sure you drink sparingly. There's no knowing when we'll get more."

Joe leaned forward and, after filling his bottle, collapsed back again and lit yet another cigarette.

The brief lull only lasted an hour, which seemed like no time at all to the exhausted troops. They were virtually out of supplies and the resumption of the fighting left them in no doubt their current positions were becoming untenable.

Chapter Twenty-nine

Somewhere in France

Louis soon forgot about Gabrielle and her angry husband. He travelled all day and, by late afternoon was searching for somewhere safe to sleep. The horizon was empty of properties as far as the eye could see, so he decided his only option was to forget about cutting across country and to take the shorter route down the narrow lane that snaked through this part of the countryside. With a bit of luck, there would be a village along the way and he would find an abandoned property in which he could rest for a while.

To his relief, the road was silent and deserted and he made good time. He began to relax and then, at a sharp bend, he suddenly heard the sound of vehicles approaching. The road was bordered by hedges too high to climb over and too thick to squeeze through. Louis increased his pace until he came to small gap just big enough for him to force his way through into the pasture behind. He was just in time. Several trucks swept past on the other side of the bushes and Louis found himself holding his breath.

The troops took some time to disappear, during which Louis pressed himself into the shrubs, hoping he would not be spotted. The lane behind him fell silent, Louis let out a slow breath and stared ahead. In the distance, set back from a winding track was a small farmhouse with a large barn by the side. There were no signs of life, but Louis had no intention of going too close until he was sure. He moved forward cautiously until he was near enough to watch the properties properly and settled down on some grass beside a tall tree to wait.

Having watched for several moments, Louis was reasonably sure the buildings were empty. Heart pounding, he crept forward towards the barn, pushed open the door and stepped inside. He made his way cautiously to the bales of straw and glanced around. This would do, but first he needed some food, which meant approaching the small farmhouse. He went back outside. The dwelling also appeared silent and deserted and, feeling more confident, he strode boldly up to the front door. Before he could knock, the door flew open and he found himself staring down the barrel of an ancient shotgun.

****

Northern France

As evening approached and the shadows began to lengthen, Jeanne turned to her father. "Where are we going to sleep tonight?" she asked. Staring into the distance, she couldn't see any woods at all and the thought of sleeping in the open didn't seem very sensible.

"I don't know. Let's keep our eyes peeled and hopefully we'll find somewhere suitable."

They were still heading towards Calais when they saw an isolated farmhouse in the distance. The shelling was much lighter here, and they approached the farmhouse with caution. There was no sign of life, but their experiences taught them not to take anything for granted.

"Hello?" Jean-Paul called out. "Hello, is there anyone there?"

There was no answer. Jean-Paul glanced at the others. "Let's go a little closer," he suggested and they all edged towards the farmhouse door. Once they were nearer, they could see the door was slightly ajar. Although there was no sign of anyone, Claudette had the oddest feeling they were being watched. She spun round, but could see nothing. Despite the warmth of the day, Claudette shivered.

"What's wrong?" Jean-Paul asked, seeing her agitation.

"I don't know. Something doesn't feel right, I can't put my finger on it…" Her voice trailed off as they heard a noise from inside the house.

"Hello?" Jean-Paul shouted again. There was no answer. He motioned for the women to stand behind him and, taking a deep breath, pushed the door open. The house was dark inside and his eyes took several seconds to adjust. At first there didn't appear to be anything out of the ordinary, then he noticed someone was sitting in the armchair facing the door. He opened his mouth to speak and then closed it again. There would be no point speaking to the man, because there was a large hole in his head and the wall behind was splattered with dried blood.

****

Somewhere in France

Startled, Louis raised his hands and looked up. The owner of the shotgun was an elderly man, his face heavily wrinkled. Behind his round glasses, the blue eyes that met Louis' unwaveringly, were pale with red veins and his remaining hair was grey.

"I don't mean you any harm," Louis began, his voice hoarse from lack of moisture.

"What do you want?" The man's tone was brusque but the finger on the trigger relaxed slightly.

"I'm trying to get home before the Boche get there. I haven't eaten and I…" Louis tailed off when he saw the man's expression harden.

"And you decided you'd rob me?" he interrupted

Louis shook his head and then decided to be honest. "I thought if no one was here, there might be some food I could take." He hung his head in disgust at the depths to which he had sunk, missing the glint of amusement that crossed the man's face.

"Well you'd better come in then." He lowered the shotgun and stepped aside, allowing a shocked Louis to enter his house. Glancing round, Louis saw the kitchen was quite sparse, but the range was lit.

"Sit down. I'll make you something to eat." The man indicated a chair near a rather rickety table

"Thank you." Louis was stunned the man had invited him in. "I'm sorry, I can't pay you."

"Don't worry yourself." The man was already cracking eggs into a large bowl and, while Louis watched, he added some chopped tomatoes and sliced cheese. "I know what it's like to flee those murdering bastards." He peered at Louis over his glasses. "You can call me Gilbert, and you are?"

"Louis."

"Where were you based?" Gilbert asked.

"The Maginot Line. At Ouvrage Brehain near Brehain-la-Ville." Louis saw little point in lying.

"Bloody useless having a defensive line stopping at the Belgian border," the man complained. He poured the egg mixture into a large pan already heating on the range. "Can't believe the whole flaming army's collapsed," he continued to himself. Seeing Louis' despondent face he said, "Don't give up, lad. There's more than one way to skin a rabbit." Louis frowned and then shook his head

"They're going to overrun the whole country. How can we stop them?"

The man shrugged "You can't. You don't have to make their lives comfortable, though." Gilbert turned his attention back to the stove, flipped the omelette and reached for some bread. "Here lad, get that inside you." He dished up the food and handed a large plate to Louis. Starving, Louis began shovelling the food in his mouth while the man watched.

"Slow down, lad. There's plenty more where that came from." He reached for a bottle of wine and poured them both a drink. Louis downed the cold liquid in one gulp, hoping to silence the voice in his head that kept reminding him of his cowardice.

Gilbert refilled his glass and watched as Louis drank deeply before turning his attention back to his food. "Not your fault you lost, Louis. You can't be held responsible for other people's mistakes; the generals, the politicians, they're the ones at fault. Not you." For a moment, Louis was almost tempted the tell the man the truth, but he couldn't do that. Gilbert would throw him out and he would be on his own again. Gilbert seemed unaware of his discomfort and continued talking. "Anyway, like I said, there's other ways to fight. We might have lost the first battle but that doesn't mean we've lost the war, eh boy?" Gilbert reached over to refill Louis' glass again and patted him on the back.

Louis nodded, his mouth full of food. In his head, the voice had changed direction. From berating him for his lack of courage, the voice now suggested that he could still be a hero; all he had to do was to find a different way.

There was silence while Louis finished the meal. As he ate, he considered Gilbert's words. He had no idea how he could fight back but, once he got home, he would go and visit his friends. Between them there must be something they could do.

****

Northern France

Jean-Paul took in the scene before him and immediately pulled the door closed, shutting out the view. He turned to his wife and daughter

"Wait here."

"What's the matter?" Claudette was pale, her imagination running riot.

"There's a dead man sitting in the chair facing the door. He's been shot. It's not a very nice sight. Looks like he's been dead some time, well a day or two anyway," he amended. "Stay here while Marcel and I have a look around. Keep your eyes open. I don't think there's anyone else here, well not anyone who's alive anyway, but I can't be sure. Are you alright to come in with me, Marcel?"

"Yes, of course." Marcel could feel the sweat forming on his upper lip, but he nodded anyway. Taking a deep breath to steady his nerves, he pushed open the door and stepped inside. The room was silent. He took another step and the floorboard creaked, making him jump. He felt Jean-Paul's steadying hand on his shoulder and he used his sleeve to wipe the sweat off his face. Avoiding looking at the dead man, he focused instead on the stairs to the left. Jean-Paul stepped in front of him, eyes scanning the rest of the room. There was no one there. They inched towards the stairs, taking care to make as little noise as possible, and began to climb upwards. There were ten steps and Marcel had reached the seventh stair when they heard the noise, the same sound they had heard from outside. This time Jean-Paul recognised it. The noise sounded like a creaking floorboard. He turned towards Marcel and raised a restraining hand. There was no need, the boy had already stopped. Jean-Paul pointed to the top of the stairs and then to the right and mouthed, "I think there's someone in there." He was pointing to the door on the right of the landing above the room where the dead body was. "Be careful!"

Marcel could feel the sweat trickling down the back of his neck and his legs felt like jelly. He inched forward, following Jean-Paul, who he suddenly noticed was armed with a small pistol. Marcel stopped in surprise, and Jean-Paul waved his arms, impatiently directing him back to the task in hand, at the same time mouthing the word "*Charles*." Marcel took a few seconds to understand that Charles must have given Jean-Paul his pistol before they separated. That would explain the brief whispered conversation he had seen between them just before they went their separate ways.

Once they were positioned on either side of the door, Jean-Paul counted silently to three. On three, Marcel flung open the door and Jean-Paul stepped into the doorway, gun in hand. Immediately, he lowered it again. Marcel, following behind him, stopped in astonishment. In the corner of the bedroom was a small child of about four or five years old. She was curled up on the threadbare carpet in the corner of the room by the window, her small fist in her mouth and there was terror written all over her face. Her face was streaked with dried tears and her long blonde curly hair was tangled and disheveled. As Jean-Paul lowered the gun, she began to scream.

"Claudette, Jeanne, come here quickly!" Jean-Paul stepped back onto the landing and shouted down the stairs, making no attempt to go near the screaming child. Within a few seconds, they were in the bedroom and Claudette edged towards the terrified girl. She scooped the child up in her arms, crooning gently until the screaming became sobs and then gradually subsided altogether.

While Claudette rocked the girl, Jean-Paul beckoned to Marcel. "Let's make sure the other rooms are empty." Seeing the child alone, with presumably her dead father downstairs, he had begun to wonder where the child's mother was. A disturbing thought occurred to him and he wanted to make sure neither the child nor his own wife and daughter made any unpleasant discoveries.

The room opposite was a bathroom and, after a cursory glance, Jean-Paul was satisfied it was empty and undisturbed. The room next to the one they had found the child in was obviously the parents' room and wasn't empty. On the bed was the naked body of a woman, covered in bruises and cuts. There was dried blood on the bed and a knotted stocking around her throat. Marcel promptly rushed back to the bathroom where he emptied the contents of his stomach down the toilet. Jean-Paul closed his eyes for a moment and offered up a silent prayer. He hoped she had not suffered too much. However, seeing the condition she was in, that was probably unlikely. Somehow, he suppressed the anger rising inside him and he busied himself trying to find something to cover the body. Finding a long, pale blue cotton dressing gown hanging on the hook behind the bedroom door, he placed the robe gently over her body and, closing the door behind him, he went to find Marcel.

"Are you alright?" Jean-Paul was concerned about the effect the sight must have had on him, but he needed Marcel's help. "We have to make sure the child and the women don't go in there," he continued without waiting for a response.

Marcel made a supreme effort to pull himself together.

"Let's go back to them, or they'll come searching for us." He helped Marcel up from the floor where he was sitting in front of the toilet and they went back into the child's bedroom.

Claudette raised her eyebrows and Jean-Paul shook his head. He didn't want to say anything in front of the young girl but Claudette could tell by the expression on his face he didn't have good news. She pulled the little girl deeper into her arms. "Can you find me some clean clothes, Jeanne?" Claudette asked. "We'll go and give her a quick wash and change her clothes… can you do something with…?" This time her words were directed at Jean-Paul and she pointed downstairs.

Jean-Paul signalled his assent. "Come on, Marcel." And together they went back downstairs to the small sitting room.

****

Catford, London

Olive went to the Post Office on the way home. Tom wasn't due until Saturday but she wanted to make sure she had the money in plenty of time. The teller gave her a strange look. Olive rarely drew out any extra during the week, especially not ten pounds, but Olive glared at him and the young man handed her two five pound notes.

Olive placed the money in her purse and hurried back to the flat. Tom had said he would be there any time after four o'clock every Saturday evening. Although she had argued that would mean leaving work early every week, he had just shrugged. Olive drew a deep breath. She would try and take back some control when he did arrive. He wanted the money, so she must be able to make him see that her leaving work early every Saturday could draw suspicion towards them. Surely he would want to avoid that? Then she realised she had the most to lose. Although he would go to prison for blackmail, she would hang for murder. He held all the cards.

****

Marcel found it difficult to touch the body and the smell made him feel sick, however Jean-Paul needed his help to move the man. Steeling himself and breathing though his mouth, Marcel helped Jean-Paul half carry, half drag the body across the floor and out through the door. Sweating from their exertions, they went back to the room and took the chair in which he had been sitting and the large blood-stained rug, outside too.

"Should we bury him?" Marcel asked.

"Yes, if we can find somewhere. Can you look around for a shovel or something to dig with?" While Marcel went into the dilapidated barn to search, Jean-Paul hunted around for a suitable place. Within a short time, Marcel reappeared with a large spade and Jean-Paul pointed to the small orchard a few metres from the back door. "Over there seems as good a place as any. You need to make the grave big enough for two."

The orchard consisted of seven fruit trees all covered in pink and white blossom, holding the promise of a bumper harvest. Marcel thought of the young couple who would never see that year's crop and, in silence, he began digging a large hole. While he was busy, Jean-Paul went back inside and tried to clean the walls, so there were no obvious signs of the brutal murder that had taken place. When Marcel finished, he went to fetch Jean-Paul and, between them, they dragged the body across the yard and put the corpse into the freshly dug grave.

"Let's go and get the woman's body while they're in the bathroom. Are you alright to help me, only I don't think I can move her on my own?" Marcel had no idea, but he followed Jean-Paul back upstairs anyway. They could hear the voices of the women in the bathroom and Jean-Paul knocked on the door and called out to reassure them it was him. When Jeanne opened the door, he told her what they were going to do. Jeanne went back in, making sure the door was closed firmly behind her.

Marcel and Jean-Paul wrapped the woman's body in a sheet and carried her down the stairs. Rigor mortis had set in, the body was stiff and awkward to move and they had to keep stopping to get their breath back. By the time they reached the yard, Jean-Paul and Marcel were both sweating. They placed her body next to her husband's and, after saying a quick prayer, refilled the hole with the soil that had been removed. When they finished, Marcel searched around for a stick to mark the grave and they both stood in silence, lost in their thoughts.

Chapter Thirty

Bethune, Northern France

Brigitte checked the envelope hidden under her mattress and smiled. She had almost seven hundred francs now and Wolfgang was due again later that evening. She frowned as she remembered his expression when she'd told him how much he owed her. Eventually, after a brief hesitation, he'd nodded and handed over the cash. She had noticed he had begun treating her differently since then; he was much more dictatorial, ordering her to do things to him instead of asking, but she didn't really mind. She found his new authority quite exciting. However, she was fed up with never going out. The Germans were obviously here to stay for a while, which meant her father and the rest of the town would have to get used to seeing her in their company. Her father was a hypocrite. He was quite happy to fawn over the occupiers and take their money, but he objected to his daughter going out with them.

In any case, she would never earn enough to go south like this, she needed to meet some new people and the best way was through Wolfgang's friends. She would have to persuade him to introduce them to her.

****

"We're pulling back to the railway sheds, lads," Woody ordered.

"If we move back much further, we'll be in the bloody sea," Rob grumbled as Joe threw one of his three remaining grenades into the road, killing four advancing German infantrymen and they took the opportunity to pull back to the corner of the street leading to the railway sheds.

Using the first one for cover, they were about to pull back further when Chalky stopped and shoved Joe out of the way, at the same time waving his arms at Rob and Taffy who were following.

"Wait!" he shouted.

"What's wrong?" Joe peered into the distance but couldn't see anything.

"I think I saw…" Chalky was waving his hands trying to disperse the dense smoke. "I'm sure I saw movement over… Yes… to the right… now!"

Joe spun round just in time to see a shape coming at him out of the thick clouds of debris and dust thrown up in the last barrage. There was no opportunity to take aim and Joe fired automatically. The advancing German's head exploded, a mass of blood, brains and bones spattering onto Joe's uniform. Before he could register this, another German came out of the dust and he fired again. By this time, Chalky was also firing, although they were unable to see if the Germans were advancing. Rob and Taffy had also opened fire and bullets were flying everywhere, ricocheting off walls and rattling across the roof tiles.

"Cease firing!" The yell came from Woody who had come forward to support them. "Chalky! For fuck's sake, Chalky! They're dead! Cease firing!" Chalky and Joe slowly lowered their rifles, suddenly aware of the comparative silence.

The rest of the withdrawal was uneventful. Much of the heavy shelling was concentrated on other areas and the noise gradually diminished. However, the wind grew stronger, fanning the flames and spreading the smoke throughout the town. Joe, Chalky, Rob and Taffy dug themselves a deep slit trench and waited. They had lost another ten men and only had one Bren gun and a few three-inch mortar bombs left. There was very little water remaining and their ammunition was dangerously low. Those who had survived unscathed considered themselves lucky; but for how much longer? "Smoke?" Taffy offered Joe one of his few remaining cigarettes.

"Are you sure?" Joe asked. "You've not got many left."

"Yeah. I'll scrounge yours tomorrow! Mind you, if this keeps up we won't be needing them. Where's the bleeding Navy and the RAF? Are we the only ones fighting this ruddy war?" Taffy lit up and watched the smoke curling lazily up into the sky.

"Get some rest, lads, while you can," Woody called across from his own trench. "Unless you'd like to take some guard duty?"

"Not bloody likely, Corp. Thanks for the offer, though," Joe answered for all of them. They finished their cigarettes, closed their eyes and tried to block out the smoke and the sound of the flames as Calais continued to burn in front of them.

Although the bombardment had stopped, the flames and smoke from the burning buildings were fanned by the increasing strength of the wind. From a distance, the whole of Calais appeared to be alight and the sky was glowing red from the fires raging unabated.

****

Northern France

Eventually, Jean-Paul nudged Marcel and, crossing the yard, they returned to the house where they found Claudette and the little girl in the sitting room. Jeanne was in the kitchen cooking some food she had found in the larder while Claudette was seated on a worn settee rocking the child.

"Has she told you her name?" Jean-Paul was anxious not to frighten the girl, so he addressed his question to Claudette.

"I'm Angelique," she introduced herself before Claudette could answer. "What's your name?"

"Jean-Paul." He smiled at her. "How old are you, Angelique?"

"You can call me Angel." She gave him a shy smile. "I'm five, well nearly five. It's my birthday soon. We're going to…" She stopped and began to whimper.

Jean-Paul gently patted her shoulder and went to help Jeanne, who was in the middle of cooking some rabbit she had found hanging in the larder. Marcel was busy preparing a green salad, having found a vegetable garden outside the kitchen window. Jeanne had also found onions and tomatoes which she was going to add to the meat.

"That smells good." Jean-Paul savoured the aroma of the cooking food. "I'm starving, but I think after we've eaten, we should move on. I don't think we should spend the night here."

"Why not?" Jeanne sounded surprised. "We could sleep in this room and then leave early in the morning. It's got to be better than sleeping outside somewhere, surely."

To Jean-Paul's surprise, Marcel was in agreement. "Jeanne's right, sir. We can take turns to keep watch, but I think we'll all be more comfortable in here."

"Alright." Jean-Paul shrugged. "Claudette?"

Claudette agreed. "The strange feeling I had is gone now. We should stay till morning. It will give Angel time to recover a little and she may be able to tell us if she has any relatives nearby. If not, we'll have to take her with us."

Although it was obvious they'd need to take the little girl, Jean-Paul realised he had not given the matter any thought. However, there was no other option; they certainly couldn't leave her behind.

"Staying here it is, then." He turned back to Jeanne. "How's the dinner doing?" He smiled down at Angel who had stopped crying and was watching him, a wary expression on her face. "Are you hungry?"

Angel nodded. She seemed less apprehensive now.

"Good. Let's eat, then." Jeanne brought over a large plate for Angel with the rabbit, bread and salad invitingly laid out in the form of a smiling face. "Look," she pointed to the meat. "There's the mouth, the tomatoes are the eyes, the bread is the beard and the salad is the hair."

Angel laughed and began to gulp down the food. Marcel hugged Jeanne. "You're really clever."

"Do we get the same?" Jean-Paul asked, making everyone laugh and then there was silence while they made the most of the first proper meal they had eaten for two days. Having finished the food, they cleared up and Claudette went upstairs to find some bedding. While she was busy, Jean-Paul switched on the wireless in an attempt to find out exactly what was happening.

The news was even worse than he'd expected. Dunkirk was holding out which was good news, but there was fighting around Boulogne and Calais. The broadcast finished with an announcement that people would be safer to go home, rather than taking their chances on the roads. Jean-Paul switched off the wireless and went to join the others.

Claudette had found them all blankets and they were curled up on the floor in the small sitting room. Angel was snuggled down with Jeanne on one side and Claudette on the other. She had not left Claudette's side since she had first picked her up and, although outwardly she seemed fine, they were all aware she must be deeply traumatised.

****

Calais, France

Now it was quiet, the fears Joe had successfully suppressed during the day while they were busy fighting, resurfaced and he found himself wondering if they were going to survive.

He lay there remembering the last time he'd seen Peggy. He could see her smiling face as he disappeared round the corner and, if he tried hard enough, he could remember how she felt in his arms and the taste of her lips on his. He wished they had been able to get married before he had been sent overseas. For the first time, he was grateful he'd slept with Elsie, even if he'd been too drunk to remember very much.

Otherwise he could have died a virgin. The morals and beliefs he had been brought up with didn't seem important anymore. He and Peggy hadn't made love, because they had been brought up to believe sex before marriage was wrong. He'd found restraining himself difficult at times and he had a feeling Peggy was only saying 'no' because of the stigma attached to women who slept with men before they were married. There was also the fear of pregnancy. He wished society was different. How wonderful to have made love to the woman he adored instead of a drunken fumble he couldn't really remember. How wonderful to have left her pregnant with his child. What if he was injured and couldn't father children in the future? Several of his friends had died today and he was sure some of them were virgins. Sighing restlessly, he changed position slightly, catching Chalky with his foot. Chalky was instantly awake, rifle pointing at Joe who whispered his apologies.

Chalky grunted and Joe watched with envy when Chalky appeared to go straight back to sleep. Joe lay with his eyes closed trying not to move and finally dozed off, only to be woken out of quite a deep sleep around midnight by the sound of heavy guns firing over their heads. This time though, the shells were going in the other direction.

Under cover of darkness, the Navy had arrived and the destroyers sitting off the coast had begun to shell the German positions.

"There you are, I was right!" Joe was exultant. "This is it, lads. The Navy'll sort them out, you'll see. Then, perhaps, they'll take us off."

"Mmm, we'll see," Chalky replied, ever the pessimist.

However, their cheers soon turned to horror when some of the shells fell short and they too came under fire. Unable to dig themselves in any deeper, they had no option but to try and sit out the barrage. Still worse was to come. At first, the naval bombardment kept the German shelling to a minimum. Then the Germans sent over Junkers 88s and Stukas to bomb the destroyers and the enemy gunners began to retaliate. For the entrenched men, exhausted, hungry and thirsty, the next two hours under German retaliation was worse than anything they had so far endured.

Eventually, the shelling stopped and, when daylight came, they gazed out to sea, only to discover the destroyers had gone.

Chapter Thirty-one

Northern France

"Did you sleep well?" Jeanne asked. "You were snoring loudly enough!"

"I don't snore." Marcel was indignant.

"Yes you do," Angel joined in. "Really, really loudly!"

Marcel blushed and was about to argue but they were all laughing so much, he smiled instead. With good spirits, they made a quick breakfast of porridge, coffee and bread and then packed up all the food they could carry.

"Are you leaving?" Angel asked. She had been watching the activity with increasing panic and they could hear the fear in her voice.

"Yes, Angel." Claudette immediately tried to reassure her. "We have to go, but don't worry, we're not going without you. We are taking you with us. You do want to come, don't you?" Claudette was concerned Angel would object. However, Angel was only worried they didn't go without her favourite doll. Relieved she was not about to make a scene, Claudette assured her they wouldn't and Jeanne went upstairs to hunt for the treasured toy. She soon spotted the figurine on the floor in the room where Angel had hidden. While Jeanne was there, she searched the small brightly decorated wardrobe and found some clothes and an extra pair of shoes for Angel. Although she hunted around for a bag or suitcase to put them in, Jeanne couldn't find one. She would have to try the main bedroom.

Jeanne hesitated before entering but she was sure Angel's mother would want her daughter cared for, so she took a deep breath and went in. Other than the bed, nothing else had been disturbed. She made her way to the large oak wardrobe where, hidden at the back behind some shoes, she located a medium sized, rather battered suitcase. Jeanne packed Angel's clothes and shoes and then checked the dressing table drawers for anything she could give Angel to remind her of her mother. She could only find some wedding photos and a couple of rings and she popped them quickly in the suitcase and went back downstairs where the others were waiting for her.

The idea of taking papers for Angel had come from Marcel who was concerned they might want to come back and find her relatives after the war. If they didn't have her name, that would be difficult. Jean-Paul agreed and had hunted around until he found some papers identifying all the family. On impulse, he decided to take all the papers with him, not just those identifying Angel. Putting them safely in the bottom of his bag, he forgot all about them. Jean-Paul took one last look round and, once he was sure they had all the food they could carry, as well as Angel's belongings, they left.

To Jean-Paul's relief, the sun was shining. They would have to travel slower today; there was no way a small child could walk at the same pace they had done for the last couple of days. Fortunately, Angel was not frightened of either him or Marcel, which meant they could take turns to carry her when she became tired. Trying to take the boredom off the monotonous journey, they sang songs and played games with her. Although they were reasonably safe in the fields and could relax a little, they still had to exercise their normal caution when crossing the roads or railway tracks. The shelling could be heard in the distance, but they were too far from either Calais or Dunkirk for the noise to be particularly intrusive.

Once they had distanced themselves from the farmhouse, Angel became chattier and seemed less traumatised. Claudette had insisted that pressing her for information would be cruel. It was best to allow Angel to talk in her own time and the others had respected Claudette's wishes and taken her advice. Angel was a lovely child and she already felt like part of the family. Marcel had never had a sister and at first he found having a little person chattering away in his ear rather strange. However, he gradually became used to her and took comfort from having yet another member in his adopted family. The affinity worked both ways and Angel increasingly went to Marcel rather than Claudette. Jeanne was touched to watch him taking great pains to amuse Angel and make sure she had every comfort.

"Should I be jealous?" she asked with a twinkle in her eye

Marcel pulled her close and hugged her. "I don't think you have anything to worry about." He took Jeanne's arm and they strolled along in companionable silence with Angelique beside them chattering away whenever she spotted different things that drew her attention. Jean-Paul and Claudette, following behind, watched with amusement and the morning passed quickly and without incident. They stopped for lunch in a small copse of trees which provided some welcome shade from the heat of the midday sun, while Jean-Paul studied the map and tried to work out exactly where they were. By his reckoning, they were near Sainte-Marie-Cheque, about a day and a half's walk from Calais, maybe longer if they had to make too many detours. They probably had enough food to last them and there were streams marked on the map from which they could get water. The big question was whether they could get there before the Germans.

****

Somewhere in France

Louis was feeling much happier after his chat with Gilbert. The old man had given him back his confidence and planted the idea of resistance in his head. From a dread of going home, Louis now couldn't wait to meet up with his friends and start planning some nasty surprises for the enemy. First though, he would call in on Brigitte. He was sure she would be delighted and probably very relived to see him.

The last signpost had stated there were only another thirty kilometres to Bethune, so if he kept going, he should be there by the following day, especially if he cut across country. The thought of seeing Brigitte cheered him up even more and, head down, a determined expression on his face, Louis left the road, jumped over the small hedge and began striding through the thickly planted wheat field.

****

Lambeth Hospital, London

The wards were busy and Peggy didn't have much time to talk to Helen when their paths crossed as they went about their duties. At lunchtime, they both stepped outside to get some fresh air. There were very few clouds in the sky and they took the opportunity to close their eyes and bask in the warmth of the early summer sun.

"According to one of the patients, the Admiralty have just announced we've lost another destroyer and a trawler." Helen's voice was low and Peggy could hear the pain. "All those poor sailors and their families, it doesn't bear thinking about."

"Any news from Jimmy or Annie?" Peggy asked.

"No, nothing. I've written to them both, though. I gave Annie your address and told Mum she could do the same." Helen gave a brief smile. "Thanks, Peggy. Mum was so grateful you let us use your address. We'll try not to overdo it, I promise."

"I don't mind, honestly. I'm glad to help."

There was silence then Helen asked, "Have you heard from Joe at all?"

"No, I haven't. It's probably just the post or he's having too much fun," she ended, trying to put a brave face on it. She was starting to get rather annoyed he hadn't bothered to write at all.

"He's definitely still in England though, isn't he?" Helen was facing the other way and Peggy couldn't see her face.

"Yes." Peggy felt her heart skip a beat. "Why? Do you know something I don't?"

Calais, France

Dug in to the sand dunes opposite Calais railway station, the few survivors of 'B' Company were pale, drawn and covered with stubble, their eyes gritty and red-rimmed from lack of sleep. Their uniforms were torn, tattered and filthy from three days of continuous fighting. Their throats were dry and sore from the cordite and the smoke and flames of the city burning all round them and their heads were pounding from a combination of dehydration and the noise from the constant bombardment. They were dangerously low on water, a situation made worse by having to listen to the gentle lapping of the waves on the shoreline behind them in the infrequent lulls in the shelling.

They could hear the steady advance of the Germans gradually overrunning the British positions in the town, coming closer with every bombardment and they braced themselves for the next attack, knowing there was nowhere else to withdraw to.

They were eating the last of their rations, when a low humming noise caught their attention.

"Oh shit!" Joe dropped the last of his biscuit and yelled, "Stukas!" All around him, men were trying to dig themselves even deeper into the sand dunes. Transfixed, Joe began to count the number of Stukas and Heinkels heading towards them. He reached one hundred and fourteen, before cowering at the bottom of the trench, covering his head with his arms, closing his eyes and praying.

The German planes attacked in groups of three, taking turns to dive bomb them, dropping a mixture of high explosive and incendiaries which left huge craters and showered them with sand and grit. The shelling was accompanied by the rattling of machine guns, a sound which could barely be heard above the noise of the bombardment, but the effects of which could be seen, the bullets whistling across the dunes spraying sand skyward. For the men dug deep into the dunes, each bomb seemed to come closer and closer and, as each one landed, Joe winced, wondering if this was the last thing he would hear.

"Parachutes!" Rob's warning came just in time.

Alerted by his shout, Joe lifted up his head and saw the approaching Germans. Aiming carefully to make each bullet count, he began to shoot at them while they spread out on the beach. To start with, they were able to shoot each man when he showed himself and hold them off without too much difficulty.

"Won't be long, and the Navy'll be here to take us off," Joe shouted above the shooting.

"Let's hope so," Taffy yelled back, although he had his doubts.

"I don't think so, lads." Woody was several feet away and his voice could only just be heard.

"What d'ya mean?" Chalky shouted

"I think we're meant to hold to the last man."

Joe stared in horror at Chalky and gulped. "That can't be right, surely?" Chalky made no comment. Joe turned to Taffy for reassurance. Taffy wasn't saying anything either. "But that's a death sentence…" Joe was stunned. He couldn't accept he would never go home. "I don't believe it," he added, a mutinous expression on his face.

"No, you're probably right." Rob spoke for the first time. "I'm sure the Navy will come and get us off. I heard from one of the 60th they're coming at fifteen hundred hours; if we hold out until then, we'll be fine."

This sounded a lot more promising and Joe immediately latched onto the lifeline Rob had just thrown him. They fought on doggedly but gradually the sheer weight of numbers, the lack of food, water and most importantly, ammunition began to take its toll. Despite this, they continued to hold on until the Germans managed to get a large trench mortar into position, directly in front of them. Their deeply-dug trenches afforded them little or no protection against this latest threat. Unlike the shelling from the field guns, which had often sailed harmlessly over them, the trench mortar's ability to fire shells that climbed vertically and then dropped directly onto them meant there was no longer anywhere for them to hide.

Bethune, Northern France

Brigitte lay back on the bed and watched Wolfgang pull up his trousers and reach for his shirt. "Why don't we go out together tomorrow evening? We could go to the cinema?"

Wolfgang stopped what he was doing and gazed down at her "I didn't think you wanted people to know you were collaborating with the enemy?"

Brigitte shrugged dismissively. "It's none of their business."

Wolfgang didn't answer. He saw no reason to take her out and spend money on her. He actually found her quite boring, although he had to admit she was more than satisfactory in bed. He pulled on his shirt and began to tuck it into his trousers.

"Well?" Brigitte pouted; she was not about to be ignored. Wolfgang saw her expression in the dressing table mirror and sighed inwardly. Perhaps he should introduce her to one of his friends. He turned towards her.

"Why don't you come with me and my friends tonight? We are only going to a bar for a drink, but I would like you to meet them."

Brigitte's face lit up. She climbed out of the bed and flung her arms round him. Wolfgang was about to push her away when he became aware of her naked body against him. He reached down and slapped her bare buttocks

"But first you can show me just how grateful you are," he whispered, pushing her down onto her knees and undoing his fly again. Brigitte took him deep into her mouth and, as she began sucking Wolfgang pushed her head into his groin and began thrusting faster and harder, his plans to share her forgotten for the moment.

****

"No!" Helen's response was too quick and Peggy eyed her with suspicion. "Well, not really. One of the men I was patching up this morning was chatting to another chap and I was sure one of them mentioned something about the Rifle Brigade being in Calais. I could be wrong though. You know how confused I get between regiments, battalions and companies and, anyway, there's more than one battalion in the Rifle Brigade isn't there? That's if I heard properly in the first place." Helen was beginning to wish she hadn't said anything. She didn't want to worry Peggy, especially if she had misheard.

Peggy felt the first niggling sensation of unease. If Joe was in France, that would explain why neither she nor Pauline had heard anything. She began to feel guilty about her earlier thoughts. Then she chastised herself. She was only surmising; she'd ask some of her patients in the afternoon to see if any of them knew anything. Normally wishing her lunch break was longer, Peggy now couldn't wait to get back to work. They weren't really meant to question the soldiers, because of the dangers of careless talk, but, if she was careful and only chose those who were willing to talk anyway, it shouldn't be too hard to ask about the Rifle Brigade.

The ward was even busier when they returned and Peggy hurried over to a young man with a filthy bandage covering his left eye. He was unconscious and she wondered if his eye was just damaged or whether, like others, he had lost it. She was unwinding the bandage slowly, not wanting to cause unnecessary discomfort when her eyes were drawn to the insignia badge on his arm.

The badge was a silhouette of a black cat sitting facing outwards on a red background. She had seen the same insignia on Joe's left arm at Christmas and he had explained the badge represented Dick Whittington's cat. She would recognise it anywhere. Her heart started to pound against her chest and she was having difficulty breathing. Surely they were in Suffolk? Joe wasn't in France. He couldn't be.

She had heard people say that when they were given bad news, the whole world stopped or went into slow motion, but she had never really understood before. A part of her mind recognised she was in shock whilst another part of her refused to grasp the fact that, at this very minute, Joe could be wounded, or even worse, dead. All the time she had believed Joe was safe and she was getting annoyed with him for not writing, he could have been fighting for his life. She felt sick and dizzy; the ward seemed to be spinning.

"Cooper, are you alright?" Peggy didn't answer. "Cooper! Peggy!" Peggy turned towards the voice that was coming from a long, long, way away.

"I think Joe's in France," she gasped before passing out in a heap on the floor.

Chapter Thirty-two

Olive reached down into her handbag and touched Kurt's letter. She had been delighted to receive another one so quickly but, because she no longer felt safe in her flat, she kept all his letters in her handbag which never left her side. There was no time to read them or even think too much, because the switchboard was busier than normal. The news from the continent was worse than ever and she hoped Kurt wasn't involved. Thoughts of him were the only thing keeping her going now.

She had no idea how she was going to get rid of the blackmailer. Fortunately she had quite a bit of money saved up, although it wasn't going to last long if she had to keep paying him. Perhaps she should move away? The thought had popped into her mind earlier, but if she did, there was no guarantee he wouldn't just notify the police. Wherever she went, the police would find her eventually and, if they didn't, the man might. The only other idea that had come to her was to try and find something on him, something she could use against him. She had a strange feeling this might have something to do with Kath but, at the moment, she couldn't think how that could possibly help her, so she filed the knowledge away.

She wished Kurt was with her. She was sure no one would get away with blackmailing Kurt. Olive frowned. She had no idea why that thought should be comforting. Perhaps deep down she felt Kurt would have understood why she'd killed Mary.

****

Joe was unable to hear his friends or even see them now. Frustrated beyond measure, he was just pondering what else he could do when the world titled sideways and he felt like he was flying through the air. The noise of the battle faded and was replaced by a strange whooshing sound and everything around him seemed to be happening in slow motion.

Joe lay on his side struggling to breathe, his body feeling like the air had been knocked out of him. Finally, regaining his breath, he gazed around in surprise. They must have taken a direct hit and the explosion had obviously lifted him up and thrown him right across the trench. With difficulty, he picked himself up and shook his head to try and clear the ringing in his ears. Then he shouted at Chalky, although he couldn't see him. Flapping his arms to clear the smoke and ignoring the sound of more incoming mortars, he peered through the dense cloud of dust and sand and finally spotted something towards the edge of the remains of their trench.

Must be Chalky, Joe thought, relieved his friend had survived the explosion. Still feeling disorientated, he began crawling towards him, then pulled up sharply. He stared at the shape in front of him in disbelief, his brain unable to register what his eyes were seeing. Shocked to his very core, Joe rubbed his eyes, closing them in the hope of erasing the sight before him. He opened them again and froze; the horrific vision was still there. Finally, Joe realised the mortar that had thrown him to the other end of the trench and left him with little more than ringing ears, had hit Chalky and literally blown him to pieces. There was nothing left, other than his head which was still wearing his helmet and was resting at an angle, chin strap missing, on the side of the trench. Joe sank to his knees, unable to take in the sheer horror in front of him. How long he knelt there, he had no idea. He only knew he couldn't move.

"Come on, Joe. You can't stay here." Woody's voice was right up against his ear. "There's nothing you can do for him now." The corporal had made his way back to their trench to pass on their last orders. "It's every man for himself, now. Get going." Seeing his words were having no effect and needing to move on to the few remaining survivors, he shouted at Rob, "Take him with you... NOW!" They were all in shock and if they didn't move soon, they would be overrun.

Somehow, Rob managed to pull himself together enough to grab Joe and, with Taffy on the other side of Joe, they climbed out of their trench and headed towards the railway station. They were joined by Woody and the few remaining riflemen. Up ahead, the German gunners had found their range and were firing straight at them with their machine guns.

****

Northern France

Gazing around at the tranquil, rural scene, it was hard to believe they were in the middle of a war zone and Jean-Paul had to fight hard to resist the temptation to stay a little longer. Unfortunately, he was only too aware the Germans were not far behind. Taking a deep breath, he stood up. "Come on, we need to keep moving." The others followed his lead with equal reluctance and, turning back to speak to Claudette, Jean-Paul noticed she was limping quiet badly. He frowned. "Have you hurt yourself?"

"No, I've just got some blisters. These shoes aren't made for trekking across country. In fact I'm not sure they're made for walking in at all."

Jean-Paul could see her footwear was holed quite badly and the dried blood on her heels where they were rubbing.

"There's nothing you can do, don't worry." Claudette was resigned. "My feet will harden up eventually and then the blisters will go. In the meantime, I'll take my shoes off whenever I can."

Marcel glanced at Jeanne who shook her head. "I'm fine. These shoes were quite well worn before we started and I don't usually suffer with my feet anyway. On the other hand, the rest of my clothes aren't doing very well..." She indicated her cardigan which was torn and covered with various muddy stains and the dried juice of berries and her skirt also appeared to have seen better days.

"You look beautiful to me." Marcel's gallant reply made Jeanne blush and, leaning forward, she kissed him on the lips. This was the first time they had kissed and Marcel was delighted she had initiated it. He had been trying to find the courage to kiss her for the last two days; now the ice was broken, kissing her again would not be so hard. Forgetting the presence of her parents, he held her close and pressed his lips against hers.

"Perhaps later?" Jean-Paul interrupted with a twinkle in his eye. "We really do need to keep moving."

Marcel sprang back, mortified. However, when he saw everyone was smiling, he relaxed. They carried on, but there was very little cover and they were torn between keeping to the perimeters of the fields, which took them close to roads and small settlements, and the dangers of being caught out in the open by the German planes.

Aeroplane activity was increasing and they had to keep diving for cover which delayed them even more. Angel was very quiet and seemed to have withdrawn back into herself. Every time a plane went over or a particularly large shell blast rent the air, she froze and had to be dragged to safety. The good humour and high spirits of the morning were gradually replaced by a dogged determination to keep going and a steadily growing despair they might not reach Calais before the Germans.

****

Calais, France

The sand was so fine, it was impossible to run through and progress was agonisingly slow. Joe was positioned in between Taffy and Woody with Rob behind them while they struggled through some particularly deep sand. They had only travelled a few yards when a murderous barrage sprayed them all in a hail of machine-gun bullets. At the same time, Joe stumbled and missed his footing. Spread-eagled, his mouth full of sand, he began to pick himself up. Aware his friends were lying next to him, he glanced to either side and then froze. They were not moving. The bullets had hit them with such ferocity, they had severed each man's head from his shoulders and would have done the same to him, if he hadn't stumbled at that precise moment. Joe knelt there, staring in disbelief, when he felt someone grab his arm and, offering no resistance, he allowed himself to be propelled along the dunes till they reached the street. His brain felt numb and he was unable to think clearly.

Rob shoved him down just as another barrage sailed dangerously close to them.

"Don't think about it. There'll be plenty of time to think later. For now, we need to get over there and out of the range of those murdering b'stards." Rob's voice was calm and didn't betray the emotion he was feeling. He pointed to the high concrete wall surrounding the station. "Somehow we need to get over the top of that, and bloody quick," he yelled as another hail of bullets sailed by so close, they could feel the rush of air above their heads. They had now been joined by all that was left of their company and, together, the men started to run full pelt towards the station. The enemy was waiting for them. They had only travelled half the distance when the Germans opened up with machine guns, spraying bullets across the street. They had little chance; men were falling all around them. Rob was right. The only way out of the gunner's range was to somehow get to the other side of the wall. But it was about ten feet high, much too tall to leap over and they were unlikely to have enough time to climb up.

****

Peggy couldn't believe she'd passed out. She had never fainted in her life and to do so in front of the patients and her work colleagues was mortifying.

"I am sorry," she kept repeating. "I don't know what came over me."

"Stop apologising, Peggy." Helen rubbed Peggy's wrists and encouraged her to sip from a glass of water. "You're only human and you've had a shock. You didn't half go white."

"I'm fine, honestly." Peggy struggled to get up. "I should get back to work."

"No, you shouldn't; not until you've drunk a glass of water, anyway." Sister Adams sounded concerned. "You're no good to anyone if you don't feel well. Just take a few minutes. I'm sure we can manage without you until then."

Knowing when she was beaten, Peggy sat back and stopped arguing. She had been sure Joe was perfectly safe doing some innocuous job and she really hadn't given it too much thought. How could she have been so stupid? And to think she'd been cross with him for not writing to her! This thought was swiftly following by an even worse one: how was she going to tell Pauline? There was no way she could avoid it, she could never lie. However, telling Pauline would achieve nothing, other than to worry her too. Peggy let out a big sigh.

"Are you sure you're feeling better?" Helen sounded anxious.

Peggy's head had cleared and she no longer felt giddy. "Yes. I'm fine now, really. I was just wondering how to tell Pauline."

Helen didn't answer, mainly because she couldn't think of anything to say. Poor Peggy, she didn't envy her that task.

"I don't know," Helen replied after a few moments. "The problem is, you're not sure of anything. He might not be in France, or in Calais, he could be in a rear party or something. Isn't there someone from his regiment you could ask?"

Peggy was quiet for a few moments. "Yes. I've met a couple of the girlfriends and Joyce, Chalky's wife. You remember, we went to the wedding? Joe was his best man." She sighed. "But if they haven't been told, then I'm going to worry them too and Joyce is pregnant. If I'm wrong, I'll upset a lot of people for nothing. And even if I'm right, there's no point in telling them, is there? They can't do anything."

"Then maybe you shouldn't say anything, at least for a couple of days."

"I can't not say anything to Pauline." Peggy was even more miserable. "What would she think if she found out later that I knew? And anyway…" She wrung her hands. "She'll guess something isn't right when she sees me at church tomorrow."

"Then you'll have to tell her the truth." Helen didn't give Peggy a chance to argue before continuing, "Peggy, the truth is you don't know anything. You're worried because some of the men you tended today mentioned the battalion was in Calais."

Peggy began to feel slightly less fraught. Helen was right. It was always best to stick to the truth and the truth was that, right now, she didn't really know where Joe was.

"Are you feeling better now?" Sister Adams was back and Peggy nodded. She was grateful for the break but all she wanted to do was to get back to work and stop being the centre of attention. "Yes, thank you. I'm really sorry," she apologised again.

"Nonsense. As long as you feel alright." Sister smiled to take the sting out of her words. "If you're better, can you go and see to the young man over by the door?"

Peggy and Helen hurried over to the patient she had asked them to tend. Fortunately, his injuries were not too bad. Other than some shrapnel in his left leg, he seemed relatively unhurt. Peggy resisted the temptation to ask him where he had come from, in case he told her something she didn't want to hear.

****

"We'll never get over that!" Joe shouted in despair. Rob was relieved that Joe seemed to have recovered, but he had to agree that scaling the wall did seem an impossible task. The Germans were slowly gaining ground and, with their numbers diminishing rapidly, one of the men ran at the wall and somehow managed to throw himself and his rifle over the top. Still, despite their desperate efforts, the others couldn't manage to do the same.

"Quick, give us some covering fire!" Joe shouted at the remaining few riflemen. "If we can't get over the top, our only chance is to try and knock a hole through the wall." Rob stared at him in disbelief.

"I know it's a long shot, but all the shelling and bombing might have damaged the structure, enough for us to break through. Then, if we position a couple of men at the hole, they might be able to hold the Krauts for long enough for us to find cover on the other side." Joe ignored Rob's sceptical expression and yelled at him, "Well, come on then, give me a hand!"

While the others started to lay down covering fire, he and Rob began to hammer frantically at the concrete with their rifle butts. Although Joe really didn't think they had any chance, they'd run out of options; they could either try and break through or wait until they were overrun or mowed down. To his astonishment, fear lent them a strength they didn't know they had, and somehow, miraculously, the wall began to crumble.

"We're in. Quick!" Rob yelled and, with relief, the few remaining men crawled through. Once on the other side, they realised there was no need to leave anyone guarding the hole. In front of them were several railway wagons and they dived for the pits underneath them. These provided perfect cover from the Germans along the entire length of the station until they reached Bastion 1, a fort on the perimeter of the harbour, facing out to sea. Here, they found the few survivors from the battalion who were frantically working on some guns which the French had put out of action before leaving.

"Well done, lads." A tired captain greeted them. "Welcome to hell! Make yourselves useful and see if you can fix those guns. Unfortunately the bloody French nobbled them before they left, not wanting them to fall into Jerry's hands. We could really do with them, so, unless you've brought a truck load of guns and ammo with you...?" He looked at each of them in turn. "No? Then lend a hand! There's plenty of ammunition, but it will be useless unless we can get the guns to fire."

For the next half an hour, while the German attack intensified, Rob and Joe helped the other riflemen in their frantic quest to mend the guns. In front of them, the few surviving Royal Marines who had landed the previous evening, tried to hold off the hundreds of advancing Germans with one machine gun.

****

Somewhere in France

The sound of vehicles was very close and Louis dived behind a hedge. He was just in time as an armoured column trundled past, followed by rows of infantry men. Louis held his breath but they were unaware of his presence. Breathing heavily, he waited until they had disappeared out of sight before making his way across the winding lane and into the meadow on the other side.

It was getting harder to avoid the Germans and Louis realised with a sickening feeling they must have overrun his home by now. He felt guilty that this was the first time he had really thought about this parents and Marcel. He had been too busy trying to save his own skin to worry about his family. Then something else struck him. If the Germans had overrun La Couture, then they had probably overrun Bethune too. He put his head down and increased his pace. He needed to get to Brigitte and make sure she was safe.

His head full of Brigitte, Louis failed to notice a small party of Germans skirting the woods in front of him. Seeing Louis heading towards them, they backed into the trees and waited for him to come closer. Louis reached the safety of the trees and breathed a sigh of relief.

"Halt! Hande hoch!" The order made him jump and his heart sank. In front of him were three Germans, their rifles trained on him, fingers resting on the triggers.

Chapter Thirty-three

Calais, France

Exhausted and dehydrated, the men fought on with dogged determination. With the water gone, they began drinking some bottles of wine they found in packing crates. They were determined not to surrender; rumours were still circulating they were going to be evacuated. However, when the promised time for evacuation came and nothing happened, their hopes faded. Eventually they ran out of ammunition. But, rather than give up, they started to throw empty wine bottles, bricks, rubble, even full wine bottles, anything they could get their hands on and which they could use as a weapon. The German onslaught continued unabated until, realising the defenders no longer had any weapons with which to carry on, the Germans again asked them to surrender. Eventually, at half past three, after three days of continuous fighting, the few remaining men of the 1st Battalion, The Rifle Brigade, were ordered to surrender by one of their last surviving officers.

Joe threw down his useless weapon and raised his hands above his head. Within minutes, the victorious Germans were swarming all over them, waving revolvers and rifles and shouting orders at them in a language they didn't understand. After searching Joe and stealing his gold St. Christopher, the Germans marched him out to a holding area where he joined hundreds of other prisoners of war, including several hundred French and Belgian soldiers. Exhausted, dazed and more than a little scared, Joe and Rob joined the other men seated on the ground and put their hands above their heads.

"What's going to happen now?" Joe's voice betrayed his apprehension.

Rob didn't answer, but his eyes showed concern. The Germans who had accepted their surrender had not been too bad; they had even congratulated them on their fighting ability, but there was no guarantee this reasonable treatment would continue.

****

Somewhere in France

Louis raised his arms. The Germans glared at him and then one of them spoke.

"Where are you going?" Much to Louis' surprise, his French was very good.

"Home."

The German stared at him for several moments then lowered his rifle.

"Go on then."

Louis looked at him warily, wondering if this was a trap. The German shook his head

"We don't want to take prisoners, so unless you want us to shoot you, get lost!"

Louis cautiously lowered his arms. Nothing happened. Taking a deep breath he stepped past them. His heart was pounding while he waited for the shot but again nothing happened and after a short distance he risked turning around. The Germans were gone and he was on his own again.

****

Brigitte left her father's café on Wolfgang's arm, ignoring the disgusted expressions on the faces of his clientele. When her mother died just after Brigitte's tenth birthday, her father had been too steeped in grief to take much notice of his daughter. Left to fend for herself, Brigitte had become first wilful, then difficult as she sought his attention. Nothing she did shocked him, so she became progressively worse. Eventually, at the age of fourteen, an older man in the village had begun paying her attention. She wasn't sure she really liked his caresses or some of the things he made her do, but when she was with him, she felt loved. She had continued to visit him until she reached the age of sixteen and then he had lost interest in her. Brigitte had no idea what she had done to upset him and in an attempt to recreate that love she had begun sleeping with the boys in the town, earning herself a reputation which finally had the desired effect. Her father was horrified, but his attention came too late. Brigitte had finally found a way to be popular. Although, at first, Louis had been just one in a line of many, somehow he had managed to creep under her defensive wall and she had found herself caring about him, in her own way. When he had stopped writing, she had immediately erected her protective shield again and assumed he was just like the others, only using her for what he could get.

The bar in Rue du Lac was full of Germans and Wolfgang immediately introduced her to several of his friends, who eyed her up with interest. Brigitte enjoyed their adulation and was soon accepting drinks from anyone who bought them. By late evening, she was feeling very drunk and was having trouble standing.

"Why don't you come outside with me?" Brigitte peered up at the tall bespectacled German, whose name she vaguely remembered was Hans, and allowed him to guide her through the throng of people to the door.

"Where are we going?" she asked. Her voice sounded like it was coming from a long way away, and she giggled.

"Just outside, Brigitte." Hans lowered his voice. "Wolfgang said you had a really clever trick with your tongue and I was hoping you could show me."

Brigitte gave an attempt at a lascivious smile. "Course I can." Her words were slurred and she was having trouble focusing. She veered to the left and Hans put out a hand to steady her. Brigitte stumbled into him and he caught her, before leaning down and kissing her. Brigitte breathed in the alcohol on his breath, linked her arms behind his neck and kissed him back. His hands began exploring her body, his fingers digging into her buttocks as he crushed her body against his. Brigitte carried on kissing him and then, when his hands moved up towards her breasts she unclasped her arms from his neck. She tried to help him by undoing her blouse, but was so drunk, she lost her balance.

Hans steadied her and pulled back, aware they were standing in full view of several cafés. He adjusted his trousers and helped her along the pavement until they came to a narrow alleyway. He guided her into the passageway and, when she slipped and missed her footing, he grabbed her arms and pushed her back against the wall.

"Ooops." Brigitte began giggling again. "I can't stand upright." Her blouse gaped open and he caught a glimpse of white flesh above black lace in the dim light.

"You don't need to." Hans shoved her down on her knees and began unbuttoning his trousers.

******

Northern France

"Perhaps we should try and get some rest and travel overnight instead?" Jean-Paul could see how exhausted they were. "We can use the moonlight to navigate by and it might be a little safer. At least there won't be many planes around and, even if there are, they probably won't be able to see us."

Too tired to argue, Claudette, Jeanne, Marcel and Angel sank to the ground and, trying their best to make themselves comfortable, they attempted to get some sleep. Jean-Paul volunteered to take the first watch and, while the others slept, he searched the map and pondered their chances. He was concerned about what they were going to do when they reached Calais. There was no guarantee they would not be stopped by a barricade like the one outside Dunkirk and, even if there weren't roadblocks, there was no certainty they would be taken off by a ship.

He rubbed his eyes and, running his hands over his face, he could feel the five day growth of his beard. He could hardly believe a month earlier they had been sitting round their kitchen table having supper with no clue about how their lives were going to change. Although they had been concerned about the threats from Germany, the war situation was a background niggle; something not as immediate as working out the type of lessons he was going to teach the next day, or trying to decide how to stop Jeanne getting involved with the Pellier boy. He could smile now when he remembered how many sleepless nights he and Claudette had spent worrying about Jeanne's infatuation with the Pellier boy, who lived a couple of streets away and had a terrible reputation. If only that was all he had to worry about now.

****

Calais, France

"My arms are killing me," Rob complained. It was some hours later and they were still sitting on the ground with their arms raised above their heads.

"Mine too. I can't feel a thing." Joe grimaced. He was about to say more when they were confronted by a burly German soldier shouting at them.

"What's he want?" Joe asked Rob, confused by the snarling soldier glaring down at him, rifle cradled in one arm as he gestured with the other.

"God knows." Rob was also puzzled, until understanding dawned on him. "I think he wants us to take our belts and shoelaces off."

"Why?" Joe frowned. "Oh, so we can't run away, I suppose?"

"Probably, although they haven't bothered to count us, so I doubt they'll be any the wiser if anyone does escape."

The German was still yelling at them, getting more agitated by the minute.

"I think we'd better just do what he says," Joe muttered when the German raised his rifle and threatened them with the butt. "At least we can lower our arms," he added. The pain in their muscles and shoulders was excruciating, but somehow they managed to take off their belts and, seeing them co-operating, the German stopped yelling. He then glared at the soldiers nearest to them and began gesturing again to encourage them to do the same.

Now the fighting was over, the adrenaline that had kept them going, stopped flowing and the exhaustion of the past three days begin to catch up with them. Unsure of their fate, and remembering the stories about the behaviour of the German armies on the Polish battlefields, they were reluctant to rest. Instead, they kept a wary eye on their captors.

They were gradually joined by more and more men, as one position after another fell to the Germans. The city was still racked by heavy shelling and gunfire as the Germans gained the upper hand. Gradually the noise lessened. The Germans were struggling to contain the thousands of prisoners. Once again, they were sitting with their hands above their heads and had been shouted at repeatedly not to try and escape, but there were so many of them, the Germans began yelling at them not to move at all.

****

Honor Oak Park, London

Peggy was grateful when her shift finally finished and she could go home. Although she appeared to be carrying on like nothing had happened and even managed to hold normal conversations, she felt detached. Arriving home, she went upstairs, took off her uniform, automatically hung it up neatly for the morning and lay on her bed. She pulled the covers around her, curled up and closed her eyes. She didn't want to talk to or see anyone. She just wanted to lie there quietly and think about Joe.

Alone at last, the tears that had been threatening since she had first heard the news, began to fall. Peggy made no effort to stop them and, sobbing, she buried her face in her pillow. She wouldn't believe anything had happened to him. She couldn't even begin to imagine her life without Joe, it was hard enough being parted from him. When he had proposed to her, Peggy had finally allowed herself to believe they were going to spend the rest of their lives together. They had even talked about children: at least one boy and one girl, and how ever many other children God saw fit to give them. They had planned a future of happiness, Joe working in engineering or somewhere similar, her nursing until the children came along and then perhaps when they were older, she would be able to go back to her career. In her mind, Peggy had seen the beautiful house, the happy smiling children and she and Joe growing old together. Surely God couldn't take all that away from them?

****

Calais, France

Unable to relax, the prisoners were relieved when the German soldiers finally made them stand up. Grateful they no longer had to hold their hands above their heads, the men fell in and began marching westwards in ranks of four with the officers at the rear. German lorries armed with machine guns drove up and down to make sure they didn't escape.

Joe yawned. "Got any food left, Rob?"

Rob shook his head. "No, nothing. Out of water too. What about you?"

"Nothing." Joe sounded worried. "Do you think they'll feed us later? If they weren't prepared for this number of prisoners, they might not have enough to give us anything to eat and drink." Joe was aware he should be more concerned about what was going to happen to him, but he was starving and food was all he could think of. Rob shrugged. He was exhausted and his throat was too dry to bother with an answer.

"Where do you think they're taking us?" For some reason, Joe wanted to keep talking, even though he was aware Rob didn't know any more than he did.

"Probably need to get us out of Calais in case the BEF counter attacks. Wouldn't be too clever to have us lot just behind their lines if it all kicks off." The answer came from another soldier. Joe could just about make out sergeant's stripes on his arm, although he couldn't work out what unit he was with because he had no cap and his uniform was filthy.

"Thanks." He couldn't think of anything else to say. He was totally exhausted and would have liked nothing better than to sit down and fall asleep. He stopped talking and tried to conserve the little energy he had left.

They moved towards the outskirts of town, passing some of their own food dumps and, encouraged by the few NCOs with them, Joe and Rob managed to grab a couple of emergency ration packs and some cigarettes before rifle butts encouraged them back into the lines. Their guards marched them until they came to Marquise and then herded them into fields. They were not given any food or water and Joe was grateful they had managed to steal something from the food dump. Having shared out their meagre supplies with those closest to them, Joe and Rob ate some biscuits and then tried to get comfortable by leaning against the hedge.

"You don't think they'll really put us down salt mines, do you?"

"I've no idea." Rob sounded exhausted. "Not much point worrying, I suppose. There's nothing we can do. I'm gonna try and get some kip while I can."

Joe didn't answer and, when Rob looked at him, he saw Joe was already asleep. Using his pack for a pillow, Rob carefully lay down. There was very little room, but most of the men were so tired a little jostling and nudging was hardly going to bother them. Others sat silently, staring into space, reliving the horrors of the past few days and mourning those who hadn't survived. While Joe and Rob slept, the sound of gunfire gradually began to recede and fade away until an eerie silence took its place.

It was this silence that woke most of the men. Although they were over ten miles away, they had still been able to hear the muffled sounds of fighting. Now, even the bombing, shelling, artillery and mortar fire had stopped. The night sky was glowing red and smoke was drifting lazily across the horizon, but the silence spoke volumes. Calais had fallen. The Germans had finally reached the coast.

Joe and Rob watched in silence while the exultant Germans celebrated. The memories of their friends were far too raw and too painful for them to discuss. Joe found himself remembering how Sparky and Johno had died. He couldn't face thinking about Taffy and Chalky or Woody... not yet. He was lucky to have survived this far, but he feared the future. He also felt guilty he was alive. Why him and not Johno? Why him and not Sparky? Sparky had children who would be fatherless. Nothing made sense anymore and, for once, his religious beliefs seemed to have deserted him. His head was already hurting from dehydration and from drinking wine when the water had run out and, trying to fathom the reasons for his survival was just adding to his confusion.

Even worse, Pauline and Peggy thought he was safely digging ditches in Suffolk. When they found out he'd gone to France, they wouldn't know he'd survived the fighting and was alive. They'd be told he was missing, presumed dead. This worried him more and more. He couldn't bear the thought of them being afraid. Somehow he would have to find a way of letting them know he had survived.

Chapter Thirty-four

Northern France

The moon was high in the sky when Marcel woke Jean-Paul. Marcel appeared tired and drawn and Jean-Paul hastened to reassure him.

"Not much further," he said and went to wake the others. After several unsuccessful attempts to rouse Angel, they gave up and Marcel offered to carry her, much to Jeanne's amusement. Marcel saw the expression on her face. "I'm not going to live this down, am I?"

"No, not if I have anything to do with it!" Jeanne gave him a hug. "Give me your bag. You can't carry a pack and Angel."

"Thank you." Marcel carefully picked Angel up and they started towards the coast. There was no noise and Jean-Paul couldn't understand why the big guns were silent. He could hear the occasional rattle of small arms fire, mortars and machine guns, but the really heavy shelling seemed to have stopped. *Perhaps they've run out of shells,* he thought, a wry smile on his face. At least he *could* smile, although there was increasingly little to be happy about. He said nothing to the others, not wanting to worry them. The only reason he could think of for the silence was that the war was over, or at the very least the battle for the coast was finished. They carried on until daylight and then stopped to have something to eat and drink. Angel was now awake and strolling along happily in between Marcel and Jeanne, just like she was their daughter.

Claudette sighed and held tightly to Jean-Paul.

"Do you think things will ever go back to normal?"

"I don't know, my love. We can only hope so for their sakes." Jean-Paul indicated his daughter, Marcel and Angel. "They're like a family, aren't they?" He smiled. "Doesn't seem possible only a month ago we were worrying about her getting involved with the Pellier boy, and now she is involved with someone we know nothing about and we have welcomed him with open arms! Furthermore, to all intents and purposes, they now have a daughter. I was just thinking how crazy the world has become over the past month."

"Everything changed when that monster took power in Germany." Claudette was angry, but quickly relented. "Still, without the war, we wouldn't have met Marcel or Angel or Antoinette, so I suppose it's not all bad. Out of everything bad, has come something good. Jeanne really likes him and I think he is right for her."

Jean-Paul sighed. "Let's hope he still feels the same when we tell him the truth." He changed the subject. "By my reckoning, we should reach the Calais road in about an hour." The silence was unnerving and he was becoming convinced they were going to be too late. There was no point saying anything until he was sure, so he kept his worries to himself and desperately hoped he was wrong.

****

Outside Calais, France

The night passed slowly. Every time Joe closed his eyes, all he could see was Chalky's helmet sitting forlornly on the side of the trench or Taffy's and Woody's headless bodies lying prone in the sand. He could hear the noise of the mortars and the machine-gun fire ringing in his ears and, although it was quiet now, every time he started to doze, he would wake up suddenly. In his dreams, the events of the past three days manifested themselves into nightmare sequences, where limbs and heads were flying around him in all directions and the smell of burning bodies filled the air. But instead of the casualties being his friends and colleagues, the maimed and mutilated corpses belonged to his family.

"You alright, mate?" Rob's voice was close to his ear and he jumped, instinctively reaching for his rifle which was no longer there. "You were shouting out in your sleep. I was worried you'd attract the attention of one of the Kraut guards."

"Thanks." Joe was completely disorientated. "I was dreaming." Joe was silent, remembering in vivid detail the last thing he had been dreaming about. He shook his head to try and clear the awful memories and to stop his hands trembling. He couldn't face thinking about his friends, not yet, so he searched for something else to say. "Seen anyone else from the battalion?"

"No." Rob shook his head. "Just us. There's so many soldiers here, though, I can't really tell. It'll probably be better in daylight. We can't be the only ones."

"No, I suppose not." Joe didn't sound convinced. "What do you think's going to happen to us?"

"Don't know." Rob sounded dejected. There was silence, then he made an attempt to sound more optimistic. "Still, if they were going to shoot us, we'd already be dead. I expect we'll be shipped off to a POW camp."

Joe hoped Rob was right. "Suppose so. Wonder when they'll notify our families we're alive. I don't want my mum worrying about me or thinking I'm dead."

"Not much you can do about that." Rob had struggled with exactly the same fears. "They'll find out eventually, I heard a KRRC sarge telling his men they've got to give us letters home. Once we're in the POW camp, we'll be able to write and tell them."

"That could be ages, though. In the meantime they'll be devastated." Joe found it was easier to worry about this than to think about other, more painful, things. He also had another reason, something he could hardly bear to admit to himself. He couldn't bear the thought of Peggy mourning for him and then getting on with her life with someone new and forgetting all about him.

****

Louis crept into Bethune and headed towards Brigitte's father's café. Everything seemed normal and he was beginning to think the Germans hadn't reached that far, when he heard the sound of marching feet ahead.

Louis hunted around frantically for somewhere to hide. He was in a narrow side street of private residential dwellings and all the doors leading onto the street were firmly shut. He ran back the way he had come, his boots echoing noisily off the cobbles.

Turning left, he found himself near a bar with some seats and tables on the pavement. The building appeared familiar and, ignoring the rather startled expressions on the faces of the few occupants, Louis rushed through the bar towards a door that led out of the back of the building. The back door led to another street and Louis raced out and made his way towards the outskirts of town. Back out in the countryside, he found cover by some bushes where he could watch Bethune and lay down panting heavily. He would wait until dark and try again.

****

Catford, London

My darling Kurt,
I do wish you were here. I miss you so much.

Olive put down her pen and tried to think of something else to say. All she could think of was that she had killed Mary and she was being blackmailed and she couldn't tell him that. She'd had no opportunity to listen to council gossip and she hadn't really taken much notice of the news either. She was stuck. She sighed and glanced at the clock. She should leave for work or she would be late. Olive shoved the unfinished letter in her handbag and, grabbing her coat, hurried out of the door.

Tom leaned back into the doorway of some flats across the other side of the road and watched Olive disappear up the street. He gave her a few moments and then headed towards the house. He'd seen her landlady leave earlier so he knew the place was empty. In his pocket was the key he'd had made: a little trick he'd learnt over the years. When he'd locked them in on their first meeting, he'd put the key in his pocket and had made an impression of it on the plasticine he always kept there for that particular purpose.

The flat was quiet and disappointingly empty of anything he could use. Tom sat down at the table and glanced around. There was nothing out of place, nothing that indicated anything other than the abode of a middle-aged spinster. On impulse, he stood up, went into the bedroom and over to the dressing table. He opened the drawer, his eyes scanning over the kind of underwear he would have expected to find and he casually rifled through countless woollen vests, and unimaginative pants and bras. Then he smiled. The lacy panties and silk stockings and suspenders underneath were definitely not what he was expecting. It looked like Olive did have a secret after all.

****

Outside Calais, France

The sun rose steadily in the sky and the German guards marched them mercilessly without a break. Joe had worn the same clothes for over a week and had not washed or shaved for nearly the same length of time. With very little to eat or drink for nearly twenty four hours, he began to feel dizzy. As they marched around a large shell hole in the highway, Joe lost his balance and barely managed to prevent himself from falling. One of the German guards raised his rifle butt menacingly and Rob grabbed his arm just in time.

"Thanks." Joe was relieved he had not been on the end of a kick or beating like many others he'd seen who'd fallen over. He was about to say more when a shot rang out

"What the fuck?" Rob twisted round but his view was obscured by the rows of men behind him.

"What's happening?" Despite craning his neck, Joe couldn't see anything.

Rob shook his head, but before he could speak, one of the soldiers in the row behind them answered, his voice raw with emotion

"Bastards just shot one of the lads for falling over and not getting up."

Joe and Rob stared at him in total disbelief.

"Bastards!" Rob burst out.

"Surely there are rules against shooting unarmed, defenceless men?" Joe was in shock.

"If there are, then someone forgot to tell this scum." Rob sounded calmer now but Joe was barely listening. He'd never really believed the rumours about how the Germans treated their captives; he had assumed most were just propaganda or scare mongering.

"They can't all behave like this, surely?" Joe voiced his thoughts out loud, not really expecting a response.

"I wouldn't bank on it." The reply came from a soldier two rows back. Joe swung round to speak to him and was momentarily shocked by the man's filthy, gaunt appearance. "I reckon they're all like it. Fucking bastards." He spat on the floor.

Joe was so shocked, he couldn't think of a suitable reply. He only hoped the man was wrong and this was just an isolated incident.

****

Lambeth Hospital, London

Helen greeted Peggy at the hospital "You look awful"

"Thanks, Helen. That's just what I need. Do my eyes look that bad?"

"Don't worry, they'll soon clear. Did you go round and see Pauline last night?"

"No, to be honest I went home, went to bed and lay there feeling sorry for myself." Helen could hear the self-criticism in Peggy's words and started to interrupt, when Peggy continued, "I couldn't face Pauline. But I can't put this off any more. I'll go to church tonight and tell her."

"It'll be much easier than you think. At least you'll have someone to share the worry with. There's nothing worse than having to cope alone without anyone." She patted Peggy gently on the arm. "Come on, let's get to work before Matron comes in."

The rest of the morning passed quickly while Peggy attended to patient after patient. Soldiers, airman, sailors, all wounded, some worse than others but all telling the same story in graphic detail. Peggy was horrified. She could hardly believe the things she was hearing and all she could see was Joe's face; Joe in an ambulance being shot up by German planes; Joe on a hospital ship being bombed by the Luftwaffe and not being able to get off.

Chapter Thirty-five

Outside Calais, France

The Germans continued their policy of shooting those who dropped out and fear became a great motivator to keep moving, but inevitably the weaker men began to succumb and Joe watched in horror while the Germans casually shot another soldier for trying to help someone who had stumbled.

"I feel like I'm in some kind of never-ending nightmare," he muttered through dry, cracked lips. There was no answer from Rob who was too busy struggling to put one foot in front of the other to answer and Joe fell silent.

In the few French villages they passed through, the streets were lined with sullen, defiant people. Children stood silently behind their parents, shocked and traumatised. Some of the French women brought out buckets of water for the prisoners to drink from, but the Germans kicked the containers over, threatening the women with their rifles and beating anyone who tried to get near the water.

By early afternoon, the sun had disappeared behind thick clouds and the rain began to pour down. Upturning their faces, they opened their mouths and drank greedily, the cool liquid easing their parched throats. Just when Joe thought he couldn't go another step, they came to Desvres, where they were herded into the football stadium. Exhausted, Joe fell on to the wet and muddy ground, too tired even to feel hungry or thirsty anymore.

In his worst nightmares, he'd never imagined his life would be like this. He closed his eyes and tried to think of a way of getting a message out. That would be a way of defying the Germans and would also reassure Peggy he was safe and would be coming back to her. He finally drifted off, only to be woken a little while later by the sound of a fight not far from where he was lying.

He sat up. "What's going on?" he asked Rob, who seemed to be paying close attention.

"One of the bloody Frogs, a Moroccan I think, tried to flog some Cadbury's chocolate and Player's cigarettes he'd obviously liberated from some BEF stores to some of our chaps. They took offence and decided to rescue them." The words were bland enough, the even tone belying the obvious anger Rob felt. The fight did not last long and the Germans waded in, restoring order in their normal fashion with rifle butts, punches and blows. The excitement eventually fizzled out and Joe could see the Frenchman lying on the ground.

"Well, he won't be doing that again." Rob spoke with a degree of satisfaction.

"He should've known better," Joe grunted. "Fancy trying to sell us our own food and cigarettes. Must be a complete idiot." In normal circumstances he would have felt sorry for the man and maybe even tried to help. But these weren't normal circumstances and Joe was too exhausted, weak, hungry, thirsty and demoralised to feel any real compassion.

****

Honor Oak Park, London

"There, there. I'm sure he's alright, Peggy." Aunt Maud patted her gently on the knee while Peggy wiped her eyes with her hanky. Maud was uncomfortable at such an overt display of emotion and glanced at her husband for reassurance. "Don't you think so, Bernard?"

"Oh yes, dear, your aunt's right." Bernard peered over his half-moon glasses at his niece and nodded with enthusiasm. "Joe's a sensible lad, not one to get himself killed. You mark my words, he'll be a prisoner or he might have even escaped and be on his way back here as we speak." He gave her a kind smile and Peggy nodded. They meant well, but they weren't really helping. There was a long silence.

"I think…" But whatever Maud was about to say was cut short by a loud knock on the front door. Maud hurried to answer it.

"Oh! Hello, Olive. This is a nice surprise. Peggy's here too." Peggy could hear the relief in Maud's voice. She didn't blame her aunt and uncle; they had grown up in an era where people didn't show emotion and, much as they loved their niece, Peggy's tears were an embarrassment.

"Do you want me to come back later then?" Olive sounded as prickly as ever and Peggy's heart sank even more. Just what she needed; her cousin gloating over her misfortune.

"No, no, of course not." Maud hastened to reassure her daughter. "Peggy's had some bad news about her young man. He's missing somewhere in France."

"I'm sorry about that, Peggy, but I expect he's alright." Olive could hardly keep the delight off her face. "You always did make too much fuss about everything." She stopped when she saw a frown pass across her mother's face. "But I am sure you must be very worried; very difficult for you." The sympathetic words almost stuck in her throat as she attempted to look concerned. There was no point alienating her parents too much.

"Yes, I am." Peggy had no such reservations. She was too worried about Joe to care about upsetting her cousin or her guardians. She stood up and glared at Olive. "I have to go now. I'm off to church to tell Joe's mother that her son may be dead!" She spat the last word at Olive.

"I'm sure she didn't mean anything, dear." Maud glanced nervously from Olive to Peggy.

"Yes she did, but it really doesn't matter." Peggy sounded resigned. "Goodbye Aunt, Uncle, I'll let you know if I hear anything." She kissed them quickly and headed for the door where Olive was standing, an expression of amusement on her face.

"He's probably deserted or found himself someone else," she whispered as Peggy pushed past her.

"You vicious cow!" Peggy hissed back. She was about to say more when she realised Maud and Bernard were watching her, so she made an effort to smile at Olive instead. "Goodnight Olive, I do hope you find someone to love you one day. It must be so hard always being on your own, knowing no one cares if you live or die."

The smug expression on Olive's face vanished to be replaced by one of fury. How dare Peggy speak to her like that? She would make her regret those words.

******

Outside Calais, France

All too soon, the break was over, the Germans lined them up again and they were marched on.

By late afternoon, Joe had lost count of the number of isolated houses and tiny settlements they had marched past, but while they walked through one small hamlet, he spotted a discarded signal pad by the side of the road. Checking no one was watching, Joe picked up the pad and put it in his pocket. His heart was pounding and he waited for the Germans to pounce on him. Nothing happened and an idea came to him. *I've got my pencil. I could write a message to Mum on the signal paper, use the safety pin from my field dressing to seal the folded paper and write the address on the front. If I could give the message to someone in one of the villages, they may be able to get it home for me. I don't really have anything to lose. If they throw the letter away, I haven't lost anything and if I'm lucky, the message will get home and at least Mum and Peggy will know I'm alive.*

He would have to wait until they stopped. Writing anything while they were moving was too difficult and dangerous. There was a German lorry, armed with machine guns mounted at the front and the back, about every fifty yards in between them and the guards watched them continually. Armed German sentries also drove up and down the length of the column on motor bikes making sure no one slipped out of the line and tried to escape.

****

Bethune, Northern France

Brigitte put on her makeup, ready to go out with her new friends. To her delight, she seemed to be in great demand and she was looking forward to another night out. She couldn't really remember much about the previous evening. Obviously Wolfgang, or was it Hans – the details were slightly sketchy – had taken care of her. She had woken up in her own bed feeling sick and with a bad headache, but was otherwise perfectly fine.

The knock on the door made her jump and she smeared red lipstick across her mouth. She wiped her lips with some tissue and shouted, "Come in."

"Ready then?" Brigitte frowned. She didn't recognise this German. He was short and stocky with rather bulging eyes and no neck.

Seeing her puzzled expression, he leered at her, revealing yellow stained teeth "You've forgotten, haven't you?" Brigitte's face wore a blank expression. "When I bought you home last night, I asked if I should pick you up today and you agreed. The name's Heinz."

Brigitte smiled uncertainly. She couldn't remember him at all.

"Wolfgang and the others are waiting, shall we go?" He was beginning to sound impatient.

"Yes. Just let me finish this." Brigitte felt better. If Wolfgang had arranged this, then she had nothing to worry about.

Heinz watched her while she applied another coat of bright red lipstick and dried her lips on the tissue. She'd been so drunk, she didn't remember anything from the night before. He smiled. Wolfgang had said to mention his name and she would do anything. He was obviously right.

"Right, I'm ready." Brigitte gave him a big smile. "Where are we going?"

"There's a big party at one of the billets. I'm sure you'll enjoy yourself." He reached for her arm and they left her bedroom and headed downstairs to the back door. Outside, there was a small Citroën. Heinz opened the front passenger door for her and she climbed in.

"Hello, Brigitte."

She spun round in surprise. In the back were three other German soldiers. To her disappointment none of them was Wolfgang. Heinz climbed in next to her, started the engine and drove off.

"I thought you said Wolfgang would be here." She was starting to feel slightly uneasy.

"He's waiting at the house." Heinz's eyes were on the road, but he reached out and rested a heavy hand on her thigh. He'd missed out the previous night; she'd been too drunk by the time it was his turn. Tonight would be different: he was first in line. His fingers squeezed her leg until he felt her wince. He released his grip and slid his hand under her skirt. "Relax, Brigitte. You're going to have a wonderful time."

****

Northern France

Now Joe had a plan, it seemed like an interminably long time before they rested again. He had hoped they would stop for a while; long enough for him to write a quick message, and then carry on. The most dangerous time would be when he was handing over the note, a task that would be much easier in the half light of evening rather than the bright light of the day. If he was seen, there was a fair chance the Germans would shoot both him and the person he had handed the message to. Joe certainly didn't want to be responsible for the death of someone else and he didn't really want to be shot either. Not for something as inconsequential to the Germans as a letter to his mum. He was shaken out of his thoughts by the harsh yell of one of the guards.

"HALT!"

Joe sank to the ground, grateful to be able to have a rest at last.

"Christ, I'm knackered." Rob's voice cracked, his face red with sunburn..

"Me too." Joe glanced around to make sure no one was listening and lowered his voice. "I've found a signals pad. I'm going to write a message to Mum and then see if I can find someone to pass the note to in one of the villages."

"That's a bit dangerous, isn't it, Joe?"

"I don't care." Joe was adamant. "I'm not going to let Mum think I'm dead, or Peggy think I'm not coming back."

"Alright, lads?" Joe spun around in amazement, delighted to hear a familiar voice.

"Sarge, you're alive! We thought you'd bought it back in the tunnel."

"Nah, take more than a few Jerries to get me. I'm glad to see you both survived. What about Taffy and Chalky?" Joe shook his head, unable to speak for a minute. "Woody?" Again Joe shook his head. Sergeant Miller patted him gently on the shoulder. "No point wondering why, lad. Just be grateful and make full use of your life, that's the best way to remember them." He caught sight of one of the German soldiers heading in their direction, "Watch out for the Kraut with the big nose; he's a mean bugger. Don't antagonise any of them more than necessary, some of them seem to be on very short fuses."

"What about escaping, Sarge?" Rob asked.

"Where are you going to go?" Sergeant Miller frowned. "The Krauts are pretty much everywhere along the coast, although some of the lads seem to think there's still fighting going on in the sand dunes in places. But there's nowhere for them to go out there other than the sea and the Navy's taken such a ruddy pounding, I'm not sure they'll keep coming back." He saw the expression on Joe's face and explained. "They've got to keep some ships back to protect the convoys and the coast or the Germans'll be able to stroll right in. Of course, if you see an opportunity then it's up to you, but be careful; they're pretty trigger happy."

The German soldier he had been speaking about had now approached, his rifle resting menacingly on his arm. In his mid-thirties, about six feet in height and heavy set, his rather prominent nose was his most noticeable feature and stood out against the pock-marked skin of his red face. With small, mean eyes and a thin lipped, surly mouth, the whole impression was of a nasty, unpleasant character who wouldn't need much excuse to be roused to violence and who would probably enjoy the experience too. Sergeant Miller stopped talking and Joe and Rob stared down at the ground, waiting for him to move on. The guard's highly polished boots were inches from Rob's feet and Joe could feel the animosity emanating from the German while he stood there watching them.

Chapter Thirty-six

Sehan, Northern France

It was late afternoon when they reached a small village called Sehan which had obviously been on the receiving end of the German shelling. Many of the buildings were just piles of rubble, whilst others were still smouldering where incendiaries had fallen and set fire to them. Jean-Paul decided they needed to find out the latest news and the only way would be to make some kind of contact with other people.

They watched the village from a small wooded area on the perimeter for nearly an hour before approaching. They had not seen any Germans and the only sounds were the normal noises of the countryside. In the distance, towards Calais, there were plumes of smoke rising into the air, but there was still no noise. Jean-Paul waited a little longer and then finally decided it was probably safe.

No one took any notice of the small party entering the village from the south end and the villagers they passed appeared shell shocked and bemused. About half way up the main street, they found a small store that was seemingly undamaged. Before Marcel and Jeanne could stop her, Angel let go of their hands and skipped ahead.

"Angel! Come back here!" Jeanne shouted and Marcel ran after her. But Angel had already reached the shop, pushed open the door and gone inside. Marcel rushed in behind her, closely followed by the others.

"Bonjour, ma petite." The lady behind the counter was smiling at Angel who had stopped in front of a stand of bonbons and was staring at them longingly.

Marcel took out some money and asked how much the sweets were.

"Fifty centimes per half kilo," the lady responded.

"We'd also like some bread, cheese, tomatoes and ham, please Madame," Jean-Paul asked. "We're together," he added.

"Of course, sir. I can only let you have one loaf and half a kilo each of cheese and ham plus half a dozen tomatoes though."

"Each?" Jean-Paul saw no harm in asking.

"Oh no. I'm sorry, that's between all of you." The woman was apologetic. "I don't have much left and, because I have no idea when I will get some more supplies, I need to put the locals first."

"I understand." Jean-Paul smiled. "Is there anywhere else I could buy some food?"

"Well there's a farm further down the road towards Calais. They always used to be happy to sell their surpluses, although now the Germans are here…" She broke off without finishing the sentence.

Nobody said anything for a moment and then Marcel asked the question they were all thinking.

"Are the Germans at Calais, then?"

"Yes, Calais fell yesterday. The Germans are everywhere."

Seeing Marcel's face, Jean-Paul hurriedly interrupted again, "Has France surrendered?"

"No, not yet …" She checked around to make sure they couldn't be overheard. "I don't think it will be long now."

"And Paris?"

"I've not heard anything about Paris. We've had no power for two days, so there's no wireless." Again she sounded apologetic but Jean-Paul hardly noticed.

He thanked her for their purchases and hurried the others out of the shop. It was inconceivable that France should have fallen so quickly and he wanted to believe this was just a setback. However, in his heart he did not really believe that was the case. The feeling in the pit of his stomach told him France would take some time to recover and he only prayed England could hold on. If not, there would be no hope at all.

Northern France

The POWs remained silent, not making eye contact until, after hovering for a few minutes, the guard went back the way he had come.

Joe let his breath out slowly. "I see what you mean." His voice was little more than a whisper.

"I wouldn't want to meet him on a dark night, or any other kind of night, come to think of it." Rob grimaced. "Look, even his fellow Krauts don't want anything to do with him." Joe could see Rob was right. The other German soldiers seemed to be keeping their distance and, although they didn't understand the words used, it was patently obvious when they spoke to him that there was none of the same camaraderie there was when they spoke to each other.

Sergeant Miller closed his eyes. "I'd try and get some sleep, lads, if I were you."

"Right, Sarge." Rob and Joe spoke in unison, but now Sergeant Miller had his eyes shut, it was too good an opportunity for Joe to miss.

"Keep a look out for me," he whispered to Rob who gave him the thumbs up and Joe took out the signals pad. Having already decided what he was going to say, Joe wrote quickly and carefully.

> *Dear Mum,*
>
> *I just wanted to reassure you I am alive. We were captured when Calais surrendered and we're going to some POW camp. I don't know where yet. I'm not wounded so don't worry about me. I'll be home soon. The war can't last forever. Give my love to Peggy and ask her to wait for me.*
>
> *Your loving son, Joe.*

He folded the note carefully and wrote the address on the other side. He had barely finished writing when Rob nudged him. Another German soldier was approaching, his rifle cradled in his arms, scrutinising the lines. Joe slipped the note in his pocket and stared at the ground, hoping the soldier couldn't hear the rapid beating of his heart. This guard was much younger, about their age, with a pleasant face. Joe raised his eyes just in time to make eye contact, the German nodded and then carried on past. Joe slowly let out his breath and, taking out his field dressing, he removed the safety pin. Checking no one was watching, he pinned the note together with the address on the outside and hastily put the paper back in his pocket.

Pleased he was halfway there, Joe closed his eyes, but he was too late. The Germans were on the move again and the guards were busy shouting at them to get up. Those who didn't move quickly enough were kicked and threatened with rifles and at least one man was shot, the sound echoing down the highway to where Joe and Rob were hastily getting to their feet, followed a second later by the sergeant. The 'pig', the nickname they had given the large-nosed guard, seemed disappointed he hadn't had the chance to attack them and they kept a wary eye on him when they set off. The threat of brutality was never far from the surface and Joe began to wonder at the wisdom of risking his neck to get a message home. He was still pondering this as they approached the village of Sehan.

****

Sehan, Northern France

While Jean-Paul was working out which direction to take, a commotion caught their attention. In the distance, there were clouds of dust in the air and the sound of something they didn't recognise. Frowning, Marcel and Jean-Paul peered into the distance.

"What's that?"

"I don't know." Jean-Paul looked around.

The noise had also attracted the attention of the villagers and, while they stood along the side of the main village street, a youth ran past, shouting, "It's the Germans, they're bringing the prisoners this way."

A gasp went up from the villagers and, as the remains of the Allied army came into view, several of the citizens crossed themselves. Jean-

Paul watched with a growing sense of despair. The prisoners carried on past, row after row, their uniforms in tatters, torn and stained with blood and general grime, their faces smoke-blackened, eyes staring and their bodies sagging with fatigue. A fight appeared to have broken out further back. From the little Jean-Paul could see, a woman had tried to defy the Germans and give the soldiers some food. A big burly German guard had attacked her with his rifle butt and then, realising the men were eating whilst his attention was otherwise engaged, he'd headed back towards the soldiers, hitting out with his rifle and kicking them with his steel capped boots. A shot rang out and another German soldier ran back. A ferocious argument broke out between the guards and Jean-Paul found himself hoping the Germans would shoot each other. Whilst their attention was focused on the argument, some villagers took the opportunity to bring out some water and gave some to the lucky men who were nearest. Jean-Paul felt sickened by the gratuitous brutality and, turning back to speak to Marcel, he caught a sudden movement out of the corner of his eye.

****

Sehan, Northern France

A commotion had broken out behind Joe. The line came to a halt and Joe twisted round, trying to look behind him.

"Food!" someone yelled and the line further back disintegrated. All Joe could see was a seething mass of bodies pushing and shoving. He gave up and turned back towards the front of the column. Then he realised, while everyone's attention was on the disturbance, no one was watching him. This was his chance and he might not get a better one.

He checked around once more and, when he was sure no one was watching, he took the note from his pocket and scanned the crowds lining the street. His eyes were drawn to a young man standing level with him. He seemed to be with a pretty girl, a small child and an older man and woman. The young man's face clearly expressed his outrage and hatred of the events he was witnessing and Joe made an instant decision. Once again checking no one was paying him any attention, he handed the note to the young man, praying he would have the good sense to hide the message straight away and not stand there staring. Fortunately the man acted swiftly and the last Joe saw of his note was the young man slipping the piece of paper into his pocket.

****

Sehan, Northern France

Jean-Paul was sure one of the soldiers had given something to Marcel. The movement was so quick, though, maybe he'd imagined it. Peering back down the wide, tree lined crescent, Jean-Paul could see the disturbance appeared to be over and he watched with the villagers while the now silent, sullen procession moved forward again. A wave of depression washed over him. How on earth were they going to get to England? And even if they did get to England, there was no guarantee they would be safe. He looked at his extended family and felt the responsibility for them weighing heavily on him, then he noticed Marcel was nudging him.

"Let's get away from here," Marcel whispered. "I want to show you something."

Jean-Paul was surprised, but there was nothing more for them here. They needed to sit down and work out their next move and the middle of the village was not the best place to do that.

****

Sehan, Northern France

Joe's heart was pounding so hard he was sure it would jump out of his chest. He waited with bated breath for the inevitable shout and subsequent rifle shot. Nothing happened. The whole transaction had taken less than a minute and attention was focused on the continuing disturbance further back. Joe stared straight ahead, not daring to look at the young man for fear of drawing attention to them. The wait seemed to go on forever but eventually the order came and they marched away. The road wound round a bend, the young man disappeared from sight and they were back out into the French countryside again. Joe felt a flush of success. He had succeeded. He had put one over the Germans and now the note was out of his hands and in the hands of someone he hoped was a patriotic Frenchman. From there his message home was in the lap of the gods.

Chapter Thirty-seven

As she strode along the road, tears of anger streamed down her face. Peggy was furious with her cousin and she vowed to get even with her. However, as she came closer to the church, her anger receded, replaced by worry about Joe and concern as to what she should say to Pauline.

The church was full and, at first she couldn't see Pauline. She was greeted by several people and, although she responded politely, her eyes roamed the hall, searching for any sign of Joe's mother. Eventually Peggy spotted her, seated near the front, talking to a couple of other women she didn't recognise. Peggy started to make her way towards them, but she was too late; the service was about to begin. Sitting down, Peggy was relieved to be next to some people she didn't know. At least she wouldn't have to make conversation. Kneeling down, she prayed hard for Joe and hoped that she would have gained some inspiration by the time the service had finished.

****

Outside Sehan, Northern France

They headed back the way they had come in silence, Marcel again carrying Angel. Finding a small clearing, Jean-Paul sat down. Angel was clinging to Marcel and it was a few moments before he could disentangle himself.

"It's alright, Angel. I won't let them hurt you, I promise. You can get down now." Marcel spoke gently to her. Eventually Angel let him put her on the ground and immediately clung to Jeanne who put her arms around the little girl and gave her a big hug. The violence had unnerved them all, leaving everyone feeling shaken and they could sympathise with Angel who had already witnessed so much brutality in her short life.

Jean-Paul gave his attention to Marcel.

"What did you want to show me?"

Marcel checked around to make sure they were definitely alone. "One of the prisoners gave me something." He put his hand into his pocket and pulled out the note.

Jean-Paul carefully undid the pin and read the scribbled message. "This is a letter to his mother to let her know he is safe. This is her address on the front."

The feelings of depression and despair that had threatened to engulf Jean-Paul vanished. Seeing the way the Germans were treating their prisoners made him so angry, any feelings of giving up were immediately replaced with a fierce determination to succeed in anything the Germans would have wanted to prevent. The message on the signal pad was not an earth shattering contribution to the fight against the Germans, just a single act of defiance by a man whose captors were sure he was defeated. Jean-Paul firmly believed that single acts of defiance like that would eventually see the defeat of Hitler and his henchmen and anything he could do to further that aim, he would do gladly.

"Now, we *have* to get to England. The soldier has entrusted you, Marcel – no, us –" Jean-Paul corrected, "with his message. He has placed his trust in us and we will not let him down. If we do nothing else, we will make it our duty to ensure this note reaches his mother."

****

Olive frowned. She was sure she'd left her underwear neatly in the drawer and not in a tangled pile. She shrugged. She'd been in a hurry that morning, perhaps she had left everything in a mess. Her fingers rested on the special black lacy corset and matching panties Kurt had bought her just before he left. She'd never owned anything like that before and she'd almost been scared to wear them. But Kurt had persuaded her. Olive blushed, remembering how he had carefully removed them later the same evening after they'd been out to dinner. In her mind, she could feel his gentle fingers undoing her bra, then cupping her breasts, sucking and licking them until she was writhing with pleasure. Then his hands slid seamlessly to her knickers, removing them gently.

Olive opened her eyes abruptly, banishing the memories to the recess of her mind. She closed the drawer, walked back into the sitting room and changed the station on the wireless. Lord Haw Haw would be on soon. She didn't really agree with the anti-British sentiments of his broadcasts but listening to him made her feel closer to Kurt.

Her thoughts returned to Peggy. She was glad her self-righteous cousin was suffering. Serve her right for being so insufferably smug. Olive hoped Joe was dead. That would be a suitable punishment for Peggy, telling her that no one cared if she, Olive, lived or died.

An idea came to her and her lips curled upwards but the smile didn't reach her eyes. Until she had met Kurt, that might have been true, but not any longer. Kurt had offered to help when Peggy's friend's boyfriend was missing. Perhaps she should ask him if he knew anything about Joe. It couldn't do any harm and what fun she could have knowing Joe's fate when Peggy had absolutely no idea what had happened to her fiancé.

****

All too soon, the service finished and Peggy raised her head to see Pauline approaching, a big smile on her face

"Peggy, I'm glad you made it. There's someone here I wanted you to meet…"

"I'm sorry, Pauline, I don't mean to be rude but I need to speak to you urgently. It's about Joe, it's really important," Peggy pleaded.

Pauline's face clouded over and she led Peggy out into the kitchen. "What's happened?"

"At the hospital yesterday there was a young man wearing the black cat on his left arm: Joe's insignia. He had just come back from Calais in France. He was wounded quite badly and said the fighting was really intense and there were just too many Germans and they were having to withdraw further and further back towards the sea. I don't know for certain Joe is there but it seems too much of a coincidence, especially when we haven't heard from him in ages…" Peggy hadn't taken a breath and, when she tailed off, needing to breathe, she glanced helplessly at Pauline.

Pauline said nothing for a moment and then, reaching out behind her for the chair she knew was there, she sat down. Her normally cheerful face was strained and pale and she suddenly looked much older.

"I think you're right. He is in France and has been fighting." Pauline hesitated. "I dreamt of him last night, a really vivid dream in which he was calling out for me but I couldn't reach him. He wasn't injured or anything," she added, seeing the horrified expression on Peggy's face. "It was more a feeling that he was scared because he wasn't sure what was going to happen to him." She reached out and took Peggy's hand in hers. A lifelong Spiritualist, Pauline had learned to trust her instincts and listen to her feelings. "I do feel he's alive, Peggy. If he was dead, I am sure I would know."

Peggy relaxed slightly. Pauline's words were comforting, even though there was no evidence to support them. "Thank you. I wasn't sure what to do. I could be completely wrong and then I would be worrying you for nothing, but if I didn't say anything and…" She stopped, tears threatening to engulf her again. Pauline got up and gave her a big hug.

"You did the right thing telling me, Peggy. A trouble shared, remember…"

Wrapped in a warm hug, Peggy started to relax and, for the first time since the previous afternoon, she felt more hopeful.

****

Bethune, Northern France

Louis crept back into town once the light had faded and headed for Brigitte's home. The café was lit up and surprisingly full. To Louis' relief, all the customers were French. He slipped into a seat in the corner and tried to see if Brigitte was anywhere in sight. A quick glance around the small café confirmed she wasn't. Louis frowned. He couldn't sit here for long; he had no money and there was no point asking Brigitte's father for her whereabouts because he was aware father and daughter didn't get on, although Brigitte had never explained why.

He stood up and was about to leave when a man spoke to him.

"Aren't you having a drink then, young man?"

Louis shook his head. All of a sudden, he remembered his army boots. He shuffled his feet under the table but it was too late, the man who'd spoken smiled. "Don't worry, lad. You're safe enough here. Do you want a drink?"

Louis relaxed. "A coffee would be great – thank you."

The man went up to the counter, ordered the drinks and handed Louis his. Louis sipped the hot liquid, enjoying his first warm drink in days and then asked, "I don't suppose you know where Brigitte is do you?"

The man frowned. "Out with the Boche."

Louis stared at him in disbelief. "You mean they've taken her?"

"Good God, no! Couldn't wait to snag herself a German, that one. You don't want to worry about her; out partying every night since they got here. It's her poor father I feel sorry for." He shook his head. "I should think her mother's turning in her grave."

Louis sat back trying to take it in. He had really liked Brigitte, obviously she didn't feel the same. He drank the rest of his coffee and stood up.

"Do you know where she is tonight?"

The man snorted. "Slipped out the back door with one of them earlier. I'd forget all about her, lad. Go and find yourself a decent French girl."

Louis nodded, but he had no intention of doing anything, not until he had spoken to her. He left the café and wandered down the street, searching for somewhere safe to wait. He would talk to her when she came home, even if he had to wait all night.

****

Bethune, Northern France

Brigitte climbed out of the car and, as it drove off she crept towards the café. Louis stepped out of the shadows.

"Nice to see you were worried about me."

Brigitte spun round and gasped, "Louis?"

"Who were you expecting? One of your Boche friends?" Brigitte recoiled at the sarcasm in his voice.

"I thought you were dead." Brigitte immediately tried to defend herself. "You should have let me know you were alive."

Louis shook his head. "Not that you'd care, but I have been running and hiding from the enemy for the past few weeks. I've had a terrible time; people trying to kill me, no food or water or anywhere to sleep. I haven't exactly had time to sit down and write love letters."

Brigitte stared at him for a moment. "It's not been easy for me either. Anyway, it's late and I'm tired." She stalked away leaving Louis speechless.

Inside the deserted, silent café Brigitte leaned back against the door and allowed the tears to flow. The party had been little more than an orgy and she shuddered to think about the things she had done. Brushing away her tears, she tossed her hair back and put the evening to the back of her mind. By the time she had climbed the stairs, she had convinced herself she'd had a wonderful time and was much better off with the Germans than Louis. After all, he wasn't even a soldier anymore.

Chapter Thirty-eight

Lambeth Hospital, London

"Where are we going, Sister?" Peggy asked in amazement. Having arrived at work slightly late after another restless night, she was totally confused by the pandemonium surrounding her. She also felt rather guilty at her feelings of relief. With the chaos all around her, she was unlikely to get into trouble for her tardy arrival.

"Gravesend. They're evacuating the wounded from France and we're sending nurses to the field ambulance stations to intercept them when they come through. One of your jobs will be to separate the walking wounded from the more serious cases. Don't worry," she added seeing the startled expression on Peggy's face, "you'll have a couple of the student doctors to help you. We wouldn't expect you to make such major decisions on your own." She pointed in the direction of several vehicles. "There should be some places on the second bus. Please get a move on."

In a daze, Peggy climbed aboard the bus and, to her relief, found Helen about half way down, also looking worried and confused.

"I saved you a seat," Helen greeted her. "How did it go with Pauline?"

Peggy quickly relayed the conversation. "Has anything happened? I didn't hear the wireless this morning."

"You know what the news is like. They think we're all idiots, so they won't tell us the truth, but it would appear we're evacuating the rest of the BEF from France."

"Have you heard anything about Calais?" Peggy sounded desperate.

Helen took Peggy's hand. "I'm sorry, Peggy, Calais fell on Sunday. They gave it out on the wireless last night.'

Peggy sat back in her seat. She tried to tell herself that just because Calais had fallen, didn't mean Joe was dead. He could have escaped; he might even be on one of the boats coming back from France. Or he might have surrendered, in which case he would be out of the fighting and on the way to some prisoner of war camp. "Sorry." Peggy realised Helen was talking. "I didn't hear what you said."

"I was just saying, I know how you feel. I have no idea where Jimmy is either."

Peggy felt terrible. She had completely forgotten about Jimmy. She reached for Helen's hand and squeezed it in sympathy and for the rest of the journey to Gravesend they both sat in silence.

****

Outside Bethune, Northern France

Louis sat by a hedge in a meadow several kilometres from Bethune, his head in his hands. He was devastated by Brigitte's actions and was struggling to change his image of her from the love of his life to a girl who would sleep with the enemy. He should really go home, but he was too upset. Deep down, Louis also suspected his parents would be happy he was no longer seeing Brigitte; they had never liked or approved of her.

The countryside was surprisingly quiet. The trees were cloaked in their summer leaves and, above him, birds circled, their mating cries the only sound in an otherwise silent world. Hearing them, Louis glanced up. The clear blue sky with delicate wisps of cloud threading their way from west to east reminded him of a day the previous summer when he had lain with Brigitte in his father's cornfield. They had made love under the warm summer sun and afterwards lay on their backs watching the clouds drift lazily across the sky. He could feel the tears pricking his eyes and he blinked them away. How could she treat him so badly? He ignored the little voice in the back of his mind reminding him that he had not been faithful either. After all, these events were unconnected. His life had been in danger, he could've been killed at any moment. He sighed. He could accept that perhaps she'd been lonely without him and if she had really thought he was dead then maybe she had been using the Germans to try and get her through the pain of losing him. This made more sense. He could understand her wanting to be comforted and his sudden reappearance had probably just shocked her into saying things she didn't mean. He smiled to himself, feeling much happier. He would forgive her and things could return to normal. For him, the relationship wasn't over. Now he just had to find a way of letting Brigitte know he had forgiven her and making her see she would be much happier with him than the Boche.

****

Northern France

Jean-Paul was concerned they were fast running out of options. It seemed the Germans had reached the channel coast, which meant it no longer offered a viable route to England. The main roads were even more congested than before, with most people now heading south. Even worse, the overflowing highways acted like a magnet to the German planes which increased their strafing and bombing, causing more panic and chaos. They tried to avoid the main routes when at all possible, but there were times when there was no choice.

He was also in a quandary. Having watched Marcel and Jeanne together, he wanted to tell the boy the truth, but it would be too dangerous to talk to him in front of Angel. However, she never left Marcel's side. He would have to try when Angel was asleep and just hope she didn't overhear anything to put them all in danger. She was only a child and would not know she shouldn't say anything.

"Is something worrying you?" Claudette asked, seeing the frown on his face and hearing his sigh.

Jean-Paul patted her arm. "I was just thinking we must tell Marcel tonight, when we stop. We'll have some food and then, perhaps you could distract Angel somehow. No, before you ask, I haven't thought how. Maybe we'll just have to wait until she is asleep. Come on, we need to keep moving."

Having made one decision, Jean-Paul felt better. *Now I just need to work out the best way to get us all out of France, and I'll have nothing else to worry about!* He smiled. If only it was that easy. *Still, one thing at a time. We need to find some shelter for the night.*

They were now back in open countryside.

"Keep your eyes open for a shelter of some sort," Jean-Paul suggested. "It doesn't have to be a farmhouse; a stable or barn will do. I think we need sleep somewhere that is not exposed to the elements."

"That sounds like heaven to me." Jeanne examined her torn and dirty dress, its original colour unrecognisable. "I would give anything for a nice hot bath, clean clothes and some warm food."

"Me too," Claudette sighed. "Never mind, the most important thing is to be safe. After all, we all look awful. Jean-Paul desperately needs a shave and so does Marcel."

"Oh, I think he looks very distinguished with a beard." Jeanne smiled at Marcel who immediately started to blush. "What do you think, Angel?"

"He's wonderful with or without a beard." Angel joined in the friendly banter causing Marcel to blush even more furiously.

****

Gravesend, Kent

As the coach approached the large stately home which had been requisitioned for the purpose of treating the wounded, the girls gazed out of the windows. Makeshift tents had been set up and, everywhere they looked, there were wounded men. Beyond the tents, several large Nissen huts had been erected in the extensive grounds behind the house. Even from a distance, Peggy could see many of the soldiers were only wearing the remnants of their uniforms and that their bandages were filthy. Following the others off the bus, Peggy and Helen were soon hard at work in one of the first tents, helping a student doctor assess the seriousness of the wounds. From here, they were moved to another tent where they patched up those whose wounds were non-life threatening and ensured those who were going straight to hospital were comfortable and would remain stable enough to survive the journey. Those who couldn't be moved would be housed in the Nissen huts behind them.

Peggy busied herself in tending to the numerous casualties, thankful most of them had reasonably minor wounds. The men were relieved to be away from the fighting and, being cared for by pretty nurses, they quickly regained their good humour, helped by a hot meal and plenty of tea to drink.

"So, darlin'. You got a boyfriend then?" one of the soldiers joked, wincing while she pulled out some small fragments of shrapnel from his thigh.

"Course she has, pretty thing like her. What's his name, love?" His companion was sporting a few cracked ribs, but was otherwise unhurt.

"Joe." Peggy smiled. "We're engaged."

"See, I told you she'd be spoken for." The second soldier gave a theatrical sigh. "Will he live, nurse?"

"Oh, I'm sure he will. It's only a few bits of shrapnel."

"Might only be a small piece of shrapnel to you, but I'll have you know it's bloody painful for me." The soldier was indignant. "Sorry, miss," he added.

"That's alright." Peggy eased out the last of the metal fragments and covered the small wound with a bandage. "There, you're finished now. If you make your way over to the soldier by the entrance, he'll direct you to where you're meant to go next. Good luck to you both."

"Thanks, miss. You look after yourself now." The soldiers wandered over to the entrance and were directed outside. Peggy had no time to watch; the next patient was already waiting for her. One after another they came, until soon, she had lost count of how many she had tended to. Every time a new casualty sat down, she found herself checking he wasn't Joe. There weren't just soldiers, there were airmen and sailors and the occasional civilian, which surprised her, until one of the soldiers explained every boat that could be sailed to France had been used to bring them back. He had come home on a small yacht overflowing with other men.

While she worked, Peggy listened to their stories in amazement. The beaches sounded dreadful with the constant shelling and strafing. She was surprised any of them had got this far. Wondering how many men had been rescued from France and whether there would be enough left to prevent the Germans from continuing across the Channel, she glanced towards the entrance. Several men poured through the gap in the tent and, for a split second, she thought she'd spotted Joe and her heart leapt. She stepped back from the man she was treating, a big smile on her face, then the soldier turned towards her and she saw he was much older. In fact he looked nothing like Joe. Her heart sank and she felt the familiar prick of tears behind her eyes. She blinked them away and returned her attention to the patient.

"Hello, Peggy." She was deeply engrossed in removing some glass from a cut over a patient's eye and the familiar voice made her jump.

"Hello, Chris." She was too upset to give more than a brief smile of her own. "I really can't talk now, there's too much to do."

"Perhaps we can grab a cup of tea later, then?" Before she could answer, he walked off to tend to the new batch of patients.

Peggy finished removing the glass and, having put a dressing on the cut, directed the patient back to the entrance. She closed her eyes for a moment and, standing up straight, rubbed the small of her back which was aching. When she opened her eyes again, Joe was standing in front of her, a sympathetic expression on his face.

"Joe!" She shouted as the image dissolved into the face of a very tall young man with dirty blond hair and pale green eyes.

"Are you alright, miss? You look done in." He sounded concerned.

Trying to ignore the crushing disappointment, she nodded. "Yes. Sorry. I thought you were someone else. I'm alright, really. Let's have a closer look at your arm." She examined the unpleasant gash running from his elbow to his shoulder and soon confirmed there was no shrapnel or glass in the wound. "You're going to need some stitches and I'm not qualified enough to do those yet. Can you go over there and join that queue." She put some clean gauze over the wound and pointed to the steadily growing queue in one corner of the tent.

"Have you heard the news?" Helen appeared beside her.

"No"

"Belgium has surrendered."

"Oh goodness!" Peggy was horrified. "What will that mean for us?"

"It'll mean we're stuck up the creek without a ruddy paddle, if you'll pardon the expression, miss." The soldier she had just treated had overheard Helen's statement. "The Germans can turn their whole army towards us now and make it even harder to get the rest of the men off the beaches."

"Wasn't there any good news?" Peggy asked, her heart sinking.

"Well they did say we had the best day yet in the air over France yesterday. " Helen seemed slightly happier. "Apparently the RAF shot down seventy-nine aircraft. Oops, there's Sister. I'd better scarper." Helen disappeared and resurfaced at the other end of the tent looking very busy.

At any other time, Peggy would have found this funny, today though she felt too despondent. Although she had seen the wounded from many different battalions and regiments, none of them were from The Rifle Brigade.

Every time another soldier entered the tent, her heart rate increased and she stared hard, hoping this time he would be there. The realisation that he wasn't plummeted her to the depths of a despair which grew worse which each successive disappointment.

"Aren't you going to stop for lunch?" Chris's voice broke into her thoughts.

"I'm not really hungry." Peggy struggled to repress the impulse to tell him why.

"Are you alright, Peggy?" Chris glanced around to make sure no one was within earshot. Not getting an answer, he was quiet for a moment and then a thought occurred to him. "Has something happened to your fiancé?"

Peggy found she was unable to answer, her throat was dry and she could feel her eyes welling up with unshed tears. Not wanting to be rude to him and unable to speak, she nodded without looking at him. Focusing her attention on the next patient, she concentrated on wiping some of the dried mud and grime off the young sailor's face, so that she could see his wound better. Perhaps if she concentrated hard enough, she would be able to control her emotions and not make a fool of herself in front of everyone. Expecting him to say something, she was surprised by the silence and when she risked a glance back, Chris had gone.

Chapter Thirty-nine

Northern France

Jean-Paul had finally decided their best alternative was to head towards the west coast. This would mean crossing German lines, but troops were very thin on the ground because the main concentration was aimed at taking the Channel ports. Hopefully, this would provide them with the opportunity they needed to slip through their advance and escape via the west coast. Having studied the map carefully, he was directing them towards the Brest, St Valery area where there was a possibility they might find a boat.

"Look!" Angel was pointing excitedly.

In the distance, across yet another field whose dried mud had hardened into furrows and ruts, there was a small barn. They stopped by the hedge and watched the structure carefully. There was no sign of any movement. Jean-Paul glanced at Marcel who shrugged and, cautiously, they began to make their way towards it. Delighted she had found somewhere, Angel kept darting forward and Marcel struggled to restrain her.

"No, Angel. We have to make sure the barn is safe," Marcel snapped. Angel stopped, folded her arms and pouted at him, a mutinous expression on her face.

"I'm sorry, Angel. I didn't mean to get cross with you. We just don't want you to get hurt." Marcel softened his tone. Although Angel was still annoyed, she allowed him to hold her hand and lead her forward.

Once they were closer, they could see their fears were unfounded and the barn was completely deserted. Jean-Paul was delighted the building was intact, there were no holes in the roof and there was even straw on the floor. Angel immediately forgot her bad temper and began picking up handfuls of straw which she threw at them.

Unable to resist, Marcel threw some back and soon Jeanne joined in, leaving Jean-Paul and Claudette watching in amusement.

"I hope the straw is clean," he remarked to Claudette who chuckled and indicated their appearance with a wry smile.

"Do you think it matters?"

"No, probably not." Jean-Paul made his way over to the far side of the barn and slumped down. He closed his eyes. After several nights of broken sleep and the discomfort of damp grass and bare ground, the straw was wonderfully comfortable and he soon dozed off.

****

Gravesend, Kent

For a minute, Peggy was angry that Chris hadn't even bothered to ask any more, then she saw him coming towards her with a large china mug in his hand. On the way, he spoke quickly to another nurse who followed him and took over from her. Taking Peggy's arm, he steered her away towards the tent flap and outside to some chairs under a large oak tree.

"Sit." His tone was firm. "No arguments. I'm a doctor and I know best. You need to drink some tea and talk. You won't be doing your job properly if you've other things on your mind and, no," he interrupted when she opened her mouth to protest, "I'm not criticising your work. Goodness, are you always this prickly?" he finished bringing a small smile to her face. "That's better. Now tell me what's happened."

Peggy hesitated and then everything came tumbling out: her fears for Joe, how she was certain he was in Calais which the Germans had captured, the worry of not knowing if he was alive or dead and the doubts because, apart from one rifleman, she hadn't seen anyone from his battalion at all, despite the hundreds of soldiers she had seen in the past few days.

"That doesn't mean he's dead," Chris assured her. "It's much more likely he's been captured. Because of the confusion over there, it could be some time before you know for certain. All you can do is to keep believing he is alive and you'll soon hear something. The longer you don't hear, the better the chances he's survived."

"His mum said the same. I can't help thinking the worst though. Seeing all these young men in such a terrible state makes the war all the more real. I keep seeing his face with their injuries." Peggy took a deep breath. "I'm sorry, you must think I'm really stupid."

"Why on earth would I think that?" Chris looked offended. "I think Joe is a very lucky man to have someone to worry about him." He smiled. "Are you feeling better now?"

"Yes, thank you." Peggy was surprised to find she did. Now she had spoken her fears out loud, they didn't seem quite so real. They hadn't gone away, just receded a little and become more manageable. She drained the last of her tea. "I should probably go back to work. Thank you again." She felt embarrassed she had poured her feelings out to a total stranger.

"Such a beautiful place, isn't it?" Chris indicated the grounds.

"Yes, so lovely and peaceful." Peggy glanced around properly for the first time since they had come outside. She was feeling much less shy now, and stood up. "And now I must go back in. But thank you, I really do feel much better now."

"Oh, you're a hard task master." Chris was also smiling. He got up from the seat and followed her back in to the tent.

Inside, it was stuffy after the clean fresh air of the grounds and the numbers waiting for treatment seemed to have doubled. Still, the tea had refreshed her and Peggy did feel better and certainly a lot less tearful. Ignoring Helen's wink, and vaguely aware that, for once, she wasn't blushing, she gave her attention to the next patient and concentrated on seeing to his injuries and making him more comfortable.

Bethune, Northern France

Brigitte was standing on the ancient bridge, staring into the narrow, fast-flowing river running alongside the town, wondering what she should do about Louis. He had caught her by surprise the previous night and she hadn't really meant to run away from him. She had thought she no longer missed him; now she knew that wasn't true. Seeing him again had bought back all the feelings she had tried to forget. She couldn't afford for him to get under her guard again. He would only hurt her and reject her, the same way all men did once they had everything they wanted from her.

The afternoon was balmy, the sun warm on her back, its rays glinting off the frothing water below. For a split second, she thought about jumping off, leaping into oblivion, then she blinked away her tears. Louis was in the past. She had new friends now, men who would help her escape Bethune. She wiped her eyes with her small white hankie and turned purposefully towards the town. Time to get ready for the evening and another step on her way to freedom.

****

Gravesend, Kent

The rest of the day was busy and time flew by.

"Right, Cooper. The bus is waiting outside. Hurry up and don't keep them waiting," Sister Adams ordered and, after putting the last of the antiseptic on the wounded arm in front of her, Peggy handed over to her replacement.

Helen was already seated on the bus. "God, what a day," she complained when Peggy sat down. "I can't wait to take my shoes off and put my feet up. Do you think it's going to be the same tomorrow?"

"I don't know," Peggy mused. "We're only really seeing the ones with minor wounds. How many do you think there are with more serious injuries, like poor Peter?"

This was a sobering thought and one Helen really didn't have the energy to contemplate. "Well, there's nothing we can do and worrying's not going to change anything. I'm going to go home and have a bath and soak my poor aching limbs. Have you got any plans?"

"No, none at all. The thought of soaking my feet sounds wonderful." Peggy yawned. "And an early night, I think. I didn't sleep very well last night or the night before. I'm going to make up for that. I don't think I've ever been this tired."

Helen didn't answer and Peggy saw she had dozed off. Yawning again, she resisted the impulse to do the same. Instead, she gazed out of the window and allowed her thoughts to wander. Inevitably they returned to Joe and whether he was alive or dead and from there to her conversation with Chris. He wasn't so bad after all, she conceded. She had felt much better after she had spoken to him. She had intended to cancel their date. The word made her feel slightly uncomfortable, their 'drink after work' sounded better, but she found she was looking forward to the evening, nonetheless. After all, whether she sat indoors on her own or went out with a friend for a drink, Joe would still be missing. She was sure he wouldn't begrudge her a chance to relax and Chris was good company. Peggy ignored the voice in her head which suggested Joe would possibly not see it like that. After all, even if he was in France, he had only just gone and he hadn't written to her for several weeks.

****

Catford, London

"Don't make me laugh!" Kath downed her drink and looked at Tom in amusement. "Course she hasn't got a boyfriend."

"Bet you anything you like she has." Tom leaned across the crowded bar. "Another pint and a port and lemon when you've got a moment." He turned back to Kath. "You've never heard mention of anyone then?"

Kath shook her head. "No. She's not exactly my bosom pal but the switchboard is full of gossips, so it's strange no one knows anything about him. Perhaps it was a long time ago and they've parted now."

Tom nodded. "Yeah, maybe."

Kath peered at him over her drink. "Why are you so interested? We've got more than enough on her to get what we want."

Tom shrugged. He had no idea really, except the idea of a woman who looked like Olive having sexy underwear intrigued him. Perhaps she had hidden depths. The thought was disturbingly exciting and he drank some beer, hoping to remove the sudden image that had popped into his head.

"I said, when are you going to see her again?" Kath repeated, an expression of irritation on her face.

"The next payment is due at the end of the week, after she gets paid. I'll pop round to remind her a couple of days before." For some reason he was quite excited by the idea. Tom stared at his beer, bemused. Perhaps they were adding something to the drink now. Maybe that would explain his strange fascination with a middle aged, unattractive spinster.

****

Northern France

"Come on, let's eat before the light goes completely. Jean-Paul! Jean-Paul!" Claudette nudged him gently. Jean-Paul opened his eyes and, for a moment, seemed uncertain about where he was, then he yawned and stretched his arms upward.

"How long have I been asleep?" he asked, his voice thick with sleep.

"A while. We've been watching the sun going down, haven't we, Angel?" Jeanne hugged the little girl.

"It's very pretty – like a big red ball." She changed the subject. "What's for dinner? I'm starving." She yawned. "I'm not tired, honestly." She glanced sideways at Jeanne.

"No, of course you're not." Somehow Jeanne managed to keep a straight face

Angel pulled a face at her and was about to start arguing but she was soon distracted by the appearance of food.

"Not bread and cheese again?" Her face showed her disappointment.

"I'm sorry, Angel. There isn't anything else, although if you eat it all up, I have saved you a couple of sweets!" Claudette replied.

Angel pondered this for a moment. "If I eat the bread, I can have a sweet?" When Claudette agreed, she took the proffered bread and began to chew, slowly and deliberately. Marcel and Jeanne took their share while Jean-Paul busied himself dividing the remains of the cheese into five portions.

We'll have to find some more food tomorrow, he thought, wondering where on earth they were going to find any. Not for the first time, Jean-Paul wished he could wake up and find he was having a bad dream. They finished their meagre meal and Angel yawned again. The sun had disappeared and the moon was now the only source of light.

"Come on, let's make you up a nice comfy bed," Marcel suggested and, for once, Angel didn't argue, instead lying down and allowing him to cover her with some straw and his jacket. Within minutes, she was asleep. Marcel made his way over to the others, sat down and put his arm around Jeanne who was sitting near the door watching the stars. The bright flashes and red glow on the distant horizon to the east and the occasional faint boom were the only signs of the war. Otherwise, all was peaceful. Jean-Paul cleared his throat.

"Marcel, how much do you know about the Nazis?" he asked.

"Not much, to be honest." Marcel sounded slightly embarrassed. "I always found the news really boring, so I didn't bother to listen."

Jean Paul hastened to reassure him. "There's no need to be embarrassed, most people didn't take any notice of the Nazis until they became a threat. You've probably gathered, we have our own reasons for fleeing from the Germans. We didn't tell you to start with, because we had to make sure we could trust you. I have known for quite a long time that we can. I was just waiting for the right time…"

Marcel nodded, then, realising Jean-Paul probably couldn't see him in the dark, answered, "Yes, of course"

Jean-Paul took a deep breath. He could feel Claudette's reassuring hand in his. "I... we, are Jewish." Marcel didn't respond, and Jean-Paul continued, "This makes us a target for the Germans. Once they have gained control of France, they will do the same here as they have already done in Germany, which is to rid the country of its Jewish population, by whatever means."

Chapter Forty

The British had now been separated from the French, Dutch and Belgian soldiers and joined by other British prisoners. The new arrivals mixed in with the marching column and two men fell in beside Joe and Rob. They waited until the guards were out of earshot and then introduced themselves.

"Andrew Sanderson, Sandy to me mates, and this is Pete, Peter Smith. We're from the Royal Sussex Regiment, captured at St Roche."

"Joe Price and Frank Roberts, known as 'Rob' – Rifle Brigade." Joe did the honours, relieved to have something else to think about. "Captured at Calais."

"How long you been over here, then?" Much to their delight, Sandy offered them each a cigarette.

"About five or six days, I think," Joe answered, drawing deeply on his first cigarette in ages.

"Oh, just weekend trippers then. Hardly worth coming, was it?"

Joe and Rob were about to object when they saw the smile on Sandy's face.

"We've been here forever," Pete sighed. "I'm beginning to forget what England looks like. Came over in September last year and we've been here ever since."

"You've not been home since last year?" Joe was horrified to think they hadn't had any leave at all.

"Oh yeah, we've had leave." Pete backtracked rapidly. "To start with, we were able to go home quite regularly, but nothing since March." He changed the subject. "The last time we went home, the civvies didn't seem to have a clue there was a war going on."

Rob nodded. "Yeah. News is heavily censored; we hadn't a clue what we were coming over to, and the civvies have got even less idea."

"Ah, that'd explain the attitude then." Seeing their blank expressions, Pete explained, "All my missus ever does in her letters is moan." He took a deep breath. "She started off by moaning about being evacuated; said they were 'orrible to her and the kids, looked down on them, like, so she came back home. Then she moaned because when she came back; all the schools were shut and she had to manage the kids all day." He stopped to draw another breath before continuing, "That was followed by... Oh yeah, the kids were running wild and getting into trouble. Not sure what she expected me to do. I could hardly go home and tell 'em off, could I?" Pete didn't give them a chance to answer before adding, "Then she started moaning about the blackout... how she couldn't see properly in the dark and London was dangerous with all the car headlights dimmed and no streetlights, so she couldn't go out at night. Where she was going at night anyway? I ask you!" Again there was no time to reply. "Then she started moaning about having to do everything all on her own 'cos I was over here having a whale of a time, according to her. Her last letter was full of complaints about all the regulations and shortages and how difficult life was for her. Not a thought about how ruddy difficult things are for me over here." Having got this off his chest, Pete lapsed into silence.

"Happily married then, are you?" Rob asked with a straight face while Joe struggled to keep from laughing.

"Course we are." Pete looked slightly affronted. "We've been married ten years now."

"There you are, Joe. Something for you to aspire to." Rob still had a completely straight face. "Let's hope you and Peggy are just as happy, eh?"

"I can't wait." Joe somehow managed to remain equally serious.

"You getting married then, Joe?" Pete asked. Having recovered from his monologue, he seemed much more cheerful.

"Yes, once I get home." The thought of not knowing how long that could be sobered him up and he frowned. "We got engaged at Christmas. She's a nurse, well training to be a nurse, in her second year."

"And you, Rob?" Sandy asked. "Got anyone waiting for you?"

"Lizzie. She's just my girlfriend at the moment, we've only known each other a few months but she's nice. Quiet like, a bit shy really. I'd like to have got to know her better, but the army had other plans…" Rob was silent for a minute, remembering her tearful face when they had parted at Christmas. He would give anything to be back with her now, giving her a kiss and a cuddle. "I've got a photo here," he pulled out a rather tattered black and white photograph showing a pretty girl with long dark hair held back from her face with a hair band. Although judging her height was difficult from the photo, she seemed to be quite small with delicate features. "Mind you, stuck in some POW camp for God knows how long is not going to do too much for our relationship. Still, hopefully she'll wait for me." Rob turned back to Sandy. "And you, Sandy? Are you happily married, like Pete?" He couldn't resist the jibe, although Pete didn't seem to have noticed.

Sandy grinned. "Yeah, something like that! I've been married for two years. Susie's her name and she's a real stunner. Blonde hair, blue eyes and a figure…" He made an hour glass movement with his hands. "And we've got one kid. He's a right little bruiser. Tommy's his name and he's nearly two. Short pregnancy!" he winked.

"Hang on a minute," Pete interrupted. "What do you mean? Happily married like me? There's nothing wrong with my marriage, I'll have you know…" Realising they were making fun of him, he stopped and grinned. "We like arguing. There's nothing wrong with a good argument."

****

La Couture, Northern France

Marie stared down at the empty grave. The priest was talking but she had no idea what he was saying. As if in a trance, she watched them lower the coffin into the ground and then she was being urged to throw some earth on top. Marie bent down and scooped a small quantity of the loose soil and dropped it onto the pine box below. Somehow this was symbolic of Jacques' life on the land and a tearful smile crossed her pale, worn face.

"Goodbye, my love," she whispered. She stood back slightly while the mourners, Georges, Christine and others from their small village, performed the same ritual. The priest intoned some more words and then the service was over. People were hugging her, shaking her hand and giving her their condolences. Marie wasn't really listening. Eventually, they all wandered off and she returned her attention to Jacques. She couldn't believe she would never see him again and she was loathe to walk away from the grave, because she would be leaving him on his own.

She felt Georges' hand on her arm, but shrugged it off.

"I'd like to stay for a while."

"Of course. We'll wait for you over there." He indicated his car.

Marie turned back to the grave, the tears running unchecked down her face. Ahead, she could only see loneliness and despair and a future without the man she loved.

****

Gravesend, Kent

"We were frightened you'd all hate us because we'd lost and put everyone in danger," one soldier said, obviously unable to believe how friendly everyone was since his return to England. "We've failed. We were supposed to protect you all and here we are being rescued and brought home by pleasure steamers, of all things."

"We're just pleased to have you safely home," Peggy reassured him.

"Thanks, luv. You've no idea how much better that makes us feel. We couldn't believe our luck when we arrived at one of the stations and they had banners up saying 'welcome home'."

Peggy lost count of how many times she had the same conversation and, when she finally had a break, she found she wasn't the only one. Helen too had spent most of the morning reassuring patients.

"It's terrible, isn't it?" Peggy mused. "Not only have they been through all that, they're scared the rest of us at home will hate them."

Helen nodded and lit a cigarette. She saw Peggy's surprised expression. "I started smoking a few days ago," she explained. "Would you like one?"

"No thanks. I'll stick to tea." Peggy drank from her cup.

Helen sipped hers and took another drag of her cigarette. "One of the chaps told me when he got picked up by a steamer, they offered him a drink and when he said he would love a beer, do you know what they replied?"

"No, go on?" Peggy urged.

"They said they couldn't serve him with alcohol until they were further from the French coast, because of the three mile limit!"

"You're pulling my leg!"

"No, honestly. He said when he was told that, he was sure we'd win the war!"

******

Hesdin, France

There were few people about as they walked through Hesdin and, those who were, watched in silence or turned away, not wanting the Germans to see the resentment on their faces. The guards hurried them along the cobbled streets, over several bridges under which the fast flowing Canche and Ternoise rivers flowed, past the equally impressive 16th Century Church of Notre Dame and back out into the countryside again.

In the distance, they saw a large chateau. The guards herded them off the road and along a private lane towards the house. On either side, there were neatly tended fields and, in the distance, Joe watched a couple of farm workers planting or picking something. The Germans marched them until they came to an even smaller track leading off to the left towards some buildings which resembled large barns. The chateau was a long way off now and the men eventually arrived in some kind of farming area. The guards ordered the POWs across a large concreted yard until they came to the buildings they had seen earlier, which turned out to be stables. The guards pushed open the doors and gestured to the stalls. Joe stopped, a wary expression on his face.

"You sure this is safe?" he asked Rob, who shrugged.

"We don't seem to have a lot of choice, do we? Anyway, if they were going to shoot us, they'd have done that by now, surely?"

Joe was still hesitating when Sergeant Miller spoke. "Spread out, lads. Move up to the end, then we can all get in." Joe ignored his misgivings and made his way towards the far end of the stable. Once there, he pushed open the door of the last stall and went in. The small cubicle felt warm and the straw seemed inviting after several nights of sleeping outside. He was joined by his friends and Sergeant Miller, who flopped down on the straw and closed his eyes, the strain of the past few days showing on his face.

Deciding that, if Sergeant Miller thought they were safe, they probably didn't need to worry, Joe, Rob, Sandy and Pete sorted themselves out some space and sat down on the thick covering of straw. Gradually they began to relax.

****

La Couture, Northern France

Once the funeral was over, Marie went back to the Laval's, but she couldn't stay there forever, kind and supportive as they were. Her strength was beginning to return and she made the decision to go back home.

"I've found someone in the village who can help out on the farm. Gaston Lafere. He's getting on a bit but he'll be glad of the extra money. If that's alright with you, of course?" Georges said.

"I can't manage on my own." Marie snapped. "I'm sorry. I didn't mean to be rude." She sighed. It was hard to think of anything other than how much she missed Jacques. "Yes, thank you. I do appreciate all your help, Georges. Perhaps the boys will be back soon," she added wistfully.

"I'm sure they will." Georges patted her arm.

Marie took his hand. "Thank you both for looking after me. I'm not sure how I would have coped without you." She could feel the tears forming again and she made a determined effort to force them away.

"We'll be across to visit you every day for as long as you want," Christine promised. "And if there's anything you need, you only have to ask." She reached over and enveloped Marie in a big hug. Marie was unable to speak for a moment. She fought away the tears again, closed her eyes and hugged Christine back.

"Shall we walk, or you would you prefer to go in the car?" George asked

Marie thought for a few moments then said with a sudden decisiveness, "I'd like to walk. It's a lovely evening and I want to see the land Jacques and I cultivated and tended together for so many years."

Christine exchanged glances with Georges, then she squeezed Marie's arm. Marie took a deep breath and, leading the way out of the kitchen, they headed towards her home.

****

"Louis, what are you doing back here?" Brigitte eyed him uneasily. They were standing by the street door in the café. Brigitte had been about to leave when Louis entered. Heinz would be here in a moment to pick her up and she was worried about how Louis would react to the German.

"I can't believe you prefer the Boche's company to mine." Louis tried hard to keep his temper. His eyes were red rimmed from lack of sleep and, after two more days living rough outside the town, his clothes were even more dishevelled than before.

"I don't want to see you anymore. Why can't you take no for an answer?" Brigitte glanced at the small clock on the wall in desperation. "You need to go." As she finished speaking, she heard the sound of an approaching car. She pushed past him and into the street, but Louis followed.

The car pulled up and Heinz leaned over and opened the passenger door. "Get in!" he ordered. Brigitte hurried across the street, followed closely by Louis.

"How dare you speak to her like that?" he yelled at the German.

Heinz eyed him up and down slowly. "Get lost, farm-boy. She's too much of a woman for you!" Louis could hear sniggering from the back of the car and his temper snapped. He stepped closer, wrenched open the driver's door and pulled Heinz out of the car. Taken by surprise, the German put up no resistance.

Brigitte screamed at him to stop, but Louis was lost in a red mist. He caught the German with two quick punches and Heinz fell to the floor. Louis stepped towards him, his foot raised, but he was too slow. Heinz saw the kick coming, rolled out of reach and scrambled to his feet. Louis rushed at him, fists clenched. The punch never landed. He was set upon by the other three soldiers who had hurried out of the back of the car to protect their friend.

Brigitte rushed forward to try and help Louis, but was shoved violently out of the way by Heinz. She fell against the car jarring her arm. Ignoring the pain, she yelled at him in protest but he took no notice, his attention on Louis who was being held by the other soldiers. Heinz managed to land one stomach punch on Louis before Brigitte threw herself onto his back, locking her arms around his neck. He spun around, clawing at her hands and Louis momentarily freed himself from the grip of the other soldiers. He flung himself at Heinz who finally dislodged Brigitte. This time she fell on the floor. Undaunted, tears streaming down her face, she stood up and stepped back towards Heinz who raised his fist to punch her. Instinctively, she moved her head to the side and he missed. But the other soldiers had now forced Louis to the ground and were punching and kicking him. Heinz returned his attention to Louis and joined in while Brigitte sank to her knees in horror, yelling and pleading with them to no avail. They ignored her and she finally fell silent, the only sound the thuds and grunts of the soldiers as their boots and fists pounded into Louis' motionless body. Fearing he was dead, she made one more attempt to stop them, throwing herself at Heinz who grabbed her arm, pinned her against the car with his body and raised his fist. Unable to move, Brigitte waited for the blow when the sound of a gunshot brought the Germans to a halt.

Chapter Forty-one

Outside Hesdin, France

"Surely we don't have to move again?" Joe groaned. He felt like he had only just closed his eyes and he really couldn't manage another step.

"It's alright, mate. The Jerries have found us some food. Smells wonderful!" Rob's words caught him by surprise and, for a moment, he wasn't sure whether he had heard properly, until the fragrance of herbs and vegetables drifted across his nostrils.

"Hot food?" Joe asked, unable to believe his senses. Sure enough, the guards brought in several large tureens which they placed near the door. Even from the back, the men could smell the stew and see the steam rising from the containers.

"Form an orderly queue, lads." One of the sergeants near the food assumed control and, despite a certain amount of grumbling, the men obeyed. The opportunity to have a hot meal was too good to ruin by squabbling about who went first. For Joe and Rob, this was the first hot meal they'd had since leaving England, over a week ago and, although the stew was very thin with few vegetables, even fewer potatoes and no meat at all, it was hot and flavoursome and took the edge of their hunger. Resting his back against one of the stable doors and feeling better than he had for days, Joe closed his eyes.

"I feel almost human."

"Yep, just need a pint to wash it down with and I'll feel right at home," Rob belched.

"Live in a stable then do you?" Pete asked.

"Ha, bloody ha." Rob was too tired to think of a clever response.

"Do you think we can smoke?" Sandy asked taking out the last of his cigarettes. The answer came immediately. A burly German guard rushed over and began gesticulating and shouting, his face twisted in fury.

"Alright, mate, no need to get your knickers in a twist." Sandy appeared surprised by all the fuss. He placed the cigarettes and unused match back in the packet, which he put in his pocket. "It was only an idea."

Joe and the others kept their faces turned away so the Germans couldn't see them laughing.

"Did he really think I was going to light up in a stable full of hay and straw? Give me some credit!" Sandy paused "On the other hand… maybe we *should* light a fire, to keep warm I mean?"

"I think you're asking to get your teeth kicked down your throat if that one sees you." Sergeant Miller's voice was low as the door flew open and the guard they had nicknamed 'The Pig' leaned in. Unlike the other guards, who had been replaced along the way, he was still with them, much to their dismay.

There was a sudden silence and Joe could hear the guard's boots scraping on the floor while his eyes darted around the stall. Joe started to sweat and had to resist the temptation to hold his breath. The guard stood there for a few minutes and then, swivelling on his heel, he headed back in the direction he had come. There were another few moments of silence and then a collective sigh of relief went round.

****

La Couture, Northern France

Marie took a deep breath and let herself into the farmhouse.

"Would you like us to stay?" Christine asked.

Marie shook her head. "No, thank you. I have to get used to being here on my own."

Christine gave her a quick hug. "Goodnight then, Marie, and don't forget, if you need anything you know where we are."

Marie stepped into the kitchen and shut the door. For a split second, she could see Jacques lying there, his blood seeping onto the floor and then the image was gone. The kitchen was quiet and, despite the warmth of the evening, the house felt cold and neglected. Marie reached over to the wireless and turned the switch. Immediately, the room was filled with classical music. She stood for a moment, fighting the memories that threatened to overwhelm her then, heading to the sink, she poured some water into the kettle, lit the range and made herself some coffee. She didn't feel tired and she didn't want to go to bed on her own, not yet. Instead she wanted to sit and remember all the good times and to pray her boys were safe and would soon come home to her.

******

Bethune, Northern France

"What's going on?" The voice was authoritative and the soldiers immediately jumped to attention, leaving Louis bleeding and unconscious on the street. Ahead was a German staff car, the officer standing by the vehicle, a weapon in his hand.

"He attacked us, sir," Heinz answered, blood pouring from his nose.

The German officer stepped closer, glanced at Brigitte and instantly summed up the situation. He turned back to the soldiers. "We are meant to be on our best behaviour. Get in the car and drive away. Now." Heinz hesitated and then reached for Brigitte's hand. "Without the girl!" the officer bellowed.

"Sir!" Heinz saluted and they hurried to comply. The car drove off and the officer strolled over to Brigitte. She was bending down over Louis, who appeared to be unconscious. He touched his hat. "My apologies, Fräulein. I would suggest you help your friend off the road and get him some medical treatment."

Brigitte seemed about to argue then changed her mind. "Thank you." She fixed the officer with a dazzling smile.

He did not appear to notice. "Good day, Fräulein." He began walking away, then stopped and turned back, his stare unwavering. "If I were you, I would keep your boyfriend away from my men. I won't always be here to protect him." His blue eyes were cold and his mouth a cruel, hard line.

****

Catford, London

My darling Kurt

I hope this letter finds you well. This is only a very short letter because you have probably just received my last one. I wondered if you could do me a great favour? I have just found out that Peggy's fiancé, Joe Price, is missing. He was last heard of fighting in Calais and Peggy is very distraught.

Olive smiled. Just the thought that her smug cousin was upset was enough to cheer her up and forget her own problems for a while.

I thought if you could find out any information at all I could go round and visit her again and try to make friends like you suggested.

Olive was quite pleased with that line, which implied she was only following his wishes.

Anyway, I'd better go now, or I won't catch the post.
Your loving Olive. xxxxx

Olive pushed her problems with the blackmailer to the back of her mind. Much as she would have loved to pour out her troubles to Kurt, she couldn't.

****

Louis came round a few hours later to find himself naked, apart from some clean underpants, lying in a warm comfortable bed, his head resting on several soft pillows. At first, he thought he'd gone blind, then he realised his eyes were shut and cautiously he tried to open them. This was surprisingly difficult; the left one seemed to be glued shut. With his right eye, he peered around trying to work out where he was. Brigitte leapt up from the uncomfortable upright chair she had been sitting in and stared down at him, concern etched on her face. Seeing her, he tried to move and winced, pain shooting through his body.

"Ouch!"

Relieved he was awake, Brigitte lashed into him

"What the hell did you think you were doing?"

Louis shook his head and then wished he hadn't. A sharp pain attacked his left temple and white lights shot in front of his eyes. "I didn't think," he muttered through bruised and painful lips. Brigitte reached for the glass she had placed by the bed and held the water to his mouth.

"Drink," she ordered. "Slowly," she added when he tried to gulp. After several sips, he signalled he'd had enough and, after replacing the glass, she sat back down, her eyes appraising his battered body.

"I'm not worth it."

"Who says?"

"Honestly, Louis, if you knew all the things I've done…"

Louis sat up slowly and with difficulty. "I don't care, Brigitte. I love you."

Chapter Forty-two

Northern France

They had heard little fighting the previous day but all that changed the following morning. Jean-Paul, Claudette, Marcel, Jeanne and Angel were woken by the sound of Stukas screaming overhead and the rumble of tanks and troops making their way through the French countryside. Behind them, the sky was lit up with flashes from the continuing bombardment of the Channel ports and they could hear the booming of the heavy guns pounding the cities. The Germans were only just behind them and, with the speed they were advancing, they would soon be overtaken.

Much to Jean-Paul's relief, Marcel had taken the news that they were Jewish in his stride. He seemed to have no anti-Semitic feelings at all, which had at least solved one of his concerns. He had also appreciated the seriousness of their position which had surprised Jean-Paul, especially after his earlier admission that he had little interest in politics. If anything, Marcel had gone up in his estimation; the boy obviously had a quick brain. He would make Jeanne a good husband, although, of course, they had to survive the Germans first.

"I think we should make for Cherbourg." Jean-Paul spoke out loud. "We should be able to find a boat there."

Used to him making the decisions, no one argued and Marcel swept Angel up onto his shoulders and began striding out in the direction Jean-Paul had indicated. The main routes were no longer clogged with refugees, many of whom were heading south rather than west. The skies ahead were also empty while the Germans concentrated their attack elsewhere, so it was safer to travel on the roads than previously.

They had to pick their way around various items scattered on the highway, including the occasional animal corpse left putrefying in the sun, but on the whole, they made good time. Marcel, Jeanne and Angel began to sing songs, occasionally Jean-Paul and Claudette joined in, but Jean-Paul was beginning to worry about Claudette, whose feet were very swollen. She had taken off her shoes a long time ago and was walking in bare feet, which was not a problem when they were on grass but the road surface was making them bleed and she took every opportunity to use the verges. Helping her across one of the ditches, he also noticed she seemed to have lost a considerable amount of weight and was now very thin.

Not having seen anyone for quite a while, they were surprised to see a ragged column of men in front of them, going in the same direction. They caught up to them and were shocked to find that they were French soldiers. There were no officers and they did not seem to have any idea where they were going.

"We were told to make for Cherbourg," one of the soldiers said. "We've been told the British will try and get us off from there and take us to England."

Jean-Paul smiled triumphantly at the others. "See, we're going in the right direction."

"I'm not sure whether they'll take civilians." The soldier cast an eye over their small party. "They may take you and the boy, because you can join up. I don't know about the women and child." Seeing their expressions, he added swiftly, "I'm sorry, I could be wrong but I don't want you to get your hopes up."

The soldier increased his speed and caught up with his comrades, leaving them standing in the middle of the road.

"He did say he wasn't sure," Claudette reminded him. "He was only speculating, wasn't he?" Even she didn't sound convinced.

"Well, we won't know till we get there, will we?" Jean-Paul replied.

The sound of an approaching lorry startled them and, terrified it was the advancing Germans, they headed for the drainage ditch.

******

Catford, London

The second page of the *Evening Standard* stated the police had arrested a young man, Stan Lipman, for the murder of a young woman, Mary Carson, whose battered body had been found at Mountsfield Park a week earlier.

Olive sat back in her chair, an expression of relief on her face. She was in the clear, or she would be once the trial was over. Olive felt a brief moment of regret for a young man who was about to hang for something he hadn't done. Then she hardened her heart. He might not be guilty of Mary's murder, but if she hadn't been there, he would probably have raped her. It was only her presence that had saved Mary, Olive reassured herself.

Now, she only had the blackmailer to deal with. Her heart sank. She had no idea what to do about him. She was convinced he was something to do with Kath, although she wasn't sure whether that was much help. Olive sighed. She would appreciate some company but there was no one she could visit other than her parents and she wasn't in the mood to listen to them harping on about her spending too much time at work and not being married.

Olive glanced at the clock and a grim smile crossed her face. She knew just the thing to take her mind off her own problems. She would go round and see Peggy, apologise for her behaviour and pretend to feel sorry for her. If Kurt did find out where Joe was, she would only be able to gloat about it if she and Peggy were on speaking terms. There would be no fun having the knowledge unless she could watch Peggy suffering. Making up her mind, she had a quick look in her larder and found some chocolate she had been saving. She placed the bar in her handbag and headed off in the direction of Peggy's house.

Northern France

There was little cover and they could only watch the approaching lorry with trepidation. To their relief, when the vehicle drew closer, they saw a French number plate. Cautiously, they stood up and dusted themselves down.

"Hey, do you want a lift?" Astonished, they spun around. The driver had the door open and was gesturing to the back. "I'm going to Cherbourg, if that's any help?" he called.

"Thank you. That would be wonderful." Jean-Paul indicated Marcel and Jeanne should climb in the back. Claudette climbed in beside the driver and waved to Angel to join her, but she shook her head and followed Marcel and Jeanne into the rear. Jean-Paul made sure they were safely inside and then climbed up beside Claudette.

"Trying to get to England?" the driver asked, letting the clutch out. The truck jolted forward. "Sorry, the clutch is playing up," he explained.

"Yes, we are," Jean-Paul answered.

"Me too." The driver wiped his right hand on his trousers and then extended it towards Jean-Paul. "Ricard Cheville," he said.

"I'm Jean-Paul, and this is my wife, Claudette. My daughter Jeanne, her husband, Marcel, and their child, Angel, are in the back." He could feel Claudette staring at him, but he ignored her. "We've not heard the news for a few days. Are the Germans still winning?"

"Unfortunately, yes." Ricard grimaced. "They started a second offensive a few days ago which is heading towards Paris. We heard this morning Italy has also declared war on us. To be honest, I think France will surrender before long. The army seems to be in total disarray and the government has left Paris and fled to Bordeaux."

There was a long silence while Jean-Paul and Claudette digested the news that their worst fears were about to come true and France would soon fall under the control of the Nazis.

Honor Oak Park, London

Peggy stared at the clothes in her wardrobe and wondered what on earth she should wear. She didn't want to dress up, or Chris would get the wrong idea, but she didn't want to look too dowdy either. She tried to ignore the nervous fluttering in her stomach. She was just going for a drink with a friend, nothing more.

She wished she'd said no, but he had been so nice to her in Gravesend, she couldn't find the words to say she wanted to cancel and, in the end, she'd said nothing. Now she was regretting her cowardice. It would have been much easier to put him off then than now. She sighed and turned her attention back to the cupboard. She eventually settled on one of her older dresses, a blue a-line dress with a white collar. She was relieved neither Ethel nor Sally were in the house, because she felt ridiculously guilty and didn't want anyone to see her.

She glanced at the clock and sighed. She would have one drink and then make her excuses. She could always say she was tired, goodness knows they had been busy enough.

****

The Road to Cherbourg, France

They continued in silence for a while. Finding the rhythm of the truck hypnotic, Jean-Paul felt his eyes closing, only to be jerked awake by the driver's soft curse. "Merde."

"Problem?" Jean-Paul questioned.

"Roadblock ahead. I thought for a minute it was German but we're alright, looks like a British one."

He eased the truck to a halt and a soldier approached the driver's side.

"Where are you going?" he asked slowly, in English.

"We're trying to get to Cherbourg," the driver replied in French. The soldier nodded and after a cursory examination went to the back.

They heard some muffled talking and then Angel's excited voice saying in French, "Chocolate, thank you."

The soldier came back to the driver and waved him on, saying, "Be careful. The Germans are not here yet, but they won't be much longer. Good luck."

Jean-Paul exchanged glances with Claudette. At least he hadn't told them to go back, although the words of the British soldiers in Dunkirk and the French soldiers on the road earlier were fresh in his mind and he was worried they would be told the same thing in Cherbourg.

Ricard eased the clutch out, this time the truck didn't jolt them forward, and they moved off slowly, making sure they negotiated the barricade carefully.

****

Honor Oak Park, London

Chris arrived promptly at half past seven to pick Peggy up and they headed towards the local pub.

"You look very nice"

"Thank you." Peggy grimaced, feeling herself starting to blush.

Chris grinned. "You don't have to keep quite this much distance between us. I won't pounce on you, I promise."

Peggy glanced across at him and realised he was teasing her. She relaxed and smiled at him. "I'm sorry, I just feel terribly guilty. I shouldn't be enjoying myself when I have no idea where Joe is, or even if he's alive." Her face fell.

Chris put out his hand and caught her arm. "I don't want you to feel uncomfortable, Peggy, honestly. Look, we'll just have one drink and then I'll walk you home. Unless you would rather go back now and we can do this another time, maybe once you know Joe's safe?"

"Would you mind if I went home now?"

Chris gave a rueful smile. "No, of course not."

The Road to Cherbourg, France

After the roadblock, they saw no one for several kilometres, by which time darkness had fallen and they had arrived on the outskirts of Cherbourg. Delighted to see the '*Cherbourg – five km*' sign, Jean-Paul's elation was short lived. The truck began to cough and splutter and then finally stopped altogether.

"Merde; merde; merde!" Ricard slammed his hand on the steering wheel. Then he relaxed. "Ah well, only five kilometres to go. Sorry folks, this is as far as we'll be going in this old thing."

They all climbed out.

"You've saved us hours, not to mention our aching feet." Claudette hugged Ricard. "Thank you and good luck to you."

"And you." He shook their hands and disappeared into the darkness, leaving them on the side of the main route into Cherbourg.

"Oh well, not far now," Jean-Paul said with an encouraging smile. "Come on, let's go."

Within moments, Angel started complaining. "I'm tired… I'm bored. Are we ever going to stop?"

Marcel groaned. Angel's whining had increased and, although he could understand why, he found himself becoming short tempered with her.

"You know why we're walking, Angel. We have to get away from the Germans and the truck ran out of petrol and, because we don't have a car or a cart, we have to walk."

Angel pouted and, folding her arms, stopped and stood still. "Well I don't want to anymore."

Marcel was about to argue with her when Jean-Paul intervened. "I think Angel is right."

Chapter Forty-three

Honor Oak Park, London

Olive arrived at Peggy's house and was about to knock on the door when she lost her nerve. Her last attempt at being friendly hadn't worked. Her motives were different this time but that was no guarantee the outcome wouldn't be the same. Deciding this was probably a mistake, she turned around and walked straight into Peggy coming up the path. Peggy was just as astonished to see her cousin and an expression of anger crossed her face, followed by something else Olive couldn't identify.

"Hello, Olive. This is a surprise. Is anything wrong?"

Olive wondered why her cousin looked so uncomfortable. Her beady eyes took in the nice dress and make up and she filed it away to think about later. Instead, she made an effort to put on a pleasant expression and hastened to reassure her. "No, no, nothing's wrong. I felt really bad about the way I behaved at mother's and wanted to apologise." She ignored Peggy's sceptical expression and rushed on. "Have you heard any more about Joe?"

Peggy stared at Olive for a long moment before shaking her head. She was still confused by Olive's apparent change of attitude and she wasn't about to forget the horrid things her cousin had said to her that easily. She was also worried that Olive might have seen her with Chris. Olive was bound to get the wrong idea. "No. Was there anything else?"

Olive ignored the overt hostility and somehow managed to keep the apologetic smile on her face. "I know I was horrible to you, but I wondered if you wanted to talk. I've bought some chocolate. I know how you love Cadbury's." Olive began fumbling through her handbag, finally pulling out the small bar. "Here."

Peggy hesitated, wondering what her cousin was up to. Then, deciding she probably had nothing to lose, she shrugged, took the offered chocolate, unlocked the front door, and indicated for Olive to step inside. "Why don't you come in?"

"Thank you." Olive stepped through the door and followed Peggy into the kitchen.

"I'll put the kettle on." Peggy pointed to the chairs and Olive sat down. There was silence while both women tried to think of something to say that wouldn't cause an argument.

"How's work?"

"I am so very sorry about Joe. I didn't mean the things I said."

They both spoke at the same time and there was an awkward silence before Peggy answered. "Well at the moment he's only missing, so he may be alright, a prisoner or even on the run somewhere in France."

"Isn't there anyone you can ask?" Olive managed to sound genuinely concerned and Peggy was unable to keep the look of surprise off her face. Sensing her plan was working, Olive continued to look sympathetic.

Eventually Peggy shook her head. "All we can do is to wait for some kind of official notification. If he's a prisoner, we probably won't be informed for a while." She fell silent.

"I'm sure he's alright, Peggy. Try not to worry too much." Olive sounded so solicitous that Peggy stared at her in astonishment and Olive flushed. "I know I haven't always been very pleasant to you, in fact I've been downright mean, but can we put the past behind us? I would very much like us to be friends."

"Why now?" Peggy still sounded suspicious.

Olive shrugged. "I suppose the war's made me realise just how important family is and, other than mother and father, you're my only relation. Can you find it within you to forgive me?" She sounded so wistful that, after a brief hesitation, Peggy put aside her animosity and banished any doubts to the back of her mind.

"Yes, of course I can." Peggy gave the first genuine smile since Olive had arrived. "Come on, let's share the chocolate!"

****

Outskirts of Cherbourg, France

The others stared at Jean-Paul in surprise, wondering if this was just a ruse. However, his expression was deadly serious.

"I think we should separate." He held up his hand to stem their protests. "Marcel can go to England and join up and fight. They will take him off in a boat, if he can find one of course, because he will be useful. We are not. We will just be more mouths to feed and, if Britain has to fight alone, she will need all her food for her own people."

"What are you suggesting?" Marcel asked, scared at the prospect of being on his own.

"I think you will stand more chance of getting to England without us. We could go south instead and settle in one of the villages near the coast."

"But what about…?" Marcel stopped, not wanting to say any more in front of Angel.

"We have alternative papers. You remember, we took them from Angel's house so we could trace her relatives afterwards if necessary."

"But there are only three sets," Claudette reminded him.

"We can always say we've lost one set. Everything will be very chaotic, I doubt we'll have any problem, especially as the three we have are in the same name. Also, if we keep going south, we may be able to find somewhere else where they will also evacuate civilians. Then we could all go."

"I don't want Marcel to leave us." Even in the dark they could see the terror on Angel's face and hear the fear in her voice. "I don't mind walking, honestly." She started to walk. "Come on. I won't complain any more, I promise."

Jean-Paul shook his head and called her back. "Angel, this is nothing to do with you not wanting to walk, I promise you. I just want to make sure we are all safe."

"I don't understand why we need to separate." Marcel argued. "Can't we all stay together?"

"Without us, you will be able to travel much quicker and we don't know how much time we have before the Germans block all routes out of the north," Jean-Paul answered. "We will head south and find another way. We can slow down because at the moment, the Germans are concentrating their attack on the north of the country. It might be months before they try to occupy the rest of France."

Marcel didn't answer. Unfortunately, Jean-Paul was making sense, but he had come to rely on him and he doubted whether he would be able to get himself to England without the help of his new family. He had also fallen in love for the first time in his life and he didn't want to leave Jeanne behind.

Jean-Paul answered his thoughts as if he had spoken out loud: "Marcel, you have proved yourself to be resourceful and brave and you really don't need us. We will find each other again once we all get to England and, if not, I'm sure we will find each other after the war. After all, we have arranged to meet up at Antoinette's, haven't we?"

"Can Jeanne come with me?" Marcel asked in desperation. "She could become a nurse or join the WRENS or something."

Jean-Paul glanced at his daughter. "What do you want to do, Jeanne?" She was surprised he had given her a choice but, before she could answer, he continued, "Bear in mind, if you go with Marcel now and they won't evacuate you, you will be stranded on your own."

Jeanne stared at her father and then at Marcel. Her heart wanted to go with Marcel, but her head was telling her something else. After a few moments, she spoke: "I would love to go with you, Marcel, but I think I have to stay with my parents and Angel."

Angel had moved closer to Jeanne and, hearing these words, she put her hand in Jeanne's and cuddled up to her, turning her back on Marcel.

Marcel wanted to argue, but he knew Jean-Paul was right. He couldn't guarantee Jeanne's safety and the last thing he wanted to do was to leave her high and dry on her own. She would be better off with her parents. Ignoring the pain that was physical in its intensity, Marcel nodded in resignation.

"You're right, I know you are..." Marcel's voice tailed off and he gazed up at the sky, wondering when these people had become more real to him than his own family and why leaving them would be such a wrench.

****

Bethune, Northern France

Brigitte stared up at Louis, unable to believe he was still with her. She knew he hadn't been home yet and she wondered if he knew about the death of his father.

"What's the matter, Brigitte?" Louis gazed down tenderly. "Is something bothering you?"

"No, of course not. I'm just grateful you're here. You have no idea how much I've missed you."

Louis relaxed. "I've missed you too." The thought crossed his mind that, perhaps now would be a good time to ask her to marry him. He glanced around. The surroundings, her father's café, were not very romantic though, and he thought he should wait until they were somewhere much nicer.

"Another drink?" Brigitte banished thoughts of Louis' father to the back of her mind. If she told him now, he would want to rush home and she wouldn't see him again. He couldn't change anything, so why upset him.

"Great, thanks." Seeing a small farm truck pull up outside the window, Louis stopped thinking of marriage and wondered about going home. He was beginning to feel guilty, but he was sure they could manage a few more days without him.

****

La Couture, Northern France

The light faded and Marie stood by the back door staring up at the stars. She wondered if her sons were still alive and were maybe looking up at the night sky and thinking about her. She hoped so. She turned away from the silent fields and stepped back inside the house, closing the door behind her. The room felt empty and she resisted the urge to sit down and weep. She still had the farm and, until she knew for certain her boys weren't coming home, she would concentrate on keeping everything going for them.

There was still gunfire in the distance. The fighting must be continuing, although she had no idea how far into France the Germans had penetrated. They must be nearing Paris. The thought sent a shudder through her. She should really listen to the wireless but she couldn't face the relentless bad news. Perhaps she would find a book to read and put a record on the gramophone. Marie frowned. She couldn't remember when she'd last played a record. Then she smiled. Of course, she and Jacques had danced the New Year in. The tears began to fall and she brushed them away angrily. If she was going to cry every time she thought of him, she would spend the rest of her life being miserable. She had to make an effort to concentrate on the happy memories instead. Jacques would not have wanted her to be sad. He would have told her to carry on fighting, not to give up hope and to remember that good news came when you least expected.

Chapter Forty-four

The next morning arrived much too quickly and, when dawn broke, Jean-Paul got to his feet and woke Claudette and Angel. Jeanne had spent the night curled up in Marcel's arms. They seemed so peaceful, Jean-Paul was loathe to disturb them.

"It's time, chéri." Jeanne stirred and Marcel also woke. Seeing Jean-Paul standing over them, he closed his eyes for a moment trying to savour every remaining minute.

Eventually, he opened his eyes again and looked up at Jean-Paul. "Time to go?" he asked and Jean-Paul nodded. Marcel stood up and Jean-Paul hugged the boy to him and wished him luck. Claudette followed suit and then it was Angel's turn. To start with, she turned her back on him then, realising she might not see him again, she clung to him, her little body wracked with sobs.

"Please, Angel, this is hard enough." Marcel was having trouble blinking back his own tears. "I will come back for you, I promise. Take care of Jeanne for me and, every night before you go to bed, look at the stars and think of me. I will be watching the same stars, just from a different place. If we see them together we can pretend we *are* together."

Angel stopped crying and she gave him a watery smile. Marcel reached for Jeanne. Her face was already streaked with tears and Marcel pulled her to him, enveloping her in his arms. Jeanne clung to him and he could feel her shaking as she cried into his shoulder, her tears soaking through his shirt. Marcel tried to break the embrace but he couldn't. He wanted to stay like this for ever. It was Jeanne who finally found the strength to let go. Raising her face until she was staring him straight in the eyes, Jeanne kissed him passionately and then, giving him one more hug, she untangled her arms and, turning back to Angel, she took her hand. Without looking back, the two girls headed over to Jean-Paul and Claudette and they began walking away.

Marcel watched them go, feeling even more bereft than he had when he had left his parents. He wanted nothing more than to run after them and he was just about to when he remembered the note the soldier had given him. If he didn't get to England, how could he deliver the message? Jean-Paul's words, about having a duty to deliver the letter, came back to him. Marcel stood undecided, torn between his love for Jeanne and his duty as a Frenchman. He turned in the direction of Cherbourg.

****

Beauraing, France

By the time they arrived at Beauraing, Joe, like the others, was completely exhausted and dehydrated. Dysentery was rife from eating mouldy bread and rotten vegetables and their uniforms were hanging off them because they had lost so much weight. Several men had dropped out of the lines and had not reappeared.

The guards marched them through the town and finally stopped in a large goods yard not far from the station. Puffs of white smoke floated gently skyward from the arriving and departing trains and they could hear the sounds of the engines as they went about their business.

"Maybe we're going the rest of the way by train?" Joe sounded more optimistic.

Rob flopped down on the floor and was quickly joined by the others. "Let's hope so. I don't think I could walk another step."

They were not allowed to rest for long, though. Within a short time, the guards roused them and marched them to the station. Standing on the platform, with the evening sun beating down and the sweat pouring off him, Joe watched the clouds of white smoke pouring from the approaching engine. His initial relief that they weren't going to have to walk was quickly replaced with dismay. The train was just a goods train and there were no passenger carriages. The engine eased to a standstill and the guards hustled them aboard using their bayonets and rifle butts.

Each closed cattle truck held about sixty men. There was no food or water and the sun shone down. The train remained stationary for several hours and the stifling heat grew. Just when Joe was sure he couldn't bear the temperature any longer, the engine fired up and the train began to move. They eased out of the station, and he felt a faint breeze coming in through the badly fitted slats in the side of the wooden panels near the top of the carriage. The train gradually built up speed and the air cooled a little.

"I suppose it's better than walking." Joe tried to think of something positive to say.

"Anything's better than walking!" Rob examined the remains of his socks. He had removed his boots earlier, despite the initial protests of the others and, after a few moments, virtually everyone else had done the same. The smell of their unwashed bodies, the sweat from the heat and the odour from their boots permeated the wagon but they were all really past caring and no one complained.

Rob closed his eyes. Joe glared at him. "I don't know how you can sleep in this heat."

"I can't, but it's worth a try. At least I can escape for a while," Rob responded without even bothering to open his eyes.

Unable to think of anything else to say, Joe closed his eyes too but he had a really bad headache, caused by dehydration and stomach ache from lack of food, and couldn't settle. Eventually he stopped trying.

****

Marcel was too miserable to notice the sun was shining. All he could think about was Jeanne and Angel and whether he would ever see them again. He could feel tears threatening to fall and angrily he shook his head. He vowed he would come back to find them. He didn't care how long it took. Hearing voices and, temporarily unnerved, Marcel dived behind a large tree then, remembering there were no Germans this far west, he came out and hurried to where the sound had come from. Marcel drew closer, he could hear the voices were English and, rounding a bend in the road, he saw several British soldiers half marching, half walking towards Cherbourg. Hastening towards them Marcel caught them up and introduced himself using the few words of their language Charles had taught him.

To his delight, they clapped him on the back and then offered him a cigarette. Marcel couldn't understand anything they were saying, however, the gesture was obvious and not wanting to offend, Marcel accepted the cigarette.

"Thank you." One of them offered him a light. Marcel wasn't sure how to light a cigarette, but he had seen others smoke so he sucked hard and immediately burst out coughing, causing much hilarity amongst the soldiers.

"'E's never had one before," said the one who had introduced himself as Dave.

"'Ere, mate, suck a bit more gently," another one, whose name Marcel thought was Les, offered kindly. Although Marcel couldn't understand the words, he understood the gestures and tried again. This time he was more successful and, although he felt really dizzy to start with, he persevered, not wanting to appear ungrateful. After a few puffs on the cigarette, Marcel began to feel less sick but he couldn't really understand why people would want to smoke at all; the taste was disgusting.

The soldiers were chatting away in English and Marcel could only make out the odd word, which wasn't enough for him to understand what they were talking about. He decided to try and ask about a boat to England and, after a few attempts, and much laughter, they finally understood him.

"You stick with us, mate, we'll see you're alright. The Navy will come and take us off and you can come with us."

****

Gravesend, Kent

They were nearing their lunch break when Peggy heard a loud scream. Turning quickly in the direction of the noise, she was surprised to see Helen standing in the middle of the ward, her hand over her mouth, her eyes wide with shock. Peggy stopped what she was doing and hurried over to her. "Helen, what on earth's the matter?" she asked.

Helen turned her horrified face to Peggy. "They've just given out on the news, *HMS Wakeful* has been sunk off the coast of France." Peggy's face was blank. She had no idea what Helen was talking about. "*HMS Wakeful* is the ship John Downey is on… Annie's husband," Helen snapped at her.

"Oh no." Peggy couldn't think of anything to say. All she could do was to hold her friend's hand and then Helen began to dissolve into tears. Peggy put her arms round her.

"What's going on here?" Sister bustled towards them. "Cooper?" Peggy quickly explained. "Do you want to go home, Macklin?" Sister asked, kindly.

"No, I don't think so, Sister," Helen sobbed. "I… it's a long story… I don't know," she finally finished.

"Right, well I don't think you'll be much good to us here, I'll have someone take you to the bus stop and you can go home." When Helen began to interrupt, she continued, "Go home to your family. Your sister will need you. We can manage without you today. It's nearly lunchtime, Cooper. Take Macklin to the bus stop and then have your lunch."

"Yes, Sister."

They walked in silence to the bus stop, Peggy unable to think of anything she could say to make things any better.

"Thanks, Peggy." Helen turned towards her.

"I haven't done anything." Peggy felt totally useless.

"Yes, you have. You haven't tried to tell me everything will be alright." She managed a half-smile and, after giving Peggy a quick hug, she boarded the bus.

****

Outside Gorges, France

To start with, Jean-Paul and his family travelled in silence. The roads were still reasonably empty and any troops they passed were either French or British and caused them no problem. Angel was missing Marcel and veered from complaining bitterly to periods of complete withdrawal that were so total, even Jeanne was unable to break through her silence. Desperately missing Marcel herself, Jeanne understood how Angel felt but, unlike Angel, she was not able to give in to her own depression and sadness.

Jean-Paul was also worried about Claudette. Her feet were badly swollen and the blisters showed no sign of healing up. Although she had long since stopped complaining, he was aware she was in considerable pain. He also noticed her legs were puffy but, when he questioned her, she shrugged off his concerns and said that nothing was wrong. He wanted to believe her when she said she knew best; she was a nurse after all, but Jean-Paul had a distinct feeling there was something she was not telling him.

He decided they would go into the next town rather than skirting round it and he would find a doctor to examine her. "Here, lean on me for a while." He took Claudette's arm and almost recoiled in shock at how thin and wasted her flesh felt in his fingers. "I think we should try to find some kind of transport in the next town." Claudette was too exhausted to answer. Lost in her pain, it was a few moments before she noticed Jean-Paul had stopped and was staring behind him.

Cherbourg, France

Before long, Marcel and his new friends were striding through the suburbs of Cherbourg. Apart from the outskirts of Dunkirk and Calais, both of which had been under heavy gunfire, Marcel had never been anywhere this big. He gazed around in wonder at the large buildings and the number of people milling about. Although the Germans had not yet reached here, he could see the fear etched on people's faces. Marcel was glad he was with the British soldiers: he had a feeling he might have been treated with a lot more suspicion otherwise. The soldiers were also glad to have him with them, because Marcel could ask for things in French. The fact that Marcel and the soldiers had trouble communicating didn't seem to worry them too much and he was grateful to them for helping him. They had already shared their rations with him and Marcel was pleased to be able to buy some food with his own money so he could repay them.

They made their way down to the harbour and, with the help of the soldiers, Marcel was able to pass through the roadblock with little difficulty. All he needed now was to get on a ship.

****

En route to Germany

After several hours, the Germans opened the hatch above them and threw down some mouldy bread, each loaf to be divided between six of them. Joe was so thirsty, he really didn't want any food, but he knew he had to eat to keep himself alive. Much to his relief, they were finally given some water. The train tracked eastwards across Belgium and into Luxembourg, before finally crossing the German border and easing to a halt near Dortmund at a place called Igel. Here, they were made to get out, while the train headed back towards France. Everywhere Joe looked, there were swastikas proclaiming German superiority. The guards began counting the prisoners and then, when they had finished, they were counted again.

"This would be funny if I wasn't so bloody tired," Rob whispered under his breath.

"P'raps they can't count," Joe croaked. He was so thirsty, speaking hurt and his lips were cracked and sore. Eventually, the guards were satisfied and they were paraded past the station staff and civilians towards another stationary goods train. Relief they were able to stretch their legs soon turned to dismay. Unlike the French, who had tried to help by giving them food and water, the German civilians jeered and spat at them. They were glad to reach the other train and stumble on board.

Chapter Forty-five

"Is something wrong?" Claudette asked

"I can hear a car coming." Jean-Paul was about to say more when the vehicle came in to view; a rather expensive car driven by a young man with a woman sitting in the passenger seat.

Pulling alongside, the woman wound down the window and asked, "Do you want a lift? We're not going far, only a little way up the road, but it might help." Jean-Paul was so used to cars driving past, he couldn't believe his ears. In fact, he was so surprised, he didn't answer and the car began to move away.

"Thank you, thank you." Claudette recovered her wits quicker than the others.

The car stopped again, the woman reached over the seat and opened the back door. Unable to believe their luck, Jean-Paul, Claudette, Jeanne and Angel piled into the back of the large car.

"Where are you going?" the man asked.

"We're not entirely sure, probably the south somewhere." Jean-Paul's reply was cagey.

"How long have you been on the road?" The woman leant round, addressing her question to Claudette.

"About two weeks now. Although it seems like forever."

"Are you hoping to go to England?"

"If we can," Jean-Paul responded. "Do you know where the Germans are?"

"No." The man scowled and then carried on, "There's very little news, to be honest. Judging by the guns, though, I wouldn't think they're too far away"

Jean-Paul realised the pounding of the artillery had become such a normal part of their lives, they barely noticed the noise anymore. "Are you trying to get to England too?" he asked.

"No, we have a duty to stay here and try to help the people. I am the Marquis Armand Belvoir and this is my wife Madeleine. We have a small chateau just a little further along and we employ several people. We cannot leave them to fend for themselves, much as we might like to." He grimaced again. "That's not meant to be a criticism. If we felt we could go, we would, believe me."

"I know you are in a hurry to go south, but would you like to come in and get some clean clothes and perhaps have a bath?" The Marchioness was smiling at Angel who was playing with a bracelet she had given her. "You don't need to stay long if you don't want to, but we would be more than happy to find you some beds for the night."

Although he was anxious to get going, Jean-Paul accepted they would probably make better progress if they stopped, had a good night's rest and replenished their stores.

"That would be very kind of you." His voice cracked with emotion. "Thank you."

"Good. That's settled then." Madeleine smiled. They turned off onto a private lane which twisted and turned and disappeared into the distance. The track was pitted and full of potholes and Jean-Paul, Claudette and Jeanne watched out of the window with interest as they drove slowly past a large orchard. On the other side, the pasture was full of cows contentedly chewing grass.

They rounded a corner and Jeanne gasped. Following her gaze, the others looked out in amazement. Tucked away, with its back to the hills was an enormous chateau, complete with ornate turrets.

"Oh, look – a castle!" Angel shrieked in excitement, her eyes wide. "Are we going there?"

"Yes, just for a little while," Madeleine replied. "You are going to have a nice bath and get some clean clothes." She turned to Claudette. "Would you like to see a doctor?"

Claudette started to argue that she didn't need to and she was perfectly well, just a little tired. Then, seeing her husband and daughter's concerned expressions, she gave in. If nothing else, he could put her mind at rest and stop her family worrying about her. "Thank you. I think that would be useful."

"We can pay for his services and for some food too." Jean-Paul was anxious they did not think he was expecting everything for nothing.

"We'll sort something out once you've had a chance to clean up and have something hot to eat," Madeleine answered as they drew up in front of the chateau and a couple of servants emerged to help them.

Madeleine spoke rapidly to the servants and they were taken to some simple clean rooms at the back of the chateau which were obviously servants' quarters and within a very short time, a doctor had been summoned. While he was examining Claudette, Jean-Paul, Jeanne and Angel took the opportunity to bathe and change their clothes. Angel had reverted back to her cheerful self and couldn't hide her exuberance at being in a 'fairy castle'. Her enthusiasm was infectious and, if they hadn't been concerned about Claudette's health, they too would have felt they had wandered into another world.

****

Cherbourg, France

The other side of the roadblock was a hive of activity with troops of numerous battalions and from several countries milling about, digging in and preparing to withdraw from the French coast. Barricades were being built and equipment and weapons that weren't in immediate use were being piled together. Seeing his confusion, Dave explained with the help of repetition, hand gestures and acting.

"Anything we can't take with us, we have to destroy so it doesn't fall into Jerry's hands. Come on, let's get some grub and find you a billet for the night." Dave was pleased when Marcel nodded immediately. Marcel's command of the English language had trebled in the short time he had spent with the soldiers and, together with a few more colourful phrases, 'grub' and 'billet' were a couple of the new words he had added to his vocabulary. They approached a makeshift tent where some harassed non-combatants were handing out emergency rations and Marcel was struck by the ordered chaos surrounding him. Although, at first sight, people appeared to be wandering around aimlessly, he could see most of them were busy and he longed to be involved and more than a fairly useless bystander.

When he reached the front of the queue, Marcel waited while a brief argument took place between his new friends and those in charge of the rations. Although the conversation was much too quick for him to follow, he presumed they were arguing because he wasn't in any kind of uniform. Eventually, they resolved the problem and Marcel took the rations offered to him.

"Flaming pen pushers," Les grumbled. They left the tent and went to find somewhere to eat their food. "He wasn't happy because you weren't in uniform, so I told him you were a French soldier who'd escaped from Calais when the Krauts captured the town and the only way you could do that was to ditch your uniform and pretend to be a civvie."

Once Marcel had understood, he thanked him profusely.

"No problem, mate!" Les seemed slightly embarrassed at such open display of gratitude. "Look, there's an officer over there, let's go and speak to him and see what we should do with you."

Marcel followed him and stood waiting patiently. A long conversation took place between the officer and Les and, when they finished, the officer strode off leaving Marcel standing beside Les who had an expression of resignation on his face.

"Sorry, mate, we can't take you. But there are some French soldiers over there. P'raps you should go and join them." Marcel turned to where Les was pointing and saw several men in French uniforms standing around, smoking and chatting. They seemed vaguely familiar, although Marcel wasn't sure why.

****

Bethune, Northern France

"Your face looks much better," Brigitte said. The swelling on Louis' face had gone down quite a bit, although he still had two black eyes and, apart from the bruising over most of his body, he seemed in much less discomfort. He knew he should really think about going home, but for the moment he was enjoying having Brigitte running around after him and catering for his every need.

"Come back to bed for a while." Brigitte climbed back in and, feeling her warm body next to his, Louis reached for her, his hands exploring the secret places he'd spent his time day-dreaming about when they were apart. Brigitte straddled him, taking care not to lean on his stomach or chest which were covered in bruises, and began to move slowly up and down.

Louis relaxed. *No need to rush home; another few days won't hurt.* Anyway, he didn't want his mother to see his bruised face; she would only fuss about him. Brigitte tightened her muscles and Louis stopped thinking and gave himself up to the pleasurable sensations flooding his body while Brigitte moved faster and faster.

****

Outside Cherbourg, France

Claudette reported that the doctor had said she was suffering from exhaustion and a couple of days' rest was all she needed. Everyone was so relieved, they did not see the look that passed between Madeleine and Armand, who had also spoken to the doctor before he left.

"Have you any idea where you want to go?" Armand asked. Jean-Paul, Claudette, Jeanne and Angel were seated at a long kitchen table, eating their first nourishing meal for several days. Armand was leaning on the range, having dismissed the servants.

"Not really, only to go south, away from the Germans," Jean-Paul answered.

"I understand." There was something about Armand's tone that caught Jean-Paul's attention. "I too have relations, a long way back I hasten to add, who the Germans would not have liked," Armand continued, making it obvious he did not want to say any more in front of Angel. He changed the subject. "I think your best bet would be to go towards the Pyrenees. There are several villages and towns you may be able to settle in and, if the Germans get that far, which I pray they won't, at least you'll be near the Spanish border and you can cross over quickly if you have to."

Jean-Paul considered Armand's suggestion which made sense.

"We can lend you a car, if you like?" Armand offered, much to Jean-Paul's amazement. "We'll fill the vehicle up with petrol and have it ready to leave by the morning, unless you would like to leave this evening?"

"We can't possible pay for a car…" Jean-Paul began. Armand raised his hand.

"We don't want paying. We can manage without one car and having a vehicle will make your life considerably easier."

Jean-Paul was overcome with gratitude and thanked Armand profusely. Relieved they would not have to walk for a while at least, Claudette answered his original question, "The morning will be perfect." She stood up and took Armand's hand. "I really don't know how we can thank you."

"No need. We're all in this together." Armand checked the kitchen clock, and then his watch. "When you get settled and no longer need the car, you can sell it. I am sure the extra money will help until you are back on your feet. Now, I'll leave you to get some rest. Good luck and remember us in your prayers." And with a brief smile, he left.

****

Marcel thanked Les and made his way over to the French troops. They were the soldiers who'd told them the British weren't evacuating civilians and one of them remembered Marcel.

"Goodness, you got here then, and they let you through, all of you?" he asked.

Marcel shook his head. "No. After we spoke to you, we decided to split up. I came here; they've gone south to try and get away from the Germans."

The soldier held out his hand. "I'm Gerard Dupré, well Sergeant Dupré, if I'm to be accurate."

"Marcel Servier. My brother, Louis, is a private in the 128th Fortress Infantry Regiment. He was serving at Ouvrage Brehain near Brehain-la-Ville on the Maginot line. I'm hoping he's gone to England and I can find him there. Then I want join up and come back to liberate France."

Gerard clapped him on the back. "Good for you. Now, about your brother. We have no idea what's happened to the French Army. Some soldiers have escaped to England, others have returned home and quite a lot have probably been taken prisoner by the Germans. If your brother is in England, there should be some record of him at one of the reception camps. How old are you Marcel?"

Marcel started to say that he was eighteen, then said with reluctance, "Seventeen."

Gerard frowned. "It would be better if you were a bit older..."

"I'm nearly eighteen," Marcel interrupted in desperation.

Gerard grinned. "That's probably old enough! Come on, I'll take you down to the harbour area. Although they're mainly using the troop ships and motor transport ships for regulars, they've also set up convoys of coasters and some Dutch Schuyts for civilians as well as soldiers. I may be able to get you on one of those."

Marcel followed him, unable to believe he might finally be about to embark for England. They passed several troops packing up equipment and others carrying wounded men on stretchers heading in the same direction. They made for the large ship moored up at the beginning of the quay, but Gerard kept going until they came towards the far end.

There were a couple of Dutch Schuyts moored up and Marcel followed the sergeant to the first one. He waited patiently while Gerard spoke to the sailor who was standing guard at the bottom of the gangplank. One minute he was standing behind Gerard and the next, the sailor had stood aside and Gerard was clapping him on the back, shaking his hand and moving out of the way leaving Marcel to climb up and step aboard. After the last few days, when everything had been so difficult, it was almost an anti-climax.

****

Catford, London

Olive counted out the exact money and placed the cash under her mattress. He was due the following evening and she was dreading the encounter. There was something slimy about him, about the way he eyed her up and down and she hadn't forgotten his hands grabbing her breast on his first visit. She wasn't under any illusion that he found her attractive. He was much younger than her, so she could only assume he leered at her to make her uncomfortable. She shuddered and tried to put him out of her head.

A brief smile crossed her lips and she thought back to the couple of hours she had spent with Peggy the night before last. Surprisingly, the evening had gone very well. After a little while, Peggy had relaxed and didn't seem the slightest bit suspicious of her motives. At least she had something positive to tell Kurt in her next letter. Hopefully there would be one from him soon, perhaps even giving her some news about Joe. She couldn't wait to watch her cousin wallowing in self-pity while she, Olive, knew exactly where Joe was and what was happening to him. Her spirits rose in anticipation and, after one more glance around to make sure everything was tidy, she headed off to work.

Gravesend, Kent

Helen arrived at work, her face pale and blotchy.

"Did you see Annie?" Peggy asked when Helen came and sat next to her on the coach.

"No." Helen shook her head. "She managed to get a phone call to my neighbour though. John's been reported missing, although nothing's been confirmed. I know this is a terrible cheek, Peggy, but could we possibly meet her at your house?"

"Of course you can. Whenever you want. Just give me some warning and I'll try to arrange for us all to go out and leave you to talk in peace."

Helen was relieved. "Thank you, Peggy. You have no idea what this'll mean to Mum"

Peggy impulsively leant over and gave her a hug. "Everything will work itself out, Helen." Helen nodded, although she couldn't really see any grounds for optimism. Her brain had been racing with questions all night. If John had been killed, would his parents let Annie stay there and, if they didn't, where would she go? There was no way Dad would let her come back home. She thought back to the shouted conversation between her parents because her mum had tentatively suggested, perhaps Annie should come back home if she was a widow. Helen had been horrified by her father's reply which was simply that she'd made her bed so she could lie in it; he never wanted to hear her name mentioned again and hadn't he made that clear when she'd left? Did she really think her husband's death was going to make a difference? Helen had never believed she could hate anyone, but at that moment she loathed her father and vowed she too would move out. She wouldn't tell him where she was going either. Even just thinking about her father made her blood boil. How could he be so uncaring and unfeeling? Annie was his own flesh and blood and she was suffering and he couldn't care less.

"Helen?"

"Sorry. I was thinking about last night. What did you say?"

"I just asked if yesterday's events had made any difference to the way your father felt," Peggy repeated and, seeing Helen's face grow dark, she added, "Obviously not. I'm sorry I didn't want to upset you all over again."

"I'm not upset, I'm furious. I never believed I could be this angry. He said John's death made no difference and, quite frankly, he couldn't care less. How could you treat your own children like that?"

Peggy was speechless for a moment. "I have no idea, but at least she has you and your mum." She was unable to think of anything else to say. Helen didn't answer and the rest of the journey was spent in silence.

******

English Channel

Marcel stood on the deck and watched the troop ships leaving until eventually only the Dutch boats were left. Soldiers were still arriving, mostly in twos or threes, others in larger groups of twenty or more. A large gathering of disheveled and dejected French troops arrived and were shepherded onto the two remaining ships, together with a number of Polish and British troops and they finally sailed. Marcel settled down for the voyage across the Channel and soon fell into conversation with some of the French soldiers, who asked how old he was.

About to say seventeen, Marcel remembered Gerard's reaction and changed his mind. "I was eighteen last week and would have joined up, but given the situation, I decided to try and get to England and join up there."

No-one questioned his statement and Marcel decided if anyone else asked him how old he was, that was how he would answer.

The journey was uneventful, although the presence of the RAF overhead was a constant reminder that they would not be safe until they finally reached England. Marcel gazed out over the calm waters of the Channel and thought about his parents and his new family. He wished they were all here with him. He was tired but his mind was restless and he was unable to settle. He suddenly remembered the note he had been given by the soldier all those days ago and he put his hand into his inside shirt pocket to check it was still there. Marcel's hand touched the paper, neatly folded and pinned and he breathed a sigh of relief.

Within a very short time, they reached Weymouth and Marcel followed his new friends off the ship. As he breathed in the salty sea air and glanced around at the unfamiliar surroundings, his ears picked up the odd word of English that he recognised and he was tempted to pinch himself. He had made it. He had reached England.

Part Three

June - July 1940

Chapter Forty-six

Jean-Paul wondered whether they had chosen the right place. The road was littered with abandoned cars, carts, bicycles and possessions and Jean-Paul felt the first stirrings of unease. Wearily, they followed the directions given to them on the outskirts of the town. Rumours were rife among those in the queue that they would not be allowed in unless they could prove they had accommodation and Jean-Paul looked at Claudette with concern. She shrugged and they decided to sit tight for a while. If they were not able to stop here, they would just move on. At least having the car made travelling more civilised. Although there was little petrol to be had, the Marquis had filled the car completely before they left and they had some spare cans in the boot. If the worst came to the worst, they could always resort to walking again, although that was not a prospect any of them relished.

After waiting for several hours in the stifling heat and only inching forward very slowly, Jean-Paul spotted a small side road that looked as if it might take them into the town. Making an instant decision, he turned off, rationalising that even if the road didn't take them in all the way, they might be able to walk the final distance if it wasn't too far. If not, they could always turn round and come back. The road was a minor one and was full of pot holes and, every now and again large piles of loose gravel which caused the car to slide. It also twisted and turned quite sharply and, after a few hundred yards they were finally out of sight of the main body of refugees.

"Where are we going?" Jeanne asked in surprise. She had been dozing in the back of the car, making the most of the opportunity while Angel was asleep. The movement of the car and the sudden silence now they were away from the other refugees had woken her.

"I think we might be safer to slip into Toulouse by the back roads, rather than allow them to register us. We have enough money to find our own accommodation and, until we see how the land lies, I do not want us to be too visible." He stopped as he heard a loud yawn from Angel who had opened her eyes at the sound of his voice. "Hello sweetheart, did you have a good sleep?"

Angel nodded with enthusiasm and stretched out her arms. "I'm really thirsty, can I have a drink?"

Jeanne handed her the bottle. "'Don't drink all the water, we don't have that much left."

"Don't worry, Jeanne." Jean-Paul watched as Angel grabbed the bottle. Her face was already flushed from the heat. "It shouldn't be too hard to find some water here and it is very hot."

Angel drank deeply, greedily slurping the water and gulping loudly, much to their amusement. Once she had finished, she looked round her and saw the houses lining the streets. "Is this where we are going to live?"

"We hope so." Claudette smiled. "Would you like to live here?"

Angel considered the question carefully; her head tilted on one side and then answered seriously, "I think so. Do they have shops that sell sweets?"

They all laughed and Jean-Paul answered, "I'm sure they do, Angel." He was about to add something else when he glanced in his mirror and saw that another car had followed them and was approaching quickly. Concerned that the vehicle might belong to the Toulouse authorities looking for people avoiding the proper registration processes, he told them all to hold on tight. They had reached the suburbs with houses either side of them and Jean-Paul speeded up.

Without further warning, he turned sharp right into an even smaller road, drove a short distance before quickly turning left and almost immediately right and then pulled up alongside the kerb.

****

Honor Oak Park, London

Peggy barely had time to open the post and read her letter from Pam confirming her visit to Dover when Annie arrived, followed closely by Helen and her mother, Patricia, who immediately gave Peggy an enormous hug.

"I don't know how to thank you for this." She had tears in her eyes.

Annie seemed even more timid than Peggy remembered and she found it hard to equate her with the firebrand who had found the courage to stand up to their dictatorial father. But, perhaps love gave you courage. Unfortunately, she didn't appear very brave now. In fact she seemed very frail and near to breaking point. Peggy's innate nursing senses took over. "Sit down, Annie. I'm sorry to hear your news."

"Thanks, Peggy. This is really kind of you and we all appreciate your help so much." Annie's voice was quiet and Peggy could only just hear her.

"Don't be silly, it's no bother at all. I'll go and put the kettle on and leave you to talk." Peggy was beginning to feel embarrassed by their continual gratitude and she was glad to have a reason to escape to the kitchen. She took her time, before returning eventually with the tea. Then, putting down the cups, she made her excuses.

"You don't need me and I've got some chores to do, enjoy the tea and take as long as you like."

****

Looking in the mirror, Jean-Paul couldn't see anything, so he turned round to take a better look. To his relief there was no one there.

He switched off the engine and looked around the area with interest. They were in a small quiet side street, the buildings either side were three storeys high and the windows were covered with brightly coloured shutters. From where he was sitting he could see balconies with flowers in pots and the fragrant smell of bougainvillea filled the air. He could hear birds singing and a dog barking in the distance, the sound of children's laughter suddenly erupted from somewhere out of sight and the whole place was reminiscent of the France he remembered from a couple of months ago. It was as if the war had not touched this street and he suddenly felt old. Was he always to be running and hiding, being solely responsible for the safety of his wife and daughter and now another small child? The strain and stress of the past few weeks was beginning to catch up with him and he fervently wished he was sitting in his own home with nothing to worry about.

He started the engine again and, after checking behind him, was preparing to pull out when, further down the street he spotted a sign outside one of the buildings. He eased the car forward to get a better look. "Look!" He grabbed Claudette's arm. "An apartment to rent. What do you think? Shall we go and see?"

Claudette gazed in the direction he was pointing and nodded. Jean-Paul edged the car forward, stopped outside the property and said to the two girls. "Wait here while we go and enquire."

Jean-Paul and Claudette climbed out of the car, walked up to the front door and knocked.

"Are we going to live here?" Angel asked.

"I hope so," Jeanne replied. "It's nice isn't?"

Angel was about to answer when the door opened and an elderly lady, dressed completely in black, peered out. There was a brief conversation, then she stood back and Jean-Paul and Claudette entered and disappeared from sight. They had not been not gone very long before they reappeared and, as Jeanne watched, she saw the old lady hand over a key and relief flooded through her. She turned to Angel with a big smile on her face. "I think the answer to your question is 'yes', Angel. Come on, let's go and have a look."

They hurried out of the car, glad of the opportunity to stretch their legs after the long journey.

"What did you say to her?" Jeanne asked.

"The truth." Jean-Paul had a twinkle in his eye. "Well as much of the truth as was needed; just that we had fled the Germans and come south." He took their suitcases from the boot, grateful to the Marquis who had insisted they take some clothes to tide them over and decent suitcases to put them in. He had insisted this would make them look less suspicious and Jean-Paul had agreed. "You're both my daughters, by the way. Is that alright, Angel?"

Angel wasn't listening. She had jumped out of the car as soon as the door opened and followed Claudette up the stairs to the first floor apartment, chattering excitedly about a new bedroom and being hungry and what time was dinner.

Jean-Paul and Jeanne followed with their meagre possessions and Jeanne glanced around with approval. The apartment was quite spacious. There were two bedrooms, a living room, kitchen and small bathroom and toilet, and a large south-facing balcony which could be reached from one of the bedrooms and the living room. The shutters and windows were open to allow the air to circulate and the rooms felt fresh and clean. The flat was quite sparsely furnished with a worn settee and table and chairs in the living room and both bedrooms only had a rickety cupboard and a couple of single beds. But after the past few weeks, the rooms seemed like the height of luxury and, for a few moments they were overwhelmed, even Angel, who for once was lost for words.

"I suggest we unpack, wash and change our clothes and then go into the main town to find some food." Jean-Paul pulled himself together first and, once the spell was broken, they all began talking at once.

******

La Couture, Northern France

Marie stared out of the window at the dark fields. Yet again she couldn't sleep. There were too many memories. Perhaps she should go away, pack up the farm and go south like her friend Isabel. But, the farm was her life and, in any case, until she knew where Louis and Marcel were, she couldn't go anywhere, so there was no point thinking like that. What would they do if they came home and she wasn't there? She had to stay to tell them about their father and the decision about the farm's future should be made by all of them, not just her.

"Well, Jacques, if you can hear me, I think I've been on my own for long enough now. I'd like both my boys home, safe and sound but, at this moment in time, I'll settle for either one of them." There was no answer and she gave a rueful smile. She often felt Jacques was with her, especially when she was in the fields. Tonight, however, she couldn't feel anything. She sighed, turned out the light and climbed wearily to bed.

Chapter Forty-seven

Bethune, Northern France

"I did speak to your mother when you were missing," Brigitte's eyes were on Louis' face. She had come back upstairs from working in the café, to find Louis ready to leave. Seeing her downcast face, he quickly explained that now things were a little quieter, he needed to go home because his parents would be worried about him.

Louis stopped by the door, turning towards her in surprise. "You didn't say." Brigitte wriggled uncomfortably. "What's the matter?"

Brigitte stared down at her hands which were resting on her knees. "I asked your mother if she'd heard anything from you and she started shouting at me, blaming me because you'd joined the army and you were missing, possibly dead and then she slapped me." She peered through her lashes to see his reaction and was pleased to see the anger in his face. "I didn't tell you, because I didn't want to cause you a problem with your parents."

Louis didn't say anything for a moment. "I'm sorry. She had no right to hit you." He leant down, tilted her head towards him and kissed her lips. Brigitte began to kiss him back, but Louis pulled away.

"I have to go home, my love. Give me a few days to make sure everything is alright there, then I'll come back and we can talk about the future." Her answering smile was fixed, but Louis didn't notice. Disappointed her ploy hadn't worked, Brigitte hardened her heart. Men always lied. She knew he wouldn't keep his word, especially when he found out his father was dead. Louis had made his choice and it wasn't her.

"When I come back, we can think about going south to escape the Germans, just you and me. A fresh start. What do you think?"

Brigitte joined in with enthusiasm, but her experience with men had taught her they couldn't be trusted so, while she was making plans with Louis for their future, her mind was already planning how she could redeem herself with Heinz and his friends once he was gone.

****

Outside Bethune, Northern France

Louis strode confidently through the open countryside. Spending time with Brigitte had raised his spirits; the beating he'd taken from the Germans had been worth every bruise and muscle pain. Brigitte had taken him back and he was more in love with her than ever. He couldn't wait until he was back in her arms again.

Although he was feeling slightly guilty about not letting his parents know he was safe, he was sure they wouldn't have worried about him too much. He was also annoyed his mother had treated Brigitte badly. He had never known his mother hit anyone before and he couldn't imagine what had possessed her. Still, he would be pleased to be home again and he would just have to make things clear to both his parents: Brigitte was his girlfriend and he expected them to treat her with respect.

He turned off the small track and onto another field. Not long now and he would be able to see Servier land.

****

Catford, London

Tom watched Olive leave and then let himself quietly into the flat. This was the third time he'd been here and he had no real idea why. He rationalised to himself that he wanted to make sure she wasn't about to double cross him, even though he knew that was unlikely. The truth was somewhat murkier. He was determined to find out Olive's secret, although he wasn't sure why he was becoming so obsessed and, even though he'd searched more thoroughly last time, he was none the wiser.

He started in the bedroom, rifled carefully through the bedside cupboard where nothing appeared to have changed and then the dressing table drawers where his fingers lingered over her underwear. An image of her face when he'd grabbed her breast came into his mind and he felt the beginnings of an erection. He dropped the knickers as if they were red hot and, shaking his head in disbelief, he shoved the drawer closed and sat down heavily on the bed. A faint rustle reached his ears and he wriggled, ruffling the counterpane. There is was again. He stood up and reached under the mattress.

Within seconds, he'd pulled out the envelope and looked inside. A smile crossed his face, this was his money, ready for collection later the next evening. He was tempted to take the cash, just to see the expression on her face when she saw the money had gone. Then he relented and replaced the envelope under the mattress. He reached further in and was rewarded by his hand touching something hard. Grinning, his heart racing in anticipation, Tom dragged a small oblong metal container towards him. To his annoyance the box was locked and he couldn't remember seeing a key anywhere. He cursed under his breath. He couldn't risk breaking the lock or she would know someone had been there. Reluctantly, he replaced his find. He would have to find a way of getting inside the box. 'Podge', one of his mates from the pub was good at picking locks. He'd ask him.

****

La Couture, Northern France

"Oh my God, Louis!" Marie was washing up at the sink with her back to the door when she suddenly heard a noise behind her. Scared the

Germans had returned, she spun round, then dropped the plate she was holding which smashed on the floor. Marie didn't notice. Standing in front of her was Louis. He was thinner than she remembered and his face bore some faded bruises, but it was definitely him. Marie's hand flew to her mouth in shock and then she was running across the kitchen towards him. She threw herself into Louis' arms, unable to believe he was really there and it was several minutes before he could extricate himself from her grip.

While she muttered over and over, "I can't believe you're really here." Louis felt even more guilty he hadn't come home sooner. "Where have you been? Why didn't you let me know you were safe? I thought you were dead or captured." Marie drew breath and tried to calm down. "No matter, you're here now."

"I've been hiding from the Germans for weeks, just trying to get back here." Louis hunted for something else to say. "Where's Papa?" When he hadn't seen Jacques on the farm, he'd assumed his father must be indoors, so he was surprised not to see him. Marie shook her head and haltingly told him about his father and Marcel.

Louis sat down heavily on the chair at the kitchen table, unable to take in everything she was telling him. He couldn't believe his father was dead and Marcel, the younger brother he'd always tried to protect, was missing.

"Would you like some coffee?" Marie was staring at him as if he was a ghost and Louis felt dreadful that he'd spent all those days enjoying himself in Bethune when he could have come back home instead.

"Yes, please." Louis stood up and gave his mother another hug. The anger he'd felt at her treatment of Brigitte was forgotten, as was his promise to take Brigitte away to the south. Marie needed him. He was the man of the house now and he vowed silently to take care of her.

****

Olive opened the door, her face a rigid mask as she tried to hide her fear. She handed the envelope to him and he pushed past her, leaving her no option but to turn towards him.

"You've got the money." Somehow her voice was steady.

"Just want to make sure it's all there, wouldn't want to be short changed, would I?" He smirked at her. "Probably best to close the door, we don't want any interruptions, do we?"

Olive shut the door and moved to the far side of the table. Tom pretended not to notice and began counting the money.

Olive tried not to show her impatience but he was taking so long. "You've got what you came for, why don't you just take your dirty money and go."

Tom laughed. "What, no tea? Or something stronger, maybe? It just so happens I've brought a little bottle along with me. Thought you might like to join me?"

Olive stared at him in disbelief. "You're blackmailing me. This isn't a social evening."

"Oh, that really hurts, Olive." Tom looked suitably miserable. "We're going to be doing business for a long time, we might as well enjoy ourselves." Olive was speechless and he took her silence for consent. "That's better. Let me pour you a snifter. Where's the glasses? Oh, they're in the kitchen cupboard, aren't they?" He was walking over towards the cabinet when she realised he must have been in her flat to know where she kept them. Her hand flew to her mouth and she recoiled in horror.

"You've been in here. How dare you?"

Tom ignored her outrage, returned with the glasses and began pouring her a drink. "Drink up, Olive. Let's toast a long and fruitful relationship."

Olive was staring at him, shock written all over her face. He grinned and moved closer. Olive backed away and he followed until she was trapped against the wall. He leaned forward, his face inches from hers.

She could smell the alcohol on his breath and, grimacing, she turned her head away. Tom grinned. "Don't worry, I haven't got time tonight. Maybe next time, though. Drink up!"

It wasn't a request.

Chapter Forty-eight

La Couture, Northern France

Gradually, over the next day, Louis told his mother something of his experiences. He didn't mention Lucie, Gabrielle or Gilbert and glossed over the beating he'd taken, not mentioning Brigitte. Instead he made up a story about being set upon by some German soldiers.

Marie was so relieved to have him home, she didn't question him at all, just listened while he told her his version of some of the things that had happened to him. She guessed there were other things he would never talk about and would probably go to his grave having never mentioned and, while her heart went out to him, Louis concentrated on not talking himself into trouble.

"Have you had any more trouble with the Germans?" he asked.

Marie shook her head. "No, apart from the first time when... when they killed your father, I haven't seen them at all."

Louis breathed a sigh of relief. He'd not seen any between Bethune and the farm, although it probably wouldn't stay like that. There was a brief silence, then Marie asked the question she was dreading the answer to: "What will you do now?"

"I suppose I'll get back to working the farm. Do you think Gaston will mind?"

Marie realised she had been holding her breath, scared he might want to go south and continue the fight against the Nazis. She shook her head. "No, I'm sure he won't. He was only filling in until one of you came home."

"Good. I'll make a start in the morning, then." Louis stood up and switched on the wireless. "Let's find out what's happening. I haven't heard the news for ages," he said, conveniently forgetting the time he'd spent with Brigitte.

****

Dover, England

The train to Dover was very busy but Peggy managed to get a seat. Pam lived with her parents and they had always made Peggy welcome, so she was looking forward to the break.

The sun was shining and, relieved to be away from the stuffy heat of London, Peggy found her spirits soaring while the train sped across the English countryside towards the coast. She gazed out of the window, watching the patchwork quilt of the English countryside speeding past. They crossed the gently rolling countryside of Kent and she saw the outline of the man carved out of chalk on the downs. Occasionally, in the skies above them, she could see Spitfires and Hurricanes, their vapour trails white against the cloudless blue sky and, in the fields outside the window, she caught glimpses of soldiers drilling or the Home Guard manning road-blocks. It was inconceivable the Germans would really invade and Peggy found herself wondering how they would cope if the worst happened.

Pam was waiting for her at the platform barrier; a tall, slim girl with slightly windswept dark straight hair.

"Peggy!" Pam's voice carried clearly across the platform causing several people to turn around. "Oh, I'm so pleased you're here." Without giving Peggy the chance to reply, Pam grabbed her friend's rather battered suitcase and hustled her out of the station where she had a taxi waiting.

"I've got loads to tell you. You must be exhausted caring for all those poor chaps. They came through here in their thousands. I helped out at the station, giving them notes and pencils so they could notify their families they were safe. I also went out collecting clothes and food for them. Some of them had virtually nothing on and hadn't eaten for days." Pam stopped to take a breath and realised she hadn't given Peggy a chance to say anything. "Sorry, I'm gabbling aren't I?" she finished. They both laughed and sat back while the taxi made its way to the outskirts of the town.

"I'm surprised you have taxis here. Doesn't the petrol rationing affect them?"

Pam grinned. "Yes, but Daddy has friends, you know?" She winked and touched her forefinger to the side of her nose making Peggy laugh again. Pam was like a breath of fresh air and, unlike any of her other friends, exactly what she needed right now. She felt herself begin to relax. The sea breeze filtered through the window and Peggy could smell and taste the salt in the air. The freshness was exhilarating after the heat of London and she knew she had done the right thing coming here.

****

Toulouse, Southern France

While Claudette cooked lunch, Jean-Paul switched on the wireless and listened to the news. His heart sank and he wondered if they had left the frying pan only to jump straight into the fire. It sounded as though the people in this part of France didn't like Jews either. Jean-Paul thanked whatever God was watching over him for Marcel's foresight in suggesting they take the identity papers of Angel and her parents. He wasn't sure how long they would offer them protection but for the moment they had given them some breathing space. Even more fortuitous, the papers had become very tatty and dirty during their travels, so much of the important information regarding first names, ages and dates of birth had become illegible. Their luck had stayed with them and it had been a reasonably easy matter of registering again. Even having only two sets of female papers had not proved an obstacle as the authorities had accepted that the other set had been lost. He had worried that Angel would object to him saying she was his and Claudette's youngest daughter and Jeanne's sister, but so far she had said nothing to contradict this. This had surprised him, until Claudette suggested that perhaps Angel was so scared of being left alone that she felt safer and more secure calling them Mama and Papa.

Fortunately, Angel and Jeanne had similar colouring. Both had blonde hair, although Angel's was pale, long and curly while Jeanne's was a much darker blonde and very straight. Not for the first time in the past few months, he gave thanks that none of them looked Jewish. His hair was rapidly thinning on top now but he still retained the firm jaw and even features that had made him so good looking in his youth. Jeanne had inherited his brown eyes, direct gaze and square jaw but there the resemblance ended. Her face was angular like Claudette's and she also had her mother's small, slightly upturned nose and full lips. Her glossy mass of long dark blonde hair came from his own mother and she had also inherited their fair skin. He sighed. With a bit of luck, they would be able to blend into French society without any problem.

Finding work also proved easier than he expected. Deciding to try and find work as a teacher, he'd set out to visit all the colleges in Toulouse, starting with the best schools and working his way down. His luck was in and, at the second college he was offered a position, albeit on probation for six months and on quite low wages. At the end of that time, if his work was satisfactory, his pay would go up. He would also have to sign a declaration stating that he was not Jewish, nor did he have any relatives who were Jewish. Trying hard to hide his distaste and not to show any hesitation, Jean-Paul signed. The Principal was delighted he had found someone so quickly to replace at least one member of his staff whom he had reluctantly had to let go thanks to the region's virulent anti-Semitic policies. They shook hands and Jean-Paul agreed to start the next day. He hurried home, looking forward to telling his family the good news.

"That's excellent, Papa," Jeanne said after he had told them. "I'm going to start looking as well, although I'm not sure where to begin."

"What do you want to do?" Claudette asked her.

"I don't know, really. I suppose I should look for some kind of clerical job. There must be plenty of that going now they'll no longer let married women work."

******

Dover, England

Pam lived in quite a large house just outside Dover. The two girls had met briefly not long after Peggy started at Lambeth Hospital. Pam was in her second year and had been assigned to mentor Peggy on one of the first wards she worked on. By then, Pam had already decided nursing wasn't for her and was searching for something else to do. However, she had not tried to put Peggy off, nor had she spent all her time complaining. The two girls got on well immediately and, by the time Pam left just two months later, they were firm friends. Peggy was really sad to see her go but they kept in touch by letter and Peggy had spent two days with Pam the previous year, just before Joe went off to Winchester. Thinking of Joe, her face clouded over and, with her usual intuitive sense, Pamela asked, "No news of Joe, then?"

Peggy shook her head. "Nothing. I feel, in my heart that he's safe but my head keeps telling me different."

Pam spoke with complete confidence. "Then you should listen to your heart. I always do and look at me." The last words were said tongue in cheek. Pam's love life was always a source of amusement to Peggy; boyfriends didn't seem to last very long and, no sooner had she got used to Pam talking about one, than she had moved on to the next.

"Who's the lucky man now?" Peggy was pleased to have an excuse to change the subject

Pam sighed wistfully. "His name is David and he's in the RAF."

"And…?"

"Sorry, is it that obvious? I think this is the one, Peggy. I can't stop thinking about him."

Peggy resisted the temptation to remind Pam she nearly always said the same thing. Instead she asked, "And because of him, you've decided to join the WAAF?"

"I know, stupid isn't it? Just think how good I'll look in the uniform though!"

"But you won't be posted to the same base, you know. In fact, I would think you'll see even less of him."

"I'm only joking." Pam grinned. "I did think about joining the WAAF but I've changed my mind. I'm not sure I would be much good at doing what I was told all the time."

"What *are* you going to do?"

"To be honest, I haven't a clue. I need to find something interesting and exciting, without having someone breathing over my shoulder all the time. A useful and worthwhile job, without being mundane."

Peggy thought for a while. "I can't think of anything, to be honest,"

"No, me neither. That's why I haven't found anything yet. Oh good, we're here." The taxi pulled up outside a large, whitewashed townhouse and Pam's mother, Cynthia, came out to greet them. There was a strong physical resemblance between Pam and her mother, although from Peggy's limited experience, Cynthia seemed a lot more sensible.

"Peggy, how lovely to see you." She gave Peggy a brief hug. "Come in and put your case upstairs. You're in the same room you stayed in last time. And then we'll all sit down and have a cup of tea and some chocolate cake. Cook made it this morning, so it's nice and fresh." Peggy returned the greeting and, after following her hosts into the house, took her case upstairs to the bedroom where she had stayed on her previous visit. The room was south facing and the sun was streaming through the open window. Peggy stood for a while gazing out over the town. In the distance, through the haze caused by the heat, she could just see the sea.

****

Louis was feeling guilty. He'd promised Brigitte he would take her away but, since he'd arrived back home he knew that was not possible, not unless he could persuade his mother to come too and that seemed highly unlikely with Marcel missing. This meant he had to stay and work the farm. He should have gone straight back to see Brigitte and explained, but he knew she would be angry and he couldn't face listening to her moaning, so he kept finding reasons not to go.

He was also wary about running into the Germans who were everywhere. He had survived his encounters with them thus far, but he saw no point in pushing his luck. He was safer on the farm for the time being. When things quietened down he would risk making the journey into Bethune. After all, Brigitte loved him, she wouldn't want anything to happen to him, she would understand the danger he could be in. There were all sorts of rumours flying around, that the Germans were shooting young men on sight or taking them prisoner and transporting them to Germany. He shuddered at the thought. No, he would bide his time and wait until things were more settled.

****

Dover, England

"Beautiful view isn't it?" Peggy spun around to see a tall, masculine version of Pam wearing a smart RAF uniform.

"Hello, Tony. Nice to see you again." She turned back to the window. "Yes, after London, the view is really peaceful and relaxing, I could stand here for hours."

"Well, make the most of it." Pam had appeared next to her brother. "They're putting together a compulsory evacuation of all but essential personnel. Because Dover's right in the front line, they want to make the town and surrounding area a military zone. You'll soon need special permits to be here"

"Oh dear, that's terrible. Where will you go?"

"London probably. Daddy has been asked to go and work at the War Office anyway, so another couple of weeks and we'll be shutting up the house and going to London for the duration. Tony's based at Biggin Hill, so he can keep an eye on the old place."

"If you've got lots of packing and things to do, won't I be in the way?" Peggy wondered if perhaps she shouldn't have come down, after all.

"Don't be silly," Pam hastened to reassure her. "You're only here for a couple of days. Anyway, it'll be nice to have a rest from trying to work out what to take and what to leave behind. Come on, let's go and have some of cook's special chocolate mayonnaise cake. I'm starving."

"You're always starving, Sis. You should be twice the size you are!" Tony teased her, winking at Peggy and the three of them went down to the kitchen.

The smell of fresh bread and cakes was stronger there and Peggy was suddenly aware of just how hungry she was. She hadn't bothered with breakfast before she left and she was ravenous.

"That smells delicious," she said, helping herself to a piece of chocolate cake.

Cynthia was nowhere to be seen and the three of them ate in companionable silence.

"Was there anything special you wanted to do while you're here?" Pam asked, licking the last of the cake from her fingers. "That was rather nice. I do hope cook doesn't find somewhere else to work while we're gone and decide not to come back to us."

"Cook's coming with us." Cynthia came in through the garden door with some fresh cut flowers in her hands. "Can you fetch the vase from under the sink," she added to Tony. "Did I hear you ask Peggy what she wanted to do?" Pam nodded, picking at the crumbs on her plate. "She might just want to take some gentle strolls and sit in the garden, you know? Don't forget, she's at work all day, not sitting around twiddling her thumbs like you."

"Oh." Pam pouted. "How boring. Is that really all you want to do?"

The idea of sitting around in the garden and taking gentle strolls sounded idyllic to Peggy, but she didn't want to disappoint her friend.

"That does sound lovely; we could do other things too, though." Peggy hoped she didn't sound too disinterested.

"How about coming to the base dance tomorrow night? You could do the strolling and sitting today and during the day tomorrow and then come and dance the night away?" Tony interrupted.

"Oh goody, a compromise!" Pam sounded ecstatic. "How does that sound, Peggy?"

Although Peggy didn't feel like going to a dance, she couldn't think of any reason to say no, at least not one that wasn't entirely selfish. She tried to appear enthusiastic.

Sensing Peggy's reluctance, Pam smiled. "They're a really good crowd, Peggy. And you don't have to dance if you don't want to, you can just sit and chat." Peggy could see she was trapped, so she gave in with good grace. "Good! That's settled then," Pam finished "And with a bit of luck, David will be there and you can meet him and tell me what you think!"

****

Stalag XXA, Poland

In the distance, Joe heard shouting. He was no longer interested and it was only with a supreme effort he responded when someone began to give him water. At first, his lips were so parched the water just trickled down his chin, but the person feeding him was patient and kept trickling small amounts into his mouth. The liquid gradually revived his body. Joe opened his eyes properly and found himself looking into the eyes of a German guard. There was no animosity in the man's face and he allowed Joe to sip the water until he had finally had enough.

Feeling slightly more human, Joe glanced around. Rob and Pete were seated on the floor near him. He frowned. Where was Sandy? He couldn't see him anywhere. He was about to ask Rob, when the door opened again and the guards appeared with large tureens of weak soup and coffee which they placed on tables at one end of the room. Those who were able to stand, formed an orderly queue, while those who were too weak to get up were fed where they lay. Joe managed to join the queue and, to his surprise, he was given a reasonable sized portion of soup, a small piece of bread and some coffee. He sat down on the floor and began to eat.

"Where's Sandy?" he was surprised to hear his voice no longer sounded hoarse and his sore throat had gone.

Rob shook his head. "Didn't make it."

There was a long silence while Joe digested this news, unable to believe yet another friend had died. He closed his eyes for a moment and offered up a silent prayer for Sandy, before opening them again, sipping the remains of his coffee and trying to remember how he'd got from the train to here, wherever here was.

He vaguely recalled the train doors opening and people shouting at him to get out. He could also remember staggering to his feet and falling onto the platform and somebody pulling him upright while the Germans counted them. Then the struggle to make his limbs work, the shouts of the guards as they beat those who fell over and his own thoughts that he should just lay down and give in to the inevitable. After that, nothing until the water being trickled into his swollen mouth.

"Where are we?" he asked in an effort to change the subject.

"Somewhere in Poland, according to one of the guards," Pete answered.

"Thorn," Rob interjected. "Well something like that anyway."

****

Catford, London

Olive stared at the door. The wireless was playing but she wasn't listening. When she'd arrived home, she had been almost afraid to go inside. She'd stood on the doorstep for a few moments and then, with trembling legs she'd forced herself to climb the stairs. The flat was as she'd left it that morning, the thick oppressive silence mocking her as she quickly locked the door behind her and pushed the table and chairs up against it. Her heart was racing and Olive forced herself to breathe slowly and think about how he was able to break in without leaving any signs. Then she realised it was obvious. He must have a key. If that was the case, she would need to change the locks. She'd been in so much shock, the idea had not occurred to her and she cursed herself for not doing something about the door while she was at work.

There had been a letter from Kurt on the mat and her heart leapt, only to sink again when she wondered if Tom had already been here and read her letter. She glanced around nervously, picked up the envelope and stared at the seals. They appeared unbroken and she relaxed. She would make something to eat and then open his letter. But somehow her fear had overcome even her desire to be close to Kurt and she placed the unopened envelope in her handbag to read the following night, once she was sure she was safe.

Chapter Forty-nine

Bethune, Northern France

Brigitte made her way across the cobbles towards the German truck, parked several metres down the street from the café. She was wearing her favourite red skirt, the material tight across her body as she swung her hips in what she hoped was an inviting way. Her white blouse, its top two buttons undone, revealing her ample cleavage, was tucked into the skirt showing off her tiny waist. The outline of her nipples strained against the tight material as she hobbled across the uneven surface in the delicate high heeled shoes which emphasised her neat ankles and long shapely legs. Brigitte ignored the discomfort, concentrating all her attention on the three German soldiers who were watching her approach with ill-disguised lust.

She had heard nothing from Louis since he'd left to return home, which just confirmed what she'd known all along. She couldn't rely on him. He had forgotten all about her. She would be better off mending her bridges with the Germans. In any case, Louis was no longer a soldier, someone people looked up to. He was just a farmer in an occupied country and he could be deported at any time. Brigitte pushed the hurt to the back of her mind and pasted a smile on her red coated lips.

"I was wondering if any of you knew Wolfgang?" She batted her long lashes at the nearest soldier, a tall thin man with an angular face and bony features.

Unable to believe that she had really spoken to him, he stepped forward and breathed in her perfume.

"Do you have his surname and regiment?" he asked politely, struggling to keep his eyes on her face.

"No, I don't." Brigitte looked disappointed, then she smiled again. "It doesn't really matter. I was just wondering if there were any parties going on. I'm rather bored."

"We were thinking of having some drinks later, when we're off duty." The voice came from behind her and belonged to an older man. Brigitte turned around, took in the small piggy eyes, large nose and fleshy face, and gave him the benefit of her most coquettish look. "Perhaps you'd like to come along?"

"I'd love to. I'm Brigitte and I live over there." She indicated the café. "What time do you get off duty?"

"We'll pick you up at about three…" He was about to say more when he suddenly straightened up and stood to attention. Brigitte spun around and found herself face to face with the officer who had come to Louis' rescue when Heinz and his friend's had attacked him.

****

Stalag XXA, Poland

After recuperating in the old dance hall, the Germans decided the men were fit enough to move and they were lined up again and ordered up the hill to the main fort. Although resting had given Joe some of his strength back, the effort of climbing the steep incline showed him just how weak he was. The guards shouted at them to move faster and resumed the previous pattern of beating those who fell over or stumbled. Before long, Joe began to question whether surviving the train journey had been the best thing. Each step was purgatory and with every breath he felt like his chest would burst, but something inside him wouldn't give up. Drawing on an inner strength he didn't know he had, he forced his feet to take one step after another and somehow reached the top.

"Halt!" The order came just in time and, while he stood there swaying, Joe fought the dizziness in his head and tried to focus on his surroundings. They were inside the grounds of the fort and in front of them were rows and rows of marquees to which they were directed. The hope his journey was finally at an end gave him just enough strength to stagger into one of the tents where he collapsed onto the straw-strewn ground. Drifting in and out of consciousness, he had no idea how long he lay there. Beyond pain, he was only dimly aware of a German soldier shouting and hitting him with his rifle butt, then kicking him with his heavy, highly polished boots.

Somehow, he managed to drag himself to his feet and followed the other men back outside where their guards began to count them yet again. Joe began to feel like he was in some surreal nightmare where people did strange things that appeared perfectly reasonable while you were asleep and only seemed ridiculous when you woke up.

The fort and the marquees were completely surrounded by a double row of barbed wire fences at least ten feet high, with watchtowers at regular intervals. In each of the watchtowers, Joe could see armed men with machine guns and rifles and, on the ground, guards with dogs, large vicious German Shepherds that barked incessantly and snapped at anyone who swayed or staggered in their direction.

****

Lewisham Council Offices, London

Olive breathed a sigh of relief. The locksmith would pick up the key from her at the council offices and go to her flat and change the locks immediately. To her surprise, he'd been very helpful and sympathetic when she'd told him an ex-boyfriend had stolen a key and kept breaking in and had offered to fit a chain too, at no extra charge. Of course he was charging a sizeable sum to do the work anyway, but Olive didn't care. She just wanted to feel secure in her own home.

"Is everything alright, Miss Cooper?"

Olive started. Kath was staring at her and she made an effort to smile. "Yes, everything's fine," she replied and was rewarded to see a look of disappointment flash across Kath's face. The expression was replaced with a smile.

"Oh, that's good. " Kath walked off, leaving Olive to her thoughts.

****

Bethune, Northern France

Brigitte gasped, but this time the officer was smiling. "Hello, my dear. How's your friend? Better I hope?"

Lost for words for a moment, Brigitte could only nod. Then she found her tongue. "Yes, he is. He's gone back to his farm…" She stopped, not sure what else to say.

"Then you are on your own?"

"Yes."

"Good, perhaps you will have lunch with me?"

Brigitte stared at him in astonishment and didn't answer. He knew she had been with the other soldiers, so why would he want to have anything to do with her?

"Well?" He sounded irritated.

"Yes, thank you, I would love to, of course I would." Brigitte gushed. She had no idea why this officer had asked her, but it had to be better than drinking with a bunch of soldiers.

"Good. My car is over there." He turned away, leaving Brigitte standing in the street, unsure as to whether she should follow him. Realising she was not behind him, he turned back. "Well? Are you coming?"

His tone brooked no argument and, putting her misgivings aside, she hurried after him. The soldiers looked at each other. "She'd have been better off coming with us," the older one muttered.

"Yeah, I heard he's a right nasty bastard," the tall thin soldier answered.

"In what way?" The third soldier was the youngest and he was still staring up the street as the car sped away.

The other two exchanged glances but didn't answer.

****

Toulouse, Southern France.

Like Jean-Paul, Jeanne did not have to try too hard to find work. She was passing the police station when she spotted a sign advertising for a clerical assistant. Deciding she had nothing to lose, she climbed the steps and entered the large hall. Seeing a reception desk, she walked purposefully towards the rather harassed woman on the other side and asked about the vacancy.

"Can you type?" She was sizing Jeanne up as she spoke.

Jeanne resisted the urge to ask her what she was looking at and nodded. "Yes, and I've done filing, general administration, reception and accountancy work."

The woman's expression brightened and she motioned for Jeanne to come round to her side of the desk. She indicated a pile of reports. "Can you type those up?"

Jeanne put her handbag down, sat on the proffered chair and began typing. The woman watched for a few moments and then smiled. "You'll do… that is, if you want the job?"

"Yes please," Jeanne replied, thinking that this was the strangest interview she had ever had.

"Good. I'm Eve, Eve Poitiers and I'm the chief clerk." Looking around, she continued under her breath, "And general dogsbody!"

Jeanne grinned; she was beginning to like this rather plump, matronly woman whose bite was obviously nothing like as bad as her bark.

"Jeanne, Jeanne Coultard." She remembered just in time to use her new name.

"Right, Jeanne, you're hired. If you want to finish those up then I'll show you round. You are alright to start today, aren't you?"

"Yes, of course."

"Good, I'll need to see your identification papers, of course." Jeanne held out her papers for inspection. After a cursory look, Eve handed them back and removed the 'Assistant wanted' sign.

"I'm going to make some coffee, would you like some?"

"Yes please, that would be lovely. Thank you."

"So, who's this, then?" The voice belonged to a tall, well-built man in his early thirties. He had wavy brown hair, a generous mouth and deep brown eyes that crinkled at the corners when he smiled, as he was at the moment.

"This is Jeanne Coultard, my new assistant and this is Deputy Commissioner Valence."

"Gabriel Valence." The deputy commissioner was still smiling at Jeanne who was beginning to blush at such intense scrutiny. "It's a pleasure to meet someone of such beauty." He was enjoying her discomfort. "When did you start working here? I am sure I would have noticed if you had been here for more than a few hours."

"I've just started." Jeanne recovered her wits and willed herself not to blush any more. He really wasn't as good looking as she'd initially thought and she was annoyed at her body for reacting to his rather obvious charms. "This morning," she continued and then stopped as she realised that she was struggling, which made it seem even more as if she liked him.

"Well, Jeanne, I am sure we'll see a lot more of each other. I will look forward to working with you." With a hint of a salute, his fingers tipped the brim of the hat he had just replaced on his head and, smiling, he headed towards the lifts.

"Well, you've certainly made a hit there." Eve sounded amused. "Just watch out for his fiancée. She's got connections with the government and she's keeps him on a very tight rein! Shame really because he's alright, apart from the fact that he knows how good looking he is, of course."

Jeanne was about to say that she had a boyfriend so she wasn't interested, when she realised that she couldn't mention Marcel, as he wasn't part of her new family story and she needed to check with her father first.

"Come on, let's go and get some coffee." Eve stood up from her desk and led the way to a small room at the other end of the large hall. Once there, she made coffee and offered Jeanne a croissant.

"They make them fresh next door and they always drop some off for us. Delicious, aren't they?" She took a large bite. Conversation stopped as Jeanne enjoyed the croissant, unable to believe her good fortune. She had not only found a job, but one that provided food as well. She couldn't wait to get home and tell her parents and Angel. She wished she could write to Marcel and tell him, but until she knew where he was, she would have to be patient and just tell him in her head.

"So, do you have a boyfriend?" Eve asked suddenly, as if she could read her thoughts.

Jeanne found herself replying before she could stop. "Yes. His name's Marcel, he's wonderful. I don't know where he is at the moment, though."

"Ah, one of those taken prisoner, is he?" Eve asked sympathetically

Jeanne nodded. It was easier to admit she had a boyfriend and lie about where he was, than pretend she didn't and, in any case, having a beau might be useful if the Deputy Commissioner pestered her.

******

Outside Bethune, Northern France

There was silence as the car sped through the French countryside. Brigitte glanced at the officer out of the corner of her eye, still confused as to why he had invited her to lunch. Sensing her unspoken question, he reached across and patted her leg. "I expect you want to know why you're here."

"I did wonder." She swivelled around so she could watch his face.

"You don't think it could be because I am attracted to you?"

Brigitte frowned but didn't answer.

"You needn't look so worried, Brigitte." He heard her stifled gasp and squeezed her thigh gently. "I was attracted to you the first time I saw you, so I decided to find out more about you. Why don't you stop fretting, relax and enjoy the ride. The sun is shining and we have all day to enjoy ourselves."

He glanced across at her, a smile on his face and removed his hand to change gear. Brigitte decided to do as he suggested and began to relax.

"You haven't told me your name?"

"Leutnant Rolf Keller. Now just sit back and enjoy the view. We can talk while we eat."

Brigitte shrugged and, realising she was not going to elicit any more details from him, she gazed up at the cloudless blue sky and tried to ignore the uneasy feeling in the pit of her stomach.

Chapter Fifty

Stalag XXA, Poland

The guards finally stopped counting. Joe's head was spinning and there were white lights dancing in front of his eyes. Although he was dimly aware of orders being shouted, Joe had no idea what they were, so he just stumbled along with the rest of the men. They staggered out of the bright hot sunshine into the dark cool interior of the main building. Joe couldn't see anything but he didn't care. At least he was out of the sun. The shuffling march came to a halt in a large, white tiled room where they were ordered to undress, wash and shave. Joe shook his head and leaned against the wall. He doubted he had the strength to take off his uniform. Within seconds, a German appeared in front of him shouting and gesticulating and, with great reluctance, Joe began the laborious process of removing the remnants of his clothes. Under the malevolent gaze of the guard, Joe took the small cotton rag and hard rock-like substance that was some kind of soap and began washing in the warm water. Much to his surprise, he began to feel better. He finished, the guards handed him a razor and Joe began to shave. The face that met him in the mirror was unrecognisable. Gaunt, hollow-cheeked and with eyes that lacked life, Joe stared at his image for several seconds before turning away as the guards ordered them towards a large pile of clean clothes by the door.

"I'm not fucking wearing this." Pete's voice was loud enough to be heard several feet away as he picked up a Belgian jacket and threw the garment back on the floor in disgust.

Joe stared at the collection of mismatched pieces taken from the captured soldiers of various nationalities and shrugged. He was too weak to really care. "At least we'll be clean."

He sorted through until he found some trousers that appeared to be about his size. He was only just finished when the guards shouted and gestured at the men to line up again. Joe waited for the interminable count, but instead they were hurried through several ancient corridors with small wooden framed glass windows to an even larger room which was obviously some sort of reception area. Here, bored officials, seated behind long wooden tables stacked with piles of paper forms, asked Joe innumerable questions until, apparently satisfied with his answers, they handed him a metal disk with a number stamped in the centre, ordering him to wear the tag at all times. Joe tied the disk onto his British Army dog tags which he already wore around his neck.

Their treatment appeared to be improving, and Joe began to relax.

****

Outside Bethune, Northern France

Rolf pulled up at a small cottage, came around to Brigitte's side of the car and opened the door for her. She took his hand and allowed him to lead her inside. The front door opened straight into a small sitting room, at the back of which she could see a kitchen. He led the way through the kitchen, unlocked the back door and Brigitte found herself in a small garden that backed onto fields. It was quiet, except for the buzzing of insects and Brigitte looked around with pleasure.

"The house was empty, so I moved in. Do you like it?"

"Yes, it's very nice." Brigitte hesitated. "What about the owners?"

Rolf's face darkened and her stomach lurched, then he smiled. "They'll have to find somewhere else, the property's mine now." He indicated a small garden bench. "Sit down, I'll make us some lunch. I have a fresh baguette, some tomatoes and brie, is that alright?"

Brigitte nodded as she made her way to the bench and sat down. Rolf disappeared back into the cottage, returning a few seconds later with a bottle of wine and two glasses. He uncorked the bottle, poured the wine and handed a glass to her.

"To an enjoyable relationship." He toasted as they clinked glasses. Brigitte gulped hers down. She was feeling increasingly nervous, although she didn't know why. Rolf was behaving like the perfect gentleman, but her instincts were telling her something was wrong. She glanced around for somewhere to put the empty glass but he reached out and took it from her, placing it gently on the ground. He was standing to one side of her and she had to shade her eyes when she looked at him. He stretched out a hand and his fingers traced a line down the side of her face. His touch was gentle and she closed her eyes. His fingers continued their featherlike touch down her neck and towards her breasts. Brigitte opened her eyes, surprised to find his face was inches from hers. For the first time, she stared into his eyes. They were almost black, the pupils enlarged. His fingers sought her hair and then he began wrapping it around his hand, pulling tighter until her head was forced back. His lips pressed down on hers and, when she didn't open her mouth, he yanked her hair making her gasp. His tongue fought its way inside her mouth while his free hand undid his trousers. Without warning, he pulled away, shoved her on her knees and the next moment had rammed his erection into her mouth, ignoring her attempts to resist him. He pushed further and further back until she began to gag.

"Come on, Brigitte. Your reputation precedes you. Show me what you can do."

Brigitte tried to ignore the nervous churning of her stomach and the warning voice in her head. Instead she told herself that Rolf was no different to all the other Germans who'd used her. His moans grew louder and she concentrated on sucking and licking, her head rocking rhythmically as he forced her back and forth. The sudden spurt of hot sour liquid hit the back of her throat and she swallowed as he pressed her head into his groin. Eventually, he pulled out, an expression of amusement on his face.

"So, did you enjoy your lunch?" She nodded. He stared at her for a moment then smiled. "I'm only joking. I'll go and get the food. Have some more wine." Without waiting for a response, he poured some more wine and disappeared back into the cottage. Brigitte gulped gratefully, wondering how long she was going to have to put up with him before she could go home.

******

Stalag XXA, Poland

Joe joined the end of the long queue of men who had finished and were waiting at the far end of the room. He had only been there a few moments when a guard came in through the small door on the right and yelled at them. Although he didn't understand, Joe followed the men in front of him. They were marched through the door, down a long, much narrower corridor, halted, lined up and made to strip to the waist. Having only just dressed, this seemed rather strange and Joe began to feel uneasy. All he could see was a door in front, through which the men were disappearing. Other men piled in behind him, the air in the corridor grew hot and stuffy and Joe began to sweat. The queue moved forward and then it was his turn. The door opened and he stepped into a small windowless room, the rancid odour of sweat and something he couldn't identify, almost overpowered him. A desk, covered in discarded paperwork and an overflowing ashtray, took up most of one wall, an old rickety wooden chair squashed in behind and, to his right there was a large metal filing cabinet, the bottom drawer gaping open, crammed tight with files. There was another door on his left. He had no time to take in anything else; a man in an unbuttoned white coat stepped in front of him, raised his hand and, without any warning plunged a large blunt hypodermic needle into his chest. Joe fainted.

He came round in another faceless corridor and was relieved to see Rob and Pete were also there, looking pale and drawn. The guards gave them little time to recover, barely enough time to put their shirts back on, hustling them towards the end of the corridor and then down two flights of cold damp stone steps to another ancient wooden door.

One of the Germans unlocked the door with a massive iron key and they were forced inside a dark, dank cellar. They saw some straw palisades lined up against the walls and were already staggering across the floor towards them when the door was slammed shut and everything went dark.

****

Outside Bethune, Northern France

Rolf reappeared a few moments later carrying two plates filled with fresh bread, ripe brie and sliced tomatoes. He placed them on the bench and then, as she reached out, he slapped her wrist. Brigitte jumped and shrank back but he was laughing.

"Take off your clothes, then you can eat." Brigitte looked uncertain and his face darkened. "Well? Are you hungry or not?" She hurried to undo the buttons of her blouse, but he interrupted. "Slowly, don't rush, we have all day."

By now, her hands were trembling. "Perhaps you could help me?" She fluttered her eyelashes at him, hoping that would please him. She was wrong.

"Stop that, lower your eyes, don't look at me, and do what I've told you." His voice was harsh and Brigitte felt a small frisson of fear.

She undid the buttons slowly and, item by item, removed her clothes until she was standing naked in front of him. He stood up and walked around her, his eyes drinking in every detail of her body. Her large firm breasts with their swollen nipples, her flat stomach and tiny waist, her wide hips and firm buttocks. He made no move to touch her, then he indicated the food.

"Eat, but remain standing so I can see you."

Brigitte took the plate and began eating, surprised to find that she was hungry. As she ate, she peered at him through her eyelashes. The slap across her bottom caught her by surprise and she yelped, nearly dropping her plate.

"I told you not to look at me." Rolf finished his food and placed his plate on the ground. He pulled out a handkerchief and wiped his hands. "Go over to the kitchen door and put your plate down on the ground. Don't bend your knees."

He watched as she walked over and bent down to place the plate on the floor. She stood up. "Did I tell you to stand up?" Brigitte shook her head and bent down again. He waited a few moments. "Now turn round and come closer."

Brigitte stood up and stepped towards him. He waited until she was in front of him then slapped her buttocks again. "I told you, look at the floor, not at me." She flushed. Her bottom was stinging and she felt vulnerable. "You now belong exclusively to me, do you understand?"

Brigitte raised her head to argue and he slapped her hard. "I didn't tell you to look up. If I find you've been with anyone else, I will punish you. Is that clear?" She nodded. "Good, then turn around and kneel down." He waited until she had done so before shoving her forward onto her hands. He slapped her hard several times and, without warning, rammed himself inside her.

******

Toulouse, Southern France

Jeanne walked slowly across the square of the Place du Capital, savouring the smells from the colourful market stalls and the numerous cafés under their stone canopies that lined its edges.

She walked down Rue Gambetta turning off in to Rue Peyrolieres and headed towards the River Garonne and the Pont Neuf bridge which linked the Old Quarter on the right bank with Place St. Cyprien on the left. Despite her eagerness to get home, she stopped and gazed down at the river, enjoying the fresh breeze that played through her hair. She closed her eyes and listened to the muted sounds of the city and the gentle rippling of the waves against the river bank and felt herself beginning to relax. She was going to love living here.

She had no idea how long she stood there, basking in the peace and quiet but eventually she opened her eyes and headed towards the left bank. Here, she followed the Rue Laganne along the course of the river until she reached Rue Benezet. It was still warm, even though it was early evening and, as she walked, she took off her jacket and rolled up her sleeves. From Rue Benezet, it was only a brief walk to the quiet side roads where they had found their apartment. The sun was still shining and, if anything, the delicate fragrance of the bougainvillea that decorated the balconies and gardens and filled the air, was even stronger than it had been in the morning. She rushed up the stairs and in through the door. Her father was sitting at the table reading the newspaper and Claudette was in the kitchen with Angel, preparing the evening meal. Jean-Paul looked relieved when she came in.

"We were getting worried about you."

"Sorry, I couldn't let you know where I was, because I have been working," Jeanne proclaimed proudly

"Well done! Where?" Jean-Paul's face lit up.

"In the police station, as a sort of clerk. It's full time and I've already started. The lady there, Eve, was very busy, so I stepped in and helped her. It was the strangest interview I've ever had!" Seeing Angel was busy helping with the food, she continued softly. "I also thought it might be useful to be working there. You never know what I might hear."

Jean-Paul frowned. "Be careful, Jeanne. The last thing we want to do is to draw attention to ourselves. The more we can slip into the background, the safer we'll be."

"Do you really think we are still in danger?"

Looking around to make sure Claudette and Angel were not paying any attention, Jean-Paul nodded, his expression serious. "Best not to worry, though." He paused. "I suppose you may be right. Working at the police station might be a good thing. Just be careful, please Jeanne…"

****

The dance was in full swing when they arrived and the noise of the music and the guests talking could be heard long before they got there. Peggy's misgivings came back with a vengeance. Never particularly outward going, she hated meeting new people. Going to a dance where she didn't know anyone was her idea of purgatory, but Pam and Tony had been good to her and she didn't want to spoil their evening. The car pulled up and she followed the others into the Nissen hut that had been commandeered for the dance. Inside, the air was stuffy and her senses were assaulted by a heady mixture of perfume and alcohol. The band was playing Doing the Lambeth Walk and several people were dancing. Pam and Tony fought their way through the throng of people, greeting several, until they reached the bar where they ordered some drinks. Peggy didn't really like alcohol, so she had an orange squash and was relieved when they made their way to a table. Sitting down, she wondered how long she would have to stay and then chastised herself for being selfish. She sipped her drink slowly and concentrated on watching the dancers while they fox-trotted and waltzed around the floor. Even if she wasn't enjoying the dance that much, she was enjoying the music, which veered from the romantic tunes of Vera Lynn and, her personal favourite, Glenn Miller, to the comic songs of George Formby.

A couple of rather drunk RAF pilots asked her to dance, but didn't pursue it when she politely declined.

"Are you enjoying yourself?" Pam's voice was loud against her ear and Peggy nodded.

"Why don't you dance?" Pam asked, swaying in time to the music

"Oh, I'm not really a very good dancer." Peggy wished she could disappear into a large hole.

"Rubbish, come on!" Tony was pulling her to her feet before she could object and she found herself on the dance floor. Having no choice, she began to relax. Tony was a good dancer and, before long, she forgot her self-consciousness and started to enjoy herself. The next dance was an 'excuse me' and, before she could say anything, another RAF man cut in and she found herself dancing with a pilot who'd obviously had a few drinks, but who behaved like a perfect gentleman. Now she was on the dance floor, a succession of pilots and RAF technicians asked her to dance and, her shyness for once forgotten, she twirled the rest of the evening away. In fact, she enjoyed herself so much, she was amazed when Pam started to lead her to the door.

"Goodness, I can't believe I've been dancing all evening," she said in astonishment as they drove away.

"You've had a good evening, then?" Pam inwardly congratulated herself.

Peggy smiled back and then her face fell. "I shouldn't really be enjoying myself, should I? Not when I don't know where Joe is, or what's happened to him..."

"So are you going to spend the rest of the war, or, at least until Joe comes back, making yourself miserable?" Pam sounded cross. "Is you being miserable going to make Joe's life better, or affect what's happening to him or bring him back sooner? Do you think he would like you to be unhappy?"

Taken aback by the vehemence in her friend's voice, Peggy considered Pam's words.

"No, I suppose not." she eventually conceded.

"Peggy, you love him, there's no doubt about that, but you can't hibernate until he comes home." Pam searched for something that would persuade Peggy she was right. "If the situation was reversed, would you want him to lock himself away and be miserable?"

"Of course not."

"Then I rest my case!" Pam glanced out of the car window. "Come on, we're home now. Do you want a cup of tea? It's the last of the non-rationed stuff. I can't believe they've rationed tea, can you? Goodness knows how we're going to manage. We'll probably have to drink gin or whisky instead!"

Chapter Fifty-one

Southern England

Marcel listened to the news that the French had surrendered in disbelief.

"What do we do now?" he asked Pierre, one of his new friends. Pierre, at twenty one, was already a veteran of the current war, having survived several encounters with the German army. He was a short, swarthy man from Marseilles who nursed a fierce hatred of the Nazis. When his unit was overrun, Pierre had managed to avoid capture by joining the millions of refugees fleeing the advancing enemy. He had met Marcel not long after they reached England.

"We'll go to London and join the Free French Forces," Pierre replied after a brief hesitation and, grabbing their few possessions, they joined the others who had also decided to fight on for France. The opportunity to go to London was too good to miss. Marcel might find someone he could ask about Louis and he could also deliver the message the soldier had given him. After all, he had the address, and it shouldn't be too hard to find.

"I don't understand how our army can just give in and go home." Marcel was stunned as they watched the large numbers queuing up to be repatriated.

"I know. Makes you sick, doesn't it?" Paul Courrière said, overhearing Marcel's words.

Marcel wasn't sure he particularly liked Paul. He could be very sarcastic, not to mention rude and abrupt. However, for once, he was in agreement. Nothing could have persuaded Marcel to go home until the Germans had been sent packing and he really couldn't understand how anyone else could feel any different.

****

La Couture, Northern France

Louis and Marie had mixed feelings about the surrender. While they both felt the humiliation of defeat, they couldn't help being relieved that the fighting was over and Marie began to hope Marcel would return home. Avid for news, they spent a considerable amount of time listening to the wireless and heard the plea from General de Gaulle. Marie glanced uneasily at Louis.

"You're not going to do anything stupid, Louis?" She stared at him but his face was expressionless. "After all, there's nothing you can do. France has surrendered and the fighting has stopped. You would be stupid to get yourself killed now."

Louis didn't answer at first and then, turning to his mother, his face full of fury, he said, "Have you forgotten they killed my father? I can't just sit back and do nothing." Seeing her expression, he calmed down and added, "Don't worry Mama, I have no intention of getting myself killed, but I'm not going to just give up and accept Germans marching all over France in their dirty jackboots." He put his hand up to stop her interrupting. "I have no idea what I am going to do yet, but I'm sure I'll think of something." There was silence and his expression softened. "Don't you want to avenge Papa?"

"Not at the expense of my son."

"I'm invincible, Mama; haven't I already survived against all the odds? You don't need to worry about me."

****

"Hello, Peggy. How are you?"

Peggy recognised his voice immediately and spun around, a smile on her face. "Hello, Chris."

"You look much better." He smiled when he saw her face fall. "No, you didn't look bad before, just tired." He changed the subject before she could answer. "Have you heard anything?"

Peggy shook her head, her face still serious. "No, but my good friend Pam pointed out that sitting around being miserable isn't going to change anything. And that if the positions were reversed, I wouldn't want Joe locking himself away and being disagreeable."

Chris gave a low whistle. "Does that mean you'll come for a drink with me, a proper one this time, not just a stroll around the block?"

Peggy laughed. "Yes, I'd love to. If you're alright with us just being friends? I love Joe. There can't ever be anything else between us. Are you sure you wouldn't rather find someone else to take out?"

It was Chris' turn to look offended. "I want to go for a drink with you because I like you, not because I'm looking for a quick pick up."

Peggy blushed and wished, once more, that she could disappear into a hole. Seeing her discomfort, Chris smiled. "Let's start again. I'll pick you up Saturday evening at seven thirty. Alright?"

She nodded and was about to say more when she spotted Helen coming towards her.

"I'll see you Saturday." She turned away and hastened over to Helen who was beaming from ear to ear.

"Jimmy's fine, Peggy. He was bought off through St Nazaire after his plane crashed. He's back at Biggin Hill."

"Helen, that's great news. I'm so pleased for you both."

"You look happier too. Have you heard anything about Joe?"

"No, but I can't keep worrying all the time. I just have to trust in God that he's alright and try to get on with my life."

****

423

Brigitte could see Louis' farm in the distance. She climbed off her bike and stood watching for a while. She had no idea whether he would want to see her again or whether Marie had poisoned his mind against her, but she had decided to cycle out to see him anyway. She felt a small frisson of fear. She knew Rolf would punish her if her found out she'd been here.

She climbed back on and began pedalling towards the farm. She let herself in through the gate and headed in the direction of the farmhouse.

"Brigitte!" Louis' voice made her look up and she was delighted to see the smile on his face. She was about to shout back when she saw Marie behind him. Marie did not look very happy and Brigitte began to feel angry. She was the one who should feel aggrieved. Marie had slapped her, not the other way round.

"Louis." Ignoring Marie, Brigitte climbed down, dropped the bike and rushed across the yard into his arms. "I've missed you so much."

"And I've missed you. I'm sorry I've not had time to come and see you but that doesn't matter, you're here now." Louis swung her round in his arms and then lowered her to the ground, his face alight with happiness.

Brigitte found herself face to face with Marie, her face unsmiling. Louis saw her expression and took Brigitte's hand.

"Now look, Mama. I know you don't approve of Brigitte but the decision to join up was mine and nothing to do with her. You had no right to blame her." He was about to carry on but the blank expression on Marie's face bought him to a halt.

"I have no idea what you're talking about."

It was Louis' turn to look confused. "You slapped Brigitte because you blamed her for me being missing."

Marie shook her head. "I don't know who's been telling you tales, Louis, but I slapped your girlfriend because she said she only went out with you because she felt sorry for you."

There was silence. Brigitte squirmed. "I only said I was sorry for you because the Germans had shot your father…" Her hand flew to cover her mouth and she tailed off in horror.

Louis stared at her. "You knew my father was dead?" His voice rose in line with his anger. "Why didn't you tell me when we were together before I came back here?"

"You stayed with her in Bethune before coming back here?" Marie was furious. "I was worried sick about you and you were too busy fucking your whore to come home?" Louis blanched at the language; he'd never heard his mother swear before. He turned around to confront Brigitte, but she was already cycling away.

****

London

Once they were safely on the train to London, Marcel began to feel nervous. What if he wasn't a very good soldier or was too frightened to fight? It was all very well *wanting* to fight the Germans but maybe he wouldn't be able to live up to his own expectations. Gazing out of the window, he was struck by the similarity of the open fields, hedgerows and narrow winding lanes, but everything was much smaller and more compact in England, and he felt homesick. The train arrived and Marcel clambered out at Waterloo station, gazing around in awe. He had never seen anywhere this big and the vastness of the station, with its numerous engines puffing white smoke into the air and the large numbers of people rushing around him, left him slightly breathless.

"Come on, this way." Paul seemed to have taken charge and no one felt confident enough to argue with him. They left the station and stepped out into the London streets. Marcel stared at the buildings around him with their sandbags and their windows criss-crossed with tape. Traffic hurtled past and busy pedestrians rushed on their way, brushing shoulders with soldiers from various countries, all proudly wearing their colourful uniforms. He felt envious of their confidence and of their feeling of solidarity. Seeing the large numbers of Frenchmen wanting to be repatriated had badly dented his faith in his countrymen and seeing soldiers from other countries only emphasised just how divided France was. Even more worrying was just how big London seemed to be. How on earth was he going to find where the soldier's family lived?

Pierre nudged him and he saw Paul asking directions. Eventually, after showing the address they wanted to get to, a man in a striped suit told them to go back into the station and take the underground to Bank and then the central line to Hyde Park. Thanking him profusely in French and broken English, they got on the underground and, after passing under the river, they changed trains and soon arrived at Hyde Park where General de Gaulle had a small flat. They each had an interview with the general who was delighted to see them, and told them to be patient because he was still in the process of setting things up. For the time being, they would return to Weymouth, to the accommodation that had been reserved for the new Free French Forces until they were given their orders. Marcel began to feel the first stirrings of pride that he was a part of something bigger than himself. He even found the courage to ask the general if his brother Louis had joined the Free French. The General promised he would find out and let him know and Marcel left feeling even more overawed by his experience.

In fact, he was so overwhelmed by his meeting with the general that it wasn't until Marcel was on the train back to Weymouth that he remembered the soldier's message. He put his hand in his jacket pocket and cursed himself loudly for not delivering the note whilst he was in London.

"What on earth's the matter, Marcel?" Pierre asked in surprise.

Marcel quickly explained about the message and that he had intended to deliver the note personally.

"I can't just hand the letter to anyone. Not after I've brought it all this way."

"Don't worry, you can hand the note in at the local police station," Pierre reassured him. They arrived back at the camp and Marcel went to ask again about his brother. There was still no news other than a message from the general stating that his brother had not appeared on any of their lists. Marcel's good mood disappeared. As all the French were now billeted in one place, he was beginning to fear that Louis might be dead. He also had no idea whether his parents were safe or what had happened to Jeanne, Angel, Jean-Paul and Claudette.

****

Honor Oak Park, London

"I finally managed to persuade her to come and see *For Freedom* with me," Colin said as they sat in the sitting room. And what does she do?" He pointed to Ethel who looked suitably embarrassed. "She falls asleep and doesn't wake up until everyone stands up because they're playing *God Save The King*." Peggy giggled and Colin continued, "And to make things worse, she snored loudly all the way through the film!"

Ethel punched his arm playfully. "I did not, you liar!"

Peggy laughed even more, then yawning, she stood up. "Right, I'm going to bed. I'll see you in the morning, Ethel. 'Night Colin."

"'Night, Peggy."

Ethel waited until Peggy shut the door

"I've got some news, Colin." She carried on before he could answer, "I've packed in my job at the munitions factory and I've got an interview tomorrow morning to be a spotter with the RAF."

Ethel waited for his reaction. She hadn't mentioned her news earlier because the last time she had, in the spring, he'd tried to talk her out of changing her job. She wasn't entirely certain whether his objections were because she would have to move away or because she was joining the armed forces.

"Are you absolutely sure that's what you want to do?" Colin asked eventually, feeling even more left out because of his reserved occupation. Despite several approaches to his bosses, his applications to be allowed to join the regular forces had been consistently refused.

"You know how fed up I am working at the factory," Ethel pleaded. "I've been thinking about this for ages. You know I have." She reached over and put her arms around his neck. "Come on, darling, please be happy for me."

Colin sighed. "Of course I am, love. I'm gonna miss you, that's all."

"I'll miss you too, but at least we'll be in the same country." She moved closer and began kissing him. After a few moments, Colin forgot to be fed up and concentrated on seeing just how far Ethel would let him go.

******

Stalag XXA, Poland

They were finally given some special pre-formatted airmail paper. "You can only write one letter and a postcard a month so use all the space." Sergeant Miller was surprised to see Joe hesitate. "Well go on, lad. Get stuck in. You've done nothing but whinge about letting your mum know where you are. Now's your chance, what're you waiting for?"

Joe looked sheepish. "Not sure what to write, Sarge. I don't want to make a mistake…"

"Well just start by telling her you're alive and you're in this wonderful place." Whatever else he was going to suggest was drowned out by the jeering of the men nearest to him. Joe began writing. After all, he had no way of knowing whether his hastily written note had ever reached home. Before long, he had covered both sides of the page and he handed his letter to the German guard.

"How long before the letter gets there?" Joe asked. No one seemed to be able to answer him and any enquiry was either met with incomprehension or, "There is a war on, you know!" in heavily accented English, or, "We'll deliver them personally for you when we arrive in England."

Great. Joe was starting to feel demoralised. *The way they're talking, the note I gave to that Frenchman's probably got more chance of getting there than this letter.*

Chapter Fifty-two

The following morning, Marcel and Pierre headed off in the direction of the town. The sun was shining and there were very few clouds in the sky, promising yet another hot, sunny day. There was a gentle breeze and the aroma of kelp assailed their senses, reminding Pierre of the smell of the beaches on the outskirts of Marseilles. Remembering a funny incident from his childhood, he began to tell Marcel, but seeing the determined expression on his friend's face, he stopped, deciding to leave the story until later. Obviously the message meant a lot to Marcel, more than just the simple act of delivering it. Taking a deep breath, so he could make the most of the fresh sea air, Pierre led the way and they hurried towards the police station.

Once there, they took turns to explain, in a mixture of French and English. The desk sergeant read the message, thanked Marcel, shook his hand and wished him luck, promising the letter would be delivered as soon as he could arrange for someone to take it. Marcel took one final look at the now, rather tatty note, and left the station. There was nothing else he could do, the matter was out of his hands and he silently wished the letter swift progress.

****

Lewisham, London

Olive was standing by the side of some bushes trying to look unobtrusive. She was watching Kath feeding the ducks. Somehow this wasn't a pastime she naturally associated with Kath, which was why she was there. Then, her suspicions were confirmed. Kath was joined by Tom and Olive's face darkened with fury. So Kath *was* involved, or was she? Maybe she didn't know Tom was a blackmailer? She watched while the pair joked together, Kath's raucous laughter reaching her hiding place several feet away. Olive felt the same rage she'd felt when Mary had taunted her. Although she couldn't hear what they were saying, she was sure they were talking about her and, even if they weren't, she knew with absolute certainty that somehow Kath was involved. She stood silently out of sight for some moments, then she walked away. Kath would regret making an enemy of her.

****

Weymouth, England

The desk sergeant had made the decision to send the message to London with the next courier who was due to leave the following morning, but then he remembered young Davis was due some leave and he had a girlfriend in London. He waited until Davis came in from his beat at ten o'clock and showed him the note.

"How about you take some of the leave you've got owing to you and go and see that girlfriend of yours? You could take this message to the nearest police station to…" He peered at the address again. "Honor Oak Park at the same time. I'm sure they'll drop it round pronto."

Andy Davis was delighted. He hadn't seen Gloria for three weeks and he was sure she would be more than pleased to see him, especially since she was always moaning he didn't get enough leave. He rushed home, changed out of his uniform and hurried down to the station. If he was lucky, he would get up to London before she finished work and surprise her.

The train was late arriving at Waterloo, but he still had some time before picking her up from the insurance office where she was working, so he headed towards Catford Police Station. When he got there, he introduced himself and handed the letter to the desk sergeant. Putting his glasses on, Sergeant Deakin quickly read the message and promised to have the note delivered immediately. As Davis left the station, he heard the sergeant shout out for one of his young constables: "Jeffries… Jeffries! Front desk, please. Quick as you like!"

Constable Jeffries appeared hurriedly through the door behind the desk, frantically brushing crumbs off his uniform, whilst trying to do up his top button. Sergeant Deakin ignored his dishevelled appearance and gave him the message with instructions to go straight round to the address.

"But, Sarge, it's my dinner break." Constable Jeffries was new to the police force and was fed up because he hadn't been allowed to join the Navy.

"No arguments. That message has come half-way across occupied France to get here, sent by some poor lad whose been taken prisoner by the Jerries. The least you can do is to deliver it before you have your dinner."

Suitably chastised, Jeffries examined at the address and then, his face noticeably paler, said with much more enthusiasm, "Good God, I know Joe, he was at school with my brother. Poor sod. I wonder where he is now. I'll get right on it, Sarge." And with that he was gone.

****

Bethune, Northern France

Furious as he was, Louis found he was quite unable to stay away from Brigitte. He slipped into Bethune under cover of darkness and found her hiding away in her bedroom.

"Louis?" She stared at him in astonishment. "I never expected to see you again." Her heart was pounding and her mind racing. If he'd been a few moments earlier, he would have bumped into Rolf who had dropped her back at the café only minutes before.

He shook his head. "I can't help myself. I love you, but you have to promise me you'll never lie to me again."

Brigitte nodded and Louis reached out for her.

Across the road, Rolf lit a cigarette from his engraved silver case, replaced the container in his pocket and leant against his car. His eyes were on Brigitte's bedroom which overlooked the street. He'd been about to drive off when he'd spotted the farm boy arrive and sneak into the café. He had recognised Louis immediately and his eyes had narrowed in fury. So, Brigitte had decided to ignore his command and was still seeing her French boyfriend. His first instinct had been to storm back into the café and have the boy arrested, but then he had changed his mind. It would be much more fun to keep this to himself and punish a completely unsuspecting Brigitte the next time he saw her.

******

Lewisham Council Offices, London

Olive was furious with Kath. Although the girl was polite enough to her face, Olive could feel the amusement in her and she ached to slap her. Lost in her thoughts, she almost jumped when the supervisor tapped her on the shoulder.

"Yes, Mr Charlton?"

"Can you come into my office please, Miss Cooper?"

Her stomach churning with nerves, Olive followed him and took the offered chair. He smiled at her. "You needn't look so worried, Olive. I just wanted to say what a good job you are doing and to tell you I am leaving in a couple of weeks. I've finally received my call up papers. Unfortunately they think I'm too old for the front line, despite all my experience in the trenches, but never mind, I am apparently young enough to teach those who *are* going to fight." He sighed and then turned his attention back to Olive. "The reason for this little chat is that I think you would make a very good supervisor and I wanted to offer you the post."

Olive stared at him in astonishment and then a small smile crossed her face. "Thank you, Mr. Charlton. I would love to."

Olive could hardly contain her joy. Being supervisor would improve her income, but more importantly, the position would give her power. Perhaps things were finally going her way. She couldn't wait to write to Kurt and tell him.

"Thank you," she said, again, shaking his hand and walking back out into the main hall, a big smile on her face. Then her face fell again. That awful Tom would want more money once he knew she had been promoted. She had to find some way of getting rid of him.

****

Honor Oak Park, London

The hammering on the door made Peggy jump. Not expecting anyone, she lowered her book and stepped out into the hall to open the door. Before she could get there, the knocking came again and then she heard a familiar voice.

"Peggy, are you there? It's me, Pauline".

Startled, Peggy pulled open the door to see a beaming Pauline waving a tattered piece of paper in her face.

"Pauline? What's happened?" she asked.

"Joe's alive! He's safe!" Pauline pushed her way in, slamming the front door shut behind her and, taking the bewildered Peggy by the arm, she led her into the sitting room.

"Look! A letter from Joe, written after they surrendered in Calais."

"But how…?" Peggy was totally confused. "If they surrendered, how did Joe manage to write a letter? How…?" She ran out of questions and let Pauline guide her to the large armchair by the wireless.

"Read it." Pauline gave her the torn, dirty note and Peggy opened the missive gingerly, frightened of tearing the fragile paper further. To her amazement, in front of her there was Joe's writing, in pencil and quite faint but still perfectly clear:

> *Dear Mum,*
>
> *I just wanted to reassure you I am alive. We were captured when Calais surrendered and we're going to some POW camp. I don't know where yet. I'm not wounded so don't worry about me. I'll be home soon. The war can't last forever. Give my love to Peggy and ask her to wait for me.*
>
> *Your loving son, Joe.*

Peggy felt dizzy. The shock of hearing, after all this time and actually seeing his own writing in front of her, was too much. She took a deep breath and then started to cry, quietly at first, then with huge wracking sobs that shook her body. Pauline said nothing, just held her tight. Gradually, Peggy recovered and, sitting back, asked, "How on earth did it get here?"

"There was a knock on the door tonight and when I went to answer it, there was a policeman there. Before I could say anything, he asked me if I was Mrs Pauline Price and when I said yes, he gave me the letter. He said he'd tried earlier but I was out. Then he smiled, saluted me and left. I was shaking so much, I had to go and sit down and when I opened the letter and I couldn't believe my eyes. I had to read the note several times and then I couldn't stop crying."

Peggy was still shocked. "Somehow, that note came all the way to England through occupied France. I can't believe it."

"No. I can't either but obviously someone up there is answering our prayers." Pauline was unable to stop smiling.

When Sally and Ethel found them half an hour later, Peggy and Pauline were so busy speculating about how the note had reached them, neither of them had heard the front door open. Seeing their tear-stained faces, Sally and Ethel immediately assumed the worst.

"Peggy! What's happened?" Sally asked.

"Joe's alive; he survived Calais. He's written us a note." Peggy waved the piece of paper in front of their faces. They were all talking at once and Peggy lapsed into silence, leaving Pauline to explain.

Seeing her expression, Pauline stood up. "I really should go now but I wanted you to know as soon as I did. Do you want to keep the note?" Peggy nodded, too overwhelmed to speak any more. Pauline hugged her goodbye and headed towards the door, let herself out and went home, feeling happier than she had in the long weeks since they had known Joe was missing.

Peggy went up to bed feeling like she was floating on air. He was safe. Her prayers had been answered. "Thank you, God," she whispered. She undressed and climbed into bed, holding his note close to her heart. With a bit of luck, the war would be over soon and he would be back home safe. In the meantime, she could stop feeling guilty about enjoying herself and go out with Chris for a drink.

****

La Couture, Northern France

Louis had gone to the local school with Gerald and Henri. Gerald was short and stocky with red hair, a slightly crooked nose which he had broken when younger and which hadn't healed properly and a wicked grin, which lit up his face when something amused him. He was by no means good looking but his humour was infectious and he'd never had any problem finding girlfriends, much to the amazement of his friends.

Gerald wasted no time in giving Louis a black and white pamphlet which he read with interest. The leaflet told them of ways they could resist the German occupation, ranging from giving them the wrong directions to turning their backs during parades.

Louis nodded slowly while he read. "They're good, but I want to do more."

"Like what?" Henri peered at Louis over the top of his glasses. Henri was taller than Gerald yet shorter than Louis. His dark curly black hair was kept short and he wore round, wire rimmed glasses most of the time because he was short sighted. However, behind the glasses, his eyes, the same colour as the rich dark fertile earth of his father's farm, were sharp and missed little. His friends had become used to him only speaking when he had something intelligent to say.

"I've no idea, there must be something, though." Louis slammed his fist into the nearest cushion.

Henri exchanged a worried glance with Gerald who looked equally uncomfortable. Although they liked Louis, he was very hot tempered and often acted without thinking. They needed some calm clear thinking now, not impetuous action that would achieve very little and could put them all in danger for nothing. Louis would need to learn to control his temper or he would get them all killed.

"I think we need to sit and work out what we can and can't do," Henri hurried on, seeing the dark expression on Louis's face. "For instance, we can't attack large groups of soldiers because we don't have any weapons or ammunition. On the other hand, we can pass on this pamphlet and maybe plan some raids on German depots and steal some of their equipment. Whatever we do needs to be simple and as risk-free as possible to start with. It also needs to be away from here, so that the Germans don't start looking for us here or carry out reprisals on our families. Agreed?"

Gerald nodded immediately and, after a couple of minutes, Louis also inclined his head. "You're right, there's no point making things easy for them."

Henri breathed an inward sigh of relief. The answer was obviously to give Louis something to concentrate on, so he wouldn't rush off recklessly without any proper thought.

"We also need to make sure we don't tell anyone anything we're doing." Henri stared at Louis. "That includes girlfriends."

Louis flushed. He knew what they thought about Brigitte. "I'm not seeing her anymore," he lied.

Henry nodded. "Good. She's a loose cannon."

Louis bit back his immediate inclination to defend her and changed the subject. "So when do we start?"

******

Jeanne stared in disbelief at the headlines on the news vendor's stand. The British had sunk the French fleet in Mers-el-Kebir and over a thousand French sailors had been killed. Jeanne gasped. Surely that couldn't be right. Why were the British sinking French ships? Her good mood forgotten, she turned away from the stand. She needed to hurry home and speak to her father. If anyone could make sense of this, he would.

"Bloody British! They're supposed to be our allies." The vendor spat noisily on the ground. Jeanne couldn't think of any answer, so she just nodded. Her thoughts went to Marcel and she wondered if he was in England and what he was thinking about this.

"Mama, Papa, have you heard the news?" She rushed in through the door to find her father twiddling impatiently with the knobs of the radio. He waved at her to sit down just as the sound of the BBC announcer began to speak. They all sat there in silence as Jean-Paul listened intently to the broadcast.

When it finished, Jean-Paul switched off the wireless and explained. "Apparently the British gave the French Navy four options. First the Admiral refused to discuss them, because the Commander of the British Navy was not of equal rank to him, then he refused all the options and appealed to Vichy France to send reinforcements. Once the British heard this, the Royal Navy was ordered to scupper the whole fleet. If the Germans had got their hands on the French ships the British would have been out-numbered and out-gunned, and the war would have been over." Jean-Paul was silent for a few moments. "Winston Churchill stated categorically that they really had been left with no option if they were to continue to fight."

Jeanne breathed a sigh of relief. She had known her father would make sense of it. Then, she frowned. "What are the French radio stations saying?" she asked.

"Pretty much what you would expect from a cowardly regime like this one," Jean-Paul sighed. "I think we should face up to the fact that living here may not be an awful lot different from being under German occupation."

"Has something else happened?" Jeanne asked

"No, but there are rumours Vichy is drawing up some more statutes aimed at the Jews. I don't know what they are yet, but it's not likely to be good news."

"What are Jews?" Angel asked curiously.

Jean-Paul cursed softly under his breath. He had forgotten Angel was there.

****

Stalag XXA, Poland

Joe was beginning to feel more optimistic. Stalag XXA wasn't too bad. At least he had his friends and the guards were less violent.

However, that night when Joe checked the lists to see where he was working the next day, he saw his number was on the list of those to be moved to another camp. Frantic, Joe checked the rest of the numbers but only Pete's was there, Rob was to remain in Thorn. After everything he had already been through, he was now to be separated from Rob too.

Feeling utterly dejected, Joe stumbled back to the cellar and told the others. It was at this point, Joe realised he was on his own and he could only rely on himself. Yes, Pete was going with him, but for how long? How long before he too was sent somewhere else? To survive the war and for self-protection, he would have to keep everyone at arm's-length, never trusting anyone completely. With that depressing thought in his head, Joe finally fell into a restless sleep.

The morning came only too quickly. Joe picked up his meagre possessions and said his goodbyes. As he left the camp with Pete, he turned round for one last look, wondering if he would ever see Rob again.

Author's Note

Lives Apart: A World War 2 Chronicle was inspired by the story of my in-laws, Ted and Brenda Taylor (nee Burge). Ted was a young rifleman, conscripted in September 1939 and sent to Calais as part of Calais Force where they fought ferociously against the German 10th Panzer Division for four days, heavily outnumbered and outgunned. Eventually, they were forced to surrendered and Ted spent the next five years in POW camps in Poland. He also spent time in a salt mine and Majdanek concentration camp. Brenda, a student nurse in London for the duration of the war, was his fiancée and she waited five years for him to come home and they were married.

When Ted was captured, he found a discarded signals pad by the side of the road and wrote a note home to his mum to say he was alive and had been captured. Somehow, that message, sealed with the safety pin from his field dressing, found its way back home from occupied France to Ted's Mum, Lou in London. She received his note a couple of months before she was officially notified he had survived.

Although inspired by them, Joe and Peggy, like everyone else in the books, are fictional characters and are not based on any real people. Ted's true story is available from Pen and Sword and all good bookshops/internet retailers and is called Surviving the Nazi Onslaught. From the Defence of Calais to the Death March to Freedom.

http://www.pen-and-sword.co.uk/Surviving-the-Nazi-Onslaught-Hardback/p/7072